RUINED

A Taylor Sinclair Novel

By Wendy Hewlett

This book is a work of fiction. All names, characters, places, and events are a result of the author's imagination or are used in a fictitious manner and any similarities to real life names, places, and events are strictly coincidental.

Runed
Wendy Hewlett
ISBN: 0992166756
ISBN-13: 9780992166755
ISBN: 9780992166748 (eBook)

Excerts in Chapter 8 from the book *The Healing Runes* by Ralph H. Blum and Susan Loughan. Copyright © 1995 by Ralph H. Blum and Susan Loughan.

ACKNOWLEDGEMENTS

The highest praise I've received from readers is from women who've written to tell me how reading the Taylor Sinclair Series has helped them to heal from their own childhood trauma.

It's taken me much longer to write the third book in the series than I anticipated. It may have taken longer without the these amazing women sharing there stories with me. Your strength and determination are a constant inspiration to me.

It is my sincere hope that Taylor's journey continues to inspire, motivate, and encourage women to heal and grow.

The editing skills of the amazing Abbie P. has been a life saver once again. I don't know what I'd do without you. I also have to thank Sherri M. who's been a devoted beta reader since the beginning. Your support means the world to me.

Lastly, to Carol M., I was overwhelmed and thrilled to receive your offer to beta read RUNED.

To all of you lovely readers for your patience in waiting for the long overdue release of this book. Your loyalty and support means the world to me.

Chapter 1

Toronto Police Constable Taylor Sinclair sat with her fists clenched at her sides. "If you're planning on leaving me chained to a desk, I may as well go back on patrol. I didn't do twelve weeks at the Academy and six weeks with a training officer so I could sit at a desk." After two weeks of nothing but admin duties and cold cases, Taylor was ready to go back to patrol. The only reason her partner, Detective Sergeant Chris Cain, took her out this morning was because she wanted her to participate in her talks to grade nine students on bullying. Taylor just observed this time, but Chris wanted her to share her experiences with bullying at the next one. God, help her.

Chris glanced at Taylor to find her staring off out the passenger window. She rubbed her hands together as she waited for her old, beloved Crown Vic to warm up and the heat to kick in. What Taylor endured just weeks before left scars - inside and out. Her black rimmed glasses did little to hide the angry red scars on her left eyelid and bridge of her nose, but those weren't the scars worrying Chris. She seemed to be unaffected by the trauma and that was worrying.

Taylor had surrendered herself to Troy Rappaport, a drug dealer obsessed with her in order to save the life of the man she loved. Rappaport's drug enterprise was crumbling around him as the police closed in. His plan was to escape the city with Taylor. He'd left Taylor tied Taylor to the end of a bed in a locked room and his brother, Brandon Moody found her there, shredding her back with a bullwhip before Rappaport stopped him. When the cavalry arrived to save Taylor, Moody was gone and Rappaport held a gun to Taylor's head. The gun discharged when Taylor made a grab for it, the bullet grazing the bridge of her nose and her left eye.

"I'm just trying to ease you into it."

Taylor whipped her head around and glared at Chris. "Do you treat all of the officers under your command differently because of their histories or is it just me?"

"Oh, for Christ's sake, Taylor. That's below the belt and you know it." When Taylor's response was to stare out the window again, Chris wanted to bitch slap her.

"Lane cleared me for full duty – physically, emotionally, and psychologically." The department's psychologist, Dr. Lane McIntyre saw Taylor on a regular basis, helping her process and heal from her childhood trauma.

They had this argument numerous times over the past couple of weeks, but every time Chris requested to take Taylor out in the field she was shot down by Inspector Worthington. It wasn't fair to Taylor because she was right, Lane cleared her for full duties on her return to work. "I'll push to get you on active cases. I don't know what else I can do."

"Fair enough. Thank you."

"You really need to start bouncing on Cail again."

Mouth agape, Taylor stared bullets at Chris. "What does that have to do with anything?"

"Just thought that might be why you're in such a bitch of a mood."

"I'm not in a bitch of a mood." Typical Chris comment. Everything related back to sex. Taylor's relationship with Caillen Worthington had been a bit of a roller coaster ride over the past month, with Cail's temper at the forefront of their issues. They broke up shortly before he was kidnapped by Brandon Moody a few weeks prior. With Rappaport's funds frozen, Moody demanded a ransom from Taylor. She hadn't seen Cail since Moody's arrest and Cail went off to the hospital.

He'd texted. He'd called. But, if she took him back before anything was resolved, he would just keep doing the same thing - get angry with her, lash out emotionally, perhaps physically, and then walk out on her without giving her a chance to explain or defend herself. Then he'd come crawling back, apologizing and telling her he couldn't live without her.

"Great suggestion. Let's just forget how much he hurt me and I'll take him back so we can have sex to improve my mood. Wonderful. It will be great, at least until the next time he gets angry. I don't know why I didn't think of that."

Chris's shoulders hunched as she winced. One of these days she was going to learn to think before making stupid comments. "I'm sorry. That was out of line. I shouldn't have said that."

"You think?"

Chris's cell phone shrieked the theme song from Hawaii 5-O, indicating the call was coming in from the Toronto Police Dispatch. She removed her foot from her mouth and answered, "Cain."

A stern male voice informed her one of the detectives in her unit requested her presence at a crime scene. The only details she was given were that a female victim had been held in her own home and repeatedly raped and beaten. "Ten-four," Chris acknowledged. "Responding with Constable Taylor Sinclair. ETA, five minutes." She checked the time on the dash and added, "Eleven forty-two."

Taylor was about to get her wish, Chris thought and proceeded to give Taylor the limited information dispatch related to her.

"You're taking me to the scene?"

"Yep. Sometimes it's better to ask for forgiveness than it is to ask for permission."

They drove to the scene in silence, mentally preparing themselves for what they were about to descend upon.

An ambulance was parked in front of the two storey residence, as were a slew of squad cars and an unmarked. The Forensics Mobile Unit, a large RV-like vehicle, snugged against the curb across the street and yellow crime scene tape circled the property, flickering in the wind. Two uniformed officers stood on the sidewalk at each side of the property, guarding the crime scene from pedestrians. Another officer directed traffic around the emergency vehicles and one stood guard at the front door of the victim's house.

Taylor stepped out of the vehicle and tugged the collar of her navy uniform jacket up around her ears as her emerald green eyes scanned the street from behind stylish black framed glasses, consciously taking in every detail from the dull grey of the clouds hanging over the prettily restored narrow brick houses to the vehicles parked on the street.

As they approached the old red brick home with white shutters and trim, Chris recognized the cop on the door. He held a clipboard in gloved hands, ready to record Chris and Taylor's names and time of entry onto the crime scene log. "Constable Allen, what have we got?"

Allen greeted Chris with a bright smile glowing against his café au lait complexion then sobered before giving her a brief summary. "Bad one, DS. Detective Stone is with the vic. She's refusing medical transportation and care. Vic's friend came over to check on her when she hadn't been able to get hold of her since early this morning. Perp was still on scene and knocked her out before fleeing. Detective Ambrose is with the friend. The photographer is recording the scene, but the rest of the forensics team hasn't entered the house yet."

"Were you first on scene?"

"Yes, ma'am. I got the call at 11:33 and arrived on scene at 11:35. The vic's friend was out for about ten to fifteen minutes, so the perp had a good head start. The second unit to arrive was on scene by 11:36 and began a search of the neighbourhood. We haven't found him yet, but the search is ongoing."

"Where was the vic when you arrived?"

"They were in the living room. The friend untied the vic, wrapped her in a robe and a blanket, and brought her down to the living room before I arrived."

"Where's Stone. I want to see her first."

"Living room. Just inside to your left."

"Thanks, Constable. Let's get a few more patrol units here. Trade off warming up in the vehicles with the officers posted outside." She held up her badge so Allen could record her badge number, then initialed the sheet and waited while Taylor did the same.

They donned paper booties over their boots and entered the foyer. The first thing they both noticed was a large, black vase, smashed on the floor with dried flowers scattered around it. Taylor placed on foot in the foyer behind Chris and was struck by a nasty vision of what the victim endured. It took her right back to the rage and violence of her own past. It probably only lasted seconds, but it felt like eons. Coming out of it, she found Chris's face inches from her own, her hands cupping her cheeks and an intense look in her brown eyes. "Are you going to kiss me?" The intensity faded and a grin worthy of a toothpaste commercial appeared on Chris's face. Taylor could have sworn her eye tooth sparkled.

"Do you want me to?"

Might take her mind off of what she just experienced. "N-no." God, even her voice was trembling. At this rate, they'd never let her on another crime scene.

"You okay?"

Taylor nodded, stifling the urge to roll her eyes. She was so sick of people asking if she was okay.

Chris kept her hands on Taylor's face, kept her eyes focused on hers.

"Can you do this?"

Taylor narrowed her eyes. "I can," she said through clenched teeth.

Chris got what she hoped for – that touch of anger to stiffen Taylor's resolve. "Yeah, you can," she said. "Tell me what you saw in your vision." Taylor's psychic abilities were a blessing and a curse. She'd been through enough trauma in her own life without having to deal with experiencing someone else's. Chris had pushed Taylor to use it in the past, but that was before she understood the pain it caused her.

"You know what I saw, what I felt."

"I know it's hard, Taylor. We know exactly what victims of these types of crimes go through. It hurts me, too."

It didn't surprise Taylor that it hurt Chris. It surprised her she admitted it.

"But, you can use it to your advantage. Do you understand?" Chris asked.

"Yeah, I get it." And she did. It was one of the things that made Chris the stellar investigator she was.

"Okay." Chris waited a moment until Taylor seemed more stable. "Ready?"

Taylor nodded again and followed Chris into the open concept living room. Everything was in black and white. The walls and carpeting were only shades off pure white with a creamy tint to the carpets and a hint of blue on the walls. A gas fireplace with a white marble surround and matching mantel sat dormant on the other side of the room. The furniture was black leather framed by chrome and glass tables. Cold, except for the vibrant painting hanging over the fireplace with splashes of bright colours.

Taylor recognized Detective Daniela 'Danny' Stone from Chris's unit. Her shoulder length dark brown hair greyed at the temples, but she made no attempt to cover it up. Taylor figured she was a good twenty pounds overweight, but she seemed comfortable with that, too. She sat on the edge of the sofa next to the victim who was wrapped in a blanket, shaking, and sobbing while Stone held her hand. Taylor could only see the top of the victim's head, her short blonde hair matted with blood and in disarray, as she sat with her head hung low. Taylor cringed as she recognized the raw wounds on the victim's wrists and ankles. She absently rubbed the raw wounds circling her own wrists courtesy of Troy Rappoport.

Two paramedics stood just inside the entrance to the living room on standby.

Stone looked up as Chris walked straight to the victim. She crouched down next to her as Stone introduced them. "Detective Sergeant Chris Cain, this is Raine Delacourte."

"Ah, shit," Chris said a little too loudly, before dropping her voice to a whisper. "Raine, I'm so sorry."

Raine's head came up slowly, her face red and puffy. "Chris..." It was said before dropping her head again, her shoulders heaving as she sobbed.

"I've got her statement, Sarge," Detective Stone began. "She really needs to go to emerg, but she's refusing."

Chris tentatively laid her hand on Raine's knee. "I get why you don't want to go, but you know better than most why it's important you do."

As Chris attempted to convince Raine to go with the paramedics, Taylor scanned every inch of the living room, dining room, kitchen, and the stairwell to the right of the front door. Bloodstains smeared the white handrail and the wall. The living room and dining room appeared untouched, but the kitchen was a mess of broken dishes and scattered cutlery. A picture frame on the living room mantle held a photograph of two women, one a fit, athletic blonde and the other a tall, slim woman with long dark hair. The photograph appeared to be of their wedding. It was obvious Chris knew Raine, but just how well? One thing Taylor was sure of - this case was going to be another difficult one for Chris.

Chris motioned the paramedics over as she moved out of the way. "Is there anyone I can call for you, Raine?"

"Bonkers ... is here. Somewhere."

"She's with Detective Ambrose in the office," Stone advised.

"Has she been interviewed?"

"Yes, Sarge."

"Okay. She can ride in the ambulance with Raine. I want her to get checked out, too." Chris turned her attention back to Raine again as Stone slipped out of the room. "Is there a family member I can contact for you?" She had a brother, if Chris remembered correctly.

"No, please don't contact my family."

Chris nodded and let the paramedics work on Raine. They had her hooked up to an IV and a heart monitor before Stone returned with Bonkers, a tiny, pixie like woman who reminded Taylor of stories she read of fairies and sprites as a kid. Her dark hair was cut in a pixie style with wisps hugging her forehead and cheeks, her delicate nose turned up slightly at the tip. Her pale green eyes were red rimmed. She wore what looked like hospital scrubs under a black Canada Goose coat hanging well past her knees.

Bonkers went straight to Raine, holding her hand and gently rubbing her shoulder as the paramedics transferred her to the gurney.

Under the blanket, Raine wore a long, white terry cloth robe stained with blood. Taylor could barely stand to look at it. She would though. She'd look at Raine's wounds, study the crime scene, and be a rock for Chris. And she'd prove to the whole damn police department she was more than capable of handling active cases.

Chris made eye contact with Detective Ambrose and gestured with two fingers for him to come to her. When he did, she whispered, "I want you with her at all times until a patrol officer takes over. No one sees her unless she knows who they are and authorizes the visit. Let's include hospital staff in there. I want everyone cleared before they go near her. Also, once you get to emerg, I want Delacourte and Cruise separated. I'll be in to interview them in a while. Don't leave them alone together until that time." Then she turned to the paramedics. "Don't take her to Toronto General."

"We don't make that call," one of the paramedics responded.

The second paramedic, a man in his thirties with receding light brown hair and gentle brown eyes, said, "Let me find out what hospital they're routing us to and we'll see what we can do." He called in on his radio and within seconds had an answer that saved his partner from the wrath of Cain. "St. Mike's."

"Thanks," Chris told him, the look in her eyes conveying relief and appreciation.

Chris waited until the door closed behind the paramedics before turning to Stone. "You called me in because you know this guy isn't done. He's going to strike again."

Chapter 2

Detective Stone faced her commanding officer with a questioning frown. "How do you do that? I haven't even given you the briefing yet." She hadn't caught on to the fact they were likely dealing with a serial rapist until fifteen minutes into her interview with the victim.

"Give it to me then," Chris ordered without answering Stone's question.

Stone flipped through the pages of her notebook. "The victim was leaving for work this morning at oh six fifteen. She opened the front door and the offender rushed her, pushing her back into the house where she stumbled and fell."

As Stone talked, Chris walked to the front door, picturing the scene in her mind. She inspected the black ceramic vase, dried flowers, and the drying bloodstain sticking some of the dried flowers to the floor. One of the forensic techs stood inside the front door, holding his clipboard in front of him while he sketched the entryway onto a blank, grid-lined sheet.

Chris acknowledged his presence with a nod as Stone continued, "She tried to get to her feet, but the offender was on her. She felt like her head exploded and the next thing she remembers she was tied to the bed and blindfolded."

Chris raised her hand for Stone to stop there. To her surprise, Taylor marched up before she could continue.

"Knocked her out here," Taylor began, pointing to the drying blood partially hidden by the flowers. "Struggles to get her up the stairs." She moved slowly, scanning every surface, pointing out a dent in the drywall at the base of the stairs and another a few steps up.

Chris felt that glowing sense of pride as Taylor carefully began to navigate her way up the stairs, keeping her feet to the outside of the steps to avoid contaminating evidence. Drops of blood on the carpeted stairs offered a trail up with blood smears on the wall and handrail along the way.

Intrigued, Chris followed Taylor up with Stone right behind her, placing their feet in Taylor's tracks. At the top of the stairs, a smeared bloodstain soiled the cream coloured carpet.

"Dropped her here," Taylor continued. "Or, he put her down to take a break." She stared down at the stain for a moment then said, "He's going to be slight. Delacourte is petite, maybe a hundred and ten pounds and he's struggling to carry her upstairs?"

White, double doors led into the master bedroom. The trail of blood drops led straight into the middle of the room and disappeared under mounds of torn clothing littering the floor. Taylor stepped over the threshold and her entire body went rigid as her mind flooded with the violence that took place here. She didn't even feel Chris grip her arm and move her to the side so she and Stone could enter. When the vision faded, Chris was in her face again, her hands gripping Taylor's upper arms. Out of the corner of her eye, Taylor caught Stone ogling her as if she was crazy. Heat bloomed and spread over her cheeks. "Sorry," she whispered to Chris.

"No. Tell me what you saw."

"It was like he was playing with her, experimenting. He called her by name, but not her name."

"Are you seeing him?"

Taylor shook her head. "It's more like I'm experiencing what's in his head."

"And what's in his head?"

"Anger, violence, humiliation, betrayal, pain. I don't know how to describe it. Jealousy. There's a lot of jealousy there." Her fist tapped her heart as she spoke.

"He feels humiliated and jealous?" Chris asked. They weren't emotions most would attribute to a violent sex offender.

"Yeah," Taylor nodded. The heat drained from her face as she stared over Chris's shoulder at the bed.

Stone stood gaping at Taylor in disbelief. She was shocked at how close Taylor's words fit with what the victim told her. "Sass. She said he kept saying Sass or Sassy."

Chris dropped her hands to her hips and turned to survey the room. "I think we're going to find that Sass is a late twenties, early thirties blonde. Athletic build. Possibly a nurse or works in the medical field."

It looked like a tornado swept through the room. The stark white duvet lay in a twisted heap at the foot of the bed. Clothes from the closet and the dresser were strewn throughout the room. Some drawers hung partially open while others littered the floor. A lamp lay broken next to one of the nightstands. Jagged shards of glass from smashed picture frames gleamed under the overhead light.

Blue nylon ropes hung from each of the four bed posts and the white sheets were stained with blood.

"Continue with the victim's statement," Chris ordered as she continued to study the room.

"She regained consciousness tied to the bed, naked and blindfolded," Stone began and went on to describe Raine Delacourte's four and a half hour ordeal that fit with what Taylor described. She'd been beaten, raped repeatedly.

"Elizabeth Cruise, aka Bonkers, used a key Raine gave her to enter the premises through the front door after ringing the bell and banging on the door just after eleven this morning. She froze when she saw the broken vase and the blood on the floor. Cruise stated she called out Raine's name and heard her scream in response. She ran up the stairs and entered the bedroom. She doesn't remember what happened after that until she came to on the floor. She did remember seeing a blue-green Mastercraft tool box just inside the bedroom door which wasn't there when she came to."

"The scene has been photographed?" Chris asked.

"Yeah. The forensic tech you saw in the foyer has begun the sketches and we're waiting on the rest of the forensics team coming in now. "

Chris walked carefully to the side of the bed and toed some clothing out of the way to reveal a long length of the same blue rope that was tied to the bedposts. Thinking of the toolbox Stone described, she said, "Mastercraft. That's Canadian Tire's brand. What do you bet they sell this blue nylon rope?"

She went to the en suite next. Towels, some wet, some tinged with blood, covered the floor. The double sinks and the shower stall showed splashes of blood mixed with water.

Taylor followed Chris into the bathroom and immediately cupped her hand over her mouth, her thumb and forefinger pinching her nose. She recognized the smell of disinfectant only it was much stronger than she was used to; so strong her eyes began to burn and water. It was all she could do not to gag. "He'd started cleaning up."

Chris glanced over her shoulder. Seeing how tightly Taylor was pinching her nose explained the sudden nasally tone to her voice. Taylor scanned the room then quickly strode back out. Chris took a minute to sniff the air, smelling some type of strong cleaner that smelled like a public pool. Like chlorine. With a gloved hand, she opened each of the cupboard doors under the sink and searched for cleaners. There was a bottle of Lysol and some Clorex wipes, but neither of them smelled like chlorine. She followed Taylor back out to the bedroom and saw her on the other side of the room with her face pressed up to an open window. "What did you smell?"

Taylor took a few more deep breaths to cleanse her sinuses of the retched smell before turning around to answer Chris. "The disinfectant. It's the same stuff they use in hospitals." She turned her face to the window again, willing herself not to think about why that particular smell remained ingrained in her memory.

Chris returned to surveying the room then asked Stone, "Have we begun door to doors?"

"I've got four uniforms knocking on doors in the neighbourhood. They should be reporting back any time now."

"Okay." She turned to Taylor, appraising how she was holding up and found her with narrowed eyes, inspecting every inch of the room just as meticulously as she had herself. It almost brought a smile to her face. "Sinclair and I are heading to the hospital. Check in with me when you get back to Headquarters."

"Ten-four."

At the bottom of the stairs, Chris approached the tech still working on his sketch and measuring distances between each piece of evidence and points at the edges of the room. "There's a strong smell of cleaner in the master bedroom en suite, but I didn't find the source. Could you make sure they swab the areas he cleaned in that bathroom?"

"Yeah, got it," the tech answered and went straight back to his measurements.

While Chris put in a call to Inspector Worthington to give him a brief report, Taylor studied the mess in the kitchen. The table was overturned, drawers pulled out, cupboards opened, and dishes and cutlery strewn all over the kitchen, plates, cups, and glasses in shards. The other rooms in the house appeared to be untouched.

When they went outside, Chris paced carefully around the perimeter of the house and found what she was looking for at a back window. The weather had been milder at the end of last week and an excellent shoe print in the dirt directly below the window was preserved by the now icy temps. Careful not to disturb the evidence, she peeked through the window and studied the view into Raine's office. The offender would have had a perfect view of Raine sitting at her computer.

"Awfully small footprint," Taylor said.

Thinking of Taylor's observations of the offender struggling to get Raine up the stairs, Chris said, "Fits with a small man."

Taylor wasn't so sure. The print screamed woman to her.

"Say it."

Taylor's eyes moved from the print to Chris who studied her rather fiercely. "I don't know. Just a gut thing."

"I know. So, tell me what you're thinking."

Taylor blew out a breath. This was going to sound ridiculous. "I just have a weird sense this print belongs to a woman."

Chris crouched down on her haunches for a closer examination of the print. It didn't necessarily belong to their offender. Hell, it could be Raine's. The one thing she did know was when Taylor got a sense about something, it was usually bang on the money.

Chris started the car then dropped her head and ran her hands through her hair.

"You know her." Taylor stated, hoping it would inspire Chris to offer the details of her relationship with Raine Delacourte.

"Yeah. Fuck."

She sat quietly, giving Chris time to pull herself together. Minutes passed and Taylor used the time to study the neighbourhood again - large brick homes with postage stamp lawns, beginning to brown with the wintery cold, but well manicured with sculpted bushes and massive trees lining the street. Christmas lights hung along the eaves and in some of the trees.

"Impressions?"

Taylor turned her attention back to Chris who sat staring out the windshield, her face pale and pained. "I think you missed something."

Chris snorted, so shocked anyone would accuse her of missing something at a crime scene she had to laugh. "What did I miss, Sinclair?"

"I think you missed one of Raine's attributes that may assimilate her to this Sass person."

"Really? And what attribute is that?" She knew her tone was defensive, but she couldn't help herself. Taylor pointing out she may have made a mistake or missed something hurt her pride. She knew it was petty, but she was used to the officers under her command being in awe of her.

Taylor wondered if Chris realized how closely she fit the profile she assigned to Sass. With the exception of being in the medical field, it was Chris to a T, right down to the other attribute Taylor thought Raine Delacourte may share with Sass. "She's a lesbian."

Chris pinned Taylor with the fire in her eyes. "What the fuck do you think that has to do with anything?"

Taylor didn't feel so sure of herself under Chris's death glare. "If what I felt in there is true and this guy felt humiliated and betrayed by Sass, she could have left him for a woman. That would really take a chink out of his pride, wouldn't it? "

"Shit." Chris dropped her head again, scrubbing her face with her hands. She had missed that. She took another minute to settle herself and then apologized to Taylor for getting angry. Taylor smiled thinly and nodded.

"One other thing," Taylor said. "He was looking for something."

"Yeah, he was. What does that tell you?" Throwing the car into drive, Chris pulled away from the curb, with the heat now pumping blissfully out of the vents, and headed for St. Michael's Hospital.

Taylor wasn't sure of the answer Chris's question. "He was looking for money or valuables?"

"Hmm. Maybe, but I think he was looking for something specific."

Taylor turned that over in her mind for a while and decided they needed more information before they could make that determination. "There was a picture on the mantle in the living room, a picture of Raine with a tall, slender woman with long, brown hair."

"Callie Delacourte," Chris answered before Taylor got to her question. "Raine took her name when they were married a few years ago. Callie was diagnosed with cancer soon after their wedding. She passed away about a year ago."

Taylor knew very well the pain of losing someone you loved, but to watch them suffer through a long-term illness, to watch them slowly withering away to nothing, had to be an absolutely horrible and draining experience. "Were you and Raine …"

Chris finished Taylor's question at her hesitation, "Lovers?" Their eyes met momentarily before Chris turned her attention back to the road. "We were lovers for a short time many years ago, but for the most part we've been friends. Not the kind of friends you and I are, but I went to their wedding." Her lips curled up briefly in memory.

13

"When Raine met Callie, she fell hard. I used to tease her about it and she'd grin like a fool, saying that one day I would fall for someone and she couldn't wait to see me experience the depth of love she and Callie shared. I figured she'd never see that day. I didn't think someone who'd never been loved could feel love, especially as deeply as they seemed to."

Taylor looked over at Chris with a warm smile. "So, does she know that day has come?"

"Ha." Chris let out a short laugh as her eyes burned. "No. I guess not." None of her acquaintances, she supposed that was a better descriptor than friends, knew about her relationship with Kate. Their lives seemed so busy and she never had the desire to take Kate to any of her old haunts. Nor did they really hang out with any of Kate's friends, although they would be tonight.

When they arrived at the hospital, they were made to wait while Raine was being treated which gave them time to interview Elizabeth Cruise away from Raine Delacourte. "How's the head?" Chris asked.

"You know I'm a nurse, right? I didn't need to be examined, Chris. I know I was unconscious and I know how to treat a mild concussion."

Her voice was as small as she was, Taylor thought. She was pretty sure she could pick the elfin woman up and carry her around all day without a problem.

"Why is it," Chris asked with a grin, "that nurses are scared shitless of hospitals?"

"Because we know what goes on in them."

"See?" Taylor couldn't help responding. "They're scary places."

Bonkers turned her gaze on Taylor for the first time, recognizing her immediately. "Yeah, well. I guess you'd have good reason to fear them, wouldn't you?" When Taylor turned red, she said, "Sorry, that's probably a sore spot. Lost my filter years ago." She tapped her head with her forefinger then winced when she hit the bump on her head. "Ow." She reached out her hand to Taylor. "I'm Bonkers. And no, I'm not telling you why people call me that. Sore spot." she said with a thin smile.

"Taylor Sinclair," Taylor said as she shook the offered hand.

Bonkers laughed. Like she didn't know her name. "All that..." Bonkers waved her hand up the length of Taylor's body and circled it in the air before Taylor's face. "And a sense of humour, too. Bitch."

"Like you'd do anything with those looks anyway," Chris said. She took out her notebook and pulled a chair in beside the stretcher

Bonkers sat on.

"OMG. You're going to make me say it all over again, aren't you?"

"I hate when people speak in acronyms."

"Good. Can we get this over with ASAP?" Bonkers smirked then added, "LOL."

Chris rolled her eyes then asked Bonkers to start at the beginning and tell her everything. Bonkers told them she grew more and more worried when Raine didn't show up for work and she wasn't answering her cell phone. By 10:30, she couldn't stand it any longer and left work to go check on her. Raine's car was in the driveway, but she didn't get a response to ringing the doorbell and banging on the door, so she used her key to let herself in. When she saw the broken vase and the blood on the floor and walls, she was scared. She called out Raine's name, heard a weak scream, and ran up the stairs. "I didn't think. I was worried about her. All I was thinking about was Raine. I saw all the blood everywhere and I thought she'd cut herself somehow, on that vase maybe, and was bleeding out. When I got to the doorway of her bedroom, there was a toolbox sitting against the door. I remember thinking that was weird. Kind of out of place, you know? Then I went through the door and ..." She covered her mouth with her hand as tears began to stream down her face.

Chris reached her hand over and Bonkers slowly drew her's away, out of reach. Leaning back in her chair again, Chris sighed. "Tell me what happened when you came to."

"God, you're such a bitch. What do you want me to say?"

Good. Get angry at me. "I want you to tell me exactly what happened after you came to."

"She was spread eagle, tied to the fucking bed. What the hell do you think happened? I untied her and covered her up. Oh, did that mess up your fucking evidence? I don't give a shit, Chris. I got her the hell out of that room and called 911." Tears continued to stream down Bonkers' cheeks, her face red and the veins in her neck pulsing as she glared at Chris.

Chris met her gaze and just sat there, giving her time to cool down. When Bonkers finally looked away, Chris said, "Who would want to hurt Raine like this?"

"No one." Bonkers shook her head as her tiny, balled up fists swiped her wet cheeks. "Who would do this?"

"Does she have any family in the area?"

"Her brother is out west. Her mom passed within a month of

Callie."

"Father?" Chris got another narrow-eyed glare from Bonkers and returned a cold stare.

Bonkers rolled her eyes and huffed. "You really are an insensitive bitch, aren't you? Her father hasn't been in the picture since she was a kid. I don't think she even remembers what he looks like."

"Have you noticed anyone paying particular attention to Raine lately?"

"No." Bonkers shook her head then winced, cupping her hand over the bump on her head. "No," she repeated.

The legs of the chair scraped against the floor as Chris got to her feet. She closed her notebook and said, "I'm going to cut you some slack on the attitude because I know you've been through a lot today, but you need to deal with your shit, Cruise. I won't be so nice next time."

"Oh, was that you being nice?"

* * *

Chris paced up and down the hallway while Taylor leaned against the wall, trying her best not to dwell on the memories triggered by being in a hospital. Going over her notes helped. Not that it would make a big difference because she remembered every detail, but if it came to a court case which could be a year or more after the investigation, her notes would be an important reminder. She wasn't sure what to do about her visions. Did she record them in her notes? Just the facts, is what they'd been taught. As Chris passed her for the umpteenth time, she asked, "Should I record what I saw or felt in my visions?"

Chris came to a stop and looked back at her as she thought about it. "Probably not. Put them in a separate report and send it to me."

A good thirty minutes later, a pudgy nurse with mousy brown hair up in a ponytail shuffled down the hall wearing bright purple scrubs. "Detective Sergeant Cain?"

"Yeah," Chris turned abruptly and headed back to the nurse. "Can we see her now?"

"She's sedated, so she may or may not be able to talk to you at the moment. She'll be going up to surgery shortly, but Dr. Atwood will explain that to you." She started back in the direction from which she had just come with Chris at her side and Taylor following behind. "Dr. Atwood will see you after you've seen Ms. Delacourte. She's just getting the reports together for you."

"That's fast." They usually had to hound the emergency doctors to release the report a day or two after the fact.

"Ms. Delacourte was fortunate Dr. Atwood was working in the ER today. She doesn't do very many shifts here anymore and she is hands down one of the best doctors on staff, if not the best."

"Dr. Gabriella Atwood?" Chris asked.

"The one and only." The nurse smiled then escorted them to a room next to the nursing station with a uniformed officer posted at the door. "I'll come and get you when Dr. Atwood has the reports ready."

"Thanks." Chris turned back to see if Taylor caught the doctor's name. The somber look on her face told Chris she hadn't overhead her conversation with the nurse. Chris held her badge up for the officer and then her breath caught when she opened the door to see Raine lying on her back, tubes and wires attached everywhere. Her face was bruised, her right wrist splinted. Bonkers sat in a chair next to her, her fingers entwined with Raine's left hand. How the hell she'd gotten in there before them, Chris didn't know.

A sob hiccupped out of Bonkers before she clamped down on her emotions. "I should have gone to check on her as soon as I realized she didn't show up for work."

"Okay, you can stop that right now," Chris said sternly. "You can't second guess yourself. This wasn't your fault and by going over there when you did, you scared the bastard off. That's going to make our job easier because he didn't get the chance to clean up or remove evidence from the scene."

"Not your fault," Raine whispered.

Chris turned to Raine, her hand resting just above the bandages on her left wrist. "Are you up for answering a few questions?"

"I never understood how you handled doing your job," Raine murmured, her words slightly slurred from the sedative. "How you could deal with this on a daily basis. I think I get it now, Chris."

Chris swallowed the knot in her throat. "Did you recognize him? Do you remember seeing him before?"

"I never got a good look at him."

"Do you leave the house at the same time every day?"

"I went back to the three shift rotation after Callie passed, so it depends what shift I'm on."

"How long have you been on dayshift?"

"Umm, three … no, four days, I think. Since Saturday."

"Okay. You routinely leave through the front door though, right?"

"Yeah."

"You don't remember anyone following you or watching you lately?"

"No. You think he was stalking me?"

"I don't know yet. I'm just trying to get an idea of your routine."

"I always leave the house forty-five minutes before the start of my shift. I go out the front door, lock it, then get in my car. I always hit the same coffee shop on the way to work. On the way home, I often pick up anything I need or hit the gym, so I don't always take the same route home like I do on the way in and I arrive home at different times depending on what running around I did."

Taylor stood silently listening. When Chris seemed to be finished with her questions, she took a step closer to the bed. "Ms. Delacourte, I'm Constable Sinclair."

Raine's eyes opened to slits then closed again.

"Have you been out to any bars or restaurants lately where this guy may have seen you?" Taylor asked.

"I haven't really been going out anywhere since Callie." She was quiet for a moment and then said, "Thursday. Bonkers?"

"I dragged her out on Thursday night," Bonkers said to Chris. "I figured a year was enough and it was time to get her ass back in the game. I went over to her place and literally made her come out with me. We went to Les Beau's, but we didn't stay very long. I never should have taken her to a place she and Callie frequented. It was pretty stupid on my part."

"Going there upset you?" Taylor asked Raine.

"Yeah," Bonkers answered for her again, but spoke to Taylor this time. "We had one glass of wine and when I realized the place was making her think about all the times she'd been there with Callie, I got her the hell out. We hailed a cab and I took her home."

"So, neither of you would have noticed if someone was watching you leave or following the cab."

Bonkers pressed her lips into a fine white line and narrowed her eyes at Taylor. "You think someone targeted her from Les Beau's?" She turned to Raine. "God, why did I force you to go there? I'm so sorry."

"We don't know where he saw Raine," Chris said. "It could have been at the hospital, the grocery store, the gym. Hell, we just don't know at this point. We don't know why he targeted her. Okay?"

Bonkers nodded, shaking loose a couple of big, fat tears that lazily slid down her cheeks.

Chris brushed her fingers over Raine's forearm. "We're going to go and let you rest, but I'll be in touch. If you have any questions or you need anything, just give me a call, anytime, day or night." She pulled two of her business cards from her pocket and handed them to Bonkers along with a booklet with a night view of the city of Toronto and the words *A Guide for Sexual Assault Survivors*. "This contains a lot of helpful information when Raine is ready for it. It explains the investigation and justice process, but, more importantly, it contains information on support programs. I'm going to have someone from Victim Services contact Raine. She'll need counseling and she'll need your support." Being nurses, Raine and Bonkers were familiar with a lot of the support programs, but it was a lot different when you were dealing with it from a victim standpoint. "Again, if you need anything, call me."

Bonkers only nodded, accepting the booklet and cards.

"Chris? When can I go home?" Raine asked.

"Aah," Chris fumbled. It wasn't a question she expected Raine to ask so soon. "It's probably going to be a few days. I'll let you know when the scene is cleared."

"Can I at least go home to pick up a few things?"

"Get me a list of what you need and I'll make sure you get it."

"But…" Raine sighed. "Okay. Thanks."

Just as Chris reached for the door handle, the door opened to reveal the nurse she'd spoken to earlier. "The doctor is ready for you now." She led them out of the emergency department to an area containing several offices.

Taylor stared at the nameplate on the door the nurse knocked on. That couldn't be the same Gabriella Atwood she knew, could it? Why hadn't she ever thought to ask Gabriella what she did for a living? She assumed Gabriella was a housewife. When the nurse opened the door, she stretched her neck trying to peer into the office. Sure enough, there was Gabriella, her long dark curls unmistakable. She raised her head and her face lit up as she got quickly to her feet.

"Taylor, I didn't realize you were here." She squeezed past the nurse and greeted Taylor with a warm hug. "How's the eye?" She took a step back and examined the ugly scar on Taylor's eyelid which her glasses helped to camouflage.

"Good," Taylor answered awkwardly, not comfortable with Gabriella right in her face. "I didn't know you were a doctor."

"Well, now you do." She grinned then gave Chris a quick hug and motioned for them to take a seat in her office.

Gabriella handed a manila envelope to Chris. "I've given you a copy of everything we have thus far. We're still waiting on some reports coming back from the lab and she will be going up to surgery shortly, but I'll have any further reports sent to your office or you can come in and pick them up."

"I appreciate your cooperation, Gabriella."

"This is a very disturbing case." Gabriella picked up a pair of reading glasses and slid them on before opening the file folder in front of her. "I don't know how familiar you are with Ms. Delacourte's injuries, so I'll give you a complete overview."

Chris opened the manila envelope and followed along with Gabriella's oral report.

"She presented with an inch long gash on the left side of her scalp and a moderate concussion. The location of this injury would point to your offender being right handed. She was raped with bruising evident in the upper thighs and pelvic area."

"No tearing?" Chris asked.

"No, no tearing."

"Odd."

Gabriella continued, "It's my understanding he held her captive in her own home for over four hours. He raped her repeatedly. How many times exactly is anyone's guess. I believe the swabs will show that a lubricant was used. Bruising, swelling, rope burns, and abraded skin are present in both wrists and ankles, consistent with being tied up. Her right ulna and radius bones are fractured at the wrist, likely a result of the way she landed when she was rushed by the perpetrator and exacerbated by fighting the bindings on her wrists. She'll be going up to surgery shortly due to the severity of this injury. There may be some nerve damage, but that remains to be seen."

Gabriella removed her glasses, lifting her head to look at Taylor and Chris. "She has several cuts, which I've indicated on the diagram included in the papers I've given you. Most are superficial, but a few of them were quite deep."

Taylor leaned over to get a look at the diagram in Chris's hand. The image showed a front and back view of the female form. The wounds Gabriella had drawn were on the left side of the chest, above the heart. She leaned in closer, running her finger over the shapes above the left breast.

ᚾᛁᛏ

"I recognize these. They're Rune symbols."

"Rune symbols?" Chris asked.

"Yeah. Quinn gave me these stones and a book called *Healing Runes*. There are twenty-five stones, twenty-four with symbols like these and one that is blank. This one..." She ran her finger over the last of the four symbols, "is shame. And this..." Pointing to the third symbol she said, "is guilt."

"Shame and guilt carved over her heart," Chris said with a frown. "What about the rest?"

The first shape looked like an r except that it was drawn with sharp angles instead of a rounded curve. The second shape was a straight vertical line. "I need to look them up."

"What else do you know about them?"

"Not much. I haven't really read the book yet. I just skimmed through it." She read about shame because that was something she felt a lot, but she hadn't had time to do much else. "I have the book in one of the boxes in my car." Taylor looked up to see Gabriella busily writing on a notepad and apologized for interrupting her briefing.

"Don't be silly, you didn't interrupt." Gabriella finished her notes and continued, "Given the level of violence, it's very fortunate Ms. Delacourte wasn't more seriously injured."

"Seriously enough," Chris stated as she returned the papers to the envelope.

"It appears the offender suited up, as no semen was recovered, but we did take several swabs. Four dark brown pubic hairs were collected and all samples were signed over to Detective Ambrose."

"Thanks again, Gabriella. When you get the rest of the results, give me a shout and we'll stop by to pick them up." Chris pulled one of her cards out and passed it over the desk.

Gabriella reciprocated by handing Chris one of her own cards. "If you need anything else from me, I'm available twenty-four seven."

In the car, Chris let her head fall back onto the headrest and closed her eyes. She needed to take a step back and go over everything again in her head. She missed the lesbian angle at the house and she hadn't asked if Raine had been anywhere recently that may have identified her as a lesbian. Taylor covered her, but she shouldn't have missed those.

When Chris lifted her head, her eyelids were heavy. "Let's hit Les

Beau's before we head back to Headquarters."

Taylor smiled and nodded her ascent. She'd been thinking the same thing. "Why do you suppose neither Raine nor Bonkers mentioned the symbols carved into her skin?"

"Good question," Chris answered and sighed heavily.

* * *

When she saw the sign above the quaint, pub-like bar spelling out the name of the place as *Les Beau's*, Taylor was surprised. She'd written *Lesbo's* in her notebook, which was how it sounded when Bonkers and Chris said the name. The way it was written in French on the sign, it should be pronounced *lay*, not *lez*. Spelling it wrong in her notebook ate at her. It wasn't like she could use whiteout to correct her error and having that error permanently in her notebook was frustrating to someone who liked everything just so. She followed Chris in the door.

A long, scarred bar ran down the wall to the right with high tables in front of it and booths to the left. Towards the back there were more tables and booths, a dance floor, and a small stage for live bands. The only thing identifying it as a lesbian bar that Taylor could see was the enormous rainbow flag hanging on the back wall. There were only a handful of patrons, which wasn't surprising considering it was mid-afternoon. Most of the customers sat at the bar, but a few were seated at tables having a late lunch. Chris approached the bar.

"Sammy, got a minute?"

"Hey, stranger." The tall, curvy bartender with a short, messy cap of dark hair finished opening a couple of beer bottles and setting them in front of a couple seated at the bar before swinging her hips down to the end to meet Chris. "Haven't seen you in here for ages, sugar. How's it going?"

"Good. Sam, this is my partner, Constable Sinclair."

"Hey." Sam reached over the bar and gave Taylor a firm handshake. "Seen you on the news so much I feel like I know you," she said with a soft laugh. "So you working or drinking?"

"Working," Chris said. "Raine was in here on Thursday night with Bonkers. Did you see them?"

"I pretty much stick to day shifts these days. Got a toddler now, so I like to be home in the evening. But, I heard they were in. I was happy to hear Raine was finally coming out and about. I hadn't seen her since Callie got sick again."

"Again?"

"Yeah, she was in remission for like two years. The cancer came back about three months before she passed and took her down hard and fast. Raine took a leave of absence from the hospital and took care of her for the last month or so. Had to be hard as hell, but Callie passed in her lover's arms. That was what she wanted. She didn't want to die alone in the hospital."

Chris cleared her throat, convinced she may be coming down with a cold or something. "Who was working Thursday evening?"

"Cherylyn would have been on bar. I'd have to take a look at the schedule to see what wait staff was on."

"Would you mind?"

Sam's expression turned dead serious. "You still work sex crimes, don't you? Something happen to Raine or Bonkers?"

"Raine's in the hospital," Chris answered.

"Ah, fuck. Like the poor girl hasn't been through enough. What hospital? I want to send flowers, maybe go see her."

"St. Mike's."

"Thanks, Chris. Let me grab the schedule."

Sam walked to the other end of the bar, spoke to a waitress, nodding towards the bar before she disappeared through a door. The waitress took Sam's place behind the bar. She noticed Chris, grinned, and headed towards them. "Hey you. Where have you been hiding?"

"I don't get out much anymore."

"Don't tell me some hot chick has you settled down and doing the domestic thing? No way in hell."

Chris laughed, but didn't deny or confirm. "Gloria, this is my partner, Constable Sinclair."

"Yeah, you're the chick on the news all the time. What happened to your hottie? I keep seeing him on the news coming out of the clubs with some red head? What's up with that?"

How was she supposed to respond to that? Taylor just stood there staring at the pretty girl with a thick mass of wavy blonde curls spilling down her back to her waist, big brown eyes, and the most cleavage Taylor had ever seen. She was worried her breasts were going to spill right out of her low cut, tight fitting t-shirt.

Chris saved her from the awkwardness. "He's being a dick."

"Being a dick following his dick," Gloria said. "Really sweetie, you need to switch to our team. The only dicks involved are of the strap on variety."

Chris doubled over laughing, not just at what Gloria said, but the look of sheer horror on Taylor's face. When she finally straightened again, there were tears staining her face from laughing so hard and Taylor was still standing there, red faced and shocked.

Sam returned and handed Chris a piece of paper with the names of the staff who worked on Thursday evening along with their cell phone numbers. "You two want a coffee or something to eat before you go back out into the cold?"

"Thanks, but we gotta get back to the office," Chris said, still wiping the tears of laughter from her eyes. "You haven't seen a guy hanging around in here with dark hair? He'd be smallish."

"Doesn't ring any bells. We get guys hanging out in here all the time. They either want to see chicks making out or they think they can pick up. You know the type," Sam said to Chris. "You used to hang out in here enough."

"Yeah, I know the type," Chris said somberly. "How about a chick named Sass? Ever hear of her?"

"Sass?" Sam rubbed her chin then shook her head. "No, I don't think so. Sexy name though."

"Okay. Thanks for this." Chris waved the paper as they headed for the door.

"Don't be a stranger. We miss you around here."

Chapter 3

They drove about two blocks in silence before Chris stopped for a red light. She glanced over at Taylor who stared blindly out the windshield. "He's not sleeping with her."

Chris was referring to Ireland Delaney, the sexy, beautiful red head who dragged Cail out of the clubs and pubs every night to make sure he made it home safely. The news and entertainment shows continued to play clips of him leaving the bars with Ireland and contemplating what happened to Taylor and Cail's relationship. Taylor wasn't sure if Cail was sleeping with her or not, but Cail's sister who was also Chris's girlfriend, Kate Worthington, kept assuring her he wasn't.

Chris sighed when Taylor didn't respond and they drove the rest of the way back to Headquarters in silence. When they reached Taylor's desk, Chris stopped. "Run the name Sass or Sassy. It's not a popular name, so you might be able to find someone between twenty-five and thirty-five."

Taylor nodded, removed her jacket and began to log into her computer as Chris disappeared into her office and closed the door behind her. She ran the name first and, surprisingly, only came up with one Sass. Unfortunately, she surpassed their target age by about twenty years. Still, Taylor wrote down her name and contact information in case Chris wanted to interview her. Next, she typed up her official report and then a secondary report detailing her visions.

Since they hadn't had lunch, Taylor made her way to the squad room and grabbed a cup of coffee. Not much of a lunch, but it was all she wanted. She just sat back down at her desk when Detective Danny Stone approached.

She stood in front of Taylor's desk and nodded towards Chris's office. "What's up with Cain?"

"What do you mean?"

"Why's she locked in there?"

"Have you tried knocking on the door?"

"It's closed."

Taylor rolled her emerald eyes. "If you knock, she'll probably open it."

"I don't want to bother her if she's upset. She knows Raine Delacourte personally. She's probably not in a good mood."

"Is it about the case?"

Stone nodded, chewing on the inside of her lip.

"Then I'm sure she'd want to know." When Stone just stood there staring at her and working away at her lip, Taylor sighed. "Do you want me to take whatever you've got to her?"

"Could you just tell her I need to talk to her about the case?"

"Fine." Taylor went back to the squad room and made a cup of coffee for Chris. When she walked through the unit and approached Chris's door, all eyes were on her. She shook her head and knocked softly on the door.

"Yeah? Come in."

Taylor opened the door a fraction and peeked in. Chris sat with her feet up on the desk. "I made you a coffee."

She waved Taylor in and dropped her boots from the desk.

Taylor closed the door behind her and deposited the coffee in front of Chris. "Are you okay? Everyone out there is scared to death to disturb you."

"Why? I'm just thinking."

"I don't know. Stone needs to talk to you about the case and she wouldn't knock on your door because she's worried you're upset since you know Raine Delacourte personally."

Chris picked up the coffee, blew on it and then took a sip, expecting the gut rot coffee the department supplied. She was shocked when it tasted as good as the coffee Taylor made at home. "Where'd you get this?"

Taylor smiled, holding a finger to her lips. "I've got a secret stash of Timmies coffee in the squad room."

With a laugh, Chris said, "I won't tell as long as you keep bringing me coffee like this."

"Deal. What do you want me to tell Stone?"

Chris sighed then took another sip of the heaven in her cup. "I'll go see her. While I'm doing that, I want you to go through what we've got so far and determine what charges from the Criminal Code apply."

Oh, yay. Taylor's least favourite part of police work. She nodded.

"When you're done that, go into the conference room and get started on a case board. Print off a picture of the vic and check with Stone. She should have the crime scene photos and the photos taken at the hospital by now. Write the details you think should be up there. I'll let Stone and Ambrose know we'll meet in there in an hour and to bring everything they've got."

"Okay." Taylor nodded again.

"Have you sent me your reports?"

"Yes."

"Okay, get started." Taylor left Chris's office, closing the door behind her again. She flopped into her desk chair and pulled out her Criminal Code.

By the time Chris joined her in the conference room fifty minutes later, she had the board nearly completed. Chris stood behind her and looked over the crime scene photos and then the notes Taylor added beneath them. She'd put up Delacourte's drivers' license photo and, beside it, a photo of her taken at the hospital.

When Stone and Ambrose walked in together, Taylor was worried they'd be pissed that she put the board together for their case.

Stone eyed the board as she made her way to the conference table. "What's up with that, Sarge? You don't usually go with a board."

Chris stood at the front of the room, leaning back against the wall with her hands jammed into the front pockets of her cargo pants, her thumbs hooked out over the edges. "I'm expanding my horizons."

Stone snorted. "Ya, right."

Chris's eyebrows popped up, but Stone was too busy seating herself and opening her file folder to notice. "You don't think I'm open to trying new things?"

Stone's head flew up and whipped around so fast Taylor nearly laughed. The look of terror on her face was priceless.

"N-no, not at all. I've just never seen you use a board before." Her gaze stayed locked on Chris's, her eyes wide.

Chris shrugged then nodded her head to where Taylor stood on the other side of the whiteboard with a fist full of dry erase markers. "My partner works well with visuals."

Stone's eyes widened again and Taylor was sure she saw anger flash through them. "Your partner?" Her eyes darted between Chris and Taylor.

"Yeah, my partner. You've met Constable Sinclair. She was at the crime scene with me this morning."

"Yeah, but … I thought she was, you know, like a secretary or something. What about Blake?"

Better to bite this in the bud right here and now, Chris thought. Before Stone went out and incited the rest of the unit. She pushed off the wall, her hands still jammed in her pockets as she stalked towards her prey. Stone sat up straighter then leaned back in her chair, trying to keep as much distance between her and Chris as possible.

"Have you ever known me to bring someone onto this team who isn't a credit to the unit?"

"No, Sarge." Stone's throat rippled as she swallowed.

"You saw Sinclair working the scene this morning. Did you find her lacking in any way?"

Tiny beads of sweat dotted Stone's upper lip. "No, Sarge. Except …"

Chris waited for Stone to continue, but she just sat there staring up at her with sheer terror in her eyes. "Except?"

Detective Ambrose, with his short salt and pepper hair and sharp blue eyes, stared over Stone's head and didn't make a sound. Smart man, Taylor thought before turning her attention back to Stone who was pretty much quivering under Chris's glare.

"Well, you know. It was kind of weird the way she could see inside the offender's head."

"Do you think Sinclair's gift is a weakness?"

Stone's head shook back and forth almost violently. "No, not at all. In fact, I was floored by how close she nailed it to what the victim told me. It was just kind of weird. I've never seen anyone channel the offender's feelings like that."

"So what's the issue with me taking Sinclair on as my partner?"

Why she hadn't kept her big mouth shut, Stone didn't know. She had no idea how to dig herself out of the massive hole she'd stepped into. "Blake," she whispered and dropped her head, finally able to break free of the death lock Chris had on her eyes.

"Am I missing something here? Have you been assigned as the caretaker of Detective Blake's career?"

"No."

"Then let me give you some advice. Worry about your own career, Detective. Let Detective Blake worry about hers."

As if on cue, Detective MaryAnn Blake sailed in and headed for a seat at the table. "Sorry I'm late, Sarge. I put those boxes in your office and locked the door. Some of that shit is worth a lot of money."

"I'm sure Constable Sinclair appreciates it, Detective." Chris continued to hover over Detective Stone. "Question for you Detective Blake."

"Yeah." Blake scanned every face in the room. The tension was thick enough to warrant a chain saw to cut through it.

"Do you have any issues with me taking Constable Sinclair on as my partner?"

Ah, okay. She thought she knew what was going on now. She voiced her opinion to the other detectives in the unit, feeling threatened by Sinclair when Chris brought her on board. Then Chris confessed to her that she was just about burnt out from working in Sex Crimes and she encouraged Blake to take the Sergeant's exam so she could take Chris's place. She felt like a fool for doubting Chris. "No issues, Sarge. I'm confident Sinclair will be a credit to the team."

Taylor raised her eyebrows. That was the last thing she expected to hear out of Blake's mouth. Blake told her to her face she hadn't earned a spot in Sex Crimes and didn't deserve to be there.

Chris backed away from Stone, addressing Blake. "How did today go?"

"Great. Good. I think. I hope. I get the results next week."

"I bet you aced it, Detective. I think maybe Detective Stone would benefit from hearing what you were doing today and why?"

Blake looked across the table at Stone, trying to convey her regret. She felt responsible for the situation Stone found herself in because she hadn't told her she now understood and accepted Chris bringing Taylor in as her partner. "I took the Detective Sergeant's exam this morning. DS Cain is grooming me to take over her position when she leaves the unit in the next six months to a year."

Every eye in the room widened, including Taylor's. This was the first she heard about Chris giving up command of her team in the Sex Crimes Unit. She was responsible for every investigation assigned to her team, the team's budget, scheduling, and other administrative duties. She reported directly to Inspector Worthington. On top of all that, she worked her own share of the cases that came to her team.

"Sarge?" Before she realized what she was doing, Detective Stone found herself on her feet gawking at Chris.

"Another problem, Stone? Don't you approve of my decision to promote Detective Blake? In the time she's been with the Sex Crimes Unit she has worked her ass off, putting in extra hours without pay, taking every opportunity to learn, not just from me, but from every detective in the unit. She puts her heart and soul into every case and doesn't give up. She's dedicated, not just to the unit, but to every officer working in it. Not only do I believe she'll do an outstanding job commanding this team, I believe there is no one better suited to the position."

Detective Blake sat with her mouth agape. She'd never heard Chris talk so highly of her. Sure, she'd been given exemplary performance reviews, but to sit there and hear her say all that made every sacrifice she made over the past few years more than worthwhile.

"I'm sorry, MaryAnn. I didn't mean any disrespect. I would be honoured to serve under your command. You know I would." Stone said her peace to Blake then turned back to Chris. "I just can't believe you would walk away from Sex Crimes, Sarge."

Chris pulled out a chair at the head of the table and dropped herself into it then ordered Taylor to sit. She waited until Taylor took a seat next to Stone, across the table from Blake. "The average life span of a cop in the Sex Crimes Unit is five years. I've been here a hell of a lot longer than that and I'm burning out. It's time for me to move on."

Seeing the doubt and confusion in Taylor's face, she added one more thing. "Before you get your panties in a twist about what's going to happen to you, Sinclair, I'm taking you with me.

"Now, Detective Stone, give us your update before the Inspector gets here."

"You'll be missed." Detective Ambrose spoke very quietly, his eyes still focused above Stone's head.

"Jesus, Ambrose," Chris said. "I forgot you were here." The tension in the air vanished as everyone broke out laughing.

And that, Detective MaryAnn Blake thought, was one of the things about Detective Sergeant Chris Cain she didn't think she could duplicate. She knew when to be hard, when to put the fear of God into her staff, and when to lighten the mood with a joke. She knew how to push you, how to make you feel pride in the job you did, how to get the best out of you. In the three years she'd been Chris's lap dog, jumping every time Chris shouted her name, the thing she most admired about her commanding officer was her ability to inspire the individuals under her command to be the best they could be. She rode you hard, but when you slipped up, she was the first person at your side to offer you a hand back up. She would tell you where you screwed up, if it wasn't obvious, but made you figure out how to fix it on your own. If you couldn't figure it out, she nudged you in the right direction and gave you full credit when you finally got there. She made you want to learn more, do more, *be* more.

Blake had to tear her eyes away and clamp down on her emotions. She began to scan the board at the front of the room and recognized the work of Constable Sinclair. She resented Sinclair from the moment she met her, yet as she scanned the board she couldn't help but feel that losing Sinclair might be as much a loss to the unit as Cain. Nah. Losing Cain was *huge*.

"The door to doors turned up very little information," Stone began. "The neighbours on either side of the Delacourte residence and directly across the street weren't home. No one saw suspicious vehicles or persons hanging around the neighbourhood recently, except a woman who lives across the street and a few houses down from the victim. She reported seeing a man dressed in coveralls and a ball cap at the victim's door this morning. She wasn't clear on the time, but said it was before seven, which fits with our vic's statement. She didn't think anything of it as the phone company had been working in the area recently. I've got a call into Bell Telephone to verify.

"Forensics is still working the scene. They'll be at it for a while yet with the mess left behind. Fingerprints lifted in the vic's bedroom, en suite, and kitchen came back as the vic's. Essentially, we have no prints and no DNA. Looks like our perp gloved up, hands and dick."

"We may have DNA from the pubic hairs collected at the hospital," Chris cut in then addressed Stone. "This may not be his first victim. When you're ready to begin the ViCLAS booklet, let me know. I want Sinclair trained on it."

ViCLAS, Canada's Violent Crime Linkage Analysis System, wasn't unknown to Taylor. Aside from studying its history and capabilities at the Police Academy, Taylor learned about the system online before she came off the streets while researching the psychology of sexual criminals at the Toronto Public Library. After studying the FBI's ViCAP system and several State systems for identifying and linking cases based on offender, victimology, modus operandi, and behavioural and forensic data, The Royal Canadian Mounted Police, Ontario Provincial Police, and Sûreté du Québec created Canada's own system.

"I'll add it to my to-do list," Stone responded.

Chris got to her feet and stood in front of the board, scanning the crime scene photos. "If he has done this before, it's only going to be once or twice. He's in the early stages here. Figuring out his MO. He made some major mistakes, the biggest being he took too much time with her. He knew she lived alone, but he didn't factor in one of her friends would come to check on her and that led to more mistakes. He had to get out fast, leaving behind the rope. More probably. We're going to find out there was more he left behind."

"The coveralls and ball cap the neighbour described were found on the floor of the hall closet," Stone added in.

"No coat," Chris said. "Unless he grabbed it on his way out. His vehicle may have been parked nearby. Sinclair, you can put checking traffic cams in the area between five hundred hours and oh six forty-five this morning on your to-do list. And since you know a bit about these Rune symbols, why don't you research them, as well."

The door opened and Inspector Cal Worthington stepped in, glaring at Chris before he walked over to the board and studied it with his hands clasped behind his back. The room fell silent, waiting for the Inspector to address them. He took his time, studying every photograph before reading Taylor's notes which included a description of the offender, the distinctive attributes they believed the victim may share with 'Sass', the details separating this offender from others such as the cuts. When he finished, he simply took a seat at the table. "Go ahead with your briefing, Detective Sergeant."

He still looked pissed as hell, Chris thought,. But, that was fine. She was prepared to defend her decision to take Taylor into the field. "Yes, sir," she responded and began from the beginning to the end covering everything they had done and discovered so far.

"You will have all of the resources available to this department at your disposal," Worthington began when Chris finished her briefing. Rising to his feet, he added, "Find this son of a bitch."

He made his way to the door then looked over his shoulder at Chris. "A minute of your time, Detective Sergeant."

"Why don't we just do it right here instead of talking behind her back." She knew she was pissing him off even more, but she was pissed, too.

"Outside, Cain," he barked.

Chris motioned for Taylor to follow her out. When the Inspector saw what she'd done he turned back. "Did I ask Sinclair to join us?"

"It concerns her, Inspector. I think she has a right to be privy to it."

"Holy fuck," Stone whispered.

As soon as the door closed behind them, Cal cut into Chris. "You know she has not been cleared for active cases."

"On the contrary, Inspector, I have a doctor's note clearing Constable Sinclair for full duties."

He looked just like Cail when he was angry, Taylor thought. His face turned red and the veins in his neck bulged and throbbed. She took a step back, in self-preservation mode.

"Your office, Detective Sergeant." Cal tromped away from them pulling out his cell phone and making a call as they crossed the unit. Taylor followed along behind Chris, scared half to death. Chris tossed her a look over her shoulder and winked. Taylor didn't like Chris putting her butt on the line like this to get her cleared for active cases. She wanted the clearance, but there had to be a better way than this.

Chris unlocked her office door, stepped inside followed by Taylor and then Cal, who slammed the door closed behind him and ordered them both to take a seat. Then they just sat there, waiting. For what, Taylor had no idea.

Ten long and torturous minutes later there was a knock on the door and Dr. Lane McIntyre stepped in. "You demanded my presence, Inspector."

Wow. Taylor had never seen Lane angry before. She was about half the size of the Inspector, but her deep brown eyes glared up at him with her hands fisted on her hips, ready to take him on.

"I was with a patient and I don't appreciate being summoned when said patient is on the verge of a very important breakthrough." Lane's shoulder length mahogany curls vibrated with her fury.

"Have you or have you not informed the Chief that Constable Sinclair is not fit for active cases?"

Lane's eyes flashed to Taylor before narrowing back on the Inspector's. "I said no such thing. What I told the Chief was how Taylor will react to crime scenes and victims of sexual assault is unknown. Does that mean she shouldn't be assigned to active cases? Absolutely not. If we didn't expose our officers to crime scenes because we didn't know how they would react the first time, we wouldn't attend crime scenes. You can't hold Taylor back from active duty because you're worried how she'll deal with it. That's my job."

"It's not like I've never been at a crime scene before," Taylor murmured. She was going to add she practically grew up on them, but that wouldn't have aided her case.

Cal took the seat behind Chris's desk and used her desk phone to dial the Chief of Police, Madison Clarke.

"Chief, you're on speaker. I've got Dr. McIntyre, DS Cain, and

Constable Sinclair with me. Dr. McIntyre informs me there is no reason to hold Sinclair back from working active cases."

"We're not going to send her into the field not knowing how she will react." Clarke's voice came through the speaker with tinny crackle.

"Do you discriminate against all victims of abuse or is it only me?" Taylor asked. She could sense Chris biting her lip to prevent a smile.

"That's not what this is about, Sinclair."

"I beg to differ," Lane put in. "We don't hold anyone else back from attending a crime scene because we're worried how they will react."

"And what if she has a complete meltdown at a scene? What then?"

"She attended the Delacourte scene with me this morning and handled herself in a very professional manner and was able to tap into the offender's motivation, his feelings. She picked up a clue to the victimology that I totally missed, although I shouldn't have," Chris said with calm authority.

Taylor just looked at her. She wasn't being completely honest by not mentioning the fact Taylor had been struck with a vision just inside the door when they arrived on scene.

"Lane?" Clarke said.

"She appears to have handled it very well. I'll schedule extra sessions with her to ensure she's coping."

"Okay. I hear we may have a serial rapist on our hands. God speed to your team, Detective Sergeant." With that the line went dead.

Cal rose to his feet, staring Chris down. "In the future, I expect you to resolve issues of this nature before taking matters into your own hands." With that he blew out of the office.

"I'll see you at six?" Lane asked Taylor with a stern look on her face.

"Yeah, I'll be there." Although, she wasn't looking forward to it. This would be Taylor and Cail's first joint session with McIntyre. Considering she hadn't been face to face with him in several weeks, she didn't know what to expect.

"Okay. I've got to get back." She ruffled Chris's hair and then disappeared out the door.

Taylor's cheeks puffed out and she blew out a long, slow breath.

Chris hiked her feet up onto her desk as a slow smile spread across her face. "That went well."

Chapter 4

Blake slowly poked her head around the doorframe into Chris's office. "Is everyone still in one piece in here?"

Chris answered with a laugh. "Fine, why?"

"You've got the biggest set of balls of anyone I've ever met." She even got a laugh out of Sinclair. "That's your stuff there, by the way." She gestured towards the evidence boxes on the floor of Chris's office before adding, "From the Lisa Harmon case."

Cail's friend, Lisa Harmon, stole various items belonging to Taylor hoping to cash them in for drug money. One of the items was the bracelet and earrings she purchased in New York for Kate's birthday. The bracelet was made up of tiny gold handcuffs linked together with a diamond on the chain between each set. The earrings were a matching set of dangling handcuffs. Taylor figured Chris made sure the items were returned to her today as Kate's thirtieth birthday bash was scheduled for that evening at Delaney's Pub, a favourite cop hang out just down the street from Headquarters.

"Thanks, Detective Blake. I could have picked them up myself."

"No worries. I was down there, so it wasn't a biggie."

Chris dropped her feet to the floor and went her desk to take her seat in front of the computer. "I've got some stuff to clear up so I can get out of here, shower, and get to Delaney's. All this party stuff is stressful." She'd never hosted a party before, but she was doing it for Kate. Chris smiled to herself. She would do anything for Kate.

"Need anything from me?" Blake asked.

"Nah. Get out of here. You deserve a break after all of the cramming for the exam."

"Thanks, Sarge. Later, Sinclair."

"Yeah, later," Taylor said quietly after Blake was already gone. She couldn't figure out why Blake was being so nice lately. She kept waiting for the bottom to fall out. "I'll get on those traffic cams and stuff." She pushed to her feet slowly, as if fatigued. At the door she turned back to Chris. "Thanks. You know, for sticking your butt on the line for me and all."

"I figure my butt in your hands isn't such a bad deal."

"Ha, ha. Perv." Taylor walked away with a smile on her face.

Yeah, she was coming along, Chris thought. Taylor handled the crime scene like a pro and she wasn't letting the media's relentless pursuit of what was going on between her and Cail, or questions about what happened to the child she'd been pregnant with at the tender age of thirteen, get to her.

Taylor studied the traffic cam videos until her left eye throbbed. She shut down her computer, removed her glasses, and put her eye patch on to give her damaged eye a rest. At the door to Chris's office, she watched Chris working away on her computer for a moment before she interrupted. "Hey, I'm heading up to Lane's office."

"Yeah, sure. I'm heading out myself in a minute. I'll see you at Delaney's?"

"Yeah." The mention of Delaney's reminded Taylor that Kate's present was in the boxes on the floor of Chris's office. "Would you mind if I searched through these for Kate's present? I'll pick the boxes up tomorrow, if that's okay." Chris nodded her ascent and continued to type. The first box held clothing, some of the expensive dresses and shoes she purchased on her book tour. In the second box, she found some of her drawings, folded neatly. Kate's present sat on the bottom next to the Rolex watch Taylor gave to Cail when she returned from her book tour. She wasn't sure what she was supposed to do with it now. The inscription on the back said 'I Love You – TGS', Taylor's initials. But, they weren't together anymore. She slipped the watch into her pocket and picket up Kate's gift.

She arrived at Lane's office a few minutes before six and found the receptionist already gone for the day. Popping her head into the doorway, she saw Lane tapping away on her keyboard, much like Chris had been. Lane looked up and smiled, then waved Taylor in. She closed the report she'd been working on and picked up a pad of lined paper, moving to her favourite chair in the sitting area. A white leather love seat sat against the wall with two matching chairs at either side of the coffee table. Taylor took her regular seat across from Lane.

"So, how are you feeling after being on the Delacourte crime scene

today?"

"Okay, I guess. It made me angry. It made me want to do whatever I can to put the son of a … you know what where he belongs."

"Those are healthy reactions. Is your eye bothering you?"

Taylor's hand unconsciously went up to cover her left eye. "I think it's just overworked. Putting the patch on forces it to rest."

"When's your next eye exam?" Lane wondered if the sight in her left eye was improving and her prescription lenses were too strong now.

"First week in January."

"Maybe you should see if you can get in before the holidays."

Taylor's response was lost to Cail's entrance. She looked over her shoulder to see him standing there with a couple days' growth of beard that made him look like a very sexy bad boy. Dark circles shadowed his eyes. He had the sexiest brilliant blue eyes framed in jet-black lashes, but they'd lost their luster.

"Hi," he said quietly, his eyes locked on Taylor. He smiled weakly and wiped his hands down the sides of his jeans. His left hand was still encased in a navy blue cast that disappeared under the sleeve of his navy sweatshirt.

"Hi," Taylor responded just as quietly, not quite a whisper. Just the sight of him was enough to fire up the desire she'd been missing so much over the past few weeks.

"Come in and take a seat, Cail." McIntyre gestured towards the love seat, but Cail opted for the chair right next to Taylor.

Taylor didn't know how she was supposed to act around him. The spicy aroma of his cologne as he passed by her had her wanting to throw herself into his arms. She sat rigidly while he took the chair next to her and reached for her hand. She drew her hands into her lap and clasped them together while Cail let out a loud sigh.

In the past couple of weeks, she'd only talked to Cail three times. Each time he was drunk and she refused to accept his calls after that. She told him each of the three times she wouldn't consider getting back together until he stopped drinking. His anger issues coupled with the drinking were a mixture she wasn't prepared to tolerate.

"Why won't you accept my calls?" Cail asked.

"You know why."

"No, I don't."

Her back was already up and they hadn't been together for two minutes. She rolled her shoulders in an attempt to ease the tension in them. "Maybe because you were too drunk to remember the calls I did accept."

Taylor could feel Cail tensing beside her. Now they were both on edge and defensive.

Lane wanted to get a sense of how they were reacting to each other and what she saw didn't impress her. "Cail has been working on his anger issues and making progress," she began.

"Maybe he should be working on his drinking," Taylor murmured.

"I'm only drinking because I'm miserable without you."

"That's funny," Taylor said. "Because your drinking is keeping us apart."

"Okay," Lane said in frustration. "Cail's drinking is an issue for you. What else is holding you back?"

Taylor was sure Lane already knew the answer, but she was going to make her say it in front of Cail. "I don't want to be that girl who has lost all of her self-esteem and stays with an abusive partner because she believes she deserves it. I've been a victim most of my life. I can't be one anymore."

That wasn't exactly accurate, Lane thought. Taylor had been a victim her *entire* life.

"I'm working on the anger thing, Tay. I wouldn't lower your self-esteem. I support your art, your writing, and your career as a police officer. Your strength is one of the things I love most about you. I wouldn't do anything to change that."

"You say very hurtful things when you're angry."

"I'm not proud of the way I've treated you, Angel. I'm sorry. You have to take anything I say when I'm angry with a grain of salt. I don't mean most of it. I just feel like I'm hurting and I want you to hurt, too. Lane's teaching me how to calm myself down and think before I react."

"You had plenty of time to think the last time. You spent all night stewing about something you knew nothing about and then you refused to give me the opportunity to explain." She felt like she was shooting down every positive Cail was bringing up, but couldn't stop herself.

"Don't you think I felt bad when I realized I'd let you wake up not knowing where you were or if you were blind and instead of reassuring you, I lit into you. I'm learning to stop and think things through before I react. I don't know what more I can do."

"Stop drinking?"

"When was the last time you had a drink?" Lane asked Cail.

"If not drinking will bring us back together, I'll stop." He didn't want to have to admit that he knocked back a couple before coming to Lane's office. He was hoping the mouthwash he used afterwards would be enough to keep Taylor from smelling the alcohol.

"How many have you had today then?"

He should have known Lane would see right through his attempt to skirt around the question. "I had a couple earlier. I was nervous about seeing Tay. I haven't seen her for a few weeks."

"How many drinks do you have per day?"

"I don't have a drinking problem. I've just been really miserable without Tay. I can stop any time."

Lane wasn't so sure about that, but decided to give him the benefit of doubt for the time being. "If Cail stops drinking, continues to do well with controlling his anger, are you willing to give your relationship another try?"

"Yes," Taylor whispered. Cail reached for her hand again, but she kept them clasped tightly between her thighs. "As long as things change. I won't tolerate any more abuse."

"What about you, Cail? What do you think needs to happen for your relationship with Taylor to move forward?"

Cail wiped his hands down his thighs. He knew Taylor wasn't going to react well to what he wanted to say. If he didn't put it out there, he'd just let it simmer until he exploded it out the next time they had an argument. Besides, he needed Lane's expertise and input to show his concerns were valid. "My biggest concern is that the violence and abuse Taylor suffered as a child has damaged her in ways she's hidden or kept buried and at any time they could come to the surface. For example, she suppresses her need for pain."

"What?" Taylor twisted in her seat to gawk at him. She couldn't believe he really said that. "What are you talking about?"

"Are you really going to sit here and deny that you get off on being whipped?"

"Oh, my God. How many times do I have to tell you it wasn't sexual. My son died in my belly. I needed to be punished. How is it any different from when your parents gave you the belt as a kid? Was that sexual? Did you get off on it?" She needed to rein in her anger. Cail stared at her with a look of disbelief on his face that made her wonder if he was purposely trying to infuriate her.

"My parents never gave me the belt, Tay."

Was he playing with her? Trying to goad her into something; trying to trap her somehow? She shook her head back and forth in quick, short movements, her mouth open in shock. "Then how did they discipline you?" Now he was looking at her as if *she* was crazy.

"People don't belt their kids into submission."

Taylor turned to Lane for support, but the pained expression on Lane's face wasn't what she was expecting. "Tell him he's wrong."

"He's right, Taylor."

Lane's voice faded away and Taylor swiftly found herself face first in the seat cushion of her mother's couch, the stench of stale cigarette smoke and the chemical, burnt plastic smell of crack filling her nostrils. A massive hand pressed down on her back as Leila's frantic shrieks filled the air behind her. Her Huggies diaper soared across the living room, landing on the kitchen linoleum with a heavy splat. The thick leather belt sliced across the delicate flesh of Taylor's tiny bottom. With each strike, Leila's screams became more frenzied and piercing, but even at such a young age, Taylor refused to give her torturer the satisfaction of her cries. She pressed her face into the seat cushion, eyes squeezed tight, and didn't make a sound.

And then she was in the back corner of the bedroom closet. She made herself as small as possible, curling into a tight ball with Leila's trembling body wrapped tightly around her. The darkness of the closet was like a tight fist, stealing her breath. Taylor desperately tried to block out the sounds of her mother's screaming by clamping her small, trembling hands over her ears.

Hot, wet tears dripped onto her shoulder and Leila whispered, "He's my father, Tay. That monster is my father."

At her young age - she couldn't have been two yet - she hadn't understood what the sounds coming from the other side of the closet door meant, but she did now. She made the same noises far too many times in her own life not to understand exactly what her mother had been suffering through.

Rick. She remembered her mother screaming his name, begging him to stop. Rick. Leila's father's name was Rick. In that moment, she wanted nothing more than to find the sorry son of a bitch and kill him with her own hands.

"Taylor?" Lane's soft voice dripped with concern and Taylor opened her eyes to find her sitting on the coffee table right in front of her, her hands on Taylor's knees.

When Taylor's eye met hers, the rage slowly dissipated and Lane thought she looked like a terrified child. "What are you feeling?"

Shaking her head as if that would dislodge the painful memories, Taylor spoke in a voice that was high pitched mixed with breathy whispers. "I thought I remembered everything from my childhood.

But, I keep getting these flashes of things from when I was really little. What else don't I remember?" When the memory of holding her dead son after he was stillborn came flooding back to her, Lane explained it was normal for someone who suffered severe trauma to suppress painful memories. It shook her more than she was willing to admit because she thought she remembered every detail of every horrible thing that ever happened to her until that point. Considering the things she did remember with terrifying clarity, she couldn't even fathom how bad stuff was for her to suppress it.

"Can you tell me about the flashback?"

"Does it matter? It's just … more, isn't it?"

"It matters."

She managed to hold back the tangle of emotions clogging her throat, unaware of the silent tears sneaking down her face as she explained the flashback. Lane grabbed the box of Kleenex from the coffee table and set it down next to Taylor. She didn't waste any time ripping several from the box and using them to cover her face, pushing her eye patch up to her forehead to get it out of the way.

She knew their mother loved them, but love hadn't been enough to save them from the horrors she was beginning to suspect and fear had occurred in that dingy little trailer home. What scared her most were thoughts of what Rick may have done to Leila.

"I can tell you what little I know from your medical records," Lane offered.

"Medical records?" Taylor dropped her hands away from her face and began kneading the damp tissues in her lap. "From when we were little?"

"Do you remember being in the hospital after the explosion?"

Taylor shook her head. She remembered everything from that day, from the smell of the fresh cut grass just before their trailer home exploded to the smell of smoke and chemicals thick in the air, the heat and force of the explosion knocking her and Leila off their feet, glass and metal shards flying through the air. "We weren't hurt." She remembered spending that night with a neighbour before being turned over to Child Services.

"Both you and Leila became very ill in the days that followed. You were suffering from malnutrition and withdrawal."

It shouldn't have surprised her. In every memory she had of the inside of that trailer there was a blue haze of smoke surrounding them, both from cigarettes and from the crack her mother and her friends smoked. She breathed it in constantly for the first five years of her life. "We were addicted to crack." Still, she didn't remember being in the hospital.

"You more so than Leila."

Leila had been at school full time. Taylor just started Kindergarten, so she would have been exposed to it for longer periods than Leila.

"You also had welts from your lower back down to the backs of your knees."

She could feel the sting of Rick's belt at Lane's words. "Leila, too?"

"No, there were no marks on Leila."

"Why not?" she heard herself asking. That didn't make sense, did it? Why would she still carry the marks of his belt days after the explosion and not Leila? Was she such a bad child he had to constantly take his belt to her?

"I don't have the answers to that, Taylor. I can only tell you what was in the medical reports."

The answers were still locked in her brain. Only time would tell if the answers would ooze out of her at some point, triggered by circumstances similar to the one which just sent her reeling into a flashback. She found herself more confused now than before Lane's revelations.

"It concerns me that you feel you needed to be punished for the loss of your son," Lane said. "It wasn't your fault. There's nothing you could have done to change what happened. But, we'll talk about that in your next session. In the meantime, there's something I want you to think about. Were you going to Sarah because you were desperate to feel or because you were desperate to forget?"

That was something Taylor really didn't want to dwell on because Lane was absolutely right. When the tail of that whip struck her back, all she felt was the physical sensations. The pain and torment of all she'd suffered, not just the sexual assaults, but losing Leila and her son, fell away. And that brought on a disturbing realization. The relief she felt at the end of Sarah's whip was the same relief she felt when she made love with Cail. The pain fell away and all she felt were the emotional and physical sensations of being with Cail. She wished she'd never told anyone about going to Sarah Johnson, wished she could bury that whole situation so deep it would never surface again.

Cail leaned against the wall just outside of Lane's office door, listening and waiting for an opportunity to insert himself back into the room. Both Lane and Tay would kill him if they knew he was listening in, but Tay never talked to him about this kind of stuff and the allure of learning more about her past was too great. It was a damn good thing Tay's mother was dead, because he wanted to kill the bitch. What kind of mother exposes her children to that?

There were a few moments of silence from inside Lane's office, so Cail seized his opportunity before he lost his nerve. Stepping into the doorway, he asked, "Is it okay if I come back in now?"

Taylor looked down at Lane and whispered, "I can't do this right now."

Before Lane could toss him again, Cail rushed forward and crouched down next to Taylor. "I didn't mean to upset you, Tay. I'm just having a hard time wrapping my head around how you could go to Sarah Johnson and let her whip you," he said with as much calm as he could muster.

When Taylor didn't respond, Lane asked for Taylor's permission and attempted to explain. "Many people who have lived through a fraction of the trauma Taylor has endured in her life, turn to drugs or alcohol to numb the emotional pain. That wasn't an option for Taylor. She gave Leila her word she wouldn't use or drink. And, for the first five years of her life, Taylor suffered due to her mother's addictions. I think that may have subconsciously strengthened her resolve to stay away from drugs and alcohol. So, Taylor turned to physical pain to help numb her emotional pain."

"It still doesn't make any sense to me. It may have given her temporary relief at best."

Taylor's head came up, her eyes locking on Cail's, pinning him with the ferocity of her glare. "And alcohol is a long term solution, is it?"

Touché. Fuck. She had him there. "Point taken. No more drinking. But, if we're going to have any chance at salvaging our relationship, Tay, I need you to be able to talk to me. I can't understand what you're going through if you don't at least try to explain it to me." He was getting his first look at the scars on her eye lid and the bright red covering most of the white of her eye. She must have realized what he was staring at because she covered her injured eye with her hand then quickly pulled the patch back into place with trembling fingers. As she lowered her hand, he grabbed onto it and felt her whole body tense. She tried to pull her hand from his grasp, but he refused to let go, fearing he'd never get the opportunity to touch her again. "Please, Angel. I know we both have work to do if we want to make this work, but I desperately want to try."

As soon as he clasped onto her hand, Taylor felt of surge of electricity travel up her arm and send shivers down her spine. This was why she avoided his touch, because now she felt the warmth of his hand over hers, the jolt of desire through her entire body, she never wanted him to let go. She wanted both of his hands on her, exploring, trailing lightly over highly sensitive skin. Strength. She needed all the strength she could muster to be able to break free, at least until their relationship was on more stable ground.

She didn't understand where he got the nerve to tell her she needed to talk to him when he walked out on her, refusing to allow her to explain.

"I love you, Angel." He pressed his lips to the back of her hand, staring up into that one brilliant green eye. "I love you."

His warm breath against her hand had her blood pounding through her veins, her breaths erratic, and Lane was still perched in front of her. She pushed herself up to her feet, whispering, "I can't do this right now." She began walking towards the door, but Cail tightened his grip on her hand, bringing her to a halt.

"Cail." Lane said his name softly, and when he turned to look at her, she shook her head.

Despite all of his instincts screaming at him not to, he released Taylor's hand and watched her walk away, praying to God it wasn't for good.

* * *

Forty-five minutes running on the track then another hour in the weight room helped Taylor sort her thoughts and burn off the raw emotions. By the time she showered and dressed, she was already thirty minutes late. She stopped into a store for a gift bag and birthday card then headed for the pub.

She planned on going back to Chris's before going to Delaney's, so she felt underdressed in a pair of faded low rider jeans, a purple cashmere sweater that stopped about an inch from the top of her waistband, exposing a strip of ripped abs. Her black leather biker jacket didn't go much lower than the sweater. She'd put her glasses back on and left her hair down.

Entering Delaney's, she had one of those moments where she wished she were about a foot shorter. It was hard to blend into the crowd when you were the tallest woman in the room. Standing just inside the door, she scanned the entire bar, surprised at how crowded it was. The sign she made for Chris hung along the wall to her right, reading 'Happy 30th Kate' and featuring a portrait of Kate on each end of the sign. Even Taylor had to admit it looked pretty good.

She spotted Cail's parents at a table with Chris and Kate and began to work her way through the crowd. Halfway to the table, she spotted Cail, his head bent in conversation with the red head. She should have brought that up in Lane's office.

Taylor leaned over the back of Kate's chair and pressed a kiss to her cheek. "Happy Birthday."

Kate jumped out of her chair and wrapped Taylor in a warm embrace. "I'm so glad you came. I was worried you'd stay away because of my idiot brother. How did the session with Lane go?"

"Fine, I guess." What was she supposed to say? She handed Kate the gift bag. "This is for you. You might want to open it instead of leaving it lying around." There was a table bearing presents against the wall, but Taylor didn't want anyone walking away with the expensive gift.

"Here, pull up a chair." Kate grabbed a chair from a neighbouring table and pulled it in beside her.

Taylor took the seat, saying hello to the Worthington's. Rose reached over and gave her hand a squeeze. She waved to Chris instead of yelling across the table over the music of the one-man band strumming his guitar on the stage in the back corner. Kate was thrilled with her bracelet and earrings, insisting on putting them on right away.

"I'm going to grab a beer. Would anyone like another drink?" Taylor asked. She got a 'no thanks' all around and excused herself to head to the bar. She found a small space to squeeze herself into and waited to get the attention of Maggie Delaney, the owner of the pub who worked the bar with a young man who Taylor didn't recognize. Maggie Delaney was a force to be reckoned with, a larger than life personality surrounded by big red hair and a boisterous laugh.

"Well, if it isn't the infamous Taylor Sinclair."

Taylor looked to her left to find herself face to face with a familiar face from her high school years. "Will St. James," she said, her tone dripping with disgust. He was still a heartthrob. He filled out some around the chest and shoulders and his hair was longer, curling on the ends to frame his tanned face. She thought he must have highlights as the tips of his bronze hair were tinted with every shade of blonde imaginable.

"You look as ravishing as ever." He flashed her a blinding grin.

"Like you ever thought of me as ravishing." St. James was always part of the cool crowd – the popular jock, always with a gorgeous girl hanging off his arm. He and his crowd of idiotic friends bullied Taylor relentlessly all through high school.

"If you only knew," he murmured. "I did my best to stop my boys from treating you the way they did. I was in a difficult position. The peer pressure made it difficult for me to keep them in line."

It wasn't a discussion Taylor was willing to have. She turned around again, waving at Maggie when she finally made eye contact.

"Aye, Taylor. It's good to see your wee face."

"It's good to see you, too, Maggie. Can I get a Coors Lite please?"

"Aye." Maggie grabbed a beer from the cooler, flipped the top off, and set it in front of Taylor with the grace of choreographed movements.

When Taylor handed Maggie her money, she refused to take it, so Taylor tucked it into a tip jar on the bar. Turning, she found herself blocked by Will and came up short. "Excuse me," she said after he just stood there. She tried to duck around him, but he just stepped to the side to block her.

"Dance with me."

"No." Taylor began to step around him again when the cowbell hanging behind the bar began to clang loudly. She looked over her shoulder at Maggie ringing it as she chanted. "Cail, Cail, Cail ..." Then the whole bar joined in until it was almost deafening. Taylor had no idea what they were up to. When she saw Cail step up onto the small stage and take the acoustic guitar from the guy on stage, she was shocked. She turned around and stood at the bar to watch him. Before she knew it, Kate was jumping up and down next to her.

"I didn't know he played," Taylor said to Kate.

"He used to have this beautiful Gibson acoustic with little mother of pearl doves inlaid all over it. He sold it to get through his last semester at McGill. As far as I know, this is the first time he's picked up a guitar since."

Taylor didn't understand why Cail went to all the trouble of going through law school and then gave it all up to become a cop. Whenever she asked, Cail just said the lure of becoming a cop like his siblings, father, grandfather and great grandfather became too great to ignore.

Cail settled on the stool then adjusted the microphone in front of him. "I'm a little rusty and my left arm is in a cast, so forgive me if this doesn't sound great." As he warmed up, practicing a few chords and strumming softly, his eyes scanned the room until they met Taylor's. His smile was breathtaking. "Here's a little Van Morrison for the woman I love."

The bar cheered wildly as Cail began to play 'Brown-eyed Girl' with his eyes locked on Taylor's the whole time, changing the word brown for green. The crowd loved it.

When he sang the *lah-ti-dah* part, he wiggled his eyebrows and had the whole place laughing.

Even Taylor couldn't help but laugh, although her face flamed. The rough, gravelly tone to Cail's voice as he sang sent shivers down Taylor's spine and a quivering deep into her belly. Why did she react so powerfully to this man? Why him? She didn't know if she'd ever know the answer to that. All she did know was he was the only man she would ever feel this way about. He was her only chance for a meaningful relationship because deep down she knew she couldn't feel this way about anyone else or let anyone else get as close to her as Cail. She couldn't imagine giving herself to any other man the way she gave herself to Cail. She missed him fiercely, but she was scared to death his pattern of getting angry and lashing out would continue or even worsen over time.

At the end of the song, the crowd began to cheer and stomp on the floor for more. "Okay." Cail grinned behind the microphone. "Here's a little thirtieth birthday present for my beautiful sister, Kate. Love you, Katie girl." He played a few bars on the guitar and stopped. "Wait a minute. I just don't think my voice can do this song justice. Who wants to hear Ireland sing Leona Lewis's Footprints in the Sand?"

The crowd went nuts. Taylor was pretty sure she was the only one not screaming and cheering. Then they began to stomp their feet and chant, "Ireland, Ireland, Ireland ..." Kate and Chris deserted her at the bar as they took off towards the dance floor in front of Cail. Grinning, Cail took Ireland's hand and helped her onto the stage. She stood slightly behind Cail, her long red curls bouncing, with one hand on his shoulder and the other curled around a microphone. Cail began to play again and the voice that came out of the red head was something that should belong to an angel. Taylor tried her best to hate her, but the song was just too beautiful and Ireland's voice perfect and lovely. The cast didn't seem to hamper Cail's ability to finger the chords.

"They make a lovely couple, don't they?" Will chimed from beside her. "Why don't we dance?"

Apparently, Will completely tuned out when Cail sang to her only minutes before. Either that, Taylor figured, or he was intentionally trying to hurt her. She turned to the right, away from Will, and began to walk away when he grabbed her by the arm. Taylor swung back around, ire burning from her bright emerald eyes.

"All I'm saying is he's been on the news for the past few weeks with that chick. Give him a taste of his own medicine. Dance with me right in front of the stage."

Tempting. But, she wasn't about to stoop to that level. "No, thank you." She pulled her arm out of Will's grip and found a spot next to the dance floor to watch Cail play. He handled the guitar like it was a part of him. How could they have spent so much time together, even lived together, and she didn't know this about him? How well did she really know this man?

Taylor turned her attention to Chris and Kate, slow dancing in front of the stage. They gazed into each other's eyes with such emotion it took Taylor's breath away. They were grinning at each other, laughing, swaying and swirling as Kate sang the words of the song to Chris.

It was such an intense, intimate moment that Taylor turned her eyes back up to Cail who watched Chris and Kate as he played, wearing a smile and sad, sad eyes. Was he feeling what she was feeling? That dark hole inside her that she wanted him to fill again – did he have one, too? She wanted that intense emotional connection back with Cail. But, she couldn't see the path to take them there.

It hurt too much to stand there thinking about it, so she made her way back to the Worthington's table.

Chris couldn't wipe the silly grin off her face. In her entire life she had loved less than a handful of people. Lane had been the only one until she met and got to know Gray, Callaghan, and especially Taylor. But, until she met the beautiful woman in her arms, she had no idea how powerful love could be. She had no idea she was capable of a love so deep. So, she couldn't wipe the grin away, even though she knew she should be telling Kate to cut it out. Truth be told, she didn't want this moment to end. Ever.

Sitting beside Rose, Taylor said, "Tell me something. Why didn't Cail pursue his career as a lawyer?"

"Ah," Rose said. "He was hired by one of the top criminal defence firms in Montréal. For the first six months he did a lot of grunt work and second chair. His first case as first chair was defending Marco Dubrovski, the son of Ivan Dubrovski, the suspected head of the Russian Mafia in Montréal. Cail got him off on a first degree murder charge and was so sickened by the whole thing that he quit the firm and applied to the Toronto Police."

"Dubrovski was guilty?"

"He was and Cail knew it from the beginning. Still, he did his job and turned down a huge bonus from Ivan Dubrovski which would have more than covered his student loans."

"He never told me. He doesn't talk about it." Yet another thing he hadn't shared about himself.

"No. It embarrasses him." Rose patted Taylor's hand. "How are you doing, Taylor? How's your eye?"

"Good. Healing." Funny how everyone asked how her eye was doing and not the wounds she received on her back from Brandon Moody whipping her. Out of sight, out of mind maybe. She was more inclined to believe it was the manner in which she received them.

Ireland and Cail finished their song and the noise level went through the roof. Taylor clapped because she didn't want to look disrespectful in front of Cail's parents. Cail said happy birthday to Kate again and told everyone to buy her shots. He helped Ireland down from the stage and then jumped down himself just as Kate and Chris arrived back at the table.

"I can't believe he got up there. Wasn't that awesome, Mum?" Kate beamed at her mother.

"It was. It's been a few years since I've seen him play. He really should buy another guitar. He could play instead of drinking every night." Rose's eyes travelled to Taylor then quickly turned away. "I'm sorry. I just can't stand to see him this way."

Holy awkward. Taylor didn't know what to say or where to look as she wondered if Rose blamed her for Cail's drinking. She ended up staring down at her lap and nearly jumped right out of her seat when an arm came around her shoulders and then that familiar surge of arousal shot through her. She glanced up at Cail.

"You play beautifully. Thanks for the song."

"You liked it?" He leaned over and pressed a kiss to her temple.

"I loved it." Taylor smiled up at him and caught sight of the mass of red hair right behind him.

"What about you, birthday girl? Did you like your song?"

Kate jumped up and threw herself into Cail's arms. "Loved it. Seeing you play and sing again was fabulous. Thank you, thank you, thank you." With each thank you, she kissed his face.

Cail laughed, hugged Kate fiercely, lifting her right off the ground. As soon as he set her back on terra firma, his mother was there to take her place. Taylor didn't hear what she whispered in Cail's ear, but he nodded and his eyes pooled as he smiled down at her.

They pulled another couple of chairs around the table so Cail and Ireland could join them. Ireland sat right next to Cail and Taylor wondered if she thought she had a chance with him. She was stuck to him like glue.

Taylor just wanted to leave. She didn't feel comfortable sitting there looking across the table at Cail with Ireland cozied up to him. Okay, so maybe she wasn't exactly cozied up to him, but it just felt weird. To give herself a break, she excused herself to go to the washroom.

She came out of the stall to find Ireland Delaney glaring at her. Even angry, the woman was beautiful. She had the most gorgeous pale skin and the few freckles dotted over her nose were just enough to be sexy. Ignoring her as best she could, Taylor went to the sink and washed her hands.

"If you ever hurt Cail like this again, you'll have me to answer to."

Taylor nearly laughed. Who the hell did she think she was? Cail's guardian? "I'll keep that in mind." Shaking her hands off, she reached for a paper towel. The Irish lilt in Ireland's voice surprised Taylor. Kate told her they all grew up together, so it was either put on or she picked it up from her parents.

When Taylor made a grab for the door handle, Ireland grabbed her arm and pulled her back. She was fed up of people grabbing her. "Take your hand off me." Taylor's voice was calm, but cold.

"He's drinking the way he is because you've hurt him so badly. The fact that he still wants you sickens me."

Ireland's nails dug into Taylor's skin right through her sweater. If she pulled her arm away, she worried how much skin she would lose. She wasn't about to justify herself to this crazy bitch. Ireland had no idea what she was talking about anyway. God knows what Cail told her while he was drunk. "Take your hands off me." She spoke very slowly, enunciating each word.

"Yeah, take your hands off her," Chris said from the doorway.

Ireland dropped her hand, then pulled her arm back and threw a punch aimed at Taylor's face. Taylor was quick enough to grab her wrist, swing her around, and pin her against the wall with her arm tucked up behind her. All she had to do was put a little pressure on Ireland's wrist and she'd scream in pain. "Would you like to be arrested for assaulting an officer?"

"I hate you for what you've done to him."

Kate arrived in the doorway, peering over Chris's shoulder. "Taylor, what are you doing to Ireland?"

"She's keeping her from punching her," Chris said over her shoulder. "Grab Cail, will you?"

"If I release you, will you walk away, or are you going to cause trouble?" Taylor asked.

"You're a sick, evil bitch. I don't know what he sees in you. You're trying to force him into a sick, twisted BDSM relationship. What kind of sicko wants a man to whip her?"

That horrible, sick feeling twisted Taylor's belly and wrenched her heart. How could Cail have told Ireland that?

"What the hell?" Cail yelled and burst through the door. "What the hell are you doing, Tay?" He pulled Taylor away from Ireland. Ireland spun around and threw her fist again. All Taylor did was take a long step backwards and Ireland missed her mark. Cail grabbed onto Ireland's upper arms. "Hey, enough. Tay hasn't tried to force me into anything. You don't know what you're talking about."

"You told me she wants you to whip her."

Taylor had enough. Chris and Kate didn't know her history with a bullwhip and she hadn't intended for them or anyone else to. She stormed out of the restroom, grabbed her jacket from the Worthington's table, and didn't slow down until she was in her car in the garage at Headquarters. She started the car up and then dropped her face into her hands. Why the hell did Cail have to discuss her private personal issues with every girl he knew?

She hoped she hadn't just ruined Kate's party. All she needed was for Chris to come after her, leaving the party because she was worried about her. She sent a quick text letting Chris know she was okay, but she was going home, not to worry about her and asking her to give Kate her apology. Then she put the car in gear and got the heck out of there before Chris or Cail could find her.

* * *

When she got back to Chris's, she realized she still had Cail's watch in her coat pocket. She tucked it into one of her suitcases, which were nearly packed. She took possession of her house tomorrow and would be moving into it over the next few days. It would be the first time in her life she would have her own home, a place where she really belonged, a place that was hers. She should be thrilled, excited, but all she could feel was betrayal and humiliation.

She got ready for bed and climbed under the duvet, snuggling in. She could hear her phone vibrating on the dresser, but ignored it.

Everything that happened during the course of the day replayed over and over again in her mind until she found herself wondering why Leila hadn't had any welts. She wracked her brain for a memory of Rick taking his belt to Leila, but she could only find memories of him stripping her, relentlessly lashing his thick belt across her bottom, her legs, her back. Leila's cries behind her becoming more and more frantic with each lash. And then it hit her like a slap to the face, a punch to the solar plexus. Rick wasn't taking his belt to her to punish *her*, he was doing it to torment *Leila*. Leila could have handled getting the belt. She couldn't handle watching her baby sister getting it. "Oh, Leila. I'm so sorry."

Her entire body convulsed with the force of her anguish, howling with the excruciating torment, until she cried herself to exhaustion and dropped like a stone into a deep sleep.

She awoke to a dark figure looming over her and shot straight up, jumping right out of the bed. In the soft light filtering in from the hallway, she finally recognized the intruder. "Holy crap, Cail. You scared me half to death." Her hands clutched her chest. "What the hell are you doing here?"

"I needed to apologize. I'm sorry, Tay. I shouldn't have said anything to Ireland."

"You think?" She glanced at the clock on the nightstand. The red letters glowed 2:15. Apparently he hadn't been concerned enough to apologize until after the bar closed. It was close to eleven thirty when she arrived home, so he stayed at the bar for two and a half more hours. "You need to leave."

"I haven't been drinking."

"And that gives you the right to break in here and scare the crap out of me? Do you know how many times I woke up on the streets with someone hovering over me like that?"

"God, I can't win for losing." Cail's fist pressed against his heart. Jesus. These little glimpses into what life had been like for Taylor on the streets physically hurt. "Can we just talk for a minute? I tried to go home and sleep, but I kept thinking what a mess I've made of things … *again*. I couldn't sleep without talking to you and trying to fix things. You wouldn't answer my calls and texts, so I came over."

Now that he said that, she realized he wasn't wearing the same clothes he had on earlier. His leather jacket was open, revealing a tight t-shirt that showed off hard, rippling abs and the square slabs of his pecs. He looked about as miserable as she felt with his eyes heavy and sad. "Say what you have to say." She remained standing on the opposite side of the bed from Cail, feeling exposed in a tank and panties.

"I don't know what to say."

They stood staring across the bed at each other while all of the things Ireland said to her replayed in her mind. "I think you should go," Taylor whispered, finally breaking the long, awkward silence.

"Don't you have anything to say? Aren't you angry?"

"Angry? I haven't gotten there yet. I'm still stuck on betrayed and completely humiliated."

"I'm so sorry, Angel. I never should have told any of that stuff to Ireland."

Good God. What else had he told her? "What's to stop her from going to the press and telling them everything you told her? She probably wouldn't even have to go out of her way. I'm sure the media is hounding her since she's been glued to your side over the past few weeks."

Cail's mouth dropped open, his eyes widened as if he was shocked by the mere thought that Ireland would talk to the media. He moved around the bed and Taylor backed up until she hit the wall then put her hands up in defence. When Cail came to a stop about a foot in front of her, she sighed in relief. Then he took her right arm and said, "Did she do this to you?"

Taylor bent her arm back so she could look at the underside of her forearm. Sure enough, there were four arced cuts shadowed in bruises and a trail of dried blood down to her wrist. She dropped her arm to her side.

"I'll talk to her."

Cail's hands glanced up and down Taylor's arms and she didn't think she had the emotional strength to push him away if he wrapped those strong arms around her. "You need to leave."

The light spilling in from the hallway dimmed. "Problem here?" Chris asked.

Kate stumbled into the doorway. "What are you doing here, Cail?" she slurred. "Haven't you put Taylor through enough already tonight?"

Cail laughed at her. "A little drunk there, Katie?"

"So? S'my birthday." She grinned. "Chris's going to give me my present. Right, Chris?"

Chris snorted. "She'll probably be out before she hits the pillow."

"Mmmm. I don't think so. I need me some birthday lovin'."

Taylor leaned back into the wall wishing they'd all just go away and leave her alone. "Maybe you could show your brother to the door first."

"You bet. C'mere asshole."

"Tay, please," Cail whispered as his hands trailed back down her arms. He took her hands and rubbed his thumbs gently over the raw, healing wounds around her wrists. "Let me stay tonight. Let me just hold you so I know we're alright."

"We're not alright, Cail. Not when you tell your friends very personal things about me that you have no business telling anyone."

Kate took a wobbly step into the room. "Was that shit true? You know, about you wanting Cail to whip you?"

"Oh, God." Taylor sank down the wall, dropped her head, and wrapped her arms around her lower legs.

"Okay, you. Bed." Chris pulled Kate out of Taylor's room and pointed her in the direction of their room before turning her sights on Cail. "You. Out." She hiked her thumb over her shoulder. When Cail began to lower himself down to Taylor, she grabbed the back of his jacket and pulled him towards the door. "Out. Now."

Cail was about to argue when he noticed the fire in Chris's narrowed eyes. "Okay." He put his hands up, giving in. "I'm leaving." He tossed a look over his shoulder at Taylor curled up on the floor. "I love you, Angel. I'm sorry."

Chris followed him down the hallway to the front door and held her hand out, palm up. "Key." He still had the key she gave him when he was staying there with Taylor, but there was no way in hell he was keeping it when it was obvious Taylor hadn't wanted him there.

Cail took a minute to work the key off his key ring and dropped it into Chris's hand. "I really am sorry for what I put her through tonight. I never should have said anything to Ireland. I was drunk and I wasn't thinking."

"I think you could write the book on how to fuck up a relationship. Get out and leave her alone if all you're going to do is humiliate her."

"I didn't mean to –"

Chris cut him off. "Shut up. Just shut your stupid trap. Stop apologizing. Stop saying you didn't intend to hurt her. Just stop fucking hurting her. Plain and simple. Get your fucking head out of the bottle and start acting like a goddamn grown up." Cail looked like a puppy who'd just been kicked after her little rant, but he damn well needed a kick in the pants. She opened the door and stood there waiting.

"That was harsh," he said with a pout as he passed through the door.

Chris didn't waste any time closing and locking the door behind him. After setting the alarm system, she went to her bedroom first to check on Kate and found her face down on the bed with her coat still on. She managed to wrestle her out of her coat, pull her boots off, and then she gave up. If Kate was uncomfortable during the night, she could take her own clothes off. She headed for Taylor's room and found the door closed. "Screw it." She knocked and walked in. Taylor must have closed the door and then gone right back to her curled up position on the floor. Her arms were folded over her head instead of wrapped around her legs, but otherwise she was in the same position.

Chris stood against the wall beside her then sank down to the floor.

Taylor dropped her arms back down to her legs and turned her head toward Chris, resting her cheek on her knee. "I've never asked Cail to whip me."

"None of my business if you did."

"The last time we were together, the night before I went to Rappaport, it was incredible. I let go of all of my fears and we … I don't know how to describe it."

"I think I get it."

"Then the morning after the Rappaport thing, I woke up and I didn't know where I was. I thought I was blind and I started to panic. Then I smelled him. All it took was his scent and I calmed right down. But, I don't know if he was pissed because I went to Rappaport or if …" She didn't want to get into explaining she had let Sarah Johnson whip her or why. "I don't know, but he was angry and he said things that hurt me to the core and then he wouldn't give me the opportunity to explain. I don't know how to get back to who we were the last time we made love."

"He doesn't know," Chris said softly.

"Doesn't know what?"

"He doesn't know the reason you went to Rappaport. He doesn't know you did it to save his life. He doesn't know you withdrew all the funds in your account for the ransom Moody demanded either. Cal thought if you wanted him to know, you'd tell him."

"Well, at least someone doesn't have a big mouth."

"Yeah, it would piss me off if my partner told people personal stuff about me. God knows what Cail told Ireland in his drunken stupors. What did Lane have to say?"

She let out a nervous laugh and said, "Long story."

They sat there in comfortable silence for a moment and then Taylor said, "Thanks, Chris."

"For what?"

"I heard what you said to Cail at the door. So, thanks, for that and for herding him out of here."

"Did you let him in tonight or did he just come in?"

"He woke me up, hovering over me, and scared the living daylights out of me."

"I took his key away from him."

"Good. Is Kate okay?"

Chris laughed. "By the time I got Cail out the door and went back to our room, she was passed out cold, face down on the bed still wearing her boots and coat. Hell, her purse was still slung over her shoulder."

A little bit of laughter turned out to be very therapeutic. Taylor felt better after the two of them had a good chuckle, right up until Chris asked, "Is that why you've been crying? Because of this stuff with Cail and Ireland?"

Taylor lifted her head from her knees and touched her cheeks, checking for tears. Her face was dry.

Chris pointed her finger at her own eyes. "Your eyes are red and puffy. Dead giveaway."

Lowering her face into her hands, Taylor sighed then rested her cheek on her knee again. "Just processing some stuff from my early childhood."

"Anything you want to talk about?"

Talking to Chris was always somehow a little easier, maybe because of Chris's history of childhood abuse. Taylor only hesitated for a moment before giving in to the need to probe Chris's knowledge of her troubled youth. "I've just been remembering some things from when I was really little, things I must have been suppressing. And then figuring some stuff out that I wouldn't have even comprehended when I was little." She lifted her head and leaned it back against the wall, turning her head so that she was looking right into Chris's eyes. "Did you have access to my medical records from back then? From after the trailer explosion?"

"Yeah," Chris whispered. "It's all in the files from the Johnson case if you want to access them."

56

Taylor wasn't so sure she did. "You knew Leila and I were addicted to crack?"

"Yeah," Chris whispered again. She wasn't sure where Taylor was going with this, but she was suddenly worried Taylor was angry with her for not disclosing everything she knew from Taylor's past.

Taylor leaned her head back against the wall and closed her eyes. "I don't remember that. Being in the hospital after … I don't remember that." She didn't know where the sudden tears came from. One second she was fine and the next she burst into tears, stuttered breaths gasping out between sobs. Chris's arm came around her shoulder, pulling her in, and she buried her face in Chris's shoulder.

"Shhhh. It's okay, kiddo."

Taylor fought back the tears and pushed herself away from Chris, mopping her face with her hands. When she was about to talk again, the tears threatened and she pushed the heels of her hands to her eyes. *Stop it!* Finally, she was able to choke out, "Leila's father."

Totally didn't see this one coming, Chris thought. Why the hell would Taylor want to know about Leila's father? She didn't respond. She just sat quietly to give Taylor time to regain control and say what she wanted to say.

"Do you know who he is?"

It took Chris a moment to think back and shook her head. "Both you and Leila have 'unknown' registered for your birth fathers. I'm pretty sure, anyway. I can look it up."

"His name is Rick. I don't have a last name, I just remember Rick."

"Taylor," Chris began, still wondering what this was all about. "He didn't …" she trailed off, knowing Taylor knew exactly what she was asking.

"No. Not me, anyway."

"Leila?"

Oh, God. Taylor hadn't gone there. She knew he raped their mother repeatedly, but she hadn't even thought that he might have been raping Leila. "Was there anything in the medical records about Leila having been sexually abused back then?"

Chris scratched her head while she tried to think. She had been focused on Taylor and barely skimmed over Leila's information. "I don't know, Taylor. Where's all of this going?"

She couldn't very well tell Chris she wanted to track the bastard down and kill him, although she knew she probably wasn't capable of that. So why did she feel this need to find him? She didn't have an answer, she just knew it was something she needed to do. For Leila? Still, she didn't know. "I guess I don't really know."

"Who was he raping?"

"My mother," she answered then added, "But, he was abusing all of us, emotionally and physically."

"I'm sorry, Taylor."

Taylor shrugged it off. "I think I'll clean up my arm and try to sleep again." She slid back up the wall.

"What's wrong with your arm?"

"The red head has sharp nails." Taylor turned her arm so Chris could see the damage.

"Looks like you're going to need more Bio Oil." Chris joked at the oil Taylor was massaging into her scars morning and night; scars from her horrifying experience in Troy Rappaport's custody. "Speaking of, do you need help with the scars on your back?"

"Thanks, but I think I'll wait until morning."

"Alright. I'll see you in the morning. If you need anything in the night, you can wake me up. I don't mind."

"I'm not going to wake you up. As it is you won't get enough sleep."

"Yeah, but it was worth it. Kate had an awesome birthday. I just hope she remembers some of it."

Chapter 5

Unable to get back to sleep, Taylor got up and went down to Chris's basement where she'd been secretly painting every night and hiding the canvases behind a bunch of boxes from Kate's apartment. She wiled away the rest of the night painting canvases for Christmas presents.

She left a fresh pot of coffee for Chris and Kate and was out the door before the two were even up. When she got to Headquarters, she changed into her uniform and slipped into Lane's office to see if she was there. She hadn't expected her to be in at this early hour, but she found Lane sitting at her desk typing away.

"Good morning," Lane smiled. "I'm just trying to get caught up."

"Sorry to disturb you. I wondered if you had a minute."

"Of course." Lane saved her document, closed the program, and stood. She motioned Taylor to her regular seat and then took hers. "Is everything okay?"

Taylor gave her a play by play of her encounter with Ireland in the washroom and then her late night conversation with Cail and then Chris, deliberately omitting the part of the conversation with Chris dealing with her early childhood. "I don't know how or even if we can to get back to where we were."

"Do you still want to salvage your relationship with Cail?"

"I love him. I want to be with him. But, this isn't the first time he's talked to one of his girlfriends about me or about us. How can I trust him again? After this and all the stuff with Lisa Harmon, I just don't know."

"He has a lot of work to do to regain your trust. I know he's trying and desperately wants things to work out between you, but talking to his friends about your personal matters is just wrong. He betrayed your confidence. I will be seeing him this afternoon and I'll talk to him about it, if you want."

"I'd appreciate it." Maybe hearing it from someone he respected would help. At Lane's nod, Taylor stood. "I'll let you get back to your reports."

She left Lane's office, made herself a coffee in the squad room, and sat at her desk to go through the traffic cams near Raine Delacourte's house again. Traffic was already beginning to get busy at six on that cold, blustery morning. There were just too many vehicles and it was too dark. Still, she went through the footage with an eagle eye, not knowing exactly what she was looking for. The description of the offender was too vague and they had no idea what type of vehicle he drove, or even if he was driving. What if he lived right in that neighbourhood? It was a possibility, she supposed. If so, would he choose his next victim from this area, too? Les Beau's was only four or five blocks from the victim's residence. If that was where he spotted Delacourte, he could be hunting right in his own neighbourhood.

She gave up on the traffic cams, not seeing any vehicles or pedestrians that peaked her interest. She went into the conference room, turned on the lights, and stood in front of the board. Studying the photos of the victim, she couldn't understand the significance of the Rune symbols he cut into Delacourte's chest. In the photographs taken at the hospital, the blood around the carvings had been smeared around her breasts and abdomen, like a crude form of finger painting. Many serial killers were obsessed with their victim's blood, some even drinking it, but she couldn't fathom why. Taylor stepped closer and focused in on the victim's breast. Fingerprints left in the blood smears may have nailed this guy if he hadn't been wearing gloves. She took a couple of steps back and viewed the board from a distance, trying to make sense of all of it, but it didn't make sense. And that was something Taylor's brain had a hard time computing. In her mind, everything had a place, an exact place, and anything the least bit disorganized frazzled her.

She scanned the bedroom photos with clothes scattered all over, drawers hanging out or tossed aside, towels littering the bathroom floor. Even the kitchen – utter chaos. What was he searching for? Or was he just throwing everything around in a rage?

"You look like you're about to beat the everlasting shit out of that board. Tell me what you're thinking?" Chris leaned against the wall just inside the conference room door, her feet crossed at the ankle and her arms crossed over her chest. Her cargo pants were a dark brown today, coupled with a button down shirt in pale green. Her favoured hiking boots adorned her feet. Her short honey blonde hair was perfectly styled, but it wouldn't stay that way. As the day wore on and she ran her hands through it, the more unruly it would become. It was a trait Taylor found endearing.

Taylor looked from Chris back up at the board, threw up her hands the dropped them to her sides. "It's all so disorganized. There's no rhyme or reason to it. Except for the carvings and I'm not sure of their significance." When she turned back to look at Chris, she was grinning, her warm brown eyes sparkling. "What?"

"You just make me so proud. The disorganization completely offends you. Has Lane ever talked to you about OCD?"

A line formed between Taylor's brows and deepened. "I don't have OCD," she shot back, even though she knew she had some obsessive compulsive tendencies.

"Easy, kiddo." Chris pushed off the wall, still grinning, and joined Taylor in front of the board. "Serial murderers, rapists, child molesters, basically come in two categories – the organized offender and the disorganized offender. You figure this guy is very definitely disorganized, which would tell us a great deal about him."

"Yeah. Like he's a sick, demented pig?"

"This is Lane's area of expertise, but, if this is a disorganized criminal, his place is probably going to be disgusting. He doesn't take care of it or take care of himself. He'll be unhygienic, disheveled. He'll either live alone or with his mother, because no one would want to live with someone that filthy. If he has a job, it will be a menial one or he may be on some sort of disability."

Taylor was beginning to see why Chris's team, and the entire Toronto Police Service, had so much respect for her. But, something about Chris's description bothered her. It sounded all too familiar. "Could he be a street person?"

"Yeah, absolutely, but I don't think he's deteriorated that far yet. Anyway, what you're looking at is not the crime scene of a disorganized criminal. He put together his kit, the toolbox Bonkers saw when she got to Raine's room. That was organized. This was preplanned. He took the time to learn her routine. An organized offender's crimes are based on fantasies. Something triggers them and they act out their fantasy, perfecting it over time. He'll learn from his mistakes."

"But, the mess he left behind at the scene suggests he's disorganized. There is nothing about the clothing strewn about that is organized."

"I don't know." Chris took a step closer to the board as she studied the photos. "Look at what he left in the closet, at what he didn't throw out."

Taylor didn't need to study the pictures to see the inside of the closet. She remembered every detail and was surprised she hadn't figured it out before Chris pointed it out. "He left the feminine clothes, destroyed the masculine – pants, button down shirts, polo shirts."

"Bonkers interrupted him, so maybe he wasn't finished. Maybe he would have gathered all of the scattered clothes and taken them with him."

Taylor shook her head. "No, look at the state of the kitchen and the en suite. That's disorganization. I think it's more likely we're dealing with a mixed offender, with elements of both the organized and disorganized criminal, which would make it more difficult to profile him and predict his behaviour."

Chris patted her chest. "Ah, the pride. You know more about profiling than most rookies."

"I read this novel once where they used profiling to catch a killer. It intrigued me and I did some research on profiling. I have more pieces of the puzzle now, but I still don't understand her."

Taylor didn't have to explain for Chris to know she was talking about Sarah Johnson, the woman who tormented and molested Taylor for most of her childhood. "That's your organized, logical mind trying to make sense out the non-sensical."

Better to change this topic, Taylor thought, before she made herself even more frustrated trying to understand Sarah Johnson and all of the others who abused and assaulted her. "I don't think he drove there," Taylor admitted. "I think it's more likely he lives in the area."

"Why?" Chris turned to face Taylor. "What's your reasoning there?"

"It's just a gut instinct, I guess. I looked through the traffic cam footage twice. It's too dark and there were too many vehicles to pick out a guy with a vague description. I don't know. He wasn't dressed for the weather and there was no men's winter coat found on scene, just the coveralls and cap the neighbour saw him in. If he drove there or took the subway, wouldn't he have dressed warmer?"

"He may have been dressed warmer under the coveralls. Plus, we don't know if some of the clothing strewn around the bedroom floor belonged to him yet."

Taylor went back to studying the board and the violence spread across it. "Can I ask you something?" She didn't wait for a reply. "Spending that much time with the victim, he didn't plan on letting her live, did he?"

Looking back up at the board, Chris shoved her hands in her front pockets. "If Bonkers hadn't gone over to check on Raine, she could very well be in the morgue right now. But, I don't think he planned on killing her."

"Why not?"

Chris stepped forward and tapped her fingertip on the discarded blindfold in one of the pictures of Raine's bed. "He wouldn't have blindfolded her if he was planning to kill her. The purpose of the blindfold was to prevent her from identifying him."

Made sense. "If he kills his next victim, are we going to lose this case to homicide?" Taylor desperately wanted to stay on it regardless of what happened.

"Even if he had killed Raine, it's still a sexual crime. These types of offenders and crimes are what the Sex Crimes Unit was created to deal with."

"Good. I want a part in putting this monster in a cell."

The edges of Chris's mouth turned up ever so slightly. "We've got about thirty minutes before the briefing and I don't have nearly enough coffee in my system."

Taylor peeled her eyes off the board and shot Chris a smirk. "Ten-four, Sarge."

"You doing okay this morning?"

"Yeah," Taylor nodded. She really didn't want to bring any of the stuff about Leila's father or Cail to the surface when she needed all of her focus on her job. "How's Kate feeling this morning?" She asked as they headed out of the room.

"The bitch isn't even hung over. After Cail told everyone to buy her shots, I thought she'd be a write-off today. She woke up before me and comes skipping into the room with a cup of coffee, all smiles and sunshine. It was enough to make you want to boot. It's just not right. How is it possible to drink that much and not be hung over?"

It made Taylor wonder if Cail was hung over every morning and, if so, why would he keep going out and getting drunk again? It was just one more thing she couldn't wrap her brain around. She couldn't comprehend anyone not wanting to be in complete control of their senses.

* * *

Taylor sat at the conference room table going through the file Chris gave her containing the reports submitted thus far while she waited for the investigative team to arrive for the briefing. Someone had turned on the TV in the corner of the room to a twenty-four hour local news station. Taylor looked up when she heard her name to find video of herself leaving Delaney's the night before. They zoomed in on her face as the commentator described how devastated she looked. Moments after she left the pub, Cail walked out arm in arm with Ireland Delaney and the speculation was that Taylor was distraught over Cail's relationship with Ireland. She supposed that was better than the truth being broadcast. Watching the two of them, Taylor was sure Ireland was playing it up for the camera. She knew she was being filmed. Odd, because Taylor scanned the entire street and didn't seen any reporters or cameras. They must have been in one of the vehicles parked along the street behind dark, tinted windows. And how did they know Cail was there anyway? How had they conveniently set up to film him coming out of different bars every night? Ireland Delaney definitely couldn't be trusted and now she had information which could really hurt Taylor if she talked to the media.

Detective Blake stood just behind Taylor watching the report play out. Bad timing, she thought, finding herself in a very awkward situation.

"Turn it off, Sinclair," Chris ordered.

Taylor looked over her shoulder to see Blake right behind her and Chris standing just inside the door. With a shrug of her shoulder, Taylor turned her attention back to the file folder in front of her. "Doesn't bother me."

Chris tried to get a read on Taylor when a breaking news alert on the TV distracted her. The video footage showed Ontario's Premier, Carl Devonshire, being led in handcuffs from his home and put in the back of an RCMP vehicle. The commentator stated that the charges against the Premier were as yet unknown. Further footage showed computer equipment being removed from both the Premier's office and his home.

"Wow," Blake commented. "Shit's going to hit the fan."

Taylor was relieved the media would have someone else to focus on. Maybe they would finally leave her and Cail alone.

Chris picked up the remote and turned the TV off. "Let's focus on the briefing, shall we?" She took a seat at the conference table as Detective Stone, Detective Ambrose, and Dr. McIntyre came in and followed suit. Then Will St. James strutted in and took the seat next to Taylor.

"Still ravishing," Will whispered beside her.

Taylor shifted uncomfortably in her seat and refused to respond. She got another surprise when Inspector Cal Worthington walked in, followed closely by someone else she recognized from her past - Detective Martine DuBois, the woman who investigated the abuse against Taylor when she was a child. Except DuBois was no longer a detective. She wore the same white shirted uniform as the Inspector. It had been a good ten years since Taylor last saw DuBois, but she remained fit and lean with her short cap of jet-black hair now streaked with grey. She was tall, but not nearly as tall as she was in Taylor's memories. Their eyes met across the room, sizing each other up before Taylor shifted her gaze. Chris looked at DuBois with a slight smile on her face and her eyebrows raised as if questioning what the heck she was doing there.

Cal stood at the front of the room, an imposing figure of authority. "Before you begin your briefing, a few introductions are in order." He motioned towards St. James who rose to his feet. "Sergeant Will St. James is on loan to us from the RCMP's Major Crime Unit."

"At whose request?" Chris asked. It hadn't escaped her that St. James's presence here and at the pub the night before made Taylor uncomfortable.

"At the request of the RCMP," Cal answered.

"Why?" Chris kept her narrowed eyes focused on St. James.

"I often go on loan to police departments across the country to offer my expertise and foster positive inter-agency relations," St. James said.

"Why now?"

It wasn't unusual to encounter resistance from officers at the police departments St. James worked with, but he was sensing something more going on here than the usual territorial resentment. The easiest way to diffuse the situation was to admit the truth. Well, sort of. "Look, I requested a transfer to Toronto so that I could spend as much time with my mother as possible before I lose her to cancer. That's why I'm here now."

Questioning him further would make her look like an insensitive bitch, so Chris backed off until she could have a more private conversation with Sergeant Will St. James of the Royal Canadian

Mounted Police.

"If you're done with your interrogation, Detective Sergeant."

Chris gave Cal a cool nod, noting the ire in his eyes.

"Most of you know Inspector Martine DuBois." His left hand went out to indicate DuBois as she moved up to Cal's side, a noticeable limp in her step. "Inspector DuBois will be filling in as head of the Sex Crimes Unit while I'm on leave beginning in the New Year."

Chris's mouth dropped open. The last thing she expected was for Cal to announce he was taking a leave of absence. She was pretty sure Kate didn't even know of her father's intention to take some time off.

"I expect your full cooperation." With that, Cal took a seat at the conference table.

DuBois pulled out a chair and sat next to him. "Detective Sergeant Cain, go ahead with your briefing."

"Detective Stone, when you're ready."

Stone's head shot up, eyebrows drawn in. "Me?"

"You're the OIC. It's your briefing, Detective."

"But, I thought ..." Stone looked around the table and decided to bite her tongue. She figured Cain would take over as the Officer in Charge given the potential for the offender to repeat. Stone took her laptop to the front of the room and quickly connected it to the overhead projector.

The briefing hadn't even begun and Taylor's head was spinning. She'd met Will's mother after one of the times Will and his friends attacked her. Taylor regained consciousness in someone's house and as soon as she saw Will, she took off. It wasn't until she made it back to where she slept at the time she realized her wounds had been tended to. The next day, Will's mother turned up at the school to check on her.

Taylor wondered how long she could handle working with Will and how she would deal with working under DuBois. She'd been terrified of DuBois as a kid. Sarah Johnson ensured she would be deathly afraid of the police, but looking back on it now, she knew she'd been a fool not to trust DuBois even though she wouldn't have been able to discuss the atrocities done to her. As Detective Stone began her briefing, Taylor glanced across the table at DuBois and found her staring back at her. She didn't even attempt to hide it, raising her carefully shaped eyebrows and suppressing a smile. Taylor dropped her eyes then chastised herself for being so weak.

"I received confirmation from the phone company that they have not been working in Raine Delacourte's neighbourhood. I think our best chance at identifying our perpetrator is finding someone who saw him in the neighbourhood or recognized him," Stone advised from the front of the room as Taylor tuned back in. "I'd also like to canvas Delacourte's workplace. It's possible our perp first came into contact with her while she was working in the emergency department at Toronto General and someone at the hospital may have seen him."

Stone looked over at Chris. She got a nod of approval and continued. "The other possibility that came to mind is social media. Elizabeth Cruise posted on Facebook that she was at Les Beau's with Raine Delacourte last Thursday evening. Having tagged Raine in the post, it was also displayed on Delacourte's Facebook wall. If someone had been monitoring her Facebook profile, he would have known exactly where to find her and may have followed her home from there."

Stone glanced over at Chris again and this time Chris added her two cents worth. "Let's canvas the neighbourhood and Les Beau's in the evening. We're more likely to find people at home after six o'clock and the night shift staff at Les Beau's begins at five or six. Get Brice McLean on board and see if he can determine if anyone has been monitoring Raine's Facebook page. Raine stops at the same Tim Horton's on the way to work every day, so let's talk to the staff there, too. Has anyone had any luck finding a woman named Sass or Sassy?"

"I only found one Sass in Ontario and she misses our age bracket by a good twenty years," Taylor answered. "She has blonde hair, but her build is far from athletic."

"Let's branch that out then. Look for a Sass in Canada that matches our vic's description, but let's talk to the Sass you found as well. This could be some sort of mommy issue," Chris said to Taylor. Turning back to Stone, she asked, "What have you got back from Forensics?"

"Not much, at this point." Stone fiddled with her laptop then turned to face the screen to study the photograph of a pair of navy blue coveralls. "This photograph shows the coveralls found in the closet by the front door. You can see a dark pattern above the left breast pocket where it appears stitching has been removed. The word *Bell* was painted over this area using White-Out, but they were able to identify the shape of the darker material as spelling *Campbell Motors* and below that the name *Mike*. Campbell Motors was a small auto service station which went out of business two years ago. I am in the process of trying to track down the owners. The coveralls are a size thirty-two, which, for a man, is quite small." Stone tapped her keyboard to display the next photo. "The cap found with the coveralls is a plain navy blue ball cap. White-Out was used here also, to paint *Bell* on the front. Dark brown hairs were collected from the collar of the coveralls and from inside the cap, so we're hoping for a DNA match."

The next photo to pop up on the screen was of the garbage pail in the en suite bathroom. At first, Taylor couldn't figure out what she was looking at, but when it hit her, the back of her hand pressed against her mouth as she desperately forced back the urge to gag.

"Eight discarded condoms were recovered from the victim's bathroom garbage pail," Stone advised.

"That's organized, isn't it?" Taylor asked. She was painfully aware of the reddening of her cheeks, especially when the grin on Chris's face made it apparent she was enjoying Taylor's discomfort. "I mean discarding them that way instead of just leaving them wherever."

"This is something my partner and I were discussing earlier," Chris stated. "If you study the crime scene photos, there are elements of a disorganized offender, but there are also elements of an organized offender. Would you like to elaborate, Dr. McIntyre?"

Lane rose and went to Taylor's board. With her hands clasped at the small of her back, she paced back and forth studying the photos at length. "Yes," she finally addressed the room. "I see elements of both an organized and disorganized offender. We know there was some pre-planning in that he knew her routine, knew what time she left the house, and he brought the tools he would need with him, such as the rope and, I'm assuming, the condoms. Certainly, those are traits we would assign to an organized offender. The chaotic state of the bedroom, clothes and towels scattered, drawers pulled out, and the mess left behind in the kitchen point to a disorganized offender. But, you're dealing with a predominantly organized offender type."

Chris's eyes skimmed over Taylor's board as Lane returned to her seat. "Our vic is gay, but we don't know if the offender was aware of her sexual orientation. Until we have another victim, figure out who Sass is, or where the perp picked up Raine's scent, it remains a possibility."

"Have you ruled out family and acquaintances then?" Lane asked.

"Raine has no family in the area. Given the state of the bedroom and the kitchen, we believe the perp was looking for something, but we don't know if he was looking for valuables or for something specific. Or he may have been throwing things around in a rage. He knew Raine in the sense he'd been watching her, discovering her routine, but does he know her more intimately? Does he work with her or know her in her daily life? Sinclair and I will question Raine again today and see if we can get any more out of her." Chris stated.

A deep line formed between the thin, arched brows of Inspector DuBois. "Have you considered the victimology written on the board describes you to a tee, Detective Sergeant?"

The slow smile spreading across Chris's face told DuBois and everyone else in the room that Chris had picked up on the similarities. "It's early stages yet, Inspector. The victimology is just a guess at this point."

"Maybe so, but be careful out there."

DuBois' genuine concern for Chris's safety elevated Taylor's opinion of her. As she listened to the briefing, Taylor's cell phone vibrated in her pocket. It was either the call from her lawyer to tell her she could pick up the keys to her house or Gray letting her know she arrived in Toronto, but she couldn't answer it or return the call until after the briefing. She was having a difficult time concentrating when all she could think about was moving into her new home. *Her* new home. Less than a year ago, she was living on the streets with no hope for the future and today she was not only becoming a homeowner, but a home owner with no mortgage. It was still hard to believe. Who knew that telling her story, or rather a softer version of her story, would make her a wealthy woman?

"Sinclair?"

Taylor jolted out of her reverie at Chris's raised voice. Every set of eyes were focused on her and she had no idea what they were waiting for. She turned her gaze to Chris who looked supremely pissed. "I'm sorry. I was just ... thinking." The heat burning her cheeks made her feel even more embarrassed.

It was Lane who relieved Taylor of her misery. "I was just asking if you could tell us about the visions you had at the crime scene."

Well, maybe relieved wasn't quite the right word because she felt even more uncomfortable having to explain her visions. "When we first arrived, I saw what was done to her, what Raine endured on that bed. Later, in her bedroom, I also felt his humiliation and a sense of betrayal."

"Yes," Lane said as she glanced up at Taylor's board again. "I can see it. DS Cain, you may be right. If, in fact, Raine was targeted primarily for her sexuality, it's quite possible the offender's wife or girlfriend left him for a woman or had an affair with a woman."

Lane shook her head as she continued to study the board. "No, there's more to it than the humiliation of being dumped, not for another man, but for a woman. Perhaps his mother was or is controlling, abusive; made him feel weak or worthless. As with the victimology, it's too early for a complete profile on the offender. What I will say is that whatever happened between the offender and Sass may have been the trigger, the final straw that pushed him over the edge. It isn't the base reason that he is acting out in this manner."

"So what we've probably got is a sociopath with mommy issues who was dumped by his girlfriend for a woman and it set him off, so he's targeting lesbians," Chris summarized.

"Antisocial personality," Lane corrected, knowing that Chris was aware of the updated terminology - she just didn't like the newer term because she felt it made the psychological disorder sound too tame. "And no, I'm saying your theory is possible *if* the offender is targeting lesbians. Perhaps it's strong, independent women he's targeting, considering it's the feminine clothes in Ms. Delacourte's wardrobe left untouched. Perhaps you're seeking a misogynist; a man who believes in the oppression of women." Lane sighed, realizing she was getting off track. "I'd like to study the reports and crime scene photos in more depth, then I'll be able to give you a more comprehensive profile. I'd also like to study the symbols carved into her chest and abdomen and see if we can't determine their meaning."

"Sinclair may be able to help with that," Chris said.

"I'll be able to help Sinclair with that," St. James said. "I have some experience with symbols. You've got the meaning of the Healing Runes written on your board for the various symbols, but there is also another interpretation called the Viking Runes."

Chris didn't want St. James working with Taylor because she knew how uncomfortable Taylor was around him. She turned to him and said, "Why don't you look into the Viking Runes interpretation and Taylor can study the Healing Runes. Bring what you have to tomorrow morning's briefing."

St. James pursed his lips and narrowed his eyes at Chris.

Chris turned towards Lane. "Detective Stone will ensure you receive all of the necessary files." Chris nodded at Stone to ensure she got the message. "My partner and I will canvas Toronto General then hit St. Mike's to see if Raine is up for a more in-depth interview."

"We'll hit Canadian Tire to see if we can match the rope and then canvas the Tim Horton's," Stone volunteered with a nod to her partner.

Runed
body

* * *

As everyone stepped away from the table, Taylor shot out the door, pulling her cell phone out of her pocket. She found a quiet spot in the hallway and placed a call to Gray's cell.

"We're at the lawyer's," Gray began without a greeting. "We have the keys, so you don't need to worry about anything. We'll meet you at the house whenever you get there."

"I don't know what I would do without you," Taylor said. God knows when she would have made it to the lawyer's office if she had to pick up the keys herself. "I have no idea when I'll finish work."

"Taylor?"

She could hear the smile in Gray's voice and it calmed her anxiety. "Yeah?"

"Congratulations. You are officially a home owner."

It wasn't until Gray said those words that it even began to sink in. Her breath hitched. *Holy, crap! I own my own house.*

It was at that moment Chris rounded the corner, like an angry bull charging towards her. "What the hell is going on with you?"

All Taylor could do was hold up her phone as if that would answer Chris's question. Then she managed to squeak out, "I own my own house."

Chris skidded to a stop and the tension in her coiled muscles fell away. "Shit. Taylor, I'm sorry." Her hand raked through her hair. "I completely forgot. Do you need to leave?" Taylor shook her head. She looked so overwhelmed, Chris took a step forward and engulfed her in a bear hug. She thought Taylor was sobbing until she bubbled over with laughter.

And the squeak became a roar. "I own my own house." Taylor grinned then broke out laughing again.

* * *

Taylor settled down at her desk while Chris was in her office with Inspector DuBois. She ran a Canada wide search for the name Sass and came up with one name in addition to the one in Toronto, a woman from Montreal – Sass Jordan, a musician.

Voices coming from the direction of Chris's office had Taylor popping her head up to see DuBois leaving. Their eyes met and DuBois gave a brief nod of acknowledgement and a lazy smile and began to walk off with a limp. Then she turned and came back to stand in front of Taylor's desk. "How are you doing, Taylor?"

Taylor, not Sinclair. DuBois was intentionally making the

conversation personal. "Good. You?"

With a quick laugh, DuBois answered, "I'm good. It's been a long time."

Taylor honestly didn't know what to say to her or why DuBois was striking up this awkward conversation. She smiled back at DuBois and nodded. Ball in your court again, she thought.

"Okay. I guess I'll talk to you soon." With one final grin, she turned and headed towards the elevators.

From her doorway, Chris waved Taylor into her office. By the time she shut down her computer and got to the office, Chris was on the phone with a sour look on her face. She raked her hand through her hair then fisted a handful of it. When she glanced up, all the colour seemed to have drained from her face.

"Damn it," Chris whispered. "Okay, send her up, but let her know I only have a minute. I'm busy on a case." She dropped the handset back in its cradle then shoved both hands into her hair. "Shit."

Taylor shifted awkwardly from foot to foot then braved the unavoidable question. "What's wrong?"

Chris collected herself then rose to her feet. "There's a lady on her way up to speak with me. If she's in my office more than five minutes, knock on my door. We need to get out in the field. I don't have time for this shit."

"Okay," Taylor went back to her desk so she could check out this visitor as she made her way to Chris's office.

Chris leaned back against her door jamb and watched the elegant Dr. Sylvie Raynard walk toward her. She'd aged very well, Chris noted. Long dark hair was pulled back from her face then fell loose down her back. The long black coat draped over her arm partially obscured the form fitting red skirt and cream silk blouse. If her smile was any wider, Chris thought, her face would split in two.

Chris didn't smile back. She let the woman hug her, but stood rigid with her hands at her side. Sylvie pressed a kiss to Chris's cheek then leaned back with her hands on Chris's shoulders and studied her. "Tu ressembles à ta mère, Christian." *You resemble your mother, Christian.*

With a steely eyed glare, Chris answered, "Elle n'est pas ma mère et mon nom est Chris." *She's not my mother and my name is Chris.* The words spilled out of her mouth in her native language without even thought. She could feel the eyes of every detective in the unit boaring into her, probably shocked at her sudden ability to speak fluent French. She motioned Sylvie into her office with a sharp nod then closed the door firmly behind them. "What do you want?"

Sylvie studied Chris with sad eyes. "I understand why you're not happy to see me, Christian."

Through gritted teeth, Chris snarled, "My. Name. Is. Chris."

Sylvie offered Chris a weak smile and a quick nod in response. "Yes, I suppose it is. Are you still so angry after all these years?"

The lid was about to fly off of what little control Chris had left. What the hell right did this woman have to come here and treat her as if nothing had happened? She took several shaky breaths, telling herself to stay calm. "What do you want, Sylvie? I'm busy with a case. I don't have time to reminisce."

Sylvie nodded, appearing appropriately berated. "I came because your mother is very ill. I thought you might want to see her before it's too late."

All Chris could manage was to stare at this woman with utter confusion and a bit of disgust. The awkward silence was deafening and painfully long. Surely the five minutes had passed and Taylor would be knocking on her door any second.

The longer Chris went without speaking, the more Sylvie felt it had been a mistake to come here out of the blue and drop this on her. But, she thought if she contacted her and requested a meeting, Christian wouldn't have agreed to it. Maybe she just needed some time to think about it and she would come around, though she doubted it at the moment. So, as long as she had Christian's ear, she would make an effort to plead Eléane's case. "It wasn't your mother's fault, honey. She couldn't protect you against him. She threw you out to save your life. It was the only way she knew of to get you away."

And the lid blew off. "Are you fucking kidding me?" Chris yelled. "She watched him beat the shit out of me for years. Years. She ignored my screams when he came to my room in the middle of the night and did things to me no little girl should have to endure. She stood by and did nothing." The entire unit probably heard every word Chris screamed out, but she was powerless to stop herself.

Sylvie took a step back as if she had just been punched, her hand slapped to her chest and horror widened her eyes. She'd known Sebastien St. Amour beat Christian mercilessly, but she hadn't known he raped her. "Mon Dieu." Her hand flew up to cover her mouth as tears slid down her rosy cheeks. "I'm so sorry, honey. I had no idea. I'm so sorry." She took a step toward Chris then stopped when Chris moved away from her.

"Get out." Chris flung the office door open, waited until Sylvie slowly retreated through it, and slammed it shut. She sunk to the floor before her legs gave out on her, unsure if she was going to pass out or throw up. She was hyperventilating, so she concentrated on slowing her breath and pushing the pain back where it belonged – buried deep inside her.

Taylor watched the woman flee in tears. She'd give Chris a few minutes to pull herself together before going to check on her. Every eye in the unit was glued to Chris's closed door, not sure what to expect when it opened.

A couple of minutes passed before Chris came sailing out with her coat in her hand and charged toward the elevators, hollering, "Sinclair."

Taylor surged to her feet, grabbing her coat from the back of her chair and her cap from her desk. She quick stepped after Chris and caught up to her at the elevators. As they stood staring at the doors, willing them to open, she could feel the steam coming off Chris.

"Fuck this," Chris mumbled, then headed for the stairwell.

Taylor closed her eyes and sighed before following Chris to the stairs. It was going to be a long day.

As soon as they got in the car, Chris donned her sunglasses. Considering they were in the underground parking garage, it wasn't due to the brightness of the sun. "We'll hit Toronto General first and then see if Raine is up for an interview." She put the car in gear and began to make her way to the exit. She had planned on sitting down with Sinclair and going over the criminal code charges and their objectives, but that went out the window with Sylvie's visit.

Studying Chris from the corner of her eye, Taylor couldn't determine if she was fine or if she was putting on a brave front. The sunglasses were the tipping point, but she still struggled with whether to broach the subject or not. Doing so would piss Chris off. Not doing so would be safer, but she thought it was better for Chris to vent rather than holding it all in. "Are you going to pretend that didn't just happen?"

"Yep." If she had any chance of making it through the work day, it had to be that way. Besides, if her mother didn't exist, how could her mother's best friend show up at her office? Didn't happen, she told herself. Now she just had to make herself believe it. And find a way to ward Taylor from the subject.

Taylor knew what it was like to be pressured into talking about a past you wanted to forget. She couldn't press Chris, but she could offer her a branch. "I'm here if you need me. That's all I'm going to say."

Shit. Will I ever get used to having friends close enough to understand what I need? Taylor could have said anything else and she would have been fine. Hell, she was even hoping Taylor would push her so she would have an excuse to yell at her. Her body started shaking. Not just a trembling in her hands, but a trembling that began somewhere deep inside her. She slowed the car to a stop and slammed it in gear, angry now because she couldn't control the trembling or the sick feeling in her gut. She got out of the car and paced, desperate to shake it all off. She'd been dead to her family longer than she'd been with them. How could they still have the ability to bring her to her knees?

Taylor watched Chris fighting for control, wondering what she could do or say to help. She opened her door and stepped out, resting her forearms on the roof of the car. "Sarge?"

Chris turned to look at Taylor.

"Raine Delacourte needs you to find the bastard who hurt her." Taylor wasn't sure if it would work, but it was worth a try.

"Yeah. Yeah, she does." Focus on the case, Chris told herself. She straightened her shoulders, lifted her chin, and got back in the car.

Chapter 6

The mouth watering aroma of bacon frying hit Cail in the face the moment he opened the door to his parents' house. He bee-lined straight to the kitchen to find both of his siblings cozied up to the breakfast bar with plates heaped with bacon, eggs, and home fries in front of them. His parents lived in this house since they were married, over thirty-two years ago. The kitchen had been recently updated with a slate floor in earthy browns and greys, white cupboards, slate countertops matching the flooring, and top of the line stainless steel appliances. It was a good investment, especially since his mother loved to cook. Across the room, the muted TV was tuned in to the twenty-four hour news station. Cail leaned over and pecked Kate's cheek. "How you feeling this morning, birthday girl?"

"Good. I had a craving for bacon and eggs."

"Ah, so this is the birthday breakfast." That explained why his mother was cooking a full breakfast on a weekday. "It's just not right that you don't get hangovers." He gave his sister another peck, slapped his brother on the back, and went around the counter to give his mother some love.

Rose Worthington, at five foot three, was more than a foot shorter than her eldest son. All three of her children shared her Celtic colouring - black hair, deep blue eyes, and fair skin. Cail wrapped his arms around her and kissed the top of her head. "What about you, beautiful? How are you feeling this morning? "

"I didn't drink enough to warrant a hangover." She reached up, cupping Cail's face to bring him down for a proper peck on the cheek. "Sit down and I'll fix you a plate."

"Actually, I stopped by to see Dad. Is he still here?"

"He left early this morning. Big case brewing by the sounds of it,"

Rose explained as she made a plate for Cail. "Anything I can help you with?"

Rose set the plate, cutlery, and a glass of fresh orange juice on the breakfast bar and Cail pulled out the seat beside his brother. "Nah. I just wanted to ask his advice about something."

"About how you're screwing up your relationship with Taylor?" Kate asked and got an icy glare. She waved her fork at him. "You need to learn to keep your big mouth shut. You can't go around telling all of your girlfriends intimate details about Taylor. It's just wrong on so many levels. You completely betrayed her. Again."

"I know I screwed up. I don't need another lecture, thank you very much."

"Stop being such a wuss and just show the bitch who's boss," Dave said. "That's your whole problem, bro. You're letting her pussy whip you."

"Keighan David Worthington. You're not too old for me to wash that filthy mouth out with soap."

As Dave sulked, Kate grinned at her feisty little mother. She would have loved to see her do it.

If it was just his mother in the room, Cail would have talked about his relationship with Taylor. But, there was no way in hell he was about to discuss his relationship with Dave sitting there. It was time to change the topic and he had just the thing to help his rocky relationship. "What are we doing for Christmas?"

"Since most of you are scheduled to work on Christmas day, we thought we'd celebrate on Christmas Eve. Gifts and brunch then dinner around five. Does that sound okay?"

"Yeah, sounds perfect. I want Tay to experience our family Christmas. She's never had Christmas before."

Dave snorted in disbelieve, but Rose reached over the counter and took Cail's hand in hers. "Then we'll give her one she'll never forget. I'll ask Gray and Patrick to join us as well."

"Chris has never had one either," Kate offered.

"You can't tell me neither one of them has celebrated Christmas before. What a crock of shit."

"David. I'm not warning you again."

"You're right, Dave. Chris celebrated Christmas with her family before they disowned her at the age of fourteen and kicked her out onto the street after beating the ever-loving shit out of her. Every Christmas morning she sat and watched her brothers and her parents open their gifts. There was never one for her. Not one gift. Unless you count the beatings her Dad gave her." Or the rapes, but she wouldn't tell Dave that. Disgusted at the thought of what Chris had endured over the first fourteen years of her life and in her brother's complete lack of empathy, Kate pushed her plate away and slid off her stool. "You make me sick." She almost ran to the front closet for her coat so she could get out of there before she lost it on her dumb ass brother.

"Kate." Rose caught up to her daughter at the closet and drew her in for a warm embrace. "Talk to me, sweetie. Please don't leave like this."

A gush of air escaped from Kate's lungs as she relaxed into Rose's arms. "Sorry, Mum. He just really pisses me off sometimes. Both of them do."

"I know." Rose leaned back, looking up at Kate and cupped her face in her hands. "We'll have a very special Worthingon Christmas for both Chris and Taylor. Don't you worry, honey. I'll see to it."

She hadn't realized how emotional she was until her mother's words had her eyes pooling. She pulled Rose to her and held on tight. "We're so lucky to have had you and Dad taking care of us all these years. I've always known we had a very special family, but until I got to know Chris and Taylor and learned a bit about their lives, I didn't really appreciate just how fortunate we've been. You and Dad accepted Chris and Taylor into our family with no questions asked. That we loved them was enough. I love you so much, Mum."

"We've made our share of mistakes over the years," Rose said with a smile on her face.

"What mistakes? You've been the best parents."

"We should have helped you to come to terms with your sexuality for one. I feel like we cost you years of happiness by waiting for you to come to us."

Kate shook her head, dislodging a fat tear from the corner of her eye. "No regrets, Mum. If things hadn't played out just the way they did, I may not have ended up where I am today. And where I am today is complete bliss and happiness."

"I'm so proud of you, darling. So proud and happy for you."

"Okay, enough of the sloppy stuff or I'll be a slobbering mess." Kate laughed off her tears and shrugged into her coat. Before she opened the door, she said, "I don't have the words to tell you what it means for you to be proud of me. I don't think I'll ever take your love and support for granted again." They shared one more hug before Kate brushed a kiss over Rose's cheek.

"Love you, Katie. Now go on before you make me cry." Rose stood at the door watching Kate, her heart filled with love and pride, until she disappeared down the street. There was no greater joy than seeing your child happy and healthy. Then, wiping the tears from her eyes, she turned to go back to the kitchen and deal with her sons, who were both healthy, but seriously lacking in the happiness department.

* * *

Dave took the opportunity of a moment alone with his brother for a little man to man chat. "Look, Cail, you're making an idiot of yourself on camera leaving the bars with Ireland holding you up every night. It's embarrassing. I know what you see in Taylor. She's a looker. But, she's a damaged looker. Better to cut yourself off from that shit, bro."

"Are you kidding me?" Cail glared at his brother. "You're the last person I'd take relationship advice from, asshole."

"I'm serious. You're wasting your time. Whatever you think you've got with Sinclair ain't going to last. Nothing good is going to come out of it." He tapped his pointer finger to his temple. "Batshit crazy, bro."

Rose walked back into the kitchen just as Cail's chair scraped over the floor and he thrust to his feet. He pushed his face to within inches of Dave's, clinging to control, and whispered hoarsely, "You don't know shit, bro. You don't know Tay and you don't know shit about relationships."

"Neither do you, by the sounds of things." Dave smirked, waiting for Cail to lose his shit and hit him. He could use a good fight to get his blood flowing.

"Boys," Rose warned, recognizing her boys were on the brink of coming to physical blows. Dave continued to smirk while Cail held a tenuous grip on his temper, staring Dave down.

"Just trying to spare us all from more of Cail's embarrassing behaviour."

"It does need to stop, Cail," Rose dared to throw out while she cleared plates. She glanced at Cail and instead of the anger she was expecting, it was hurt and defeat she read in his expression. He stepped away from Dave and sat back in his chair, dropping his face to his hands. Rose let out an audible sigh and signalled for Dave to leave the room.

Dave rolled his eyes, but did as his mother bid. "I'm just going to change my laundry over," he announced, heading to the basement.

Taking Dave's vacated seat, Rose brushed her hand up and down Cail's back. "Talk to me, honey."

Cail rubbed his hands over his face before turning to meet his mother's gaze. "I asked Dad once how I would know when I met the right woman. He said he couldn't explain it, but I would just know." He huffed out a short laugh. "He was right. I knew the first time I laid eyes on Taylor Sinclair. I could spend days just looking at her. Those almond shaped eyes, bright green and exotic behind dark lashes. Exotic, yet filled with such sadness. That long, elegant nose, high cheek bones, and strong jaw, full lips. The sound of her deep, raspy voice. She has the most beautiful smile, but it's so rare you see it." He stopped there for a moment, realizing what he must sound like. "It's not just her physical beauty, but her huge heart and deep inner strength despite everything she's been through. I want what you and Dad have, Mum. I want it with Tay. Is that too much to ask?"

With a smile, Rose took one of Cail's hands in hers. "Relationships are always difficult, Cail. With Taylor's … problems, it's going to be harder than most."

"You think she's too damaged for our relationship to work, too."

"No, honey, that's not what I said. I just meant you'll have to work harder for it. She'll need you to be patient and understanding."

And I've been everything but, Cail thought. "Doesn't matter anyway," he said, defeated. "I've screwed things up so bad this time, I don't think she'll take me back." He glanced up at that moment to see Taylor on the TV screen across the room. The sound was muted, but he didn't need the sound to see the pain in her expression as she stormed out of Delaney's and fled down the street. Pain he put there betraying her trust yet again.

"Cail," Rose whispered, giving his hand a reassuring squeeze. "You need to talk about it. Holding it in will destroy you." She wondered if he realized the expression on his face as he watched the TV screen was just as pained as Taylor's.

Admitting to his mother how much of an ass he'd been to Taylor was not something Cail wanted to do. He shook his head, unable to look his mother in the eye.

Rose waited patiently, watching the changing expressions on Cail's handsome face as he struggled to find words. Minutes passed in silence until Rose decided a little prompting may help. "It isn't just Taylor's issues affecting your relationship. I heard you yelling at her the morning after she'd been abducted by Troy Rappaport."

His temper flared once more and he was thinking of Lane when he took a deep breath then another before he allowed himself to respond.

"She wasn't abducted," he rasped through gritted teeth. "She went to him. She left our bed and went to him."

"Is that why you've been so angry with her?" It was time to set her son straight. Her husband wanted to leave the decision of telling Cail why Taylor had acted the way she did up to Taylor, but leaving Cail in the dark when it was effecting his relationship was wrong. "Have you asked yourself why Taylor gave herself up to a man she despised?"

"Of course I have. She was worried he would hurt someone close to her – Gray, Kate, or Chris. That's the only reason she would have done what she did, but she should have trusted us to keep everyone safe."

"She did it to keep *you* safe, Cail."

"No." Cail shook his head almost violently. "Don't even go there, Mum. She didn't do it for me. She could have woken me up and talked to me. She didn't. She took matters into her own hands when she should have talked to Chris, if not me. She should have let us do our jobs and she wouldn't have gotten hurt." Lifting his casted arm, he added, "*I* wouldn't have gotten hurt." He could picture the room Rappaport held Taylor captive in. He could picture her kneeling at the end of the bed with her wrists in restraints, pulled tight so that her arms were stretched out in front of her. He could see the blood left behind after Rappaport's brother, Brandon Moody, found a bullwhip in the room and used it to tear Tay's back to shreds. He could still smell the coppery scent of her blood, taste it in his mouth.

This was exactly why Cail needed to hear the truth. For him to go on blaming and resenting Taylor was wrong and unnecessary. Rose reached a hand up to Cail's cheek and turned his head so that she could look him straight in the eye. "He told Taylor he had people watching you 24/7, including people you trusted." She knew that would get Cail thinking because there was an investigation into the police officers on Rappaport's payroll at the time he took Taylor. "She was given the option of giving herself up to Rappaport or he would have you killed." Cail shook his head in disbelief and Rose firmed her grip to keep his eyes with hers. "We both know he could and would have done it."

The way he treated Taylor when she woke up with bandages covering her eyes after her ordeal with Rappaport and Moody was partly due to his anger at her for abandoning him in the bed they had shared to go to Rappaport. He had no sympathy for her injuries because he believed she caused them herself by the decision she made without consulting him or Chris. His hand covered his mother's on his cheek and he closed his eyes, turning his anger inward. God, he was such a fool, making assumptions instead of asking for the truth. "Why the hell didn't anyone tell me?"

"Your father felt it was Taylor's place to share certain things with you … or not."

Cail's eyes opened and met his mother's again. "Certain *things*? There's more?"

Rose sighed then pursed her lips. She'd gone this far, she may as well go all the way. "When Moody contacted Taylor demanding a ransom, she went to her bank and tried to withdraw the entire amount. The money for her house had already been transferred into a trust account, so she was only able to get half of the money. If she'd been able to, she would have withdrawn the funds allocated to her house in order to save you, Cail. In fact, she tried to do just that."

That had been another bone of contention for him. They had talked about buying a place together and then Taylor just up and bought a place on her own. He'd already given notice at his apartment and hadn't found a new place yet. He had until the end of the month to find a place or he'd be staying with his parents for a month or two.

The morning after the whole Rappaport fiasco, Taylor told him if he walked out without allowing her to explain, they were done. And he'd walked out without thinking it through. God, what had he done? "I'm so scared I've lost her and damned if I don't deserve it."

"Did your session with Lane not go well yesterday?"

Cail got up, went around the counter, and pour himself a cup of coffee. He held the pot up, looking at his mother and she shook her head. He waited until he was seated beside her again before attempting to tackle his mother's question. "It wasn't what I expected." He let out a short laugh at his understatement. "I have a real hard time understanding some of the things she does. I know it's my problem, but I just wish she could talk to me about it."

"You mean like why she let someone whip her?" Cail's head whipped around, shocked by his mother's question, but she just laughed. "Heard you yelling at her that morning, remember."

Was there an end to his giving away Taylor's secrets? he wondered.

"What do you do when you're really hurting, honey?" Rose asked.

"Apparently, I get angry and try to hurt the person I think is making me hurt."

Interesting, Rose thought, but totally not where she was going with this. "Let me put it this way, what have you been doing the past few weeks while you've been hurting?"

Duh, he thought. He just had this conversation with Tay and Lane. "I've been drinking. And before you say anything else, I know it doesn't help."

"No, it doesn't. My point is that when we're in pain we try to alleviate it. It's natural. But think about how intense Taylor's emotional pain must be. When you're in that much pain, resorting to physical pain as a distraction isn't all that surprising. We see it all the time with people cutting."

He got that part, he really did. But resorting to allowing someone to whip you? "She voluntarily went to Sarah friggin' Johnson and let her whip her with a bullwhip."

"Mmm." Rose got up to get back to clearing the dishes, patting Cail's hand before walking away. "The bigger the hurt, the more desperate the distraction."

Chapter 7

Chris was much steadier when she pulled into the parking lot of Toronto General Hospital. "Keep your eyes open for anyone remotely matching our description, anyone watching us or overly interested in what we're doing, anyone inserting themselves into our investigation."

"I know what to watch for," Taylor responded.

The cold grip of winter was giving them a break today with the temperature a few degrees above freezing and the sun shining down on them. Chris glanced over at Taylor and caught her staring up at the foreboding building in front of them with the sourest look on her face. She wanted to laugh, but she knew why Taylor had such disdain for hospitals. She looked up, taking in the modern façade of brick and glass. "I can handle this if you want to wait in the car."

Taylor glared at Chris, wondering if she would ever stop trying to protect her from every little uncomfortable situation. "No, I don't want to wait in the damn car." Whatever prompted Chris to ask was at least enough to take her mind off her own problems because she was grinning now. "What?" Taylor asked in exasperation.

"Nothing." Chris continued to grin and headed for the entrance to the emergency department. "Just thinking that my partner is pretty damn bad ass."

Taylor mentally braced herself for the smell of sterilization, the sound of urgent pages, the chaos of medical staff rushing around, sick people crying out or moaning, and everything else that made hospitals what they were – nightmares from her past. A warm blast of air slapped her in the face as soon as the sliding glass doors slid open, bringing with it a good dose of that sickly disinfectant smell. The waiting room was filled to capacity with people staring blankly into space or huddled together in small packs. Taylor scanned every face, noting subtle reactions to her uniform then turned her attention on staff – the guy mopping the floor, too intent on his work to notice any newcomers; the nurses behind a wall of glass, busy typing away at computers or rushing around doing God knew what.

Taylor followed Chris to one of the glass enshrouded cubicles. The woman on the other side barely spared them a glance over her red tartan reading glasses before calling out, "You need to register at triage." She went right back to banging away at her keyboard.

Chris pull a black leather wallet from her back pocket, open it, and slammed her badge and ID against the window with a resounding crack. Taylor stifled her laugh as the woman jumped so high she nearly fell out of her chair.

"DS Cain. Toronto Police. I need to speak to someone in charge."

The deep brown eyes took their time peering over the reading glasses this time. They scrutinized the badge then focused in on Chris before welling up. "Oh, God. You're here about Raine." She got slowly to her feet, looked all around, and then sunk back into her chair. "I'll just…" she faded out, pointing to her phone as she picked up the handset. Taylor took note of her shaking hands as she dialed. She couldn't hear what the woman said, but it was short and sweet. When she hung up, she told Chris someone would be with them shortly then scurried off through a doorway.

"I think she went to change her underwear," Taylor snorted and got a backhand in the upper arm from Chris before she started laughing herself.

The person sent out to greet them was Raine's pixie friend, Bonkers. She bee-lined straight for Chris. "Have you found him?"

"No, not yet. We need to talk to the staff, especially anyone who regularly works on Raine's shift."

Bonkers seemed to shrink at Chris's words, her shoulders hunching as if deflating. "That shouldn't be too difficult. The shift on right now is Raine's. How do you want to do this?"

"I need a list of everyone on Raine's shift – nurses, doctors, and any support staff. While you're getting that, it would be helpful if we could wander around, observe, and talk to people. We won't get in the way."

Hands on her hips, Bonkers blew out a long, slow breath. "Doctors have their own rotation. It doesn't match up with any particular shift, but I can probably get you the doctors call schedule for the last month. Nurses and support staff shouldn't be a problem, but I'll have to get them from nursing administration."

With a nod of her head, she turned to lead Taylor and Chris through the sliding doors leading into the emergency department. A swipe of her ID card opened the doors and Taylor instinctively pressed the back of her hand to her nose. It didn't seem to matter how hard she tried, she couldn't suppress her reaction to this environment. She tried to ignore the nausea and light-headedness and focus on studying the various staff members and their reactions to her uniform. What she was seeing wasn't quite what she expected though. Several staff members dressed in a variety of brightly coloured scrubs looked at her with curiosity first then with concern. Bonkers was speaking, but everything sounded muffled, as if she had cotton in her ears.

Then Chris was in her face, her hands on Taylor's biceps, pushing her until the backs of her knees hit a chair and she dropped into it. Chris's cold hand pushed on the back of her neck until her head was between her knees. Taylor was glad no one could see her face as she stared at the floor between her feet. Then a wall of fear slammed into her chest. Would Chris see this as an excuse to put her back on desk duties? Was everyone right about her fitness for active cases?

A pair of tiny running shoes splattered with a rainbow of bright neon colours appeared in her field of vision and she recognized Bonkers' voice as the petite form crouched in front of her. "Have you had anything to eat today?"

Why would she ask that at a time like this? Taylor wondered. She shook her head then regretted the movement as the dizziness nearly took her under.

"Breathe, honey."

Oh, yeah. Good idea, Taylor thought. Breathing through her nose would definitely lead to her throwing up, so she inhaled through her mouth.

"I'm going to prick your finger to get a blood sugar count. You'll just feel a tiny prick."

Taylor tried to pull her finger out of Bonkers' grasp, but she was incredibly weak and Bonkers had a surprisingly good grip for such a tiny person. Taylor lifted her head in time to see blood dripping from the end of her finger as Bonkers touched a little strip of paper attached to some kind of hand-held machine to it. She had no problems with the sight of blood as long as it was anyone else's. Maybe it was because she was already feeling lightheaded, but that tiny drop of blood made her head spin again. She dropped it between her knees again.

A cold cloth pressed to the nape of her neck and Bonkers retreated, her tiny running shoes replaced by Chris's boots. "I'm sorry," Taylor whispered as Chris crouched in front of her.

She glanced up to see her cap in Chris's hands, but she couldn't remember taking it off. She waited for Chris to say she should have stayed in the car. She wasn't such a bad ass now, was she?

Chris took one of Taylor's hands, gave it a squeeze, and leaned in close to Taylor's ear. "It gets easier," she whispered. "You desensitize the more you're exposed to it."

Taylor pulled off her glasses and moved the cloth to cover her face. She removed it when she felt a hand on her shoulder. Bonkers was back and handed her a little container of juice and a half an egg salad sandwich wrapped in cellophane.

"Your blood sugar is quite low. You'll feel better after you have these."

It wasn't until Taylor looked up that she realized they were in a private little exam room and not out in the hallway. How far had Chris pushed her? Taylor took the apple juice and set the sandwich on her lap. She took a couple of sips and was surprised to find that little bit of juice was easing her dizziness. When she made no move to unwrap the sandwich, Chris did it for her then handed it to her. "Eat."

Taylor turned her head away. "I feel sick. It's the smell of the disinfectant."

"Yeah, I know, kiddo. But, you're going to feel better after you eat it."

Taylor wrinkled her nose at it, took it from Chris, and studied it for a moment before taking a bite. It was tasteless, but she managed to get the whole thing down and finish the apple juice. She looked at Chris and apologized again.

"Yeah, you were just trying to cop a free snack, weren't you?" They shared a quick laugh and then Chris turned serious. "You've been up since we got home last night, haven't you?" At Taylor's nod, she asked, "So why haven't you had anything to eat in all that time?"

This was the last thing Taylor expected to be chastised for. "I don't know. I just … didn't think about it." She'd gone days at a time when she lived on the streets without eating and never fainted. She didn't have a reaction at St. Mike's Hospital the day before, but she also had a hearty breakfast that morning. Come to think of it, that hearty breakfast was the last thing she ate. "I'm sorry," she said. "I'll make sure I eat breakfast from now on."

"Stop apologizing. You haven't done anything to be sorry for."

Despite Chris's words, Taylor still felt like she let Chris down.

When Bonkers came back in with the call lists Chris requested, Chris asked her to take them to the nursing station where Raine spent most of her time as the head nurse on her shift. She found chairs for Chris and Taylor and they settled in to observe for a while.

It didn't take Taylor long to recognize the logic in the chaos. As patients came in, the names were written on a large white board set up like a spreadsheet. Each nurse appeared to be assigned to specific rooms. There were employees whose only duty appeared to be portering patients on gurneys back and forth to x-ray, the Operating Room, or wherever. Paramedics constantly came and went, often igniting a flurry of activity. There were also clerks, working at the nursing station entering data into their computers or making calls, cleaning staff, kitchen staff delivering meals or picking up trays, cops, doctors, even therapists of one sort or another. And that was before you added in the patients with their family or friends in tow.

"We've only been sitting here for ten minutes. Imagine how many people are through here on an eight hour shift." As she spoke, Taylor scanned in every direction. "How are we supposed to determine if someone fitting the vague description we have crossed Raine's path?" When she didn't get a response, Taylor turned to find Chris's head tilted to the side as she stared at the ass of a young nurse bent over in front of a computer terminal. Taylor batted her arm.

Chris jerked around to glare at Taylor.

"Are you checking out her butt?" Taylor whispered with disgust.

"I'm observing," Chris replied with a guilty grin. "Did you see the tat at the small of her back? Cute."

Taylor went back to watching everyone while thoughts of what the tat might have been ate away at her.

They spent another half hour observing before Chris had enough. They began interviewing staff members who didn't seem to be involved in an emergency. No one noticed anything out of the ordinary or anyone paying particular attention to Raine. They didn't think she did anything to warrant someone attacking her or singling her out.

Taylor met back up with Chris at the nursing station. They didn't get anywhere with their interviews. On a good note, two women asked for Chris's number. On the downside, three asked for Taylor's. Chris joked about it on the way back to the car, but Taylor wasn't laughing. "Cheer up, three *guys* asked for your number, too." Taylor gave her the stink eye which made Chris laugh even more. "One of them wasn't bad looking."

"You mean the one who fits the loose description of our offender?" And was a good six inches shorter than Taylor.

That stopped Chris's laughter. "Oh, yeah. He kind of did, didn't he? But," Chris held up a finger. "If he was our perp, he would have asked for *my* number."

"Unless," Taylor held up a finger, mocking Chris. "He is our perp and he asked for mine to throw us off."

They arrived at the car and Chris stared at Taylor over the roof. "What's your intuition telling you?"

Taylor made a sour face. "That he really just wanted my number."

"Then why did you just say all that stuff about him being the potential perp?" Chris popped the door locks.

"Because he fits the loose description of our offender," Taylor said before getting in the car. "And my intuition could be wrong."

"I doubt it."

"Anyway, I counted eight guys that met the description while we were in the ER."

"Needle in a haystack. Still, it wasn't a waste of time."

"Why, because you got a great view of that nurse's butt?"

Chris's jaw dropped as if she was completely offended by Taylor's question. "I was checking out her tat. It was really nice work." She dropped the gearshift into drive and prepared to fight traffic on the way to St. Mike's.

"In the market for a good tattooist, are you?"

Chris laughed. "Yeah, maybe."

"Do you have any?"

Chris just smiled and raised her eyebrows at Taylor, which frustrated Taylor. She was asking for a reason, not because enquiring minds need to know what ink Chris hid in mysterious places. She rolled her eyes then put them to better use by scanning the pedestrians and traffic as Chris drove. But now she was wondering about Chris's possible tats and where they might be because she'd seen Chris in a bikini and hadn't seen any ink. *House.* She completely forgot about her new house. She could think about that and get the scary tat images out of her head.

They drove for about five minutes before Chris said, "Eight? Seriously? You saw eight slight, dark-haired men? I don't think I saw eight men, never mind eight matching our vague description."

Taylor couldn't help laughing. "That's because you were too busy looking at womens' butts." She got another back hand to her upper arm for her efforts. "Ow."

Chris glanced briefly at Taylor and resumed driving. "I suppose you've got all of their names, too?"

Why that embarrassed her, Taylor wasn't sure. "Yes," she mumbled. "I checked their ID and wrote their names in my notebook."

Chris just grinned.

* * *

Raine Delacourte's right forearm was heavily bandaged and elevated with pillows, her right eye swollen and bruised. When she recognized Chris, she covered her mouth with her left hand and wept silently.

Chris leaned over the bed to hug her awkwardly. She let Raine cry herself out before straightening and then pulled up a chair next to the bed and sat holding Raine's left hand. "I've got a lot of questions for you. Do you think you're up for it?"

Raine nodded.

"I know you told Detective Stone what happened, but I need you to tell me again. From the beginning in your own words. Okay?"

With another nod, Raine began to tell the story again, beginning at the point the offender rushed her when she opened her front door. When she got to the part where she woke up blindfolded and tethered to her bed, she stopped for a moment to regain her composure. "The first time he raped me, it wasn't how I expected a rape to be. It wasn't as violent as I would have expected. I was struggling, trying to fight despite the restraints, but he wasn't as violent as I expected, you know?"

Taylor was surprised by Raine's admission. Though she had no vaginal tearing, Taylor attributed it to the offender's use of lubricant. It seemed very odd though. She'd never heard of a rapist using lubricant before.

"I mean he was rough, but not violent. Do you understand?" She looked pleadingly at Chris.

"Yeah, I get it."

"And he would touch me. Not like someone who hates you, but like a lover. Like he was committing every part of me to memory with his hands."

"Describe his hands for me. Were they callused? Soft?"

"I don't know. I think he was wearing gloves the whole time."

Raine continued to describe her four hour ordeal in graphic detail.

At one point, he climbed on the bed and straddled her. She was sure he was fully clothed. He had jeans on at least. She could feel them against her skin. "He said something like, 'Just tell me why?' I don't know what he was talking about."

"Can you describe his voice?" Chris asked.

Raine closed her eyes and tilted her head. "No, not really. He never really spoke in a normal voice. It was more of a hoarse whisper. Like he was gritting his teeth, angry, but he didn't yell. It was like an angry whisper. I'm sorry. I don't know how to describe it."

"That's okay. You're doing great. Keep going."

"He said, 'Why, Sass? Why? She wasn't yours.' And I didn't answer because I didn't know what he was talking about. That must have pissed him off even more because he slapped my face." Her left hand came up and brushed lightly over her face, feeling for the damage. Dropping her hand again, she continued, "He started crying then. I'm sure he was crying. He went downstairs for a while and I could hear glass breaking, like he was throwing my glasses and dishes at the wall or something. When he came back up he went into the bathroom. The next thing I know, the doorbell rang and then Bonkers is calling my name from downstairs and I thought, 'Oh, my God. He's going to get Bonkers.' I heard him come out of the bathroom and I could hear Bonkers coming up the stairs. It sounded like he hit her with something when she came into the room. I heard her make a noise, like a grunt, then a thud. Someone ran down the stairs and the front door slammed. I was crying and calling Bonkers. I didn't know if she ran out or if he did."

"Do you remember anything about this guy you think might help us identify him?"

Raine sighed deeply. "Only what I've already told you."

"Think about when he rushed you at the door. Can you picture him? Did you get a look at him? Notice anything?"

Raine closed her eyes again, trying to take herself back to that moment. He came at her, head down with a ball cap on, so she hadn't gotten a look at his face. And the coveralls were baggy, hiding his form. When she fell, a sharp pain shot up her arm from her wrist and she was pretty sure her eyes were squeezed shut, wincing in pain, when he clocked her on the side of the head. "I didn't get a look at his face. Just the hat and the baggy coveralls. I'm sorry."

"Don't be sorry. You're doing great." Baggy coveralls? They were a size 32 which was small. This guy must have been tiny. There was something else nagging at Chris. Raine said he grew angry and slapped her and that didn't add up for her.

"Great?" Raine wept. "I can't tell you anything about this guy."

Chris took Raine's hand again and gave it a squeeze. "Every little bit you tell us helps. Okay? You really are doing great." Releasing Raine's hand, she passed her some tissues. While Raine dabbed her eyes, Chris asked, "What about scents? Did you smell any cologne? Anything like that?"

"No, not cologne. Something though. Soap maybe." Raine shook her head slowly. "No, it was more of a chemical smell. Like a heavy duty disinfectant. Or chlorine, like they use in pools."

"Like the stuff they use in the hospital?" Taylor asked.

Raine looked up at Taylor as if she hadn't realized she was there. "Yeah, actually. It kind of smelled like the stuff the cleaners use at work."

"Did you have any of that type of cleaner at home? The kind they use at work?" Taylor asked.

Raine's face flushed. "You're not going to bust me for taking a jug of cleaner from work, are you?"

"No. We don't care about that," Taylor said. "Where did you keep it?"

"It's in the bathroom cabinet. Underneath the sink. Why? What does the cleaner have to do with anything?"

"It's just a detail we need to clear up," Taylor said as she scribbled in her notebook.

Her partner definitely had a nose for the job, Chris thought. Maybe a quick trip to the Forensic Sciences building was in order. "The way this guy tossed your bedroom and the kitchen appears as if he was searching for something. Any idea what that might be?"

"Searching for something?" Raine's brow furrowed and her left hand came up and massaged between her brows. "Are you sure? I can't imagine what he would be looking for."

"He may have been looking for valuables, but he didn't take any of your jewelry."

"Well, he left in a hurry. Maybe he didn't have time to take it."

"You're probably right," Chris said. "When are they cutting you loose?"

"Tomorrow, I hope. They want a neurologist to take a look at my arm then I should be able to go."

Chris frowned, raking her hand through her hair. "Wiggle your fingers."

Raine laughed. "So, you're a doctor now too, are you?"

"That's why they're calling in a neurologist, isn't it? You've got nerve damage."

"Relax," Raine rasped. She wiggled the fingers of her right hand very slowly to appease Chris. "They're just being cautious."

The normal movement of Raine's fingers eased her concern, but Chris was still worried about her. "Do you need a place to stay until you can get back in your house?" With Taylor moving out, her spare bedroom would be free again and she could put Raine up until her house had been cleared and cleaned up.

"That's sweet of you, but Bonkers insists on taking care of me at her place." A slight smirk appeared on Raine's face as she looked into Chris's eyes. "You're not hitting on me, are you?"

Chris laughed. "You wish." She stood and took a step towards the bed. "Seriously, though. If you need anything, call me. You've got my cell number, right?" Raine gave a short nod in response. "Okay. If you think of anything else, call. I'm available twenty-four seven."

"There you go hitting on me again."

Laughing, Chris said, "Yeah, you're just too hot to resist right now." She got a quick snort from Raine.

* * *

Cail slouched in Lane's waiting room with his head hung low. He hadn't had a drink since he met with Taylor and Lane the day before and he hadn't slept a wink last night.

His mother's words played over and over again in his mind, like a song on repeat only it wasn't lyrics or music flowing through him. He felt sick when he thought of how he treated Tay when the only reason she'd gone to Rappaport's that day was to save him. He should have known she wouldn't give herself up to that bastard unless there was no other choice.

His appointment with Lane wasn't until late afternoon, but he'd been so distraught he came straight here from his parents'. Lane wasn't even in her office, but he sat there hoping she would fit him in when she got back. Now, he felt like he needed to talk to Chris to fill in the rest of the details he didn't know. The problem with that was he would run into Tay if he went down to Chris's office and he was pretty sure Tay didn't want to see him after last night. He pulled out his phone, intending to send a text to Chris, just as Lane walked in.

Lane took one look at Cail and motioned for him to follow her into her office. "You look like hell, Cail. What's going on?"

Now that he had Lane's attention, he wasn't sure what to say. He'd never felt this emotionally wrecked in his life. One thing he was sure of was he never wanted to feel like this again. "I've made a real mess of things and I need to fix it. I need everything to be right again and I don't know if that's possible." He slumped down into one of the comfy leather chairs and covered his face with his hands. "Just tell me what I need to do to get her back. Please, just tell me what I need to do."

The Worthington kids were like family to Lane. She watched them grow up with her own children and it was difficult to see Cail like this – broken, filled with pain. The one glimmering light was both Taylor and Cail essentially wanted the same thing - to get back to where they were before the whole Rappaport debacle. She settled into the chair next to him, placed her hand on his knee, and spoke softly, "You're asking the wrong person, Cail."

"Could you get her to come here so we can talk?"

"She's working a major case with Chris. I can't just pull her off an important investigation to talk."

"Please, Lane. I feel like I'm falling further and further into an abyss, like I'm slipping further and further from her." Further and further into a nightmare where he existed without Tay. There was an enormous weight on his chest, squeezing his lungs.

"You know I can't discuss Taylor with you. What I can tell you, because she asked me to discuss it with you, is that she's very concerned that you're revealing intimate personal details about her to your friends."

"I know I screwed up. I don't need another lecture about what I told Ireland. I was drunk and upset. I don't even remember what I said."

"Oh, dear God, Cail."

Lane flopped back in her chair with a groan, slapping her hand on her forehead. It was the first time Cail saw her lose her professional composure when she was at work. He was concerned, but he wasn't sure why she was so upset. She knew he'd talked to Ireland.

"You need to speak to Ireland. Find out exactly what you said to her."

"Why? She told Tay what I said."

"You need to find out everything you said. If you don't remember, God knows what you've told her. She could go to the media and make a fortune. They would take it as truth because she's been filmed with you on a daily basis over the past few weeks."

"She wouldn't talk to the media."

Lane sat up in her chair with an exasperated sigh. She started to say something then stopped herself, let out another sigh then started again. "Cail, how do you suppose the reporters have known what bar you were at, what time you would be leaving, and the best place to set up to get a good shot on any given night?"

"No." His mind reeled. What Lane insinuated couldn't possibly be true. He hadn't really been paying attention to the videos they were playing of him and Ireland leaving the bars. Most he hadn't even seen. In the short bit he saw at his mother's of Tay leaving Delaney's the night before the camera was certainly in the best position to catch Tay walking back to HQ. If Tay's car had been parked in the other direction, they would only have gotten a shot of her back.

"Look at some of the videos again, Cail. Watch Ireland in them."

He refused to believe Ireland had anything to do with the reporters showing up. They'd been friends since childhood, she wouldn't do something like this. "You've known Ireland as long as I have. I can't believe you would accuse her of setting this up."

"Watch the videos and we'll talk about it when you come in for your session this afternoon." With that, she patted his knee and stood, dismissing him.

Cail got to his feet slowly, his mind still reeling, trying to remember the videos he had seen, but he just hadn't paid attention. Except for the pained expression on Tay's face in the video this morning, he couldn't recall any details. He was in Lane's waiting room and didn't even remember walking out of her office, he was so distracted. It probably wasn't safe for him to drive at the moment, so he decided to walk down to Delaney's. Maggie would probably let him borrow her laptop and he could sit in the relative privacy of the back room and pull up the videos from the news station's website.

* * *

Chris headed to the address Taylor had for Sass Levinsen. "Any thoughts on the case?" Chris asked as she drove.

Taylor faced the window, scanning in all directions as they inched their way through heavy traffic. She sighed and turned to Chris. She had to try to put this delicately because she wasn't sure how Chris would react given her association with Raine. "Do you think she's holding back?"

"About what?"

"Do you think she knows what the guy was searching for?" Taylor winced, waiting for Chris's response.

There it is, there's that intuition kicking in. Chris smiled and glanced over at Taylor. "Anything else about what she said bothering you?"

Taylor squirmed in her seat wondering if Chris realized just how uncomfortable she was making her. "The slap when he was supposedly angry. That's more of a girl reaction. And the lube. What rapist uses lubricant?"

"I can't tell you how refreshing it is to work with someone who's on the same wavelength as me," Chris grinned. "You think she was raped by a woman."

"It would explain the baggy size 32 coveralls and why the offender struggled to get Raine up the stairs. But, it can't be, can it? I mean, how often do you investigate female rapists?"

Chris very nearly blurted out that Taylor was raped by a woman. "It's rare, but it happens."

Taylor closed her eyes for a moment to shake loose the memories of Sarah Johnson. "She left out the symbols carved into her chest again."

"Yeah, I know."

"Makes you wonder what else she's leaving out, doesn't it?"

Chris pursed her lips and nodded. Raine was holding back, but why?

It took them over an hour in traffic to get to Sass Levinsen's apartment, have a two minute conversation to rule her out as their Sass, and get back to Headquarters. Chris told Taylor to take a few hours, go to her house, and they would meet up later to go back to Les Beau's.

On the way home, Taylor stopped at a grocery store to pick up some necessities. She stood at the entrance staring at the doors trying to talk herself into going in. Grocery stores were scary places. There was only one exit. You could get caught in the middle of an aisle and have no escape. On top of that, there were just too many choices. How were you supposed to decide what brand to buy? You didn't have to worry about all of these choices when you were dumpster diving, which was where she got most of her meals before she came off the streets. When she lived with Cail, he either did the grocery shopping or came with her because he knew she had anxiety attacks every time she she went into a grocery store. Kate always did the shopping at Chris's.

She took a deep breath of cold, clean air and tried to blow out all of the butterflies in her stomach, shaking her hands out at her sides. She could do this on her own. She could do it without Cail holding her hand and making the decisions for her. Yeah, she was strong and independent. She took two steps forward and a blast of warm air hit her followed by the earthy scent of fresh produce as the doors slid open. She faced her first decision - cart or basket? She was only picking up a few things, but was it enough to warrant a cart? Cart, she decided. She could use it as a weapon if need be. Or, at the very least, it could act as a barrier between her and a predator. But, the basket could be used as a weapon, too.

"Tay?"

Taylor turned and came face to face with Cail. "Hey, how are ya?" His smile and dimples made her belly melt to goo.

"Good, good. Do you want a hand with your shopping?"

How had he known she was here and needed him? She just stared at him, not knowing what to say.

Cail ran a hand through his hair and then gestured back towards the door he just entered. "I was just walking down to see Lane and I saw you standing out front staring at the doors. I thought maybe you might want some help."

Was it wrong to accept his help when they were at odds? Were there rules for this kind of thing? "I just need to pick up a few necessities like milk and coffee and stuff. I got my house today."

"Oh, yeah? Congratulations." He bent over and picked up a basket and motioned her to proceed ahead of him. "You know, I was kind of hoping we were going to do the house thing together."

Taylor stopped and turned back to face him. This wasn't a good idea if they were going to end up arguing again.

Cail raised a hand to stop her from saying anything. "Don't worry. I know it's my fault. I'm happy for you, Tay. I really am. You deserve to have a beautiful home of your own." He steered Taylor towards the dairy section.

"Thank you."

"I had a talk with my mum this morning and she told me some things I was unaware of. It made me realize just how big a fool I've been."

Taylor didn't say anything. She just let him talk as he helped her pick out cream and milk.

Cail put the items in the basket, turned to Taylor and took her hand. "Angel, will you let me take you out for coffee so we can talk?"

"Cail..." Taylor pursed her lips and frowned. They were better off talking during their sessions with Lane.

"Please, Angel. I know I've made a lot of mistakes. I need to ask you what happened. I need to hear everything from your perspective. I think it's the only way we're going to be able to heal from all of this and move forward. I just want to get back to where we were, you know?"

God, yes. She knew. "I don't have a lot of time, right now. We're working a big case."

"I could pick you up early tomorrow morning. You're always up really early. Pick a time and I'll be there."

"You'd pick me up at four in the morning?"

"Yes," he said, grinning. Taylor laughed and it was the first time he'd seen that beautiful smile in way too long. He couldn't resist brushing his fingertips down the groove between her high cheek bone and strong jaw and when she leaned into his touch his heart filled.

Chapter 8

As Taylor drove down the narrow lane leading to the gated back entrance to her new house, the sky blazed orange, yellow, and red, as if someone set it on fire. She slowed as she approached the gate and looked up to see the warm light radiating from her windows. She stopped the car and just stared up at the welcoming glow and it hit her. This was her home ... with electricity and running water. Cold *and* hot. Her chest tightened and a lump lodged in her throat at the enormity of the situation. She was a street rat. Had been for over sixteen years. She'd lived in some horrid conditions, but ... that was all over now. She had a safe place that she could return to every night and no one would ever kick her out.

She caught a movement out of the corner of her eye and looked up the lane to see a figure emerging from her gate with a round belly protruding from a long coat. She smiled to herself at the sight of Gray and watched her walk towards the car. Taylor popped the door locks and reached over to open the passenger door.

Gray leaned her head in. "You okay, hon?"

Taylor's eyes began to burn and she nodded. "I'm just really ... overwhelmed, I guess. This is big. It's a long way from where I was this time last year."

Gray squeezed herself into the passenger seat and leaned over, as best she could with her belly in the way, and hugged Taylor. "It's okay to cry. They're happy tears. The best kind."

Taylor took her glasses off and buried her face in Gray's shoulder. She squeezed her eyes shut tight and shook her head. She wasn't going to cry and ruin this monumental moment. "I'm so glad you're here with me for this. I miss you so much."

Gray circled her hand over Taylor's back, calming her. "Sharing this moment with you is the highlight of my year."

Taylor snorted. "You just got married and you're pregnant."

"Well, it's in the top three."

The shared a good laugh. Taylor loved having Chris as a best friend, but Gray felt like coming home. She felt like family. "How's Gracie?" Taylor leaned back and placed her hand on Gray's growing belly. She had some kind of weird attachment to Gray's baby. Placing her hand on Gray's belly, she was always able to get a sense of the baby or a vision of her in the future. "She's really growing now, isn't she? You're still singing to her and she loves it. Callaghan, too."

With a smile, Gray placed her hand over Taylor's and slowly moved it to the side of her belly. Taylor felt the kick and jumped then started laughing. Her grin faded as she remembered feeling her own child moving and kicking in her belly. "That's the best feeling in the world, isn't it?"

"There's really nothing better." They sat there quietly for a moment with their hands joined on Gray's belly enjoying Gracie's kicks then Gray reached into her pocket and pulled out two remotes. "Think you're ready to check out your new home?"

Taylor puffed out her cheeks, gazing up at the luminous windows. A slow grin spread across her face. "Yeah. Let's do this." She put her foot on the gas and headed for her gate as Gray pressed the remote to open it. Once inside the gate, Gray pressed the second remote that opened the garage. If the media figured out Taylor's address, the gate and garage allowed her to get into her house without being harassed by cameras and questions. It was perfect.

Taylor retrieved the groceries, shuffled some boxes around in the back of the car, and grabbed the box with the Runes in it. They stepped into the house through the garage door into the finished basement with laminate floors and walls painted a light sage green. The gym equipment Taylor had scheduled to be delivered and set up tomorrow was already in place. "Gray?"

"I thought it would be a nice surprise to have it all delivered and set up for you today."

If her arms were free, Taylor would have given Gray a big hug. She leaned over and kissed her cheek. "Thank you." They made their way up to the main level which was open concept with beautiful, wide-planked hardwood floors stained a deep, dark brown. A floating staircase against a rustic red-brick wall led up to the second level.

Taylor got a shock at the top of the stairs as a bunch of people yelled out, "Surprise!" There was a huge sign across the brick wall that read, 'Welcome home'. Chris was there, holding hands with Kate. Cal and Rose were there. Gabriella was there with her entire brood - Jackson, her husband, and her kids, Arianna, Nate, and Greg. Even Gray's housekeeper, Maggie was there. Callaghan came and took the box and grocery bags out of her hands and gave her a kiss on the cheek. "Congratulations and welcome home." The next thing Taylor knew, she was engulfed in hugs from every direction. She was so stunned all she could do was stand there with her mouth agape trying to take it all in. System overload.

It took her a while before she registered the furniture she purchased had also been delivered a day early. Maggie was busy putting dishes away in the kitchen surrounded by granite counters, dark wood cabinets, and stainless steel appliances. The dining room table was a deep brown with eight high-back chairs set around it.

In the living room, two taupe leather couches faced each other over a dark brown coffee table. Two matching chairs were set at the side of the coffee table facing a massive flat screen TV hanging on the brick wall. Taylor hadn't purchased a TV.

At the opposite end of the room from the kitchen, the office/art room had already been set up with her art table and a new desk and computer.

Gray took Taylor's hand. "Are you okay? Is this all too much?"

Taylor nodded slowly. Her mouth still hung open and she couldn't stop looking all around, taking it all in and trying to process that this was all hers.

Gray led her over to one of the couches and sat her down. She looked over towards the kitchen and caught Maggie's eye. Maggie just nodded, understanding what Gray wanted by the worried look on her face.

Maggie brought a cup of tea over and placed it in Taylor's hands. "Congratulations, Taylor. Your home is gorgeous."

Taylor nodded then stared into the cup of tea. The mug was one of the set matching the dishes she and Gray found online. "How did all of this stuff get here?"

Gray circled her hand over Taylor's back again. "I arranged for everything to be delivered today instead of tomorrow. I thought it would be a nice surprise to have everything set up when you got home from work. I'm sorry, Taylor. I should have thought about how all of this would affect you."

Taylor reached for Gray's hand. "No, I'm sorry. I didn't mean to sound ungrateful. It's just so much to take in." She looked towards the floating staircase. "Maybe I could just go to my room for a few minutes and try to settle myself." She just wanted to get away from all of the people and let everything soak in.

"Go on up then," Gray said, taking the mug from Taylor's hand and setting it on the coffee table. "Take as much time as you need."

Taylor walked up the stairs knowing everyone was staring and wondering if she lost her marbles. She knew she would have to apologize for her rude behaviour, but she had to get away from everyone. At the door to her bedroom, she stared in, admiring the huge sleigh bed, already made up with her new sheets. A pleasant aroma soothed her, a mixture of clean linen and new wood. Across from the bed, a gas fireplace with a marble mantle served as the focal point before two taupe suede chairs separated by a dark wood end table. A throw rug in multiple earth tones covered the dark plank floor boards between the bed and the sitting area. Taylor's favourite part of the room was directly across from her and she felt herself drawn to it. The huge window overlooked the street below and the three storey abandoned warehouse across the street. The window ledge was about twelve inches deep with a sill of slate grey marble which matched the fireplace's mantle and surround. Taylor had been dreaming of perching herself here to watch the world go by on the street below. She slid onto the sill and brought her knees into her chest. The brown brick warehouse across the street featured boarded up windows on the main floor. Some of the panes of glass in the windows of the second and third floors were broken. To most it would be an eye sore. To Taylor it had the potential to be a respite for street kids - a place where they could go and not be asked any questions. A safe zone in the middle of a war zone.

When she was little, Leila used to sing *Wind Beneath My Wings* to her when she was trying to get her to go to sleep. She could picture the sign above the entrance to the now empty warehouse - *Beneath My Wings* - with a huge set of angel wings hugging the words. She was going to need a heck of a lot more money to make that dream come true. She could write another book, perhaps.

"You okay?"

Taylor turned to smile at Chris standing in the doorway and nodded. "I'm home."

* * *

Taylor took the Runes and The Healing Runes book into the office while everyone was busy eating pizza. She sat down at the dark wood desk and opened the book to the page she was familiar with; the only page she'd taken the time to read - Shame.

Shame from the past throws a shadow across today's sun. How long have you been a child of Shame, standing alone outside the schoolyard fence, watching the other children as they play?

Drawing this rune signals a time when the Shame you have lived with for so long can be understood and healed, dissolved into memories and pictures that belong only to the past.

From the time she began seeing Dr. Lane McIntyre, she'd been advising Taylor that in order to heal she had to talk about her trauma. This chapter on Shame gave the same advice.

When the time is right, you will find the courage to tell just one person what happened - just one.

That's what she was trying to do with Lane ever since Quinn gave her the Healing Runes.

Imagine a day when you are free from all feelings of Shame. A day when you are no longer suffering from the painful experiences of your childhood... Realize that you have survived your pain, and honour yourself for your commitment to the healing journey. For it is one of self-acceptance, self-love, and self-care. A noble journey out of the shadows and into the Light.

"Is that the Rune book?"

Taylor looked up to see Chris leaning against the door jamb, watching her. She closed the book and answered with a nod.

"May I?" Chris held out her hand.

Taylor hesitated. She knew Chris would go straight for the chapter on Shame and read it. She handed the book over and sat there looking down at the floor while Chris flipped through the pages. She knew exactly when Chris found the chapter and she drummed her fingers against her thigh while she waited.

"Taylor?" Chris whispered.

Her eyes flitted up to meet Chris's and what she saw in her expression she felt to her core. *Pain.* The pain of Chris's own tortured childhood. Chris had never healed from her shame either and the visitor in her office today brought it all to the forefront. "The time is right, Chris. We both need to heal from our feelings of shame."

Chris pursed her lips and flipped through the pages again until she found the chapter on Guilt, the third symbol carved over Raine's breast. As she read through it, all she could think about were Sylvie's words, telling her that her mother was very ill and asking her to see her.

The Rune of Guilt fosters healing by reminding us of the need to make amends. For those who seek to heal situations from the past - for what was done or left undone - this Rune counsels you to open your heart and act. Is there a letter to be written, a call to be made, someone you must sit with face to face, a prayer to be said? Now is the time to bring order, clarity and peace to the chaos of the past.

Chris read through to the end of the chapter. She wasn't the one who should be making amends for her guilt - her mother should. And, maybe that was why Sylvie came to her today. If her mother was nearing her end, would she want to make amends with Chris? Why? To save her own soul? She could have tried to reach out to Chris any time over the past sixteen years, but she hadn't. Not until she was faced with being condemned to hell. She wasn't doing it for Chris. She was doing it for herself.

"This isn't about us, Taylor. We have to figure out how this applies to our offender. Why did he carve these particular symbols into Raine's chest?"

"He thinks Raine should be ashamed, that she's guilty of something?"

"For being gay? For loving Callie?" If their offender really was a woman, that theory would be blown to hell.

"Maybe Callie is our Sass. According to Raine, he said 'Why, Sass? She wasn't yours.' Maybe he wasn't asking *why, Sass?* Maybe he was asking *why Sass?* Not referring to Raine as Sass, but asking her why she took his Sass away from him?"

Or her, Chris thought. That theory would work with a male or a female offender. "So," Chris tossed the book onto the desk in front of Taylor and sat on the edge of the desk. "You're thinking about telling *just one person* your story?"

"Not thinking about it. Doing it. I've been trying to tell Lane what I remember and the memories that have been coming back to me."

"Is it helping?" What she just read in Taylor's Rune book made it seem like there was hope for healing from the pain and putting it behind her, but she didn't trust it. Didn't believe it.

If Taylor answered this correctly, it could inspire Chris to talk about her past after all these years. The problem was, she couldn't lie. "It is and it isn't. With me, it's stirring up memories long buried. Lane thinks that's a good thing, though." She was making a mess of this. She certainly wasn't making a positive case for Chris to talk. "I just feel that I need to get it all out before it destroys me, you know?"

"Yeah...I know." Chris lifted herself off the edge of the desk and walked away.

* * *

They walked into Les Beau's dressed for a night out. Gray had done a weird triple braid thing on each side of Taylor's scalp and pulled the braids to the back of her head, pinning them together and then letting them fall loosely down her back with the rest of her hair. It was complex, but it looked really cool. She wore a black sweater and jeans, topped with her long black leather coat and a pair of kick ass black military boots.

Kate wore faded jeans and a royal blue sweater hugging her gentle curves. The colour electrified her blue eyes. She left her curly black hair loose to sway against her back.

Chris traded her cargo pants in for a pair of black dress pants. She covered a black tank with a white, button-down shirt and left it untucked.

The bar looked much different at night. The lights were dimmed and the music playing through the sound system turned up. It wasn't exactly crowded, but there were a lot more people in the bar than when they came in mid-afternoon yesterday. Chris led them to the bar, her hand clasped with Kate's. The woman behind the bar wore her sandy brown hair in short curls. She was laughing with a group of patrons as she mixed some fancy cocktails. After she delivered the drinks and collected the money, she glanced down the bar and her eyes bulged when she recognized Chris. The smile faded from her face and she wrung her hands on the bar towel she was holding and made her way down the bar. "Chris? Long time no see."

"Cherylyn, this is my girlfriend, Kate, and my friend, Taylor."

Cherylyn's dark brown eyes flashed to Kate and then right back to Chris. "Your girlfriend? I thought you didn't do commitment."

"Aah..." *Awkward.* Chris turned to Kate trying to get a read on her reaction to Cherylyn. Kate's eyebrows shot up and Chris thought, fuck it. She grabbed on to Kate's face and brought her in for a kiss that made Taylor turn her red face in the opposite direction. Chris pulled away, her heavy lids fluttering open, and focused on Kate. A smile bloomed on both their faces and Chris spoke loud enough for Cherylyn, and a lot of the other patrons, to hear. "This one is worth it. Long term."

A woman down the bar turned in her stool, bringing her shapely legs and high heels around before sliding off the stool and smoothing down the skirt of her charcoal business suit. "Well, well, well. This is cause for celebration. Cherylyn, get these ladies a drink on me."

"Kate, Taylor, this is Crown Attorney Alexa Nash," Chris said.

"We've met," Kate said. "How are you, Alexa?"

"I would have been better if I'd known you were one of us, Kate. I had no idea." Alexa gave Chris and Kate a quick hug and then turned her sights on Taylor. "Taylor Sinclair," she purred with a grin that could only be described as predatory. She looked at Taylor as if ready to devour every inch of her.

Taylor took a step back, increasing her personal space. "Yeah, hello. Lovely to meet you."

"Easy there, girl," Chris said. "Taylor's straight."

"I could make a great case for turning you, Taylor. We could start with Caillen Worthington. Any man that let's you get away has to be a complete fool."

Taylor straightened and stared Alexa down. "Sorry. That topic's not open for discussion."

Alexa threw her head back, her russet waves bouncing, and laughed. "I love a woman who doesn't kiss and tell. I like you, Taylor."

They moved to a booth across from the bar. Their plan was to hang back and observe, interviewing staff as the opportunity arose. Taylor made sure she was facing the door and when Alexa came over to join them, she got up and let Alexa slide in so that she remained on the outside.

Chris leaned forward in her seat. "Were you in here last Thursday, Alexa?"

Her eyes went up and to the left before answering. "Thursday? Oh, yes. I was working the Trebec case and came in for a drink around seven."

"Did you see Raine and Bonkers?"

Alexa deflated and slouched back in her seat. "I heard about Raine. I'm so sorry. Yes, I spoke to them while they were here. It's the first time I've seen Raine out since Callie passed."

"Did you see anyone paying particular attention to Raine?"

"Both Raine and Bonkers attract attention, but neither one of them were giving off the vibe that they were into hooking up. It was nice to see Raine, but she's definitely not over Callie yet."

While Chris questioned Alexa, Taylor's eyes surveilled the bar. Their group generated the attention of everyone in the place, customers and staff alike, which didn't surprise Taylor. With her notoriety, she expected it now. It could also be curiosity in Kate. Chris was known for cutting her lovers loose the moment they started to get serious, so seeing her blatantly claim Kate as her girlfriend would come as a shock to this community. The bartender certainly seemed upset about it. She kept throwing daggers at Chris and Kate with her eyes.

A waitress with short, wavy brown hair who kept looking over at them, stood at the end of the bar. She was shorter than Taylor, but just as muscular. When she noticed Taylor watching she quickly turned away, but every time Taylor glanced over at her, she was staring their way again.

Laughter brought Taylor's attention back to the table. Alexa was telling a story about a trial, but Taylor was only half listening and missed the punch line apparently.

"Anyone ready for another drink?" The waitress who'd been hanging around at the end of the bar stood next to Taylor with a round tray balanced on her left hand. Her name tag identified her as Lian.

Taylor pointed to her name tag. "How do you pronounce that?"

"LeeAnn," she answered.

"Martini, dry with two olives." Alexa slid her empty glass to the edge of the table.

Chris and Kate each ordered another drink and Taylor passed. "She's new here, isn't she?" Chris asked.

"Lian? Yes, she's been here for a month or so."

"Was she here on Thursday?" Taylor asked Alexa.

"I don't think she was working that night, but she may have been hanging out in here. She comes in for a drink every now and then. Odd little duck, that one."

"How so?"

"I don't know, just a weird vibe. She's always watching everyone, but doesn't say much."

"Does she come in with friends?"

Alexa shook her head. "I've never seen her with anyone, but I don't pay much attention to her." Alexa smiled and winked at Taylor. "Not my type."

Lian delivered the round of drinks to the table and Alexa insisted they be put on her tab. She took a sip of her Martini, set it down and then grinned fiercely. "There's my girl. Would you mind?" She indicated that Taylor let her out of the seat.

Taylor stood, watching Gloria, the blonde bombshell who they'd met when they were in the day before, charging towards them. Heat spread upwards from Taylor's neck into her cheeks when she remembered Gloria's comment about dicks of the strap on variety. Chris caught it because she started laughing. Gloria and Alexa came together in a collision, embracing each other and locking lips. Alexa swung Gloria around so she was facing Taylor. "Honey, have you met Taylor?"

"We met yesterday. You're not trying to steal my wife, are you, Taylor?"

That sounded weird, calling another woman her wife. Taylor could hear Chris laughing again. "Tempting, but no," she answered.

"What about Kate? Have you met Chris's *girlfriend*, Kate?" Alexa asked.

Gloria's mouth dropped open as she turned to face Chris and Kate. "Oh, my God. Chris. You really are doing the domestic thing, aren't you?"

Chris was still laughing from Taylor's red cheeks. "Yeah, Gloria this is Kate."

Gloria grabbed Kate's hand and held it between both of her own. "Sweetie, you must be something special to have hooked this one, let me tell you."

"Oh? Please do," Kate said with a sly grin.

Taylor offered up her seat to Gloria and went to wander the bar, chatting with staff when she could. Two men huddled at a table in the back corner, laughing and clanging their drinks together like they were celebrating their good fortune. Taylor leaned against the wall. Neither one of them would fit into a size 32 coverall, but Taylor kept an eye on them nevertheless. It creeped her out to see them ogling the women swaying and gyrating on the dance floor.

In her peripheral vision, Taylor watched a tall, slim waitress with short, platinum blonde hair slither up to her and lean against the wall at her side, facing her. "You," she purred, "are one sexy, bad ass in that outfit. And you're not gay. What are you doing here, Constable Taylor Sinclair?"

Taylor continued to watch a couple across the room who kept glancing at her and whispering to each other. "Is it a crime for me to be here?"

"Honey, it's a crime you're not gay."

Taylor snorted before turning her head to study the woman

standing next to her. Icy blue eyes rimmed in dark liner stared up from under thick, dark lashes. Her tongue darted out and slid erotically across her lower lip.

"You're all the same. One track minds. All of you," Taylor said.

"Is that a crime, officer?"

"I suppose not." Taylor glanced down to read her name tag. "Were you working last Thursday, Cameron?"

Cameron shrugged one shoulder. "Word's already spread like wildfire that you've been asking about Raine. I'll answer your questions, but I want something in return."

"Is that right?"

"You don't remember me, do you?"

Taylor studied Cameron's face trying to place it in her memory. Darker, longer hair. Younger. Much younger. "Cammy."

Cameron's eyes widened. "So, you do remember."

"I remember." Taylor sighed. Would her past ever stop creeping up on her? she wondered. "What is it you want?"

"Answers, mostly."

"Answers to what?"

Cameron shrugged again, a tight lipped smile on her face.

"Do you have information about Raine or not?"

"I'm going on break. Give me fifteen minutes of your time and I'll tell you what I saw on Thursday night." Cameron turned and walked away.

Taylor stared after her. Did she call Cameron's bluff, take a chance she didn't see anything, like everyone else they'd spoken to so far? What could she possibly want from Taylor after all these years? What answers? Taylor pushed off the wall and charged after Cameron. She followed her down a dark hallway and burst through a heavy steel door into the alleyway. She paced up and down, checking the shadows before approaching Cameron, who just lit up a cigarette. She leaned back onto the brick wall exhaling with a smirk. The stench of rotting food and stale urine reminded Taylor of a lifetime spent rummaging through dumpsters scrounging for scraps in alleys just like this. Taylor forced those thoughts from her mind. "What answers do you want? I don't understand."

Cameron turned her head and blew her smoke away from Taylor before turning back. "I want to know why you did what you did for me?"

"Why? It was wrong, that's why."

"You risked your life saving me and you didn't even know me. You got me to a Dr. Ripkin's and then you disappeared. You didn't even let them look at your injuries."

"It was a safe place for you. It wasn't safe for me."

"Then why did you risk it?"

Taylor paced, searching the alley again, checking the shadows just in case. She was fourteen when she snatched Cameron away from her handlers. Taylor watched them for years. She knew all the handlers and players in the child prostitution ring that enslaved Cameron. Normally, it was a matter of thwarting the recruiters. Occasionally, the opportunity presented itself to steal one of the kids away from the ring and she took it. In Cameron's case, one of the handlers caught on before Taylor could get her away. Her years on the streets made her a fierce fighter by the age of fourteen and Taylor knocked the guy out, but not before she sustained a few injuries.

Cameron watched Taylor checking every nook and cranny, toeing garbage bags aside and peeking behind dumpsters. She took a long haul on her cigarette and then another before losing patience. "That's all I want to know. Why you did it."

"I told you. It was wrong."

"Did they have you? Before you saved me, were you one of his girls?"

"No." Taylor stopped pacing and faced Cameron. "They tried to take me a few times, but I always got away."

"Was it because of what you were going through? Because of what Sarah Johnson was doing to you?"

Taylor clenched her jaw. "You're intent on making it about me. It wasn't about me."

"Wasn't it?"

"Should I have stood by and watched them exploit little girls and boys?"

"We had a name for you, you know? I mean, the ones you got out."

Taylor's brow creased, her nose wrinkled. Did they form a club, these kids, or what?

"*Frigg, the Liberator.* You were this mysterious entity who most of us thought was a superhero or a ghost or a figment of our imaginations. We had creative little minds back then." Cameron dropped her head to stare at the ground and took another long haul on her smoke. She blew it out slowly. "My daddy sold me to Zheng when I was seven."

Taylor rubbed the heel of her hand over the tight muscles in her chest. Seven. She'd seen Zheng's crew with kids as young as four, but still, the thought of a seven year old being made to do what those kids were forced to do was sickening.

"I was eleven when you got me out." One last draw on her cigarette and Cameron snuffed it out under her boot. "A girl left the bar last Thursday night right on Raine and Bonkers' heels. I don't know if she's got anything to do with what happened to Raine, but she was staring at them the whole time they were in the bar."

"Any idea who this girl was."

"Yeah. She's serving your table." Cameron pulled the steel door open then looked over her shoulder at Taylor and just stared for a moment. Then she stepped through the door and it banged closed behind her.

Taylor walked down the alley to the street in front of Les Beau's and took several deep breaths through her nose, flushing the stench of the alley from her sinuses. Frigg the Liberator? Really? She wasn't some super hero and definitely not one that should be named *Frigg*. She just couldn't stand what Zheng's organization was doing. It didn't take much to master the patterns in their comings and goings. All she did was take advantage of opportunities. She knew when a recruiter was about to grab a kid just by watching them. Often, all she did was distract the kid so they didn't walk into the trap. There were countless times when she followed handlers taking the kids to 'dates', but it was much harder to intervene in those circumstances and some kids didn't want to be 'liberated'.

Just as it had been easy for her to watch Zheng's players, it had been easy for them to catch on to her. Running had been her saviour. They couldn't catch up to her.

Kate watched Taylor through the window for a moment. She stood on the sidewalk, a despondent expression on her face, staring off into the night. She wished there was something she could do to free Taylor from the despair she seemed to carry around with her. She popped her head out the door. "Taylor? Why are you standing out there in the cold?"

Taylor shook herself out of the past and made her way back inside. "Just needed some fresh air." She followed Kate back to their booth and gave Chris an update on what Cameron said about Lian.

They pulled Lian aside and questioned her, but she insisted that leaving right after Raine and Bonkers was a coincidence. She went straight home because she had an early shift the next morning. If she was staring at them, it was only because she was interested in Bonkers.

"Trust me, kid. Bonkers isn't interested in you," Chris said.

Lian looked hurt, but she just shrugged her shoulder and said, "Yeah, I know."

"How does everyone know Bonkers isn't interested?" Taylor asked on the way back to the booth.

"Because she's asexual. That's why everyone calls her Bonkers."

"Doesn't make her crazy." Taylor had never experienced sexual attraction or desire until she met Cail, so she understood what it was like to be asexual. If you weren't attracted, you weren't attracted. It wasn't Bonkers' fault. Maybe, like Taylor, she had good reason to be asexual.

Chris knew what Taylor was thinking. They had a conversation similar to this not long after they met. "No, it doesn't make her crazy."

* * *

Taylor left Chris and Kate at Les Beau's and went to Chris's to pick up the rest of her stuff. It worked out better than she could have planned because she was able to get her paintings and supplies out of Chris's basement without anyone being the wiser. Sneaking them into her new place under Gray's nose wasn't a problem either. She and Callaghan had already gone to bed.

Taylor settled in the office with a hot cup of tea and fired up the iMac. The first thing she wanted to do was a little more research on Runes. It turned out that a Viking God, Odin, had invented the Runic alphabet made up of Rune symbols.

The Healing Runes version of the four symbols - Humour, Fear, Guilt, and Shame - seemed like what the offender wanted the victim to feel. Except for humour, that one didn't make any sense. The Viking symbols - Flow, Standstill, Signals, and Constraint - didn't fit for her, but she hadn't read up on their meanings.

It was when she explored Norse mythology a little further that she came across the name *Frigg*, a Goddess and the wife of Odin. She was said to have the gift of foresight and the power to change the destiny of all beings if she so chose. Okay. This was getting a little weird. Taylor shut down the website.

She logged on to Facebook and went to Raine Delacourte's page mostly for a picture of Raine. Her profile pic showed Raine with Callie. Taylor clicked on the picture to enlarge it then started scrolling through Raine's profile pics. Most of them were of Raine and Callie together. The older the pictures, the healthier Callie looked. Cancer had taken its toll on this poor woman. She looked healthy in her wedding photos and in the photos Taylor assumed were taken on their honeymoon. They'd gone south. White sand beaches, azure seas, and breathtaking sunsets. Taylor stopped on a picture of Callie Delacourte in a black bikini.

Couldn't be, she thought and leaned into the computer screen to get a closer look at the scars over Callie's left breast.

Chapter 9

Taylor perched in her window seat and saw Cail walking towards her house from the subway. He really got up in the middle of the night to take her out for coffee. She slid off the cold marble and made her way downstairs. She didn't want Cail to wake up Gray and Callaghan by ringing the bell, so she was at the door when he climbed the steps. "Hey, you made it."

Cail grinned up at her, his dimples deep and his blue eyes had some of their lustre back.

He reached for her hand and leaned in to brush a kiss over her cheek. "And you, beautiful Angel, don't look dressed to go for coffee."

She wondered if he realized how badly his hand was shaking. She wasn't sure if it was nerves or alcohol withdrawal. Taylor glanced down at her workout gear clad body – shorts, tank top, and Nikes. "I thought we could just have coffee here. Is that okay?"

"Yeah. Sure." He thought she'd be more comfortable on neutral territory. The invitation into her house had to be a good omen. Taylor took him straight up to the kitchen and offered him a seat at the breakfast bar. The place was gorgeous. Exactly what he would expect for Taylor - a rustic, warehouse/modern luxury combo. The kitchen was like something out of a magazine with its granite counters and top of the line appliances. "This place really suits you, Angel."

Taylor scanned the room before locking eyes with Cail. Her lip curled up slightly. "It's going to take some getting used to. I'd show you around, but Gray, Callaghan, and Maggie are still sleeping."

Her new home was as overwhelming to her as grocery shopping, Cail thought. She opened the cupboard door to get coffee cups and he wasn't surprised to see every mug lined up to perfection. She'd done the same thing at his apartment. "Gray and Callaghan are here?"

"Gray has a room for me at her place, so I wanted to give her the same back. She doesn't have to stay at the Grand when she's in the city anymore."

"And she brought Maggie, too. Bonus."

"Ah, I think that was just to help get everything moved in and set up. Maggie will be going back up to Balton today." Taylor set the two mugs of coffee on the counter and took a seat next to Cail.

"That's too bad."

"Yeah." Taylor stared down into her mug, waiting for Cail to start the conversation. She could feel his eyes on her, but he hadn't tried to grab her hand or touch her like he usually did.

"Will you tell me what happened? Starting after we went to sleep that night. That perfect night." Memories of the last night they spent together haunted Cail. Despite everything that was going on with Rappaport and the dark bruise marring her beautiful face, Taylor had smiled and laughed like he'd never seen her before. It was rare to see her smile, but her face lit up that night.

When he looked at her now, all he could see was a deep and penetrating sadness which he felt right down to his bones. Knowing he was responsible for that sorrow devastated him, pulverized his heart. And he had no clue how to put a smile back on that stunning face, in those gorgeous eyes.

Taylor's body shuddered involuntarily at the thought of their last night together. The night she let go of her fears and inhibitions. It *had* been perfect. She exhaled a blast of nervous energy and then just let it all spew out. "I woke up with the bruise on my cheek throbbing and I was getting ready to go down to the front desk and ask for an ice pack when Rappaport called my cell phone. He said he had people watching you around the clock. People you trusted. If I didn't go to him, you would be dead. If he didn't call someone at pre-arranged times, that person had orders to kill you. I couldn't risk it, Cail. I couldn't put your life on the line because of my past."

She told him about getting Rappaport to give her a few hours before meeting him at Union Station and spending that time trying to find a way to save them both. But, time ran out and she left the information and clues she'd found on Chris's desk and went to meet with the devil, praying Chris could finish what she started to ensure Cail's safety.

His mother had been right. Tay gave herself to that animal for him. "Why didn't you wake me up, Tay? Instead of going alone, why didn't you let us help?"

"Don't you think I thought about it, Cail? If we all stormed into Headquarters and tried to work out a solution, he would have known. And he would have followed through on his threats. Two of the cops on his payroll played hockey with you. One of them worked on your shift. He had people close to you keeping tabs on you."

He had to let that go. He knew he did. She had valid reasons for doing things the way she had and he had to respect that. "Will you tell me what happened when you were at Rappaport's condo?"

Taylor shifted in her seat then sat there turning her coffee cup round and round. This could be the deal breaker, but she stood her ground. "No, I'm not going to discuss what happened in that condo with you." The time for that discussion had been the morning after the whole Rappaport ordeal, but he walked away from her, ending their relationship. She turned her head to face him. "There are intensely private and personal things about me you've discussed behind my back with people I don't even know. I want to trust you, Cail. I want to be able to talk to you." Even she knew for a relationship to work there had to be trust. "But, I can't."

Taylor's lips were pursed tightly, her nose flared, brow drawn in, and eyes glossy. He hurt her deeply and perhaps irreparably. All this time he'd walked around in a rage, believing Taylor was to blame, and it was him. He did all the damage to their relationship. If he hadn't been so judgemental and stubborn, they wouldn't be in this predicament. All of the air left his lungs, his whole chest burned. He stood slowly, head spinning to the point he thought he might black out. "For what it's worth, I'm sorry."

The walk across her living room to the stairs leading down to the front door seemed to take forever. The more steps he took forward, the further the door appeared to be. When he finally got outside, he just stood there trying to draw air back into his flaming lungs. He really needed a drink.

Taylor watched him walk away with her mouth hanging open. Was that it? He wasn't even going to attempt to make things right, to rebuild what they lost? She turned back around in her stool and dropped her face into her hands. Her only chance at ever having a relationship just walked out the door. Again.

"Taylor?" Gray placed her hand on Taylor's shoulder. She heard the last part of their conversation and understood why Taylor was hurting.

Taylor lifted her head and tried to draw her lips up into a smile. "Hey. Good morning."

"Is it?" Gray slid onto the stool Cail just vacated. "Taylor, you just moved into your very own home. You should be ecstatic, yet I've never seen you so despondent. And I'm not just talking about what just happened with Cail. You were like this yesterday."

Taylor folded her arms on the counter and lowered her head, resting her cheek against her forearm. "There's just so much going on right now – Cail, this case we're working on, crap from my past. There's too much going on in my head. I feel like I need to write it all down and lay it out in front of me so that I can make sense of everything." Like a case board. Maybe if she could see it all written down, she could deal with it bit by bit. Treat it all like an investigation – define the problem, identify solutions, choose the best procedure to solve the problem.

"That sounds like a good idea," Gray said.

Or not. Her crap wasn't an investigation. The problem was, having spent a lifetime avoiding dealing with her crap, she didn't know how to begin to deal with it. "I watch Chris and Kate or you and Callaghan and you make it look easy. I want what you have. With Cail. But, it doesn't look like we're capable of having that kind of relationship."

"Of course you are, Taylor. If you both want it and you're both willing to work at it, there's no reason you can't have it."

"It doesn't look like he's willing to work at it."

Gray rubbed circles over Taylor's back. "Do you want to know what I saw walking out of here a few minutes ago? I saw a man in pain. If he didn't love you, he wouldn't be in so much pain, Taylor."

"I know he loves me, but there is something different about him this morning. Maybe he's decided I'm too much work and who could blame him?"

"Oh, sweetie. Loving someone is never too much work. Think about it. You love him. How much work would you be willing to put in for him?" Gray slid off the stool and retrieved a bottle of water from the fridge. "I'm going back to bed." She leaned over and pressed a kiss to Taylor's cheek. "You," she poked Taylor's shoulder, "can either let him walk away or ..." She dropped her voice to a whisper, "Go get what you want."

Taylor sat up and watched Gray walk away. When she got to the stairs she looked over her shoulder with a mischievous smirk and winked then climbed the stairs humming.

Did she text him, phone him, run after him? Or let him go? She shot off the bar stool, grabbed the first jacket she found in the closet by the front door and was out the door before she could get it on. The frosty air smelled of mornings and new beginnings, although dawn was still a couple of hours away. She sprinted towards the subway, but Cail hadn't gotten as far as she thought. The silhouette of his tall, muscular frame appeared lonely on the sidewalk ahead, only a block from the house. He walked slowly with his head low, shoulders slumped, and his hands in his jacket pockets. "Cail?" He stopped walking, but didn't turn around. "I thought you wanted to talk. Why are you walking away?"

Cail turned around slowly. It was cold enough they could see their breath and Taylor wore workout shorts and a light jacket. He shivered just looking at her. "It just hit me how much I've been hurting you. I don't want to hurt you anymore, Angel."

"Then let's work through our problems and fight to get back what we had." She closed the distance between them and stared into his eyes. "That's what would make me stop hurting, Cail."

"If things are going to work between us, I need you to be able to talk to me about your past. I've screwed that up, Tay. I'll set Ireland straight, but I can't undo what I've done." He reached up and cupped her cheek and she laid her hand over his. "I don't know how to fix the damage I've done."

"You can't undo it, but you can earn back my trust. I know it's going to take time and I need to know you're not discussing my personal issues, but I want to get back to where we were before Rappaport ruined everything, Cail. I want it more than anything."

It wasn't Rappaport who ruined everything. It was his reaction and behaviour. His own stupidity. Cail leaned in and pressed his forehead to Taylor's. He couldn't blame her if she didn't want him back. To hear her say she wanted to fight to get back what he'd ruined, floored him. "You do?"

She could only think of one way to answer. She pressed her lips to his.

Cail inhaled a sharply through his nose, but didn't return the kiss. He never thought he'd feel those soft lips against his again and he savoured the moment.

Taylor began to pull away with the pain of rejection shooting through her heart. Then Cail's hands cupped her cheeks. He cocked his head and dove in, devouring her mouth. She felt the burst of heat all the way to her toes. Her fingers plunged into his soft curls, massaging his scalp and holding his mouth to hers. Everything faded – the cold, her past, the case…their issues. He dropped his hands to circle her waist and drew her in tight with his body. Her hands slid over his shoulders to his chest. She wanted inside that jacket, wanted his skin touching hers. And then a thought snuck through – Ireland's angry words in the pub bathroom. She jerked back, stepping away from Cail, and cupped her hand over her mouth. "I'm sorry. I shouldn't have done that."

"Angel?" Cail took a step forward and cupped Taylor's face in his hands, tilting her head up so he could look in her eyes. "We both want the same thing, right? We both want to get back to where we were?"

"Yes."

He could tell by the frown on her face there was a but coming.

"But, we're not there yet, Cail. And I don't know how to do it. I don't know how to fix what's wrong between us."

Cail smiled. Wide enough that his dimples appeared. "I think I might have an idea on that. We'll start over, a fresh start. Let me take you out to dinner and a movie?"

"A movie?" Taylor stared at Cail as if he'd grown a third eye.

"Any movie you want. I'll even go to a chick flick if that's what you want."

"A chick flick?"

It wasn't like Taylor to repeat his words back to him and she had a look of confusion on her face. He'd told himself he would try to be more understanding and patient with her. Taylor wasn't anything like the other women he'd dated. Her past made her different from anyone he'd ever known. He promised himself he would try to be more sensitive to her needs. So he took a moment to try to figure out her confusion and then it clicked. She'd never dated before him and he hadn't exactly wined and dined her. She hadn't experienced a lot of the things most people had in life. "You've never been to a movie theatre, have you?"

A deep rose flushed her cheeks and she shook her head in answer.

He couldn't imagine anyone of their age never having experienced watching a movie at the theatre, but that was one of the ways he had screwed up their relationship the first time around. He would constantly need to remind himself to think about what she had or hadn't experienced and why. But, for now, he'd thoroughly enjoy seeing her experience things for the first time. "I'll pick you up after work tonight. I'll pick the restaurant and you can pick the movie."

Taylor continued to stare, dumbfounded, before she finally asked, "What's a chick flick?"

Cail couldn't stop laughing, even though Tay wasn't laughing with him. When he caught the annoyed expression she wore, he stifled his laughter long enough to blurt out, "A girlie movie."

"Oh." Her checks were burning again. What the heck was a girlie movie? She didn't want to ask and have him laugh at her again.

"So, you'll come out on a date with me? We'll start over?" Cail asked.

When they were at the academy and Cail pursued her relentlessly, he'd been extremely patient with her. Over time, she came to trust him. Starting over might help, but would it change the way he reacted when he became frustrated and angry with her?

"I know I've been a jerk" Cail said. "I'm seeing Lane and working on anger management. It will be better this time, Angel."

"Will it?" It was out of her mouth before she could filter her thoughts. She was aware she sounded sarcastic and winced.

"It's when you're hurting yourself or putting yourself in danger that I lose control. Or when Kate was in danger. That's when I lose it. I feel so helpless and I can't stand to see anyone I love suffer like that." He brushed the backs of his fingers over her cheek in a soft caress. "I need to learn how to deal with it in a healthy manner. I'll get there, I promise."

He cupped her cheek in his palm again and Taylor absently leaned into his touch. She wanted to believe him, but the taste of betrayal was still strong in her mouth.

"Please tell me you'll let us start over. I need to prove to you that I'm worthy of your trust. I know that. Starting over is the only way I know how."

"Okay," she conceded, her breath freezing as it met the icy air. Maybe he was right. Maybe it was the only way.

Cail pressed a kiss to her forehead and then took a step back from her. "Go home, Angel. It's too damn cold out here to be wearing shorts."

* * *

"What's up?" Chris asked as Taylor let her and Kate in the front door.

Taylor eyed Chris as she led them up to the main level and headed for the office. She had dark circles under her eyes this morning, as if she hadn't slept a wink last night. And, instead of her usual cargo pants and hiking boots, Chris was wearing low-waisted grey dress pants, a cream silk blouse and a blazer. On her feet she wore a pair of dress boots with a low heel. She glanced at Kate, but Kate just smiled as if all was right with the world. "I found something on Facebook you need to see." She settled in the desk chair and brought up Raine Delacourte's Facebook page, found the picture Callie, and clicked on it, enlarging it on the iMac screen.

"Holy shit," Chris said. "Raine knows a lot more than she's telling us."

"They're the same symbols carved into Raine's chest," Taylor said.

"What do they mean?" Kate asked.

The symbols were carved over Callie's heart in the exact position as they were now carved into Raine's. Taylor quickly explained the meanings of the symbols, both the Healing Runes and the Viking Runes interpretations.

"The Viking Runes make no sense to me," Taylor said. "Whoever did this, had to have had the Healing Rune interpretations in mind."

Chris agreed with Taylor that the interpretation of the Healing Runes seemed to be more fitting to the crime. "So, who carved those symbols into Callie Delacourte and why? And why target Raine? Because she was married to Callie?"

"I looked for a similar case against Callie Delacourte and came up blank," Taylor admitted. "I found very little info on Callie."

Chris realized she knew little about Callie's background. "We need to go see Raine. Print out that picture of Callie with the scars and we'll take it with us."

Taylor pulled the picture out of the laser printer and followed Chris and Kate out to the kitchen. Chris made a bee-line for the coffee pot.

Gray pulled a mug out of the cupboard and turned to see the threesome heading towards her. "Good morning." Grinning, she bent to give Chris and then Kate a hug. "I didn't expect to see you two this morning."

"That better not be decaf," Chris said.

"It's not. I'll make you a pot of decaf if you want though, Gray." Taylor moved to the cupboard to extract the decaf coffee, but Gray brushed her off.

"No, it's fine. I'm making a tea. I've kind of gone off coffee."

"Gone off coffee?" Chris shuddered. "Sacrilege!"

Gray leaned into Taylor and whispered, "How did it go with Cail?"

"He wants to start over." She didn't bother hiding her response from Chris and Kate. "Like from scratch. He wants to take me out on a date tonight, dinner and a movie."

"And?" Chris asked. "Are you going?"

Taylor shrugged, wincing a bit. "When I go out in public, the media tends to show up."

"They didn't show up last night," Kate said.

That was true, but Taylor still didn't trust going out and not being accosted by reporters. With any luck, they were losing interest in her. "Maybe the lesbian community is a little more respectful of people's privacy than most." The last time she went out to dinner, the other patrons in the restaurant started posting on social media that she was in the restaurant and, within minutes, the place was surrounded by journalists and photographers. She ended up getting clocked in the face with a video camera trying to make it to the car.

"Why don't you just invite him over here for dinner then?" Chris asked. "You could watch a movie on your new TV after a romantic dinner."

Taylor glanced up at the large screen TV. "Where did that come from anyway? I didn't buy it."

Gray grinned. "Sorry. I can't live without TV."

Taylor laughed and nudged Gray's shoulder with her own. "Since when? You've always got your nose in a book."

"Blame Patrick. He's got me addicted to watching the news."

"The news?" Patrick asked as he hit the bottom stair.

Gray's face tinged with pink. "Okay, okay. I may be a little bit addicted to some of these reality shows."

Patrick laughed as he moved in behind his wife and kissed her neck. "Just a little, eh?" He grabbed a cup of coffee then turned on said TV and changed the channel to the twenty-four hour news. The story on the province's Premier, Carl Devonshire, was front and centre. They announced the charges against him involved a child pornography case which explained why his home and office computers were seized. Then the story switched to an announcement by the Liberal Party stating they were electing a new Provincial leader who would take over the duties of Premier. The image on the screen showed a man in his fifties with salt and pepper hair in a sleek business suit. He was surrounded by two younger men in their thirties. The announcer identified him as Sebastien St. Amour, a corporate lawyer who was expected to win the leadership. He was accompanied by his two sons, Armand and Alexandre.

The sound of a coffee cup hitting the floor and smashing startled everyone. Chris swore and bent to pick up the shards littering the floor at her feet.

"Chris?" Kate laid a gentle hand on her shoulder.

"Shit, sorry. I guess I have butter fingers this morning." She raised her head, looking for Taylor. "I hope this wasn't an expensive cup."

"No, don't worry about the cup." Taylor grabbed some paper towels, bent to help Chris clean up the mess, and retrieved another cup from the cupboard, making Chris a fresh coffee. She didn't say anything, but it was unlike Chris to have butter fingers and her face was a bit pale. Something had upset her. Taylor looked back at the TV screen, but they'd moved on to other news.

* * *

The drive to St. Mike's was unbearably quiet. Taylor scanned all around, chancing a glance at Chris every few minutes. She could tell Chris was deep in thought, though she showed no emotion. Chris parked the car and was out of the vehicle before Taylor could get her seatbelt off. She quickly caught up and matched Chris's pace.

"Got the picture?" Chris asked.

"Yeah." She wanted to ask if Chris was okay, but was afraid of her reaction.

When they reached Raine's room, they found the door open and a lady inside making up the bed. Chris whirled around and headed for the nurses station. "Raine Delacourte?" she asked the nurse sitting in front of a computer, holding up her badge for the woman to see.

"Ah. She was released this morning. She left about twenty minutes ago with a petite woman."

"Shit," Chris murmured as she shoved her badge back in her pocket.

"Should we head to Bonkers' condo?" Taylor asked.

Chris shoved her hand through her hair before meeting Taylor's eyes. "I've got something I need to do first and I'm going to ask you to keep it to yourself."

Taylor raised her eyebrows and she waited for Chris to continue as they walked back towards the elevators. To her surprise, Chris punched the up button instead of down, but still didn't say anything.

Once the elevator doors closed them into the small box, Chris said, "My mother's here. In the hospital."

"Oh." Was that why Chris had been so jumpy? Taylor wondered.

"The lady who came to see me yesterday is my mother's best friend. She told me my mother is dying and wanted to see me. I didn't want to see her. She made her choice when she kicked me out and disowned me. I don't owe her anything." Chris's hand found its way through her short hair again. "Right?"

"Right," Taylor answered.

"So why do I feel so damn guilty for letting her lie here dying?"

Taylor felt like a fish out of water. She had no idea how to handle this. "Have you talked to Lane about it?"

"No." Chris made a fist and rubbed it against her chest. "I couldn't sleep. I can't breathe. I figured if I came here and got it out of my system, I'd start feeling normal again. I will, won't I?"

Oh, geez. "I don't know, Chris. I just know that talking to Lane always helps me." That only seemed to make Chris worse. Her breaths came in short wheezes. "Try some slow, deep breaths." Taylor put her hands on Chris's shoulders and coached her through some breathing exercises until she was breathing easier.

"If you ever tell anyone about this, I'll have to kill you," Chris said. She couldn't bare for anyone to think she was weak.

"Like I'd tell anyone," Taylor said.

The elevator doors opened again and they followed signs to a nursing station. Chris showed her badge again and asked to see Eléane St. Amour. It was at that moment Taylor understood why Chris dropped her coffee. Sebastien St. Amour, the man on the TV favoured to become the next Premier of Ontario, was the same man who abused her for the first fourteen years of her life – her father.

The nurse gave Chris the room number and directions to it. Outside the door of room 1412, Chris braced her hands on her knees and took a few more deep breaths.

"Are you sure you want to do this?" It was easier dealing with her own past than watching Chris suffer through this, Taylor thought.

"No, but I need to do it." She straightened, resting a hand on Taylor's shoulder. "I need you to stay with me, no matter what she says. Okay?"

Taylor nodded her assent.

Chris eased her way into the private room, unsure what to expect. The woman laying in the bed appeared child-like in size. She didn't remember her mother being that small. Or that old, she thought as she got a better look at the frail woman with honey blond hair streaked with grey. She'd lost a lot of weight. Tubes and wires were everywhere and the monitor beside her displayed her vitals and the rhythm of her heart. Chris studied the screen for a moment. Considering the woman was supposedly on her death bed, she was relatively stable with a strong pulse and average blood pressure, not too high or too low.

When she turned her focus back on the woman in the bed, a pair of big blue eyes stared up at her.

"Christian?"

It wasn't the smooth voice Chris remembered from childhood, but the gravelly voice of someone who smoked five packs of cigarettes a day. Or one who lay in a hospital bed with tubes in her nose for days on end without a drink.

"Est-ce que je suis en train de rêver?" *Am I dreaming?*

"Non. C'est moi." Chris picked up a cup of water with a straw in it and helped her mother to take a few sips.

"Merci, Christian." A bony hand with an IV in its back snaked out from under the covers and gripped onto Chris's with surprising strength.

Chris stared down at the hand clamped onto hers and tried to pull away. "I'm Chris. Just Chris."

"You chose a name to spite me."

"I didn't come here to argue with you." Chris tugged a little harder on her hand and gained her freedom.

"Why did you come? No, let me guess. Sylvie. She couldn't keep her nose out of it."

"You never told her the truth, did you?"

Eléane's eyes closed and for a moment Chris thought she actually might cry. But, that would mean she cared and Chris knew she didn't. She never had. When those blue eyes opened again, they were as cold as they'd ever been.

"Do *you* want the truth, Christian?"

"Like I would believe anything you had to say." Chris walked to the window looking out to the brick of another wing of the hospital just a few feet away. She didn't come here to dredge up the past or to argue. She just wanted to end the turmoil gripping her ever since Sylvie came to visit her. "How long do you have left?"

"Days. Weeks maybe."

"Why aren't you at Sunnybrook?" They had a new, state of the art Cancer Centre at Sunnybrook. It didn't make any sense that she wasn't there, especially with the money her parents had.

"It's too late for any heroics, Christian. Besides, your father wanted me close."

The selfish bastard, Chris thought. He couldn't drive a few extra miles to see his wife where she'd be getting the best care. "He's not my father." The anger in her voice surprised even Chris. She got another surprise when Eléane cackled behind her. She turned to look over her shoulder and found Eléane holding her stomach as she laughed then began coughing. It was Taylor who went to her and helped her sit up enough to take another drink.

When she settled down, Eléane patted the bed at her side and said, "Come, sit, mon cher. Let me tell you a story." When Chris didn't move, Eléane sighed and began her story anyway. "When I was twenty-eight, I left your father. I didn't even take the boys. I just high-tailed it back to Ste. Thérèse thinking my parents would take me in. They didn't, of course. They were furious with me for leaving Sebastien. I was forced to take a job and get myself a little apartment. I met a man. A man I fell in love with and we had an affair."

It all began to make perfect sense – the hatred Sebastien St. Amour always had for her. She wasn't his. Some of the tension drained from Chris's shoulders and she took a step towards the bed.

"I was going to file for divorce and marry him, but Sebastien came into the café where I was working and dragged me back to Toronto. He had me guarded around the clock so I couldn't run again. Then I discovered I was pregnant." Eléane turned her head so her blue eyes met the deep brown of Chris's. "I'm sorry, Christian. I'm so sorry for all of the pain I've caused you. I'm sorry I wasn't able to protect you. I don't expect you to believe me or to forgive me, but I kicked you out that day to save your life."

"You're right. I won't forgive you." Temper flaring, Chris couldn't stop herself. "You heard me screaming at night and you did nothing."

"No. You made that up. Sebastien would never … you hated him. You said those things because you hated him. You screamed during the night because you wanted me to think that, to get back at him for all the times he beat you."

Chris took a step back. It was like she'd been slapped in the face. How could her own mother believe Sebastien over her?

"Listen to me, mon cher. You must go to confession. This … this homosexuality. It's an abomination."

"An abomination?" Chris yelled. "You think your daughter is an abomination, yet it's okay for your husband to rape children?" She smirked when Eléane flinched. "I've got news for you, Eléane. I won't be going to confession. I'm gay. I'm a lesbian. I love fucking women and I'm going to keep doing it."

The monitor at the side of the bed began to beep, but Chris stalked forward, closing in on her prey. "I've fucked a lot of women over the years. Does that bother you, *Maman*?" Jesus, she was an abomination, but it was okay for Eléane to have an affair while she was still married? "Is that more of an abomination than standing back and allowing your husband to beat and rape your illegitimate child?"

"It's lies, Christian. You're lying."

"Chris?" Taylor stepped between Chris and the bed just as two nurses ran into the room.

"We need you to calm down, Mrs. St. Amour." While one of the nurses attended to the monitor, the other one insisted Chris and Taylor leave.

"You're the biggest hypocrite I've ever met," Chris tossed over her shoulder as Taylor led her from the room.

Taylor could almost see steam shooting out each time Chris exhaled. She watched her pace back and forth in front of the elevators, not knowing what to say.

"I shouldn't have gone in there," Chris said. Looking up at Taylor, she added, "I'm sorry for being so crude."

"Why were you?"

Chris stopped pacing and shoved her fingers through her hair. "Because it hurts like hell listening to your mother call you an abomination. I needed to hurt her back."

"I'm sorry." Taylor didn't know what else to say. How could her mother be so blind to what was happening to her daughter under her own roof? Or did she just refuse to believe it? "Why do you think your mother ran from Sebastien St. Amour? Did he beat her, too?"

"I don't know why she ran. I never saw him lift a hand to her, but he was, for lack of a better word, dominant. He expected to be obeyed and she definitely obeyed him."

"Is that why she never stepped in when he beat you? Was she afraid of him?"

"Probably," Chris answered. "But that doesn't excuse her, Taylor. She let him beat me for fourteen years, rape me for three years. I don't buy that she believes I'm lying because I hated him. She *knew*. She had to have known." If she was wrong and her mother really had no idea, she would bloody well prove it.

* * *

When they arrived at Headquarters, Chris had a calmer mind and a plan. Her mother would accept the truth before she died. She went straight to her office, closed the door, and pulled up the records from the night her parents kicked her out some sixteen years ago. The file included the medical records of the tests performed at Toronto General Hospital that night which proved beyond a doubt she had been raped repeatedly over a long period of time. She printed the medical records and put them in a sealed envelope before Taylor knocked on the door and popped her head in.

"I got a positive result back from ViCLAS for a like crime that took place in Banff, Alberta six years ago. The victim, Lily De La Cruz, was raped. The Rune symbols were carved into her chest and she nearly died of asphyxiation. She was strangled by hand. Oddly enough, she was saved when a friend came over to check on her and the suspect fled. Lily De La Cruz named her ex-lover, Siobhan Silva as her attacker. Silva was convicted and did five years in a federal penitentiary."

"Let me guess," Chris began as she got to her feet. "She went into witness protection. Where's St. James? I think we just discovered why that bastard inserted himself into this case." She spotted him on the other side of the unit, sitting at a desk, tapping away at the computer keyboard with his head cocked to the side, trapping the phone between his ear and shoulder. She started to make her way to him when her cell phone rang and she stopped to answer it. "Cain."

"Sarge. It's Stone. Someone accessed Raine Delacourte's place. The seal on the door is broken. We searched the house and no one is here, but we found something. The edge of the carpet in the bedroom closet is pulled up. We pulled it back and found a safe in the floor beneath it. It's empty."

"Son of a bitch. Raine went back to the house and emptied the safe."

"Do you want us to track her down, Sarge?"

"No." Not yet, Chris thought. "Come back to the office. We're going to have a little briefing."

Chris sent Taylor into the conference room to update the board with the new details then went back into her office, leaving the door open this time. She sat down at her desk, realized she was missing something and sent Taylor a text message.

When you've finished what you're doing, I need coffee.

She picked up the sealed envelope on her desk and took it down to the desk sergeant in the lobby and asked him to have a uniformed officer deliver it to Eléane St. Amour at St. Mike's. That should give her mother some interesting reading material to keep her from getting bored in her cozy private hospital room.

* * *

Chris leaned against the wall at the front of the conference room while she waited for the team to assemble and get settled into their chairs around the table. She had Taylor turn the board around at the side of the room so no one could see the updates yet. As soon as everyone settled, Chris honed in on Detective Stone. "Stone, why don't you give us an update of any new evidence or information that has come in since our last briefing?"

Stone got to her feet. "Um, well, there's not really anything new except that Detective Ambrose and I went to the victim's house this morning to take another look at the crime scene. We found the seal on the front door compromised and did a search of the house. No one was there, but we found the corner of the carpet in the master bedroom closet sticking up. When we pulled it back, we found a floor safe. It was unlocked and empty."

"So, it appears that Raine Delacourt went back to the house and emptied the safe," Chris said.

"Or the suspect did," Stone added.

Chris pushed off the wall and stepped up to the conference table. "No, not the suspect. He spent considerable time in the closet when he had Raine tied to the bed. If he didn't find it then, he didn't find it by going back to the house a second time without creating more of a mess." She stuck her hands in her pockets and glared at Stone. "You had a good look at Raine's Facebook profile, didn't you?"

"Yes, Sarge."

"Did you find anything that might relate to this case?"

Stone shook her head. "Just the post that Bonkers tagged Raine Delacourte in saying they were at Les Beau's."

"Did you look through Raine's photos?"

"Yes."

"And found nothing relating to this case?"

Stone's brows drew together and her face flushed. "No, Sarge."

Chris opened the file folder on the table and drew out the photograph of Callie Delacourte wearing a black bikini with white sand and azure seas behind her and placed it directly in front of Stone. While Stone picked it up and studied it, Chris eyed Will St. James for his reaction. The bastard just sat there, smiled and shrugged his shoulders.

"Oh, my God. She's got the same carvings as Raine." Stone looked up at Chris with eyes bulging.

"Anything back from ViCLAS, Detective?" Chris asked.

Uh-oh. When Chris called her Detective, she knew she was in deep shit. It was the way she said it. "Um, I haven't checked yet this morning."

"You haven't checked yet?" Chris swallowed her anger. It wouldn't benefit anyone if she exploded on Stone. "Why not? Wait." Chris put her hand up in front of her. "Don't answer that." It would just piss her off even more. She turned to Taylor. "Who filed the ViCLAS report?"

"I did," Taylor answered. "You said you wanted me trained on it."

"Did Stone help you?"

Taylor's face flushed. Stone was supposed to train her on it and answering Chris's question would get Stone in more trouble than she was already in. "Detective Stone was busy, so I just went ahead and did it myself. It wasn't her fault, Sarge."

"Without any training, you just went ahead and did it yourself?" Chris had to remind herself Taylor got a hit back and fairly quickly, too.

"It wasn't that hard," Taylor answered. "I had the case information. It was just a matter of answering the questions and submitting the report."

"That's why you got the hit back and not Stone," Chris said more to herself than the group assembled around the conference table. She should have figured Taylor could handle something like that without assistance. Chris went to the side of the room and as she pulled the board back to front and centre, she said, "ViCLAS came back with a hit for a like crime out of Banff, Alberta about six years ago. Would you care to give us an update on that case, Sergeant St. James, since you were the Officer in Charge?"

All eyes went to Will St. James, who stood slowly with a grin on his face. "Well, it seems you've found me out, Detective Sergeant. Callie Delacourte was indeed the victim in that case although her name at the time was Lily De La Cruz and she had recently broken up with her girlfriend, one Siobhan Silva. Siobhan liked to believe she was psychic and often did readings using Runes. She was abusive during their two-year relationship, which was why Lily ended it. Siobhan went a little crazy on her one night when she believed Lily went out on a date. She was convinced Lily was cheating on her because the Runes told her so. It was the last straw for Lily and she moved out without telling Siobhan she was leaving or where she was going.

"The night Siobhan found Lily and attacked her in her apartment, she nearly killed her. I believe she thought she did kill her, but Lily was still breathing when Siobhan was forced to run from the house. A friend of Lily's came to check on her and scared Siobhan off." St. James opened up his messenger bag and pulled out a file folder. From the folder, he produced an old photograph of Siobhan Silva and slid it to the middle of the table.

"That's Lian," Taylor said.

"Lian?" St. James asked.

"She works at Les Beau's as a waitress. Has done for about the past month."

"Ah, makes sense." St. James lowered himself back down to his chair. "Six weeks ago, Raine Delacourte placed a memorial to Callie Delacourte in the Toronto Star. We believe that's how Siobhan discovered Lily's new identity and where she'd been living for the past six years."

"Why the fuck didn't you tell us this from the beginning?" Chris asked.

"I'm not authorized to share certain information."

Chris imagined, for one blissful moment, drawing her weapon and shooting Sergeant Will St. James right between the eyes. Through gritted teeth, she asked, "Do you realize, you complete idiot, that if we had this photograph yesterday, we would have Siobhan Silva in custody now?"

St. James only shrugged again. "We'll get her. We know she works at Les Beau's and they should have her address on file."

Chris slapped her hands on the table and dropped her head, mentally counting to ten before she ended up throttling him. She refused to look at him when she raised her head. "Sinclair and I will track down Raine Delacourte and find out what she took out of that safe. Stone and Ambrose, head over to Les Beau's and get a full name and address for the waitress named Lian and pick her up." She picked up the file folder then slapped it against the table hoping to get a reaction from St. James at the sudden loud noise. She got nothing from him, but Stone winced. Shaking her head, she walked out of the room.

When Taylor poked her head into Chris's office, Chris sat at her desk with her hair sticking up in all directions. "You okay?"

Chris glared at her. "She's not going to be at Les Beau's. We spooked her last night when we questioned her. She'll be in the wind, damn it."

"Which is why you gave that assignment to Stone." Taylor moved into the office and sat in front of Chris's desk.

"Not just a pretty face, are you?" She grinned then grabbed her coat from the back of her chair. "Let's go pay a visit to Bonkers' condo."

* * *

Bonkers let them into the apartment and offered them a seat in the living room. She said Raine was resting in the guest bedroom and went to make coffee. Taylor wandered to the window and looked out at the city spread out in front of her. Bonkers had an excellent view of the CN Tower and the downtown cityscape. She was twenty-five floors up from street level with a long balcony facing south.

The living room was what Taylor would consider very feminine. The carpet was a soft rose colour and there were floral prints on the sofa and chairs. A large screen TV sat on a long TV unit. Beside the TV and on the tables throughout the room, were a variety of little fairy figurines. A large painting on one of the walls depicted a fairy scene also. Very whimsical, Taylor thought.

Bonkers brought a tray in, set it on the coffee table, and proceeded to pour coffee for everyone. She left Taylor and Chris to add their own cream and sugar and added cream and three heaping spoons of sugar to her own.

"Want to explain to me what you were doing on my crime scene this morning, Bonkers?" Chris asked as she sipped her coffee.

Bonkers' eyes widened and she set her cup down with trembling hands.

"What? You didn't think I'd find out?" Chris asked.

"No, it's not that." Bonkers stuck her hands between her thighs and sighed. "I tried to talk her out of it. She wouldn't listen."

"What did she take from the house?"

"Clothes and stuff, I think. She went upstairs and came back down with a black duffel bag."

"Where's the duffel bag now?"

"She took it into the room with her. Why? She needed clothes and stuff, Chris. Is it really a big deal?"

Chris didn't answer. She took another sip of her coffee then rose to her feet. "It's time to wake sleeping beauty up."

Bonkers jumped up like she was going to protest then sank back down into her chair when she caught the expression on Chris's face – the icy glare that froze people in their tracks. Taylor raised her eyebrows at Chris, a slight smile curving her lips. She wondered if Chris practiced that look in the mirror to perfect it. If she had, it was probably years ago. She had it down to a T.

Chris opened the door to the guest room slowly and quietly. Raine was lying on her back staring up at the ceiling. She barely turned her head to see Chris and Taylor before turning her eyes back to the ceiling. "I'm not up to talking at the moment." Her voice was laden with tears, cracking with emotion.

"Too bad," Chris said, scanning the room. There was no sign of a black duffel bag in the pastel green room. Soothing colours, Chris decided. There wasn't much in the room aside from the double bed and a dresser. Two pine end tables held elegant lamps with fairies dancing over the shades. It seemed the fairy theme ran through the entire apartment, including the large painting hanging over the bed above Raine's head. Even the quilt on the bed featured fairies and tied in the wall colour.

Taylor closed the door and leaned against it as she studied the room. There were two other white doors in the room. One, Taylor figured, would lead into a closet. That would be where they'd find the black duffel bag, unless it was under the bed. The other door was slightly ajar revealing a grey bathroom counter with a white cabinet beneath it.

Chris took a file folder out of the messenger bag slung over her shoulder then tapped it against the side of her leg as she stared down at Raine. "What did you take out of the safe in the floor of your bedroom closet, Raine?"

Raine's eyes widened before narrowing to glare at Chris.

"What? You didn't think we'd find out? You left the carpet turned up in the corner." Chris watched a tear slide out of the corner of Raine's eye and slowly run down her temple. It disappeared into her hair line and still, she didn't answer. Chris removed the picture of Callie from her file folder and plopped it down on Raine's belly. "Take a look at that."

With a sigh, Raine picked up the photograph and held it up in front of her face. Her hand fell heavily to her side, releasing the photo. "Damn you for being so good at your job."

"It's time to cut the crap, Raine." Chris eased herself down onto the bed next to Raine. "You know who your attacker was. You've known all along. What was she after? What did you remove from your safe?"

More tears. They flowed more freely now. Raine pulled a tissue from the box on the nightstand and made an attempt at mopping them up. "It's all she had left. That woman took everything Callie had. Left her with practically nothing. She barely escaped with her life." Raine struggled to sit up. Taylor moved in to help her then fluffed the pillows behind her to make her as comfortable as possible.

"Tell me," Chris said. "The whole story, Raine."

Raine mopped up more tears. "Callie was involved in an abusive relationship when she lived out in Banff. She had money, an inheritance from her parents. She left it in the bank accumulating interest and didn't really think about it. She got out of the relationship after the woman went a bit crazy on her one night. Callie packed up and left.

"A few days later, she tried to change banks as a precaution and discovered her inheritance was almost all gone. Out of more than a million dollars, only a hundred thousand remained. Callie withdrew the funds and she's been carrying around the cash ever since."

"That's what you took out of the safe? That's what the woman who attacked you was after?" Chris said.

Raine nodded. "This woman – Siobhan something – she discovered where Callie was living and attacked her. She did the same thing to Callie that she did to me, only she strangled Callie and nearly killed her. She would have, if a friend of Callie's hadn't come over to check on her.

"It was my own fault. I never should have submitted Callie's picture with the memorial announcement. I wasn't thinking."

"Why weren't you straight with me from the beginning, Raine?" Chris asked. "Why try to hide it?"

"It was stupid." Raine held her good hand out in front of her and when she saw how badly it was shaking she fisted it in her lap until her knuckles turned white. "She didn't get what she came for, did she? I knew she would come back and I wanted to be waiting for her with a gun. I wanted to kill her. For Callie. For myself." She let out a short, self-deprecating laugh. "It would have been self-defence, right?"

"You idiot." Chris took her good hand and gave it a squeeze. "Where were you going to get a gun?"

"I hadn't figured that part out yet," Raine said, looking up from under thick eyelashes.

Chris shook her head and repeated, "You idiot." She stood then and walked towards the closet. "I want a look at the duffel bag you brought out of your house, Raine."

Taylor watched the look of innocent stupidity across Raine's face turn to panic as Chris reached for the doorknob.

Chris opened the door and found the duffel bag was lying on the floor. She grabbed the end and dragged it out, surprised at how heavy it was. Raine sat up and scooted to the side of the bed as Chris pulled the long zipper across the top of the bag. *Holy shit.* Bundles of one hundred dollar bills filled the entire bag. She reached in and began shifting the bundles around. Her gut told her it was more than just cash Callie was hiding. Beneath the cash she found two gunmetal grey lock boxes and pulled them both out, setting them on the blonde laminate floor. Both were locked. She cocked an eyebrow at Raine. "Keys?"

"I-I don't have the keys, Chris. Honestly, I don't. They must be in with Callie's stuff somewhere."

"I can open them," Taylor said to Chris.

Chris had forgotten about Taylor's knack for picking locks, a skill she acquired living on the streets. She slid one of the boxes over to Taylor. "Do it."

Taylor pulled a set of picks from the inside pocket of her uniform jacket and sat on the floor with her legs crossed, pulling one of the boxes onto her lap. It took her seconds to open it. She lifted the lid then turned it back toward Chris.

Fitted snugly into a foam base was a Sig Sauer P226 9 mm and two clips. Chris carefully removed the gun from its bed and checked to insure it wasn't loaded before replacing it. Her lips pursed as she glanced over at Raine who had her head bowed. Yeah, Raine knew there was a gun in the lockbox. "Hadn't figured that part out yet, eh?"

Raine's head shot up. "I didn't know. I've never opened those boxes or seen Callie open them."

"I'm so fucking fed up of bullshit today, it's not funny," Chris said. A pounding headache beat at her temples. Not surprising. There was only so much crap one person could stand in a day.

"Have you got a permit for this gun, Raine?" Taylor asked. "And before you say that you didn't know about the gun again, let me just tell you that ignorance is no excuse in matters of law."

Chris couldn't help herself – she shot Taylor a quick smile. Raine was on her feet, her mouth open, but nothing coming out.

"No?" Chris asked.

Raine closed her mouth and shook her head then plunked herself back down on the mattress. Chris slid the second lockbox over to Taylor and kept her eye on Raine as Taylor went to work on the lock. It sprung open seconds later and Chris took it from her before she could open the lid and went to sit next to Raine on the bed. "Do you want to tell me what I'm going to find in here before I open it up?"

Raine, head bowed again, spoke softly. "I don't know what's in it."

Chris popped the lid up and still Raine kept her head down. "Not the least bit curious to see what's inside, Raine?"

Raine sat up a bit straighter and lifted her head. "I'm tired. I'm not feeling so good. I need to rest."

Ignoring her protests, Chris pulled two Canadian passports out of the box. She opened the first and found Callie's photo with the name Jasmine Delacroix. Did she have another alias ready in case she had to run from Siobhan again? Chris wondered. The other passport contained Raine's photo with the name Skye Delacroix. Both were issued a year and a half ago, just before Callie got sick again. "Did you pick your new name, Raine, or did Callie pick them?"

"You don't know what it was like for her," Raine insisted. "She lived in constant fear of that woman finding her again. You can't blame her for being prepared."

"So you admit to knowing about the passports?"

Raine, cast resting in her lap, rubbed her left hand over her forehead. "Callie told me about the passports, yes."

Chris placed the passports back in the box and removed a black velvet bag with a drawstring. She placed it in her palm and felt the weight of it then pulled the strings apart and peeked inside. A slew of glittering gems stared back at her. Chris studied Raine, but saw no reaction. She poured some of the stones into her palm. "Any idea where Callie got these babies?"

With a sigh, Raine said, "They belonged to her parents. It's all she had left from them. Those and the money Siobhan didn't gamble away."

"Did Siobhan know about the diamonds?" Chris asked.

"I don't know. Really, I don't."

Chris was willing to bet she did. She was certain they were what Siobhan was searching for in Raine's house. She put them back in the lockbox and then put both of the lockboxes back in the duffel bag and closed it up. "I'm taking the bag with me, Raine and before you get your panties in a knot about it, you'll get all of it back, except for the fake passports, as long as none of it comes back stolen."

Raine just nodded, looking defeated.

As soon as they got down to the car, Chris arranged for twenty-four hour surveillance on Bonkers' condo and on Raine Delacourte. Not just to prevent Siobhan from coming after her again, but to keep an eye on Raine. She wasn't being honest with them and Chris had no idea why.

"Thoughts? Impressions?" Chris asked.

"She knew the contents of that duffel bag," Taylor answered.

"Oh, yeah she did."

"So, what else is she trying to hide?"

"That's the question, isn't it?"

The car filled with the ring tone on Chris's cell phone and she grabbed it from the clip on her belt. It was Stone reporting in that Lian Logan did not show up for her shift at Les Beau's today. Stone and Ambrose went to the address Lian gave to her employer, but it was phoney. She was in the wind.

Chapter 10

Chris headed straight for her office and began rifling through her drawers looking for Advil or Tylenol. Her headache had grown to epic proportions. When she found no headache remedies, she slammed the drawer shut and kicked the desk for good measure just as Taylor appeared in the doorway with a bottle of Advil in one hand and a bottle of water in the other. "Thank you," she said as she accepted both. "You're a life saver." She didn't waste any time in swallowing three of the gel caps. The tension in her neck and shoulders was phenomenal. "I could really use another coffee and then I need to go up and see the Inspector." She dropped down into her desk chair and leaned her head back."

"You sure you're okay?" Taylor only braved the question because she was extremely worried about Chris now. It wasn't like her to get headaches or look so pale.

"I will be if these Advil ever kick in."

Taylor began to walk away to get Chris a coffee when she called her back. "Yeah?" she asked as she popped her head around the door frame. Chris had her eyes closed now and didn't bother to open them as she spoke.

"On your way back, send St. James in here and come in with him."

Taylor winced. "Yeah, okay."

St. James was sitting at the same desk he'd been working at that morning when Taylor came back with a mug of coffee in each hand. She made her way over to him, wondering what he was doing all this whole time. Was he working on this case, another one, or something completely unrelated to his job? His head popped up as Taylor approached then he resumed his intense focus on the computer, hitting a couple of keys to blank out the screen. "DS Cain would like to see you," she said then steered back across to Chris's office without waiting for his response.

Taylor set a mug gently in front of Chris, worried about waking her up when her eyes opened. "Sorry, I didn't mean to disturb you. How's the head?"

"If this is what you deal with on a regular basis, I don't know how you do it." Chris picked up the mug, breathed in the warm aroma, then took a slow sip while Taylor settled into one of the chairs on the other side of the desk.

"The trick is to get the Advil into you when you first feel the headache coming on," Taylor said. "The longer you leave it, the harder it is to get under control."

"Fuck," Chris said without much punch.

She was about to ask Taylor if she'd told St. James to get his ass into her office when she heard Detective Stone mutter 'fucker' moments before said fucker showed up in her doorway.

"Close the door and take a seat, Sergeant," Chris said.

St. James closed the door, sat down next to Taylor, offering her a grin and a wink. She rolled her eyes at him and shifted in her seat.

Chris set her mug on the desk with a thump as she glared at St. James. "Do that to my partner or any other female in this department again and I'll report you for sexual harassment."

He snorted before he realized she was serious. "Are you crazy?"

"Not as crazy as you are if you think we're going to tolerate your bullshit in this department. Would you like to explain why you've been taking up space in my unit for the past two days? What exactly are you working on, St. James?"

Crossing his arms over his chest, he narrowed his eyes and said, "That's none of your business."

"Oh, but it is. You've inserted yourself into my unit, supposedly to work on the Delacourte case, yet you haven't contributed a damn thing to the investigation. In fact," she raised her voice. "If it hadn't been for your fuck up, we'd have had the suspect in custody. Now she's in the fucking wind and it's on you if she hurts anyone else."

St. James surged to his feet. "I explained to you this morning that I couldn't divulge certain information."

Chris placed her palms on her desk and slowly pushed up from her chair, leaning heavily on the desk. Her voice was icy cold and calm. "I'll repeat my question. What have you been working on for the past two days?"

He crossed his arms over his chest again, staring Chris down, and didn't respond.

Fine, Chris thought. If he wanted to be a stubborn ass, she'd take another route. "If it isn't directly related to the Delacourte investigation, you can get the fuck out of my unit and stay out. If it is related, you'd better have two days worth of work on my desk by the end of the day along with the case file for the Lily De La Cruz case. I want everything you've got, including the crime scene photos."

With that, Chris walked out of her office. She headed for the stairs, hoping the few flights up to Inspector Worthington's floor would give her a chance to cool off.

* * *

Martine sat across the desk from Cal Worthington reading through some papers as Cal worked on his computer. Chris tapped on the doorjamb and had both of their heads popping up. Cal nodded to the chair next to Martine without changing his serious expression while Martine grinned. Chris sat down next to her, still trying to formulate the right words. "Inspector, we've had a setback in the Delacourte case due to information withheld by the RCMP."

"I've heard," he muttered, continuing to tap away at his keyboard. "Technically, he's not in the wrong, Chris."

"That's bullshit," she huffed. "If he'd even slipped us the picture of Siobhan Silva yesterday, she'd be in custody now. Why is he so hell bent on protecting the identity of someone who's not even alive?" Before she finished the question, the lightbulb went on in her head and she shot out of her chair. "Shit. It's not Callie Delacourte he's protecting. It's Siobhan Silva."

Cal leaned back in his chair and steepled his fingers together. "That was my impression."

If Chris hadn't been so twisted up about her mother, she'd probably have come to that conclusion before now. She paced back and forth, gears spinning in her head. "Why? Why is he protecting her? What's she got that the RCMP wants?" It wasn't a lightbulb that went off in her head this time - it was a big, fat shiny diamond. "The diamonds."

"What diamonds?" Cal asked.

"Raine Delacourte went right back to her house when she left the hospital this morning and emptied a safe concealed under the carpet in the bedroom closet. She removed the contents in a black duffel bag and took it with her to Elizabeth Cruise's apartment. We've got it now, but among the contents was a bag full of diamonds."

"Bingo," Cal said. "Where's St. James now?"

Oh, shit. Chris winced. "Hopefully, still downstairs in my unit. I kind of gave him an ultimatum before I came up here."

"Does he know you brought those diamonds into evidence?"

"No. The duffel bag is still in the trunk of my car. I was in a hurry to get to my office when I came in, so I haven't taken the bag in or recorded its contents yet."

A slow smile spread across Cal's handsome face. "He'll still be in your unit then. He's not going anywhere until he finds those diamonds." He leaned forward, placing his elbows on the desk and clasping his hands. "Who else knows about them?"

"Raine Delacourte, Sinclair, and myself."

His smile became a full out grin. "Get Sinclair up here."

* * *

Chris and Taylor took the elevator down to the garage, retrieved the bag of diamonds from the duffel bag, and then took the elevator back up to Inspector Worthington's office. They counted out twenty-four blue tinged diamonds. Worthington signed and dated the seal on the evidence bag and secured them in his safe.

Once that was done, Chris and Taylor went back down to the garage and brought the d and pulled out evidence bags. They counted and recorded everything, sealed it in evidence bags, and then Taylor took it all down to the evidence room while Chris typed up the report.

Chris could see Will St. James on the other side of the unit, working away on his laptop. She waited, watching him after she submitted the report. She knew he saw them come in with the duffel bag and figured he would be itching to check to see if the diamonds were on her list. He lasted about three and a half minutes after she filed the report to turn to the desktop computer. His brow furrowed as he focused on the desktop's screen and then his face turned red, the veins in his neck bulged. He picked his cell phone up off the desk, dialed a number then got up and paced as he talked, his free arm waving dramatically. She wished she could hear the conversation. *Bastard. See how he likes it when information is withheld from him.*

Chris was smirking when her desk phone rang. She picked it up as she continued to watch St. James. "Cain."

"Hey, DS. It's Sergeant Wilkins on the desk. I've got a Dr. Sylvie Raynard asking to come up and see you. Says it's important."

Fuck, Chris thought. Had her mother sent Sylvie back here after reading the reports she sent over? Why the hell had she done that anyway? She didn't need to prove anything to that woman. Her stomach summersaulted in her belly.

"DS?"

Shit. It wasn't Wilkins's problem. She couldn't expect him to deal with Sylvie. She'd have to suck it up and do it herself. "Yeah, send her up." She stuck her head out of her office doorway, relieved to see Taylor back at her desk. "Sinclair," she yelled, then dumped herself back into her chair. When Taylor showed up in the doorway, she told her to come in and shut the door. "I did something really stupid," she said.

"What?" Taylor stood where she was, not sure what to do. Chris's face was a bit green.

"I sent the medical records from the night my parents kicked me out to my mother at the hospital," Chris admitted. "It contained proof I'd been sexually assaulted over a long period of time."

"You want her to know the truth."

Chris shrugged, her face screwed up like she was in physical pain. "The lady who was here yesterday is on her way back up. I think my mother sent her. I need you to stay in here with me."

"What? Why?" Coward, she thought. She wanted to be there for Chris, but this seemed above and beyond.

"So you can stop me from doing anything I'll regret later."

"Oh, Chris." She still didn't trust herself not to become violent, even after finding out she wasn't her father's biological daughter. Taylor sat, determined to be there for her friend even if she was dreading listening to whatever this lady had to say.

Just to be on the safe side, Chris removed her weapon from the holster at her hip and locked it in her desk drawer.

* * *

Taylor got up at the soft knock and opened the door. The woman on the other side was elegantly dressed in a black skirt with a cream blouse and killer stiletto heels in shiny black. A long black coat was draped over her arm with a small black purse clasped in her hand. Taylor offered her hand. "Hi, I'm Constable Taylor Sinclair."

"A pleasure," Sylvie smiled, but it didn't reach her eyes. "Dr. Sylvie Raynard." She shook Taylor's hand then turned to Chris. "I wasn't at all sure you'd see me, Christian."

"Chris," she spat through clenched teeth.

"Sorry, mon cher. It's habit. I've thought of you as Christian since you were a baby." She attempted another sad-eyed smile then turned back to Taylor. "Would you mind giving us a few minutes?"

"She stays," Chris said. "Say what you have to say." *Then get the hell out of my office.*

Taylor closed the door behind Sylvie and while the woman took a chair, Taylor remained on her feet in case she had to intervene.

"I've just come from visiting Eléane at the hospital," she began. "She's very upset, Chris."

Finally, Chris thought. Did she realize how insulting it was for her to insist on calling her Christian? Obviously not. "You think I give a shit about her being upset? What the hell do you think she did to me for all those years?"

Sylvie raised a hand, palm out. "I know, cher. Neither of us deserve your sympathy."

Chris leaned forward, eyes narrowed. "You didn't know."

"I should have," Sylvie said as tears pooled in her eyes. "I treated your wounds. I should have asked more questions. Hell, I should have reported your father the first time your mother brought you to me." She flipped the clasp on her purse and pulled out some tissues, dabbing under her eyes.

Chris wanted to roll her eyes. "Why are you here, Sylvie?"

"Eléane wants to see you again. Will you go see her, Chris? Please?"

She never should have sent those records over to the mother. The last thing she wanted was to see her mother's face with the same pity etched all over Sylvie's face now. She didn't think she could stand that.

"Please," Sylvie repeated.

"I'll think about it," Chris agreed, more to get Sylvie to leave than anything. She had no intention of facing Eléane.

"Okay." Sylvie pressed the tissues to her eyes. "That's good. That's all I can ask."

Taylor waited until the woman was gone then asked, "Will you go see Lane?"

"I'm fine." Chris slumped back into her chair, relieved that was over and hoping it was all behind her now. The familiar sick feeling would start to fade now, wouldn't it?

* * *

With his laptop bag slung over his shoulder, Cail wrapped on the door of Ireland's apartment. He waited a few minutes, listening for signs of life inside the apartment then wrapped on the door again. He was about to knock again when a shadow passed over the peep hole. "Ireland, open up."

He heard the slide of the chain then the dead bolt slicking open before the door eased open a few inches. Ireland's pale green eyes stared out at him, half closed. "What the hell, Cail? It's way to early for a social call."

It was past ten. He knew Ireland was a night hawk, but he thought he showed great restraint in waiting for a decent hour before showing up at her place. "We need to talk," he said.

"Ooh, you look so serious. What's going on?"

Cail sighed. "Are you going to let me in or do I have to do this standing in the hall where all your neighbours can hear us?"

The door slid open while Ireland pulled her silk, emerald green robe closed over her small breasts and tied the belt at her waist. "Coffee," she groaned and walked to the kitchen.

Cail set up his laptop on the breakfast bar while Ireland got a pot of coffee going. He cued up one of the videos of the two of them leaving a club. When Ireland crawled onto the bar stool next to him, he hit play on the video. Cail stumbled and wobbled, Ireland supporting him, down the sidewalk towards the camera. He paused the video as Ireland swept her hair over her shoulder, her eyes directly on the camera. "I've studied every video out there of us leaving a bar over the past couple of weeks. In every one, your eyes meet the camera. You knew the camera was there. You knew exactly where it was."

"Cail-" Ireland began before Cail cut her off.

"Do you want to explain to me how the media, or at least one member of the media, knew where I was every night, when I'd be leaving, and exactly where to set up to get the best shots of us?" Her eyes were wide open now, Cail thought.

"Are you accusing me of setting the whole thing up?"

Cail snorted and shook his head. "That's exactly what I'm doing. Are you going to deny it? Because I tracked down the videographer, Ireland."

"Shit," she said on a huff and ran her fingers through her hair, throwing it over her shoulder like she'd done so many times on camera.

"Was it money? Is that why you did it?" He was willing to forgive her if she had a good reason. Hell, he was hoping for a reason to forgive her. He really didn't want to believe Ireland would so easily sell him out.

"No." A line formed between her brows, her pale green eyes hardened. "Do you have any idea how difficult it is to make it in the music business? I've been busting my ass for over a decade, getting nowhere. That bitch is on the news for five minutes and she's an instant celebrity. What's she done to deserve it?"

Cail mentally counted to ten. "You did it to get attention? To further your career?"

Ireland slid off her stool and went to pour the coffee. "God, you make it sound so … self-serving." She poured two mugs then set them and some cream and sugar on the breakfast bar. Instead of returning to her stool, she stood at the bar across from Cail and doctored her coffee, closed her eyes and sighed at the first sip, the heat of the coffee sliding down her throat to her belly as much of a comfort as the caffeine.

Cail just watched, waiting for her to show an ounce of remorse, but it wasn't there. "It's okay to make a fool out of me in order to further your music career, but you get upset when I make it sound self-serving?" That seemed to get to her. Her freckles stood out as her face paled.

"I-I didn't mean to hurt you, Cail."

But, she had. She'd taken a lifelong friendship and twisted it into something ugly. "I need to know everything I told you about Tay. I need to understand where you got this idea that she wanted a BDSM relationship with me."

Ireland's mouth dropped open. She snapped it shut then blindly stared off in the direction of her living room window.

"Word for word," Cail said. "Everything I told you that involves Tay."

She took a few sips of her coffee, set it down, then met Cail's eyes again. "Why bother, Cail? She's no good for you. Can't you see that?"

"I'll decide who's good for me." He counted to ten again. Between Ireland and Dave, he was fed up with people telling him Tay was too damaged for their relationship to work. "You don't know Tay or anything about her."

"I know enough. You don't live a life like she has and come out of it normal, Cail. Ask Lane. She'll tell you how messed up that woman is."

She couldn't even say Tay's name. Was it jealousy? he wondered. *That woman* is the love of my life. She's had a hard life, but Lane is helping her. And, Lane will tell you that Tay is deserving and capable of a healthy relationship. It's me who keeps screwing up, like betraying her trust telling you stuff about her. So, are you going to tell me what I told you?"

"I'm just trying to look out for your best interests, Cail. I thought if you were seen in public with someone, she'd leave you alone. You deserve better."

"Not only did you use me to try to further your career, you tried to ruin my relationship." Jaw clenched, he slammed his laptop closed and shoved it back in his bag. Standing, he slung the bag over his shoulder. "I don't know what effect it will have on your career, but your plan to ruin my relationship failed. You did succeed in ruining another relationship though - our friendship. You're not the person I thought you were, Ireland." He turned to leave and Ireland ran around the breakfast bar, grabbing onto his arm.

"Cail, wait. It wasn't like that. Please."

"Friends support each other, Ireland. They wouldn't sabotage a friend's relationship." He pulled his arm from her grip and continued towards the door.

"Please, don't leave like this," Ireland pleaded, following behind him. "Tell me how to make it right between us." When he pulled open the door, Ireland was in panic mode. "You didn't tell me anything, Cail. I got it from another source. You wouldn't spill anything on her."

Cail spun around. Very few people knew about Taylor's propensity for bullwhips. He was about to ask her who the hell her source was when his brother strolled out of the hallway with sleep mussed hair and wearing nothing but black boxer briefs.

"Hey, bro," Dave said, and made his way to the coffee pot.

"Jesus fucking Christ." Cail's blue eyes shot flames at Ireland. He spun around again and slammed the door behind him. He had to leave as he was in serious danger of hurting his brother. It wouldn't surprise him if the whole media tip off thing was Dave's idea. Hell, he probably coerced Ireland into doing it. He punched the down button and paced back and forth. He supposed he shouldn't have been surprised when Ireland rushed down the hallway in nothing but her flimsy robe.

"Cail, please?" Tears streamed down her blotchy face, her eyes already red and puffy. "I couldn't bear watching how much she tore you apart. I just wanted you to get over her, to stop hurting."

The elevator door slid open at that moment and Cail stepped in. Ireland's hand shot out to hold the door open. "Go back to your lover, Ireland," Cail said as he punched the button for the lobby. "I have no interest in anything you have to say."

Chapter 11

Taylor and Chris went back to Raine's neighbourhood armed with photographs of Siobhan Silva. No one on her street recognized Silva, so they continued on, heading towards Les Beau's. If Taylor was right about Silva living in the area, Chris figured they might get lucky.

They'd been at it for an hour when a wet snow began to fall. Taylor was already chilled to the bone. The dampness made it even worse. She stepped into a vape store about a block and a half from Les Beau's and showed the picture to the clerk, a young east Indian with a short beard and kind eyes.

"Yeah, that's Lian. She do something wrong?"

"When's the last time you saw her?" Taylor asked, ignoring his question.

"A few days ago, I think. She comes in a couple of times a week to buy juice."

Taylor glanced over her shoulder at the wide open window in the store front. "You ever notice which way she goes when she leaves?"

"Sure. She just lives across the street there." He nodded out the window. "Above the variety store."

Taylor looked out at the apartment above the store. Bingo, she thought. "Thanks for your help."

"What did she do? Kill someone?"

Taylor walked out, leaving his question hanging in the air. She pulled out her cell phone and called Chris, who was making her way down the opposite side of the street. When Chris answered, she said, "I think I found her apartment." She started across the street as Chris came out of the variety store.

"Yeah, me too." She stopped and looked up at the apartment.

"How do you want to handle it?" Taylor said into her phone even

147

though she was standing next to Chris now.

Chris looked over at her, rolled her eyes, then dropped the phone from her ear and ended the call. "You think she's still here?"

"Only one way to find out." Taylor stepped up to the black door next to the store, turned the handle, and was surprised to find it unlocked. A long narrow staircase led up to the second floor. At least it was clean and didn't stink of stale urine. She climbed the stairs as quietly as she could with Chris following up behind her. The door at the top was also painted black. Taylor stood on one side of the door while Chris took up a position on the other side and they listened to the muffled sounds of a TV playing inside. At Chris's nod, Taylor knocked on the door.

She knocked again after a few moments, but the only sounds were coming from the TV. She couldn't hear anyone moving around inside. "Not here," Taylor whispered.

"Unless she saw us out the window," Chris whispered back. She needed a warrant. She pointed at the stairs just as the door at the bottom opened. Siobhan Silva stared up at them then took off in a flash. Chris let Taylor go ahead of her due to her superior speed.

Taylor took the stairs two or three at a time and shot out of the door onto the sidewalk, searching up and down the street. She couldn't see Silva anywhere.

"Go that way," Chris ordered, pointing east as she started west, checking in store windows and alleyways. Knowing in her gut they'd lost her, she turned back just as Taylor flew out from around the corner.

"She had a car parked out back."

Damn it, Chris thought. They'd left her car back near Raine's. "Description?"

"Silva Toyota RAV 4." She rhymed off the plate number and Chris grinned.

"Call it in. I'm going to work on a warrant."

* * *

Taylor clipped the two-way radio back on her belt. "The plate comes back to a Gold Caravan."

"No surprise there. The car is probably stolen, too. With any luck, we'll find the vehicle before she ditches it." Chris checked her watch. The warrant would be coming through any minute. They'd opted to wait inside the variety store to keep warm. The snow was coming down heavier now and the wind had picked up with face numbing intensity.

Just as the warrant came through, Will St. James pulled up to the curb. "Fucker," Chris muttered under her breath. He looked sharp in his fitted grey suit and gold tipped hair. She didn't suppose he needed a warm coat when all he did was sit on his ass in an office or in a warm car. He stepped up onto the curb, grinning like it was his calling card.

Chris pushed the glass door open and stomped out into the frigid air. "What are you doing here, St. James?"

"Thought you might need some help."

"F'er," Taylor muttered so only Chris could hear her.

Chris had to turn her head and press her lips together to keep form laughing at Taylor's inability to say the F word. She paced up and down the sidewalk until she regained her composure. St. James probably thought she was fuming and that was fine with her because, truth be told, she was furious with him. She held onto that anger and stepped up to him. "I get the feeling you're sitting back watching us do all of your work for you, so you can march in at the opportune moment and scoop the bust."

St. James raised his eyebrows and smirked. "Now why would I do that?"

"Because you're a lazy asshole?" Chris mimicked the smirk that quickly dropped off St. James's face.

"I've put a hell of a lot of time and effort into this case, so back the hell off, DS."

Chris stayed where she was. "What is it, exactly, that you're here to help us look for, Sergeant?"

"Evidence."

Chris rolled her eyes and stalked off to the black door leading up to Silva's apartment with Taylor right on her heels and St. James bringing up the rear. When they reached the top, Chris turned to St. James and waved her hand at the door. "Why don't you do the honours?"

St. James took a couple of steps run at the door, hit it with his shoulder, and bounced off without budging the door. "Solid," he said, rubbing his shoulder. He leaned back and gave it a good kick, hitting right beside the deadbolt, and still it didn't budge. Two more kicks had a similar effect.

"I can open it," Taylor said.

St. James continued to rub his shoulder. "Go for it." His right leg was tingling from the force of his kicks.

Taylor took out her pick set and went to work on the deadbolt lock with St. James staring over her shoulder. "That's not entirely legal."

"Big guy like you can't break the door down," Chris said. "Have you got another suggestion?"

"Battering ram, but it would take time to get one here."

While they bickered back and forth, Taylor finessed the lock, smiling when the deadbolt clicked open. She turned the handle and opened the door a fraction. "We're in."

"Make sure it's not booby trapped," Chris ordered.

With the door open a fraction of an inch, Taylor searched for strings or lines that would indicate the door was rigged. "It looks clear." She eased the door open all the way and sighed in relief when nothing happened.

Chris surveyed the living room. It was sparse, with a faded blue couch and a pine table supporting a small TV, tuned to the twenty-four hour news station. There were no knick-knacks or pictures anywhere. "Take the living room, St. James. Sinclair, you've got the kitchen. I'll take the bedroom and bathroom. Any electronics will be taken in to Brice McLean."

Taylor headed for the kitchen, pleased to see it was neat and clean. She'd seen some horrific kitchens during her time on patrol - sinks filled with dirty dishes and bugs crawling all over them. Nasty. She pulled on a pair of purple nitrile gloves then started with the drawers. The first one held cutlery - two each of forks, knives, and spoons plus one paring knife. The second drawer was empty, but the third contained a file folder. She pulled it out and placed it on the counter before opening it. Staring back at her was an eight by ten image of Raine Delacourte walking out of her house with Bonkers carrying the black duffel bag. She flipped to the next photo which showed a vehicle pulling into a parking garage attached to an apartment building. Taylor was sure it was Bonkers' building. She couldn't see the occupants of the car, but she was willing to bet it was Raine and Bonkers. The next photo showed Taylor and Chris going into the building and the next was of them coming out with the duffel bag. Taylor tried to picture where the photo was taken from. There was another apartment building across the street from Bonkers', so the photo had either been taken from the lobby of that building, the street, or a vehicle parked on the street. She hadn't noticed any pedestrians when they were entering or leaving and she'd taken a good look around. That left the lobby or a vehicle. The street had been lined with parked cars, but she hadn't seen a silver RAV 4. Based on the angle of the photo, Taylor figured Silva was in a dark blue minivan parked directly in front of the entrance to the building across the street.

"I've got a laptop," St. James said from the doorway to the kitchen. He held the MacBook up for Taylor to see. "It's password protected. Not much else in the living room."

Taylor closed the file folder. "We'll take it in for Brice."

"What ya got there?"

She figured it wouldn't hurt anything to show St. James what she found. He'd see the photos sooner or later anyway. "Surveillance photos. Looks like Silva has been watching Bonkers' building.

"You got someone posted there though, right?"

"Yeah."

St. James helped Taylor finish searching the rest of the kitchen then they both headed down the short hallway to the bedroom to check on Chris.

The double bed in the bedroom looked like someone just rolled out of it and the heaping pile of clothes in the corner made it obvious laundry day was overdue. Chris was on her hands and knees with her head inside the closet.

"What have you got?" St. James asked.

Chris leaned back on her haunches and looked up at Taylor and James. "I was hoping to find the Mastercraft toolbox Bonkers saw, but all I've found is cardboard boxes filled with shoes, clothes, some framed pictures, and other personal items. Looks like Silva didn't bother unpacking most of her stuff."

"The toolbox was probably in the car, along with her camera." Taylor held up the file folder. "She took some surveillance shots at Raine's house and Bonkers' building this morning."

Chris held out her hand for the folder and flipped through the pictures. While she was doing that, St. James opened the drawer of the bedside table. "Likes her toys," he said.

Taylor cringed when he held up a bright pink dildo. "I'll check the bathroom." She'd leave St. James to play with the toys."

"Any lube?" Chris asked. They may be able to match it to the lube used on Raine.

"Nope." St. James held up a strap on. "But, we've got this."

"Bag it," Chris said. "The rest of the toys as well."

There wasn't much to check in the tiny washroom. What Taylor was looking for was a jug of the disinfectant used to clean up in Raine Delacourte's bathroom, but she didn't find one.

When they had exhausted their search, they headed back down to the street, bracing themselves against the wind and snow. Chris glanced at her watch. "Are you going back to the office?" she asked St. James.

"Eventually."

"You want to take the evidence back and log it in?" All they had were the sex toys, pictures, and the laptop. "I'm cutting Sinclair loose and I've got something I need to take care of."

"Yeah, no problem." He took the file folder and stepped off the curb.

"Hey," Chris called. "You mind giving us a lift back to my car. It's parked over by Delacourte's house."

"Sure."

"Are you going to see your mom?" Taylor asked. "I'll go with you."

"Go home, Sinclair. Enjoy your hot date with Romeo." She rolled her shoulders, attempting to alleviate some of the tension. "I'm not sure if I'm going to see her or not." The guilt was eating at her again. In a matter of days, her mother could be dead and she would feel sick having left things the way they were now. She never should have sent those damn reports.

* * *

Chris turned the car off then rested her forehead against the wheel. Either she went in and talked to Kate about what was going on with her mother or she ignored it all and hoped the ache in her gut would go away eventually. She wanted to ignore it all. Put it all back in the deep recesses of her mind and pretend it wasn't there. That's what she'd been doing for the past sixteen years and it was working okay so far, wasn't it? She was a high-functioning kickass, respected Detective Sergeant.

She lifted her head and looked at her little house with warm lights beaming from the windows. The woman inside had become her world. Would she lose Kate if she didn't make the effort to heal from her past? Would she end up like Taylor and Cail, fighting to get back what they'd lost. "Fuck." She let her head sink back down to the steering wheel. She wanted it all with Kate. Maybe Taylor was right. Maybe it was the right time to heal from their pasts.

She got out of the car and made her way inside, feeling like she was wearing a necklace of concrete slabs. She walked into the house and sniffed the air. She didn't know what Kate was cooking, but it smelled heavenly.

Kate took one look at Chris and turned the oven off. The lasagna could wait. "What's going on?"

Chris flopped onto one of the stools at the breakfast bar and dropped her head into her hands, elbows supporting her. She ran her hands through her hair and lifted her head. "I did something really stupid."

Kate couldn't help smiling. "Not you?"

Chris snorted. It wasn't something you heard her say. Ever. "Yeah, me. I should have waited until I cooled down. I reacted. I didn't think of the consequences until it was too late."

"Chris? What's going on?" Kate sobered up pretty quick with the seriousness of Chris's tone. She moved around the counter, stood behind Chris, and wrapped her arms around her. "Talk to me."

"That's what I'm trying to do." Trying, but not doing a very good job of it. "My mother's in the hospital. She's dying. Cancer."

"Oh, Chris. I'm so sorry."

"I went to see her."

"Oh."

"She was still in complete denial about my father sexually abusing me. So, when I got back to the office, I printed off the medical reports from the night they kicked me out and I had them sent to her in the hospital."

Kate sighed. "Maybe it wasn't a stupid thing to do. Maybe she needed to see what was in those reports."

Chris lifted her head until her eyes met Kate's. "Do you really think so?"

"Yeah." Hell, she'd love to give that woman a good piece of her mind. She hoped having the evidence in front of her was a hell of a wake up call. "She needed to know the truth, Chris. Especially if she's close to death. What is it they say? The truth shall set you free."

Was that what her mother was looking for? Was that what Taylor was trying to tell her she needed to do? God, she had no idea what to do. "She wants to see me again."

Kate buried her face in the curve of Chris's shoulder and hugged her tight. "We'll go together."

A gush of air escaped Chris's lungs. "Thank you." God, she was never letting this woman go.

* * *

Taylor had texted Cail to let him know she was working later than expected, so she was surprised to find him sitting on her couch watching TV with Callaghan and Gray. She climbed the last few steps, crossed to the couch, and dropped like a stone.

"You look exhausted." Gray picked up the remote and muted the TV.

"I think it was the cold. It just drains the life out of you." She probably shouldn't have sat down because now she didn't want to move.

One of Gray's perfectly shaped eyebrows rose slightly. "Why don't you go up and take a hot shower? You'll feel better. We saved you a plate. I'll heat it up for you when you're done in the shower."

Taylor rolled her head until she faced Cail. "You ate?"

"Yeah, sorry." Cail reached for Taylor's hand and gave it a squeeze. "I didn't know how long you'd be."

"S'okay. I don't want to go out anyway." Taylor closed her eyes, enjoying the warmth of Cail's hand in hers and the little zing travelling up her arm.

"You could have your date tomorrow night. Bring Cail to the Crawford Gala."

Why did Gray have to say that? Now Taylor felt obligated to bring Cail to their publisher's Christmas Gala. The media would be swarming the place and champing at the bit to get the dirt on whether or not they were back together. How was she supposed to respond to their questions? She'd been hoping to make an appearance then sneak out, avoiding the media as much as possible.

"You don't have to bring me along, Tay. I understand if you want to go solo."

Now she felt even worse. It wasn't that she didn't want him to go. It was walking into another media frenzy she was hoping to avoid. "What are we going to say when fifty million reporters ask if we're back together?"

Cail grinned at her. "Yes?"

But, they weren't. Not really. They agreed to start over. That didn't mean anything was solved. Taylor peeled herself off the couch. "I'm going up for that shower."

Cail waited until Taylor disappeared up the stairs. "Does she seem more desolate than usual or is it just me?"

"She's definitely more depressed than I've ever seen her," Gray said with a sigh.

"Because of me, do you think?"

"I couldn't say, Cail. I haven't had a chance to speak to her." She hadn't had more than a couple of minutes alone with Taylor since she and Callaghan arrived in Toronto and those few moments were that morning when Cail walked out on her.

"I know she's got a lot on her mind," Cail said. The discussion he heard between Taylor and Lane played through his mind. "I figured she'd be elated with getting her own house. I mean, it's a huge step for her, right?"

Callaghan felt the tension building in Gray's hand, entwined with his over her belly. At seven months pregnant, he didn't want his wife getting upset. "Look, Cail, we're friends and I don't want you to take this the wrong way, but you should be talking to Taylor instead of grilling Gray for information."

"I'm not trying to press her for information. Gray, I'm sorry if I gave you that impression." For some reason, he seemed to be very good at screwing things up lately. Cail rubbed his hands over his face then looked up at Gray again. "I know she's hurting. I know she has repressed memories from her childhood resurfacing. I don't know if it's that making her so sad, if it's me, or if it's a combination of things. I also know she's not comfortable talking to me about any of her stuff right now." Despite the fact he hadn't spilled any of Taylor's personal stuff to Ireland, he still felt responsible. He understood why she lost her trust in him. "I guess I just wanted to make sure you're there for her. I don't expect you to tell me anything. Tay will open up to me when she's ready, but she needs someone she can talk to in the meantime."

The fact that Taylor's childhood memories were resurfacing was news to Gray. "What repressed memories?"

"Oh, shit." He figured Gray knew at least that much. "I can't talk about it. Tay already distrusts me for betraying her confidence."

Gray's one eyebrow shot up. "What secrets have you divulged now? And to whom?"

"I didn't. She just thinks I have."

Gray's patience wore thin. "Well, for God's sake, Cail. Why haven't you set her straight?"

"Haven't had time for that conversation yet. Besides, she may not believe me."

"Maybe what we need to do is all sit down and get everything out on the table." A family meeting is what they needed, so everyone was on the same damn page.

"Oh, yeah. She'd *love* that."

* * *

Taylor wrapped one towel around her body and one around her wet hair and made it as far as her bedroom window. She perched on the window sill and gazed out at the falling snow. It was a heck of a lot prettier when you had a warm house to watch it from. When she lived on the streets, snow could be deadly. At least, the cold temperatures could.

As she watched the snow, movement at the end of the street caught her eye. A lone figure stalked up the street on the opposite sidewalk and, judging by the size, it was a child. The clothes and gait said male. He wore baggy jeans and a sweatshirt with the hood pulled over his head. His head was down, but she knew by instinct his eyes scanned for danger. Street kid. She didn't know how she knew, but she was sure of it. She was even more sure when he glanced over his shoulder before tucking down the laneway beside the abandoned building across the street. She'd bet money the kid was sleeping in that building.

"Taylor?"

Taylor jumped at Gray's voice. She'd been so wrapped up in the kid, she hadn't heard anyone coming up the stairs.

"Sorry." Gray made her way across the room to Taylor. "I didn't mean to frighten you. Why are you sitting in the dark?" She looked out the window and smiled. "Looks like we'll have a white Christmas."

Taylor's palm covered her still racing heart. "I guess." She leaned her head against the window.

"Want to talk about why you're so sad?"

Taylor stared out into the night. A faint light flickered then disappeared in a third floor window of the warehouse and Taylor saw herself in a similar situation not so long ago, trying to stay alive in a freezing cold building with no heat. She should be happy to be in her warm, safe home. In less than a year, she went from street rat to having everything she ever dreamed of and more. "I know I've been really down lately, but I just don't seem to be able to pull myself out of it."

"Is it that woman who's been with Cail on the news?" Gray had an idea she was the one Taylor thought Cail broke her confidence with.

"I don't know." Taylor lifted her shoulders and let them drop. "I guess that's part of it."

Gray hoisted herself up onto the window sill with her back against the window. "I don't suppose you've had time to write everything down, but I think that was a great idea. I always find writing very cathartic. It helps get it all out and you may have an epiphany."

The thought of what Rick put Leila through still ripped at her. She continued to stare out the window.

"You've just been through a traumatic experience with Rappaport. It's not surprising you're feeling miserable, Taylor."

"It's not that. Or that's not all of it." Taylor told Gray about the flashback she had in Lane's office and her realization that Rick gave Taylor the belt on a regular basis to hurt Leila.

"Don't you dare feel guilty for that," Gray said with force. "It wasn't your fault. You were just a little girl. There was nothing you could have done to change what happened."

Taylor pulled the towel from her head, her hair tumbling down her back like a small avalanche, and pressed it to her face. "It would be like you being forced to stand back while someone did that to Gracie. It would have destroyed Leila." She was heartsick over Leila's suffering. She knew she couldn't have prevented Rick from doing the things he did. It didn't make her feel any better knowing it.

Gray winced at the thought of someone harming her daughter and wondered where the hell Taylor's mother was when her daughters were being mistreated. She sure as hell wouldn't be able to stand back and watch someone hurt her child. She wondered what threats Rick made to Leila to force her to do just that. "All of that was so long ago, Taylor. Don't give him the power to make you suffer still. Don't give him your power. He's not worth it."

"I don't know how," Taylor said into the towel. "It hurts. I don't know how to make it stop."

"Turn the hurt into something else, something empowering. It's okay to be angry at him and to use that anger for something good. It's not okay to let him continue to hurt you."

Taylor was so tired. Tired of feeling like this, tired of all the monsters out there, preying on those weaker than them. "I am angry at him." So angry she wanted to track him down and kill him. "But, it still hurts. I feel sick every time I think about it."

"Realizing Rick's motives has come as a shock, but the pain will ease in time." It would always be there, Gray thought. But the severity would wane. "Have you been sleeping?"

"A little," Taylor answered after a brief hesitation.

"Did you sleep at all last night?" Nightmares or night terrors interrupted Taylor's sleep on a good night. She imagined Taylor was getting even less sleep than usual with these revelations coupled with her other issues. She was surprised the poor girl was getting any sleep at all. She didn't get a verbal answer to her question, but Taylor shook her head. There was another reason Taylor wasn't sleeping. She slept better and had fewer nightmares when Cail was with her. "Why don't you let Cail sleep with you tonight? Just let him hold you so you can get a few hours sleep."

Taylor wasn't at all sure she could 'just sleep' with Cail. Not because she didn't trust him. She didn't trust herself. Her body missed him and it didn't seem to want to listen to reason. She didn't think she could resist the temptation of touching him, loving him if he was lying next to her, holding her, his strong arms and his scent embracing her. "I don't know if that's a good idea."

"Tay?" Cail whispered into the dark room.

Taylor's head shot up. Cail stood in the doorway, backlit by the light in the hall. His silhouette emphasized his shape in tight jeans and a long sleeved t-shirt - lean waist and hips, broad shoulders, muscular arms. Taylor unconsciously ran her tongue over her lower lip. *Yeah, so not a good idea.* "I need to get dressed," she whispered to Gray.

Chapter 12

Taylor came out of the en suite dressed in black yoga pants and a navy Toronto Police sweatshirt. Gray was gone and Cail was sitting on the end of her bed in the glow of the bedside lamp.

"Nice room," Cail said. It was painted a pale, dusty blue with dark wide planked floor boards and dark furniture. Her duvet cover had a white background with swirling designs in dark browns and pale blues. "Peaceful. I suppose tranquil is the right word."

"Yeah." Taylor took another tentative step into the room, twisting her hands in front of her. It did feel tranquil, like a sanctuary. Not that she ever had a sanctuary, but it's what this room felt like to her. "It's calming."

Cail jabbed a finger at her, grinning. "Yes. That's exactly what it feels like." His smile faded. "It's what you deserve, Tay. A place where you can feel calm and grounded."

He sounded like Lane. Maybe he was spending too much time with her. She didn't want him becoming a armchair therapist and constantly telling her to breathe. That would just be annoying. She walked over to the window, leaning back against the sill.

"I have something to tell you and I'm not sure how you're going to take it," Cail said.

His head cocked to the side, he smiled and his dimples appeared, but his bright blue eyes were squinting, as if he was in pain. Taylor's fingers gripped the sill as she waited for him to continue.

"I went to see Ireland."

Taylor stood a little straighter, every muscle in her body tensing. "Okay."

"She set the whole thing up, Tay. She used me, hoping the media attention would further her music career."

That information came as no surprise to Taylor. It was pretty obvious that Ireland set them up to be videoed coming out of the clubs.

He got up, walking towards Taylor. "I'm sorry, Angel. I had no idea what she was up to." He slid his hands around her waist and drew her close.

The tension in her body ratcheted up a few degrees before she relaxed into Cail's embrace. His strong arms cocooned her in a safe, warm nest. She pressed her nose into the curve of his shoulder and breathed in the spicy cologne mixed with the scent that was uniquely Cail, relaxing her even more. Her arms found their way around his waist and she let out a deep sigh. This felt more like home than the house they were standing in.

Minutes passed with them just holding each other. Cail turned his head and brushed his lips back and forth across Taylor's temple, knowing it would soothe her. "I have something else to tell you, but I understand if you don't believe me."

"What?" Taylor whispered. She couldn't bring herself to care what he was saying at the moment. His heart was thumping against her chest, tightening her nipples and shooting pangs of desire straight down to her core.

"I didn't tell Ireland anything about you. She got her information from another source."

Taylor leaned back and stared into Cail's eyes. He was telling her the truth. "What source?"

"I'm pretty sure it was Dave."

"Dave?" How could that be? How could Dave know about her history with a bullwhip?

Cail knew exactly what she was thinking by the confused look on her face. "He was at the crime scene, at Rappaport's. I don't know exactly what he told Ireland, but he saw the scene with your blood on that bed and the bullwhip lying there." He could see the scene perfectly in his mind. He knew what it would have done to her to be restrained, helpless. It made him sick to his stomach that she put herself in that horrific situation and, for what, to save him? Was there no end to the pain her caused her?

"You never told her that I wanted you to..." *Ugh.* She couldn't even bring herself to say the words. "Hurt me? That I wanted some weird sexual relationship?"

Cail shook his head. "No, Angel." He should have known he hadn't said those things to Ireland. For one, it wasn't true. And two, it just wasn't like him. "I never said anything about you to her."

"You don't think she knows the rest of it? You think Dave got the idea from the crime scene?" Taylor asked.

"I don't see how she could know. I think Dave may have put her up to this whole thing."

"Why? Why would he do that?"

"It just seems like something he would do. He's my brother, but he can be a real asshole."

Taylor sank back into Cail's embrace. "It's a relief. If any of this gets out, I can deny lies. I can't deny the truth."

"It's not going to get out, Angel. If it does, I'll go to the media and fix it." He'd do anything to keep her in his arms like this.

"No offence," Taylor murmured into Cail's shoulder. "But, I doubt anyone would consider you a reliable source at the moment."

After watching all of the videos of Ireland and himself, he couldn't argue. "I'm sorry, Tay. For all of the pain I've caused you. I judged you for something I didn't understand and I never gave you the chance to explain. I never even considered there could be an explanation."

"There isn't." The last thing she wanted to do was talk about this, but it had to be done at some point and the sooner she could put it behind her, the better. "I don't know how to explain it. That first time she took her whip to me, I went somewhere beyond the despair I was living in."

"It was an escape," Cail said.

Taylor leaned back just far enough to meet Cail's eyes and in them she saw compassion. "You *do* understand."

Thanks to his mother, he thought. "I can't imagine what it must have been like for you. I had no right to judge the way you coped with it all." Cail leaned in until his forehead rested against hers and closed his eyes. "Thank you," he whispered.

"For what?"

"For trusting me enough to talk to me."

It hadn't escaped Taylor's attention that Cail was aroused. Their bodies were pressed together. She couldn't touch him like this and not feel that zing of pure pleasure zipping through her entire body. She supposed it was the same for him. "I need you to leave."

"Angel?" He didn't want to let her go.

"If you stay, we're going to end up in bed." Or right here against the window sill. Or on the floor. A shudder began at her neck and ran right down to her curled toes at the thoughts running through her head.

"Would that make you happy?" It would make him happy and he'd love to see her smile again, to break through some of the sadness lingering in her eyes.

"It would make my body happy. I'm not sure my head's ready for it."

Cail nudged her nose with his. "Then I'll leave."

Taylor hugged him tighter, rocked her hips into his and shuddered when he gasped. He brushed his lips over her left eye, the one with the scars. It was so gentle, like he was trying to heal her with his lips.

"Does it hurt?"

Taylor shrugged. Physical pain didn't bother her much. Compared to some of the pain she'd experienced in her life, the eye injury was nothing. "Not any more. Do they bother you? The scars?" So many people commented on her beauty, but to her they were empty compliments. She didn't feel beautiful. Even without the scars.

"No, Angel. Does it bother you?"

"I feel like the outside matches the inside now. I know my heart is good deep down, but there are a lot of scars. A lot of dark places."

He didn't agree. "There is so much light in you, the dark places have nowhere to hide." She touched on the dark places inside of her every now and then, but never elaborated on it. He wondered if letting Sarah Johnson whip her was one of those things she considered part of her dark side. She'd been a child, alone on the streets, trying to cope as best she could. Why had he needed his mother to explain it to him? Why hadn't he seen it on his own? "I love you, Tay. I admire your strength, your will to survive, and your determination to make something of yourself despite it all."

Taylor pressed her lips to Cail's. It seemed like a good way to end the line conversation.

Cail cocked his head and deepened the kiss. Here was love, bliss, passion. Being with Tay eclipsed every other experience in his life. The intensity never waned. A touch of her lips sent shock waves through him. The glint in her eye melted his heart. Her response to his touch humbled him and filled him with joy. He slipped his hands under her sweatshirt and grazed the tips of his fingers up her back, pausing when he came to a thick, ropey scar then tracing it across her back. He knew Brandon Moody whipped her when Troy Rappaport took her. He knew he hit her hard enough to flay her back wide open, but feeling the terrible scars beneath his fingers made it all the more real. "Oh, Jesus, Tay."

She stiffened in his arms and pushed her hands against his shoulders, but he splayed his hands over her back and held her in place. Her head turned to the side, eyes cast down. "You have nothing to be ashamed of, Tay. You put yourself in grave danger to save the lives of the people you love; to save my life. Your strength and courage are enviable." Her eyes flicked to his, flashing heat before they lowered again. Cail brushed his lips over her temple and whispered, "You blow me away." He knew he was making her uncomfortable with his compliments, but he couldn't help himself. She awed him.

Taylor needed to put some space between her and Cail or she was going to do something she might regret. It felt so good to be in his arms again, even with the unease his words brought. She wasn't some hero who saved his life. She never should have gone to Rappaport. She turned to face the window and rested her palms on the sill. "No, you were right. I should have woken you up that night. I should have trusted you and Chris."

"I wasn't right, Angel. I know it's hard for you to trust and I gave you reason not to." Cail winced inwardly. The last thing he wanted to do was remind Taylor of his betrayal of her with Lisa Harmon. "You can't go back and change anything." God, how he wished that were possible and he could change his own behaviour over the past couple of months. "And it all worked out in the end. We're all safe."

His arms came around her, his hands splayed over her lower abdomen and her palms slid over his hands until their fingers intwined.

Dwelling on the past was trapping Taylor in her melancholy mood, she supposed. Cail was right. She just wished there was some way of making all of it not hurt so much. She relaxed into him with his chest warming her back.

"The only thing we can do, is learn from our mistakes," Cail said. "So, I'm making you a promise. I won't judge you or jump to conclusions. I'll try to be more aware of what you've been through and ask if I don't understand something. And I'll never discuss you, or us, with anyone without your consent."

Taylor took a deep breath then turned her head to look into Cail's bright blue eyes. Trust. Communication. Those were two things she knew had to be present for a relationship to work. He was trying to give them to her. "Okay," she whispered.

"Okay." He brushed his lips over her temple then nodded towards the window. "Not much of a view."

"I like it. I like watching the movement on the street."

"That decrepit old building is an eyesore though."

Taylor shook her head. "You see a rundown old building. I see something entirely different. I want to buy it."

She felt like an idiot when Cail laughed.

"What on earth for?"

The way she saw it she had two choices - keep her secret dream to herself to avoid further embarrassment or share her dream with him to see if he still laughed at her. "I'd turn it into a refuge for street kids."

"Tay, there's tons of shelters across the city."

At least he didn't laugh at her this time. "Do you know why I never went to shelters?"

"No."

"You may get a hot meal and a warm bed for the night, but you had to give your name."

Cail didn't say anything. A picture of her out there on the cold streets flashed through his mind. A little girl so scared to give her name, she stayed out in the cold and dumpster dived for her meals.

"If I can find a way to open a refuge, the kids wouldn't be required to give their name and they'd get more than a hot meal and warm bed. They'd be able to come in for medical attention, education, or just to hang out in a safe place. The only requirement would be that they're clean or want to get clean. There'd be a medical detox ward, therapists, teachers."

"Tay," he whispered. He had no words, so he just tightened his arms around her and nuzzled her cheek. "What can I do to help?"

* * *

Chris walked into the hospital room hand in hand with Kate. Her mother's frail body lay in the bed, her eyes closed. Tubes protruded from her nose and the back of her hand, but the monitors had been disconnected. She wondered what it must be like to lie there knowing the end was near.

Sylvie sat next to the bed, holding Eléane's hand. A slight smile appeared on her face, but her eyes emitted a deep sorrow.

"This is my partner, Kate," Chris said. "Kate, this is Dr. Sylvie Raynard, my mother's friend."

Sylvie rose to her feet making a tsk sound. "You used to call me your aunt, Chris." She held her hand out to Kate. "It's a pleasure to meet you."

"Likewise." Kate shook Sylvie's hand, noting the firm grip, then reached for Chris's hand again.

There was a metal cabinet on wheels sitting next to Eléane's bed with the envelope Chris sent over lying on top of it. If she could take the damn thing back without Eléane having ever seen it, Chris would snatch it up and run. But, it was too late for that. She swiped her free hand through her hair, suppressing the urge to pull it out of her head.

"You should have come alone, Christian," Eléane said in her tired, raspy voice. "This is family business."

Chris's eyes drifted from the envelope to her mother. She hadn't moved a muscle except for opening her blue eyes. Chris wondered if she'd been awake all along, waiting to see if they talked in front of her before she cracked her eyes open. "Family business? I suppose I should leave then."

Eléane drew in a rattling breath and exhaled sharply. "I didn't ask you here to argue, Christian-"

"Chris." She hadn't been Christian Elise St. Amour for over sixteen years.

"Chris, please?" Sylvie said. "She's very weak. She doesn't have much time left."

"Karma's a bitch, isn't it?" Chris wanted to kick herself as soon as the words were out of her mouth. Her mother gasped and Sylvie's mouth dropped open. Not that they should be shocked at her comment. "What? It's the truth."

Her mother's bony hand reached out and pulled the envelope from the cart, her trembling amplifying out to the envelope until Sylvie took it from her.

"Your mother has some questions about the papers you sent her," Sylvie said.

"No." Chris took a step back. "I'm not answering any fucking questions."

"I owe you an apology, Christian." Tears pooled in Eléane's eyes, gathering like tiny diamonds in her thin lashes. "I didn't want to believe Sebastien was hurting you in that manner."

"In that manner? Well, isn't that fucking polite."

"Chris," Kate whispered. "Give her a chance."

Chris's fury turned to Kate. "Give her a chance? Do you know how many fucking chances she had to help me, to protect me from that monster? She did nothing. For fourteen years he beat the shit out of me while she stood by and watched. For three years he raped me and she..." Chris gestured air quotes with her fingers. "...didn't want to believe it? Fuck that."

Eléane sucked in stuttered breaths, exhaling in wheezes. "Je suis désolé, mon cher. Je suis très désolé."

Chris's face flushed red, the vein at the side of her neck throbbed, and her eyes bulged, ready to shoot laser beams of death. Kate pulled on her hand, dragging her toward the door. "Excuse us for a moment," she said to Sylvie and Eléane. As soon as she got Chris out in the hall, she whispered, "Take some deep breaths before you give yourself a heart attack."

Chris leaned back against the wall and did as she was told. She couldn't help herself. Every time she got near her mother she went on the defensive. The woman made her angrier by the minute.

"Just what is your goal here, Chris? Is it to hurt your mother as much as possible or to try to ease the pain you're carrying? Because, at this rate, you're going to feel worse when you leave here than you did when you came in."

"Maybe we should leave," Chris said. "This isn't going to help anything. Or change anything."

"What is it you want to change?" Sylvie asked.

The sick feeling that's been in my belly since you showed up at my office, Chris thought. She wasn't surprised Sylvie followed them into the hall. If someone was making her best friend as upset as Chris was making Eléane, she'd be interrupting them, too. "I don't know, Sylvie. It's about sixteen years too late for this."

Sylvie closed the distance between Chris and herself, her heels clicking against the floor tiles. "There must be something we can do to give you both a bit of peace before she passes."

Chris's eyes burned and she let out a 'huh' sound that was halfway between a laugh and a sob. She leaned her head back against the wall and squeezed her eyes shut. "My whole life I've been dealing with abuse or the effects of it in my head. But, yeah, let's all look for some peace so *she* doesn't have to die with the guilt of what she's done."

"I said peace for both of you." Sylvie reached for Chris's hand, but Chris pulled away with such force it looked like she was going to backhand Sylvie. Sylvie didn't flinch. "I can't imagine how difficult your life has been, Chris."

"I'm not looking for your pity."

"And I'm not giving it. But, I would like to try to help, to give you the change you mentioned."

"I don't want your help. The time for that help was the first time

Sebastien St. Amour raised a hand to me. Instead of doing that, she stood back and watched." Chris jabbed a finger at Sylvie. "And you patched me up for her." She left unsaid the fact that Sylvie had a legal obligation to report suspected child abuse to the police. "For fourteen fucking years. Do you have any idea how many broken bones I had that never even got an X-ray?"

Sylvie's head bowed and her fingers brushed across her cheeks. "I read the reports." She spoke so softly, it was barely audible.

"So, what? The two of you wanted me to come here so you can try to absolve some of your guilt? Is that it?"

"Non," Eléane's weak voice came from the doorway. "Nous ne méritons pas votre pardon, Christian." *We don't deserve your forgiveness, Christian.* She clung to the doorframe, as if that was the only thing holding up her ravaged body. "Nous vous avons demandé ici pour que vous puissiez commencer votre guérison." *We asked you here so you could begin your healing.*

"Pfff." Chris rolled her eyes. "And how were you planning to do that?"

"By making Sebastien pay," Sylvie answered. Her tears dried up and a slight smirk appeared. "Please come back in and sit down. Eléane needs to get back in bed." Sylvie led Eléane and her IV pole back into the room and got her tucked into bed.

Chris and Kate followed them into the room and pulled two more chairs up.

With her pillows fluffed behind her, Eléane examined Kate from head to toe with cold blue eyes. "Who are you?"

"My partner, Kate," Chris answered. "Kate, that's Eléane St. Amour."

"What do you mean, partner? Are you just sleeping together or do you have a long-term relationship?"

Chris stared at her mother. She hadn't expected questions about the seriousness of her relationship. She hadn't expected her mother to acknowledge her relationship. "We live together. I want to spend my life with her."

Kate's head whipped back and she fought the grin threatening to spread across her face.

"How much does she know?"

"Pretty much all of it," Chris answered. Kate was the only person she ever really talked to about her past. She gave Taylor and Gray the short version, but she told Kate, minus the grisly details, because Kate demanded full disclosure if their relationship was going to move forward.

Satisfied with Chris's answer, Eléane decided it was safe to speak in English. "What Sebastien did to you, cher, was torture for me. It was my punishment for leaving him and having an affair."

"Then why did you stay?"

"I tried to leave with you, Christian. Several times. I was never successful and when we were brought back, it wasn't me he hurt. I couldn't risk running again. I couldn't risk him killing you."

Her damn eyes were burning again. "Why didn't you tell me this before?"

"I needed you to hate me, so that when the opportunity arose for me to get you out, you wouldn't try to contact me again."

"That was your plan? Get me to hate you then shove me out the door with nothing but the clothes on my back?"

"You're alive today, mon cher. If I hadn't done that, I don't think you would have survived to see your fifteenth birthday."

"Why the fuck didn't you just call the police?"

"Tsk." Eléane scrunched her nose up and pursed her lips as if she just sucked on a lemon. "Such language."

"Sebastien is well connected, Chris," Sylvie said. "Why do you think I never reported the abuse?"

"I called the police the first time he beat you." Eléane's voice slurred and her eyes looked like they were weighted down. "It didn't end well."

"She needs to rest," Sylvie said.

"I'll have plenty of time to rest when I'm dead. We need to finish this."

"We couldn't go to the police with Sebastien's influence." Sylvie waited until Chris's eyes met hers. "But, you have influence there now, too."

"No." Chris wasn't sure whether to believe them or not. She was used to her mother being a complete bitch. She didn't trust this woman who seemed to have some compassion. She stood and moved her chair back to the corner.

Sylvie jumped up and followed Chris across the room. "It's the only plan we can come up with to make him pay."

"He's gunning for Premier. The minute I file charges, the media will be all over it. Do you have any idea what that will be like for me?"

Movement to her left brought Chris's eyes up and she was sure her heart stopped when she recognized Sebastien St. Amour in the doorway. It was like she was transported back in time to when she was scared shitless of the bastard. His bulky form in a grey suit made him look like a stainless steel refrigerator.

"What the hell are you doing here?" His deep voice boomed and he looked at Chris like she was dog crap on the bottom of his shoe. "Ellie? Why is this person in your room?"

"She's resting," Sylvie said. "Please keep your voice down." She took a long step back at Sebastien's glare.

"I asked you a question." Sebastien was at the side of the bed in two strides. He grabbed Eléane by the upper arm and yanked her right out of the bed. She flailed, trying to gain her footing, then slid to the floor when he released her arm.

"Hey," Chris yelled. She was at his side before she had time to think it through. "Keep your filthy hands off her."

Sebastien swung around, leading with the back of his hand, and caught Chris solidly on the right cheek. She nearly joined her mother on the floor. She bent over for a second then came up with her Glock in her hand, pointed at Sebastien's chest. "That's assault on a police officer. Turn around and put your hands behind your back."

"Christian, please. Just go. Please." Eléane pushed up to her haunches and sent her daughter a pleading look. "It will be fine if you go."

"Do you think you can threaten me? Do you know who I am?"

In Chris's opinion, people who led with 'Do you know who I am?' were narcissistic assholes. "Yeah. I know who you are." She hoped it was only her ears picking up the tremor in her voice.

Chris nudged Kate towards the door and backed out of the room. She didn't take her gun off Sebastien until she could no longer see him. She marched to the elevators with steam coming out of her ears and her face throbbing like a bitch. Punching the down button, she paced back and forth. "Can you imagine that behemoth beating up on a child? Coward bastard."

"Chris?" Kate spoke softly.

"Fucking, fucktard, piece of fucking shit."

"Chris? Please holster your weapon."

Chris looked down at her right hand. She hadn't even realized she was still holding it. She looked around, noticed the nervous glances from staff and patients, and slid the Glock into its leather home at her hip. "Sorry," she said to everyone in the area. "Police." She held her badge up then returned it to her pocket. "Had a bit of a situation."

The elevator doors opened with a ding and Chris thought, thank fucking Christ. She ran inside and jabbed the close door button until the doors met in the middle. Then she took a deep breath, leaned back against the wall, and slid her eyes over to Kate. "So, how'd you like my family?"

Their eyes met. Kate raised her eyebrows. Chris raised hers.

By the time the elevator doors opened on the main floor, they were laughing so hard they had to hold each other up.

* * *

The laughter relieved some of the tension, but that sick feeling was back in Chris's gut by the time they settled into the car. She wasn't just sick about sending her mother those files. She couldn't help wondering what abuse her mother endured after they kicked Chris out of the house. Did he beat and rape Eléane once she was out of the picture? Even Sylvie looked scared shitless of the bastard. God, she shouldn't have left them there with him. "I'm going to get a restraining order."

"Against who?" Kate asked.

"Sebastien."

"You think he'll come after you?"

"Not for me. For Eléane." She turned north onto Yonge Street, heading home. The least she could do was make sure Eléane wasn't abused while she was dying. "I'll post a uniformed officer on the hospital room door." Thinking about Sebastien's size, she added, "Maybe two."

Kate laid her hand on Chris's thigh. "She's got so little time left, Chris. Is it worth making yourself a target?"

"I won't be making myself a target."

"If you prevent him from being able to see her, you'll piss him off. Right now, you may not be on his radar. But, if you do this, you'll be in his crosshairs." And that wasn't taking into account damaging Sebastien St. Amour's reputation at a time when he was gunning for Premier of Ontario. If word got out he may be abusing his wife, his political career would be in the trash and he would blame Chris for it.

"I'm not a helpless kid anymore." She could bloody well protect herself. She'd never shot anyone before, but she would fucking A defend herself with her gun if he tried to hurt her.

"This is a man with connections. We don't know if those connections are judicial, political, criminal, or a combination of those." Kate sighed and leaned her head back against the seat, turning her head to look at

Chris. "Just think about it before you do something you may regret." Or, worse, do something to put yourself in grave danger, Kate thought. "Please."

Chris glanced over at Kate and let out a sigh of her own. She already regretted going off half-cocked and sending those reports to Eléane. She really did need to slow down and think this through. "This is why I'm a better person for having you in my life."

"Aww. That's the sweetest thing you've ever said to me."

"That's not true." That made it sound like she never said anything sweet to Kate. "I tell you I love you all the time."

Kate grinned. Every now and then she had to pinch herself to make sure this wasn't all a dream. "I love you, too."

Chris pulled into the driveway of their small bungalow and pulled the key out of the ignition. "I'm going to let you show me just how much." She leaned over the centre console and captured Kate's mouth, going in hard and fast. Lust punched low in her belly as she brushed a line of sweet kisses across Kate's jaw.

"Why are we making out in the car when we have a house free of guests?" Since Taylor moved out, they had the place to themselves and it sent their sex life into the stratosphere. Not that she was complaining. She'd just rather be making out in the nice warm house. "Besides, we need to get some ice on your cheek. Your eye is already turning black."

"Not the first time he's left bruises on my face." Chris swirled her tongue over the hot spot just below Kate's ear that drove her crazy.

"You never told me your injuries weren't properly treated." Kate shuddered and tilted her head to give Chris better access, but Chris pulled back.

"What would be the point?"

Kate brushed the tips of her fingers over the darkening bruise on Chris's cheek. She supposed Chris was right because it only made her sicker to know more details of the abuse she suffered. "Sylvie was right. You can still lay charges."

"Kate," Chris sighed. The problem was, Chris didn't think she could do it.

"What if he wins the Provincial leadership? He'd be Premier of Ontario, Chris. He should be in a cell, not Parliament."

Chris sighed again and rested her forehead against Kate's. "Let's hope to hell he doesn't win." That sick feeling in her belly was back, replacing the punch of desire. Chris straightened in her seat and shoved her door open.

When they got into the house, Chris flopped herself down on the couch while Kate wandered into the kitchen.

"Want a beer?" Kate asked.

"No, thanks." Chris's stomach couldn't handle a beer. Damn Sylvie for coming to her office. She was fine until Sylvie showed up.

Kate came into the living room with an ice pack wrapped in a tea towel. She crawled onto the couch, straddling Chris's lap, and held the ice pack to Chris's cheek. "We should have arrested the bastard."

Chris closed her eyes on a sigh. Her hands slid up Kate's thighs, coming to rest at her waist, her thumbs sneaking under her sweatshirt to graze over the soft, warm skin of her belly. "I never should have gone to see Eléane. That part of my life was behind me until I walked into that room and stirred everything up again."

Kate snorted. "It wasn't behind you, babe. Buried maybe, but not behind you."

"You're wrong."

Kate cocked her head, studying Chris's face - the furrowed brow, eyes squeezed tight, lips pursed. "If it was behind you, you wouldn't be reacting so much right now."

"I don't know what I'm supposed to do."

"Will you talk to Lane?" Kate leaned forward and pressed a kiss to the worry line between Chris's brows.

Taylor's words popped into Chris's head - *it's time for us to heal from our shame.* Lane had been there for her since the moment she was kicked out and she still hadn't told Lane her story. Maybe it was time. "Yeah. I'll try."

"Whatever you decide, Chris, I'm here for you."

Chris wrapped her arms around Kate and pulled her in tight, burying her face in the curve of Kate's neck. For so long, no one had loved her. She didn't know what it was like to be loved until this woman became a part of her life. It didn't seem to matter what she did or what she said, Kate stood by her. Solid. Strong. "I love you so much."

Somehow the ice pack ended up clenched in Kate's fist. She dropped it onto the couch, circling her hips against Chris's. It wasn't until she felt something hot and wet slide down her neck that she realized Chris was crying. She'd spent nearly all of her non-work hours with Chris over the past six months and she'd never seen her cry. She'd seen her angry and knew it was one of the ways she channeled the hurt inside her. She'd seen her laughing and knew that was a coping mechanism at times as well. But, she'd never seen strong, resilient Chris break down in tears. She tried to pull back, but Chris tightened her arms around her.

"Just hold on for a minute," Chris whispered into Kate's neck. She kept going back to that moment when Sebastien St. Amour walked into the hospital room; back to that scared, helpless, detested kid. She told herself no one would ever make her feel like that again and here she was at thirty years of age, right back where she started from.

Kate's arms slid around Chris's back and she held on. "Whatever you need, I'm here for you. I love you."

"I need *you*." Chris lifted her head and found Kate's mouth, brushing her lips lightly over Kate's and the shrill ring of her cell phone pierced the air. "Shit." Chris grabbed the offending device from her hip, tapped the screen, and put it to her ear. "Cain."

"Chris, it's Raine. I need you to tell this neanderthal you have posted at Bonkers' door that it's okay for me to leave."

"Leave to where?"

"I'm flying out to spend a few weeks with my brother out west."

Despite the fact Chris would rather Raine stayed under her protective eye, she couldn't legally prevent her from going. "Okay, put him on the phone."

"Jeffreys," a deep male voice said.

"This is Detective Sergeant Chris Cain. Make sure Ms. Delacourte gets to the airport safely, then you can report back to your sergeant for reassignment."

"Ten-four, DS."

Chris ended the call and dropped the phone onto the couch beside her. Maybe Raine would be safer out west until they could apprehend Siobhan Silva.

"That have to do with your case?" Kate asked.

"Yeah."

"Do you need to go?"

Chris shook her head. "No."

"Good, because I think you mentioned something about needing something."

"You. Always and forever."

Kate grinned. "Mmmm. I like the sound of that."

Chris touched her lips to Kate's, so warm and soft. She tilted her head and took the kiss deeper and her cell phone sang out the theme to

Hawaii 5-O. Chris smiled, her lips still pressed to Kate's.

"I wish you could turn that damn thing off," Kate huffed.

Chris picked up the phone again. "Cain."

"DS Cain, this is Colin Andrews in dispatch. I'm sorry to disturb you. We've received several calls from a Dr. Raynard. She says it's urgent she speak with you. I've got her number."

Chris blew out a breath. "Yeah, give it to me."

Sylvie answered on the first ring, her voice tense. "Chris, it's Sebastien. He took your mother out of the hospital against medical advice."

"What? What the hell did he do that for?"

"He said her place is at his side while he's campaigning for the Provincial Leadership. There was nothing I could do. Eléane is conditioned to obey him."

"Jesus."

Kate slid off Chris's lap and sat next to her, her hand resting on Chris's thigh.

"I don't think there's anything I can do," Chris said. "If she went with him willingly..." What the hell did Sylvie expect from her? "Will he hurt her?"

Silence.

"Sylvie? Will he hurt her?"

"No, I don't think so." Sylvie's voice was as soft as a whisper.

"I don't understand why you're telling me this." Chris plunged her hand into her hair and pulled.

"She's your mother. I thought you'd want to know."

"She hasn't been my mother for a long time. Her choice."

"I'm sorry I bothered you." The line went dead.

Chris threw the phone to the other end of the couch. Now she felt guilty as hell again. "What the hell am I supposed to do? I haven't heard boo from these people in sixteen years and all of a sudden they expect me to jump in and fix their problems."

Kate didn't have to ask what was going on. She'd heard most of the call. "I don't think there's anything you can do even if you wanted to. Eléane made the decision to go with him."

At what cost? Chris wondered. What would he have done to her if she refused? "So why do I feel so damn guilty?"

"Don't." Kate crawled back into Chris's lap and cupped her face in her hands. "You've got nothing to feel guilty about."

"You saw the way he treated her in that hospital room. She said she's tried to get away from him in the past and he just hauls her back. Do you really think she went with him willingly?"

Kate sighed heavily and leaned in, touching her forehead to Chris's. "No. Probably not."

Chris leaned over, reaching for her cell phone and dialed Sylvie again. "Maybe there is something we can do," Chris said.

Chapter 13

Taylor changed into her uniform and was crossing the lobby when she spotted Chris outside on the sidewalk pacing back and forth. She changed directions and went outside. "Chris?"

Chris turned at Taylor's voice, in mid exhalation of the cigarette she was smoking. Last night's snow had been cleared from the sidewalks and the pristine white was now a grey, slushy bank riding the curb.

"I didn't know you smoked." Taylor didn't mention the dark bruise on Chris's right cheek.

Chris looked down at the cigarette wedged between the first and second fingers of her right hand. "I quit five years ago."

"I take it things didn't go well with your mother last night."

Chris laughed. It was either that or cry. "No. Not so good."

"Want to talk about it?"

Chris started pacing again and took a long haul off the cigarette then ran through the whole story for Taylor.

"So what are you going to do?" Taylor asked.

"The first thing I'm going to do is go up to see Lane." She glanced down at her watch. "She's squeezing me in."

"Good." Taylor nodded. "That's good."

"While I'm up there you can go over the case notes again. See if there's anything new in from forensics. We need to find Silva."

"Should I check in with Brice to see if he got anything off her laptop?"

Chris glanced at her watch again. "Nah. He wouldn't have had time to take a look at it yet. I'll check in with him later this morning."

They began walking inside. Chris had five minutes to get up to Lane's office and she was dreading it. "So, how did your date go?"

"We didn't go on a date."

Chris stopped and studied Taylor's face. She looked more rested than she had and not quite as melancholy. "Are you okay?"

"Yeah. We talked."

"Just talked?" Chris grinned and wiggled her eyebrows as she started for the elevators again. Taylor didn't have to answer. The red flush in her face was answer enough.

"We didn't have sex," Taylor said. Why she felt the need to explain that to Chris, she had no idea. "We talked and snuggled. That's it."

Weeks ago Chris probably wouldn't have understood that, but she'd spent hours snuggling with her lover the night before and it had been everything she'd wanted at the time. She needed comfort and Kate seemed content to give it to her. "So things are good between the two of you?"

"Better. I think we're getting there." Taylor hit the elevator call button and turned to face Chris. "In case you forgot, I'm only in for a half day today."

"Yeah, you've got a meeting with your publisher."

Taylor wrinkled her nose and Chris laughed. "Why are you dreading it?"

"I think I'm probably in trouble."

"Why?"

Taylor shrugged. "I haven't been returning my publicist's calls."

Chris was still laughing as they stepped into the elevator. "Taylor?" She hit the buttons for the Sex Crimes Unit's floor and Dr. McIntyre's floor.

"I didn't want to deal with any of it."

"That's not going to make it go away. Why does she keep calling you anyway? What does she want?"

"Different things. Interviews or offers to appear somewhere. There's been modelling offers and stuff like that."

"Does Cheryl Starr still contact you?" Cheryl Starr was a reporter for the National News Network and she always treated Taylor with respect.

"Now and then."

"Can you give me her number?"

The doors slid open and Taylor stepped off holding the door open. "Anything I need to know about?" She took out her phone and pulled up Cheryl Starr's number then handed her phone over to Chris so she could put the number in her own phone.

Chris shook her head. "It depends if Sebastien interferes with my plans today."

"You're going to threaten him into taking your mother back to the hospital?"

Chris handed Taylor her phone, glancing at her watch again. "I gotta go."

Taylor let the door close, worried for Chris. Sebastien St. Amour didn't seem like the kind of man to take threats lightly. This wasn't a day she wanted to be away from Chris. Damn Tony Crawford for insisting she attend this stupid meeting. She walked into the Sex Crimes Unit and found it mostly deserted. There were a couple of detectives left over from the night shift and none of the day shift had arrived yet. She liked this time of the morning when she could get a head start without being interrupted. She headed for the conference room and stared at the case board. It was sorely out of date now with the new information they'd gathered. Updating it helped to organize her thoughts, so she collected reports and printed off some pictures and brought them into the conference room.

* * *

Silence hung in the air like a thick fog as Chris sat in the plush leather chair across from Lane, hands clenched between her knees.

"Chris, I don't have a lot of time," Lane said.

Chris glanced up at her and drew her hand through her already tousled hair. The sickness in her belly worsened with each passing second. She shouldn't have had that damn cigarette. "A friend of my mother's came to see me a couple of days ago."

Lane's spine straightened and she slid to the edge of the chair, leaning forward. "Chris? What's going on?"

"She's dying. My mother."

"Oh, no you don't." Lane's usually soft blue eyes turned to ice. "You will not feel guilty because some woman who used to have a hold over you is ill."

"Used to?" Chris asked, because it sure as hell felt like she still had a firm grip. Her hand slid to her belly as if that would ease the roiling in her gut. She took a deep breath and told Lane about the two visits to her mother's hospital room.

"Do you feel threatened?" Lane asked.

Chris pointed to her cheek. "The man backhanded me in the face. Hell, yeah, I feel threatened."

Lane sighed. "Chris, I think it's wise to stay out of this situation. Do not come between your mother and your father."

"He's not my father." For sixteen years she kept the identity of her family secret. She was still leery of revealing the identity of the man who made her life hell. But, it was time. "Sebastien St. Amour is not my father."

Lane's body jerked as if she'd been struck. "Sebastien St. Amour? The one poised to become Premier?"

Chris screwed up her nose. The mere mention of his name disgusted her. "Yeah, that one."

"Good Lord, Chris. I know your parents. I've worked with Eléane on charity events and committees for years."

And that was the main reason Chris had never divulged who her parents were. They were well known in the elite social circles of Toronto. The pain in Lane's face - in the deep line between her brows, the crinkles at the edges of her eyes, the pursed lips, and the glossy eyes - made her feel even sicker than she had over the past few days. "I know."

"God." Lane surged to her feet and dashed to the window, staring out at the bleak, grey day, her hands gripping the window ledge so hard her knuckles were white. "Damn that bastard to hell." She wanted to strangle Sebastien St. Amour with her own hands. She wanted to slap Eléane St. Amour silly for not protecting her daughter all those years. Eléane volunteered at the Secret Garden, an organization devoted to the support of abused women and children, for God's sake. *What a bloody hypocrite.*

"Lane?" Chris didn't know what to do. She came here hoping for some relief from the pain, emotional and physical, that knotted her stomach since the moment Sylvie Raynard walked into her office. All she succeeded in doing was upsetting Lane and making herself feel even worse.

The phone on Lane's desk rang and she swung around and grabbed the receiver, pressing it to her ear. "Yes," she barked. "I'm going to need a few more minutes. Please have him wait in reception." She placed the receiver into its cradle and then sank into the chair behind her desk, dropping her face into her hands.

Chris got to her feet, stepped around the coffee table, and sunk her hands into her pants pockets. "I'm sorry."

Lane lifted her head and met Chris's gaze. "Sorry? Chris, you have nothing to be sorry for. I'm angry. Furious. Not at you. At myself, for not seeing through those people. At them, for being imposters." She shook her head. "I've been in this job for a long time. I've heard some horrific stories. But, I've never had friends, people I associate with regularly, be revealed as monsters." She wanted to go back home and take another shower, feeling dirty by association. She wondered how Chris must feel and realized this wasn't about her. Chris came to her for help, not to be saddled with guilt over Lane's reaction. "I'm sorry." She stood and walked to Chris, taking her hands in hers. "How are you feeling? What do you need?"

Chris shrugged. She had no idea what she needed. "Taylor said talking about her past is helping."

"You've refused to talk about it for more than half your life, Chris. Why now?"

"I don't know. I've had this horrible, sick feeling in my gut since my mother's friend came to see me. I just want it gone. I can't stand feeling like this."

"And you believe talking about the abuse you suffered will relieve the sick feeling?"

Yeah, sounds pretty far fetched. She shrugged again. "You're the psychologist. You tell me."

"I don't know that it will eliminate it completely, Chris, but talking about it will certainly help you start to process your trauma. It's not a quick fix."

"Fuck."

"Chris." Lane shook her head. She was used to Chris's foul mouth by now, but it still annoyed her. She glanced at her watch and winced. "I'm out of time."

Chris left Lane's office with the roiling still curdling in her gut and an appointment to return after lunch.

* * *

The team was assembled around the conference table when Chris arrived. She approached the board first, studying the changes Taylor made and that flutter of pride swept through her.

Turning to the conference table, she made eye contact with everyone at the table - Taylor, MaryAnn Blake, Danny Stone, Kenny Ambrose - and then her eyes pierced St. James's. "Did you get the laptop to MacLean?"

"Uh," St. James began. "I thought our people would be better equipped to handle that."

Already in a rotten mood, Chris seethed. God help her, she wanted to hurt St. James in that moment. "Get out." The calmness of her tone surprised her. When St. James did little more than sit there staring at her, her temper flared even more. "Get your sorry ass out of my briefing."

"You can't kick me out. You don't have the authority."

"Bet your ass, I do. You can come back when you decide you want to work with this team instead of against us. Thanks to you, Silva's in the wind. And now this business with the laptop. This case is the jurisdiction of the Toronto Police, not the RCMP. You take orders from me. So get your sorry ass out of my briefing. Now."

He calmly closed his daytimer, stood, and walked out of the room. Everyone else sat frozen in their seats. Chris dropped into a chair and called up to Inspector Cal Worthington, requesting he look into getting Siobhan Silva's laptop back from the RCMP. When she hung up, she said, "Give me an update, Stone."

"Detective Ambrose and I were able to track the coveralls to a Mike Messini. He passed away about a year ago and his wife recently donated four pairs of the coveralls to a Salvation Army store. We talked to a clerk who remembers selling them to a petite, dark haired woman about two weeks ago."

"So she has another three pairs on hand. Anything else?"

"Ah, no. That's it."

Jesus fucking Christ. What was wrong with these people? "Sinclair?"

Taylor glanced from Stone to Chris then gave a run down of the events of the previous evening and the search of Silva's apartment.

"So, at this point, we've lost her," Chris said. "I'll speak to the Inspector about putting her face on the evening news, but she could be any damn where by now." Chris needed that friggin' laptop. Damn St. James all to hell. "We put out a BOLO for her with a description of the vehicle, although she's probably dumped it by now. Stone, get in touch with forensics again. See if they've got anything that will help locate her." With that she pushed away from the table and stormed out of the room, yelling, "Sinclair."

Chris grabbed her jacket from her office and took the stairs up to Inspector Worthington's office with Taylor pacing behind her. "What a fucking shit show. I don't know what the fuck is up with Stone, but she's dropping the ball on this one."

Better to keep her mouth shut, Taylor thought. She didn't want to piss Chris off any more than she already was. Besides, what was she supposed to say to that?

Chris marched to Inspector Worthington's office and came to an abrupt halt in the doorway. Martine DuBois sat in his chair typing away on the computer and Worthington was noticeably absent. "Where is he?" she asked.

DuBois glanced over her shoulder with a sultry smile. "Good morning to you, too."

"Shit, sorry. Good morning. Where is he?"

DuBois' dark eyes sparkled with her deep laugh. She swung her chair around to face Chris and leaned back. "He'll be right back. Anything I can do for you?"

"Do you know if he made any headway getting Silva's laptop back?"

"Brice should have it within the hour."

"I want St. James out of my unit."

"I'm afraid that's not going to be possible," Worthington said from behind Chris.

She turned around and stepped aside to give him room to enter his office. He brushed by her and set a steaming white mug bearing the Toronto Police logo on the desk in front of DuBois and took a seat in front of the desk, cradling his own cup between his palms.

"He's using us and sabotaging our case."

Worthington set his cup on the desk with an audible sigh. "Do you think I don't see that, Chris? Don't you think I want him gone as much as you do? I've expressed my concerns to the Chief and, for some reason, she won't budge. We're stuck with him for the time being, so do your best to work around him."

Chris didn't like it, but if Worthington couldn't get rid of St. James, there was no way she was going to be able to. "Do you think we could get Siobhan Silva's face plastered all over the news?"

"Let's give it another day or two."

"She could be in the wind by then."

"She's not going anywhere. Not without the diamonds."

True that, Chris thought. "Okay. We'll keep digging."

On the way to the elevators, Chris said, "I want you to look into the diamonds angle. See if you can find any reports of a diamond theft out west going back ten years or more." It may not bring them any closer to finding Silva, but at least they'd have a better idea of why Will St. James was firmly entrenched in her unit.

"Got it," Taylor said.

"And keep it to yourself. No one else knows we have the diamonds."

They got in the elevator and Taylor was surprised when Chris hit the button for the garage. She figured they'd be going back to the office. "We going out?"

"I've got a personal thing to take care of. You can use the computer in the car to research the diamonds."

* * *

Chris parked in the main parking garage at Sunnybrook Health Sciences, took out her cell phone, and called Sylvie.

"Hey, I just parked the car. What room are you in?"

"Why don't I meet you at the main entrance?" Sylvie said.

"Yeah, sure. I'll see you in a minute."

"Do you want me to wait here?" Taylor asked when Chris ended her call.

"No, come in with me." She didn't want to go in there alone. At the very least, she wanted a witness, just in case.

As they entered the lobby, Sylvie crossed to them with brows drawn in and her mouth pursed in a fine white line. It shouldn't have concerned Chris, never mind make her heart skip a beat. She'd long since stopped caring about her mother, hadn't she?

"What's going on?" Chris asked.

"It's not good, I'm afraid. Her condition has deteriorated. The oncologist is with her now and they're getting her settled in. We should be able to see her as soon as they're finished." Sylvie didn't look at Chris as she spoke. She stared off to some point in the distance.

It dawned on Chris how hard this must be for Sylvie. She'd been Eléane's closest friend for as long as Chris could remember, always there to support her and help her deal with the fallout of a controlling and abusive husband. "How are you holding up?"

Sylvie's dark eyes flicked to Chris's and widened, as if the last thing she expected was for Chris to show some compassion. She ran her hand down Chris's arm and gave her hand a squeeze. "I'll manage. What makes this more difficult is Eléane refused to fight from the moment she was diagnosed. She has no desire to live."

"Can you blame her? He made her life miserable."

"And yours. I'm so sorry I didn't do more to change that, Christian."

"I didn't come here to talk about the past." She didn't want to think about it never mind talk about it.

"Of course. Let me buy you a coffee and we'll go up."

Chapter 14

The woman lying in the hospital bed looked smaller and much more frail than the woman Chris had seen just the night before. Prongs in her nose fed her oxygen and an IV line pierced her left arm, but otherwise no machines monitored her.

A woman in bright purple scrubs leaned over her and pressed a stethoscope to Eléane's chest. She listened for a moment then removed the device from her ears and draped it around her neck. "Hi. I'm Stephanie, the nurse assigned to Mrs. Elias."

Sylvie chose the fake name they were using to keep Sebastien St. Amour from finding Eléane.

"Sylvie Raynard," Sylvie introduced herself. "I'm her closest friend." She waved her hand to Chris, who stayed by the door. "And this is her daughter, Chris."

Stephanie nodded with a compassionate smile. "It won't be long. If there's anyone else you want to come in, now is the time to call them."

"What do you mean, it won't be long?" Chris asked.

"A matter of hours," Stephanie said. "Her respirations are slowing and her organs are beginning to shut down."

"Can't you do something?"

"She has a DNR order, so all we can do is keep her as comfortable as possible while she passes."

Chris looked to Sylvie, expecting her to intervene, but she just walked to Chris and grasped her hand. "It's what she wants, Chris. We have to respect her wishes."

All of the colour drained from Chris's face when she walked in the room. Taylor had no idea what to do for her. Chris had been estranged from her mother for more than half her life, but losing her still had to be hard.

184

"Alright. Okay." She'd seen death plenty of times and under much worse circumstances than this, so why was her head spinning? "I really just came to make sure she was settled in and that St. Amour couldn't find her."

"He's already called," Stephanie said. "Or, someone did. He was told Eléane St. Amour was not registered."

"Wow, that was quick." Chris hadn't expected him to start calling around the hospitals until at least late afternoon.

"I'm afraid that's my fault," Sylvie said. "She couldn't stand at that rally this morning, so Eléane's sons propped her up between them and then dumped her in a chair backstage as soon as they were done with her. I snuck her out. I'm sorry, Chris. I couldn't wait until they took her home."

"No, no, it's fine. I was thinking maybe he should be notified anyway. If she's only got hours left, maybe he should be here."

"I'll call him, but not yet. Not until she's nearer the end." Sylvie released Chris's hand and went to Eléane's bedside. "It's what she wanted."

Chris stepped out into the hall and called Kate on her cell phone, updating her on her mother's status. Then she said to Taylor, "Take my car and head back to the office so you're not late for your meeting."

"I'm not leaving you here alone. I'll wait until Kate gets here."

Chris smirked. "Crawford will kill you if you miss that meeting, won't he?"

"There's still plenty of time. I'm not leaving until Kate arrives."

* * *

Taylor sat at the massive table in a conference room at Crawford Publishing with Gray at her side. They'd only been sitting there for a few minutes, but it felt like hours to Taylor. She drummed her fingers on the surface of the table until Gray's hand covered hers.

"Sorry. I feel like I'm in the principal's office at high school waiting for my punishment."

"No doubt," Gray said with a grin.

Emma Brinkman walked into the room carrying a banker's box and dropped it onto the table with a great *thud*. Her mousy hair was tied up in a knot at the back of her head and she pushed her purple framed glasses up her nose as she looked down it at Taylor with a glare. Taylor sank back in her seat, wishing she could disappear, as Emma began removing file folders from the box and slapping them onto the table top.

"You're angry with me and I owe you an apology," Taylor said. May as well get it out there from the start.

"You signed a contract with Crawford Publishing, Ms. Sinclair. You're in violation of that contract." Emma punctuated her words by slapping another folder down.

"I'm sorry I haven't returned your calls. I've been working a big case." Gray's hand slid across her thigh, giving her a reassuring squeeze. That just made her feel guilty because she'd been ignoring Emma's calls long before she started working on the Raine Delacourte case.

"Take it easy, Emma," Tony Crawford, CEO of Crawford Publishing, said as he entered the room and took his seat at the head of the table. He was a distinguished looking man in a fitted charcoal suit and dark hair slicked back. "Taylor's here now, so let's lay it all out."

Literally, Taylor thought as Emma slapped another folder onto the growing stack. Then she slapped her hand down on top of them.

"We have here some of the offers which have come in since the release of *Leila's Locket*."

"Some of the offers?" Gray asked with wide eyes.

"Mmm," Emma answered. "We've weeded out the inappropriate ones." She took a seat across from Taylor and Gray and pulled a thick folder off the top of the stack, opening it in front of her. "This is requests for interviews." She looked up at Tony. "Should we go through them all?"

"I don't think that's necessary at this time," he answered.

"Am I expected to give interviews to every one of those?" Taylor asked. She thought she was done with all that crap. She spent over a month travelling around North America on a publicity tour. Wasn't that enough?

"Not all of them," Tony said. "But, we do expect you to give a few. Emma, why don't you give us a quick overview of the ones you've given highest priority."

Emma smirked at Taylor over her glasses before lowering her head to the file. "Top of the list is a request from Cheryl Starr. She's doing a documentary on your life and would like you to participate in it."

"Participate?" What did that mean? Was she supposed to answer Cheryl's questions about her life or what?

"Yes, participate. She wants you to be in the documentary, visiting old haunts, reminiscing about your younger years and your years on the streets."

"No." She had no desire to relive all of that and couldn't understand for the life of her why anyone would want to make a documentary about it.

"She's offering a handsome fee." Emma leafed through a few pages then passed one over to Taylor.

Taylor took one look at the sum and laughed. "This is some kind of joke, right? You're mad at me for not returning your calls, so you're pranking me."

Emma looked Taylor in the eye with a straight face. "It's no joke, Taylor."

Taylor focused in on the amount again and all she could think about was the abandoned warehouse across the street from her house and how far that money would go towards fixing it up. She looked up at Emma again. "Have you got other offers like this? People offering crazy amounts of money for my story?"

"Not just for your story, Taylor. We've got offers for modelling and acting jobs. We've even got an offer from an art gallery to show your art work."

"Put Cheryl Starr's in the maybe pile and I think we better go through the rest of these."

"We'll leave you to it then," Tony said, rising from the table. "Gray, shall we go to my office?" He offered her a hand as she struggled to get out of her seat with her swollen belly, his eyes twinkling as he tried valiantly to suppress a grin.

It took a couple of hours for Taylor to go through all of the offers and that was with Emma giving a quick synopsis of each and the dollar figure associated with it. Taylor decided which offers went in the 'maybe' pile and which ones went in the 'no' pile.

Emma opened another fat folder, telling Taylor it contained requests with no monetary value. Taylor was about to tell her to put them all in the 'no' pile before Emma told her the first request was for her to visit a group home for children in the system, either orphans or kids who'd been taken from the care of their parents by Child Services.

"Yes," Taylor said.

Emma's head flew up to meet Taylor's gaze, her brows reaching up into her hair line. It was the first time Taylor gave a definite yes. "You'll do it?"

"Yes," Taylor repeated. These were the people she tried to reach with *Leila's Locket*, but there was little hope of these kids gaining access to the book. If she could make a difference in their lives, give them a glimmer of hope, she'd do it.

They went through the rest of the pile and Taylor left the conference room with a big box of maybes to go through and make final decisions on. She was relieved to hear that Tony sent Gray home with a driver hours before. She barely had enough time to rush home and shower before she had to be at Crawford Publishing's Christmas Gala. It was another obligation she dreaded since the media would be lining up out front and shouting their miserable questions.

She left the box in her car and ran up the stairs to the main level of her house and nearly ran right into Cail sporting a flashy tux. She had to stop and just admire him for a moment, her eyes drifting down and then up that fantastic, rangy body adorned so brilliantly in black and white. He was grinning at her when she reached his striking blue eyes and heat rose up from her chest, blossoming over her face. "You look great."

"Thank you. I'd say the same, but ..." Damn, he put his foot in it already. How did you finish a sentence like that without offending her? "Um, I assume your not wearing that to the Gala."

Taylor glanced down at her jeans and black leather biker's jacket and wished she could get away with doing just that. "No. It'll just take me a minute to shower and change."

"Oh, no you don't," Gray said from the living room couch. She was dressed in what Taylor could only describe as a gown - an ice blue wonder with long, lacy sleeves and a wide, flowy silk skirt which would be comfortable with her baby bump. "Jump in the shower and I'll be up to help you with your hair, makeup, and dress."

Taylor groaned. "Please don't tell me you got me a dress." Gray tended to find dresses for Taylor that left more skin exposed than covered.

"No," Gray smiled. "I figured you could wear one of the lovely dresses you bought while on your book tour."

Thank heaven, Taylor thought. It was too darn cold to be running around in a skimpy dress that made her uncomfortable and extremely vulnerable.

"But, I'll be doing your makeup and your hair."

* * *

Taylor chose a hunter green, form-fitting velvet dress with longs sleeves. It would be warm and felt Christmassy, not that she knew what Christmassy felt like. When she came down the stairs, she was surprised to see Chris and Kate waiting to leave with them. Chris wore a tuxedo with a red cummerbund and bow tie that matched the hue of Kate's dress. She'd never seen Chris wear something like it before and was a little jealous. Taylor was much more comfortable in pants than a dress.

"You didn't have to come, Chris," she said. "How's Eléane?"

Chris shrugged. "She passed late this afternoon."

"Oh, Chris." Gray rose from the couch with some help from Callaghan and she wrapped Chris in her arms. "I'm so sorry, honey."

"It's no big deal. She wasn't part of my life."

"It still has to hurt," Gray said. "She was your mother."

"No, she gave up that right, remember." Chris waved Gray off before she could say any more. "I don't want to talk about it. I just want to go to the Gala and enjoy my real family."

Gray smiled and cupped her hand on Chris's cheek. "Then that's what we'll do."

"Did Sebastien show up?" Taylor asked.

"No, he sent my brothers to make sure she was really dying. They didn't hang around once they saw it wasn't a lie."

"Christ, that's cold," Callaghan said as he wrapped a cashmere shawl over Gray's shoulders.

Taylor stepped up and hugged Chris, whispering, "Despite how you felt about her, I'm sorry for your loss. If you need anything - a shoulder or an ear - I'm here."

"Yeah, thanks." Chris's arms tightened around Taylor before releasing her and stepping back. "Let's get this party on the road."

When they settled into the limo, Gray asked, "So, are you going to do the documentary with Cheryl Starr?"

Taylor nodded, her eyes lifting to the abandoned warehouse out the window. "I'm thinking about it."

"I'm surprised. I didn't think you'd touch that with a ten foot pole." Gray leaned in and whispered in her ear. "I got the impression that you were motivated by the money and that's not at all like you, Taylor."

Taylor kept her eyes on the abandoned warehouse as the limo pulled away from the curb. "I'll explain it to you later." She couldn't help but feel Gray was disappointed in her. That hurt, but she was sure she'd understand once she revealed her plans.

"Since you're all here," Cail began, "My parents are having Christmas dinner at their place on Christmas Eve and you're all invited. They said to come around eleven for brunch and presents and we'll have dinner around five."

"That sounds lovely," Gray said. "Please tell them we'd love to come."

"I will, thanks Gray. What about you, Chris? Can you make it?" Cail asked.

"Yeah, sure." She usually volunteered to work over Christmas since she didn't have anyone to spend it with, but this year she had Kate, Kate's parents, Taylor, Cail, Gray, and Callaghan. Shit, she'd have to go Christmas shopping. *Ugh.* It wasn't her favourite time of year after the miserable Christmases she spent with her family as a kid. Plus, she hated shopping.

Cail took Taylor's hand and smiled into her bright green eyes. "What about you, Angel? Will you come?"

Taylor looked over at Chris to make sure she'd have the time off work then shrugged. "I guess, yeah. Is there something we should do? Something we should bring?" She had no idea what was involved in celebrating Christmas with the Worthington's.

"Just bring yourself," Kate answered. "That's everything we need."

The limo pulled to the curb at the venue and Taylor tightened her grip on Cail's hand. "Don't say anything to the reporters, no matter what questions they yell out."

"Okay," Cail said and nodded.

"Promise me. Don't engage with them."

Cail leaned in and pressed a chaste kiss to Taylor's lips. "I promise." He thought she was overreacting until they stepped out of the limo and the questions came fast and furious from every direction. There were a lot of questions about them getting back together and if Cail had a drinking problem. Those he expected. But, somehow he'd forgotten just how brutal these reporters were, firing their rude and inappropriate questions. They were still inquiring about what happened to the baby Taylor had when she was still a child herself. To her credit, Taylor didn't even flinch. Her eyes were focused on the door at the end of the red carpet area. Cail wrapped his arm around her waist as he smiled and waved, but inside his blood boiled at the injustice of what they put Taylor through. She didn't want their attention and she certainly didn't deserve their constant reminders of her nightmarish past.

"Almost there, Angel," he whispered. Her tense muscles vibrated against him, but to look at her you'd think she was having the time of her life, grinning from ear to ear and waving at the crowd.

"Taylor? Cail? Can we get a picture of the two of you together?" Someone called out and Cail slowed, turning towards the voice and giving his dimple infused smile. That he didn't have to force. With Taylor on his arm, he was filled with joy. Taylor turned with him, posing, and he couldn't help himself. He leaned in and kissed her temple.

He figured she would be pissed at the public display of affection, but she turned to him, her lips pursed together as she tried to look stern and failed. She broke out laughing then planted a quick kiss on his lips.

"Well, that will answer one of their questions."

Taylor rolled her eyes, still grinning.

She was surprised to find that she was actually enjoying herself. She consciously blocked out the horrid questions and focused on Cail with his arm wrapped around her. She spotted Cheryl Starr behind the rope barrier a few feet away and walked over to her. "I'm sorry I haven't responded to your offer. I haven't had time to go through it yet, but I'll take a look at it this weekend and get back to you."

Cheryl's head flicked back as if she'd just been slapped. "You're considering doing it?"

"Yeah," Taylor nodded. She'd told Cheryl no so many times, she wasn't surprised by her reaction. "I'll give you a call next week."

"Are things okay between you and Cail again, Taylor?" Cheryl asked before Taylor could walk away.

Taylor looked into Cail's bright blue eyes and smiled. "We're working on it."

When they finally made it inside the venue, Taylor asked, "Are you okay?"

"I'm fine. Why?"

She wanted to roll her eyes at him again. "They directed some pretty harsh questions at you." Usually when they were surrounded by the media, the ugly questions were for Taylor. This was the first time many of them they were directed at Cail.

"It's fine, Tay. It's my own fault. I made a fool of myself and I sincerely apologize for putting you through that."

Taylor narrowed her eyes. "Your attitude or perspective has changed drastically in the past few weeks. What happened?"

Grinning, Cail lifted her hand to his mouth and kissed her palm before pressing it to his cheek. "I had a long talk with my mother and she set me straight."

"Huh. Remind me to thank her."

* * *

As they were being served dessert, Tony Crawford began speaking from behind a podium set up on a low platform at the front of the room. He talked for a few moments on the successful year and Crawford Publishing's plans for the future.

"Every year at this time, as you know, we like to celebrate our top selling authors. Coming in at number three this year is an author who's been with us for the past five years. He released two novels this year in his popular Detective Dan Fawkes series. Please join me in congratulating Billy Duvane."

As the room filled with applause and a few hoots, a somewhat pudgy man with salt and pepper hair and an ill fitting brown suit made his way to the podium. Tony shook his hand and presented him with a crystal, book-shaped trophy and an envelope. Duvane raised the trophy over his head and cried, "Yes! I finally broke the top three."

"Congratulations, Billy. Well deserved, my friend." Tony waited a moment for the applause to die down as Duvane left the platform. "I apologize to our number two author as this is the first year in the more than ten years she's been with Crawford Publishing that she hasn't captured the top selling author spot. We jokingly refer to her as our bread and butter. She also released two new novels this year despite getting married and starting a family. *Strength of Innocence*, which was released just a few weeks ago, sits at number one on the New York Times Bestseller List. Please join me in congratulating the lovely Gray Rowan."

Callaghan helped Gray out of her seat and escorted her to the podium where she too received a crystal trophy and an envelope while the audience cheered.

"I didn't know they called her bread and butter," Taylor laughed. "We'll have to tease her about that one."

"I wonder who knocked her out of the number one spot," Chris said, staring at Taylor with raised eyebrows.

"Oh, I don't think so. They're fiction writers." There was no way *Leila's Locket* could beat out Gray's two novels over an entire year.

As Gray returned to her seat, Tony said, "That leaves you guessing who our top selling author of the year is. Well, I can tell you that this person is brand new to Crawford Publishing and the book outsold any other title we've released since my grandfather started this company. For the first time since I began working at Crawford, our top selling author is a non-fiction writer with a unique story. Please join me in congratulating the author of *Leila's Locket*, Miss Taylor Sinclair."

Taylor sat there staring at Tony, unable to comprehend what she just heard. Surely he made a mistake.

Cail stood and gripped the back of Taylor's chair to pull it out for her, but she wasn't moving. He leaned over and whispered, "Tay? You need to go up there."

People were beginning to get to their feet, clapping and cheering, as Taylor rose. Thank God Cail held on to her arm and led her up to the front of the room or she didn't know if she would have made it. She wished someone warned her. She'd prepared herself for the onslaught of people outside the venue, but she hadn't known she'd be centred out inside.

Tony handed her the trophy and envelope and the crowd began to chant, "Speech, speech, speech." Tony stepped back and nodded at the microphone.

Oh, crap. What was she supposed to say? This reminded her of having to speak at the Police Academy graduation ceremony. She thought she wouldn't have to do anything like that again. She stepped up to the podium. "Uh…"

The room filled with laughter which made Taylor laugh as well. "Sorry, I really didn't expect this. I mean, how on earth did my little book outsell two Gray Rowan novels?"

The applause began again and Taylor waited until it calmed down. "The reason I wrote this book was to give strength to the kids who are still living out there on the streets, the kids in group homes and foster homes who are losing hope at their dire circumstances. I'm happy to report that it is making a small difference, but it's really not enough. There's a reason kids live on the streets. It's not because they want to. Often, like me, it's to escape an intolerable living situation. Going to school or to government run shelters is not an option because it's not safe to give their names. There's literally no reason children should be abandoned to abusive and neglectful living situations in this day and age. There's more we can do and I'm hoping I can make more of a difference by opening a refuge for street kids; a safe place they can go to for a meal, support, a warm bed, without having to reveal their identity.

"It's still in the planning stages and there's a long way to go. I want to thank Tony and the rest of the staff at Crawford because if it hadn't been for them, I wouldn't even have a chance of opening a resource like this. And, if it hadn't been for the encouragement and support of Gray Rowan, there wouldn't be a book titled *Leila's Locket*."

Taylor bowed her head then walked back to her seat, her face on fire with the embarrassment of everyone gawking at her.

When she got back to her table they were all standing and Gray was the first to embrace her.

"That's why you're considering doing Starr's documentary, so you can build a resource centre for street kids," Gray whispered in her ear.

Taylor shook her head. "Not build. The warehouse across the street …"

Gray leaned back to look into Taylor's eyes, grinning. "You've been sitting at your bedroom window staring out at that building and planning what you can make it into."

"Well, I didn't think of it as planning at the time. I thought I was just daydreaming, until I saw the amount of money Cheryl Starr was offering. I didn't mean to blurt that out up there. It just came out."

"Oh, Taylor," Gray said with tears in her eyes. "I'm so proud of you."

Chapter 15

Taylor spent the next morning in her home office going through media records of jewelry robberies between ten and thirty years ago and came up with nothing that matched the description of the diamonds sitting in Inspector Worthington's safe. She called Chris and reported her findings.

"I thought I told you to take the weekend off to get settled into your new house," Chris said.

"I'm at home." She was surprised Chris didn't want her to work. Even though they seemed to be at a standstill, there were things she could do, like staking out Silva's apartment to see if she came back or canvassing the neighbourhood.

Chris laughed. "Okay, if you insist on pursuing this over the weekend, expand the search to five to ten years ago."

"Alright." There was a moment of silence over the line then Taylor asked, "Are you doing okay? Is there anything you need?"

"I'm fine, Taylor. It's sad, but I really didn't even know her anymore, you know?"

"Will you go to her funeral?"

"Yeah. Probably."

"If you need me to go with you, I'm there, okay?"

"Yeah. Thanks. I may just take you up on that."

Taylor went right back to searching the internet when she got off the phone and hit pay dirt about half an hour later with a jewelry store heist that took place five years ago. She called Chris back.

"We only have half of the diamonds. Exactly half."

"You found it?"

"Yeah, and get this, the thieves left a message written on the wall in Rune symbols."

"Holy fuck. I'm coming over."

The call ended abruptly and Taylor was left staring at her phone. She shrugged it off and Googled 'Rune symbols' while she was waiting. She could have kicked herself for not doing that simple thing days ago. She figured the symbols were tied to the meanings in the Rune book she had, but that was clearly not the case. She wrote out the symbols that were carved into Callie Delacourte, aka Lily De La Cruz, and Raine Delacourte, then found them on the list she brought up from her Google search.

When Chris arrived ten minutes later, she was in the kitchen making coffee.

"Where's Cail?" Chris asked.

Taylor shrugged. "I don't know. He went home after the Gala last night."

"Oh, I thought maybe you two were back together," Kate said.

"We're getting there, but I want to take it slow."

"Smart." Kate rubbed her hand up and down Taylor's back, secretly pleased when Taylor didn't flinch at her touch. "I hope it all works out."

"Yeah, me too." Taylor poured a coffee for herself, Chris and Kate and took them into the office. Gray sat at the desk typing on the iMac. Taylor took them to her art desk where her laptop was set up.

"Run me through what you've got," Chris said.

"Do you need me to leave?" Gray asked.

"No, you're fine. Anything Taylor found on the internet is public knowledge."

"It is. I found it on the website for the Banff Gazette." Taylor opened her laptop and brought up the page.

Chris narrowed her eyes at the screen as Taylor gave her a synopsis of what she'd read. "Five years ago there was a robbery of a jewelry store in Banff, Alberta. They'd just taken possession of 48 blue diamonds. The police figured it was a professional job with some inside help. The thieves had the codes for the security system."

"Any employees matching Silva's description?"

"No," Taylor said. She looked up at Chris, smiling. "But, they had an employee who stopped showing up for work after the robbery. She hasn't been heard from since."

"Fucking A." Chris shoved her fingers through her hair and leaned over Taylor's shoulder as she pulled up the video surveillance of the robbery that the RCMP in Banff released in an attempt to identify the perpetrators. Chris, Taylor, and Kate focused on the screen as two individuals entered the store and disarmed the security system. They were dressed all in black, faces covered with only their eyes visible. One was tall and lean, the other shorter with an athletic build.

"Who's case is this? No, wait." Chris held up her hand like she was stopping traffic. "Let me guess. Will St. James."

"Bingo," Taylor said. "There's more." She placed the piece of paper with the symbols she had copied in front of Chris. "I Googled 'Rune symbols' and it turns out there's a Runic alphabet. The symbols carved into Callie and Raine, match the symbols used in the Banff heist, spelling out L.I.A.N."

"L.I.A.N," Chris repeated. "Lian?"

"Yes, but look at this." Taylor pulled the piece of paper in front of her and wrote out two names then turned it around for Chris to see. She'd spelled out LILY and SIOBHAN then scratched out the last two letters of Lily's name and the first five of Siobhan's, drawing a circle around the remaining letters - L, I, A, and N. "Looks like they've been signing their work," Taylor said. "And they didn't start with this diamond heist. They were notorious out west for close to a decade, always leaving this signature behind. After the diamonds were stolen, they went cold. There were no further robberies by the Rune Crew, which is what they were dubbed by the media."

"Fuck me. Callie Delacourte is the second thief." She fit the body type of the tall, slim person in the video.

"Siobhan Silva was in prison at the time of the diamond heist, though," Taylor said. "She may have been involved in the prior heists, but she couldn't have done this one."

"We need to speak to St. James," Chris said. And Raine Delacourte, she thought. Did she head out west to recuperate with her family or was she up to something more sinister? Just as she was thinking that, her cell began ringing. "It's Raine," Chris announced and answered. She was about to question her about how much she knew of Callie's past, but Raine's voice came through panic stricken.

"Chris, thank God. I can't reach Bonkers. She hasn't turned up at work today and she's not answering her cell or her home phone. Please, Chris. You have to find her."

Oh, shit. She should have kept an officer on Bonkers' condo. Siobhan Silva didn't know Raine skipped town. "Okay, listen to me, Raine. I'll find her. I need you to stay calm and I'll call you back as soon as I can. Okay?"

"Yes. Oh God, Chris. If she's hurt, I'll never forgive myself."

"Is someone there with you?"

"My sister-in-law."

Chris talked to the sister-in-law in hopes of getting her to calm Raine down. Then she, Taylor, and Kate jumped in her car heading for Bonkers' condo.

* * *

Chris raced through the city with lights and sirens, arriving at Bonkers' apartment building within minutes. When Bonkers' didn't answer their call from the building entrance, she dialed the superintendent's number and requested access to the building.

The man who came to admit them into the lobby was in his late fifties with thinning hair, more salt than pepper, and suspenders holding up his baggy jeans.

"I'll need to see some ID," he said, but Chris was already pulling out her badge.

"Detective Sergeant Chris Cain," she said. "We need to do a welfare check in apartment 2502."

"Yeah, yeah," he said and shuffled to the elevator, punching the up button.

They rode up in silence while Chris chanted over and over again in her head, 'Please let her be okay. Please let her be okay.' She didn't need Taylor's intuitive powers to know something was very wrong. According to Raine, Bonkers' never skipped out on work and she never would have not gone in without calling.

The superintendent used his master key to open the door to apartment 2502. Chris was about to go through the door when Taylor put a hand on her shoulder to stop her. "Why don't you wait here while Kate and I check the apartment?" Elizabeth Cruise was a friend of Chris's and she'd already been through enough this week without discovering what may be waiting inside the apartment.

"I'm fine," Chris said. "I need to do this."

Taylor nodded and the three of them entered the apartment, weapons drawn, clearing room by room before moving down the hall to the bedrooms. They checked the guest room and the attached bathroom before moving to the closed door of the master.

This time Kate placed a hand on Chris's shoulder and their eyes met. Chris shook her head. There was no way she wasn't going into that room. Kate nodded and Chris eased the door handle to the right then swung the door open, gun aimed into the room. They didn't need their weapons. Silva was long gone.

Bonkers sat on her haunches on the bed, bent forward with her face planted in the duvet and her hands tied behind her back with blue, nylon rope. Taylor stepped forward, pressing two fingers to the carotid artery on her neck. She shook her head.

Chris let out a wail that sounded like a wounded animal and sunk to the floor with Kate crouching next to her, arms cocooning her.

Taylor traced her footsteps back to the door so as not to disturb any more evidence than necessary. "We need to move out to the hall and call in forensics."

"The living room will do," Kate said, helping Chris to her feet. "She needs to sit down."

* * *

The three of them stood in the bedroom doorway as the medical examiner examined the body of Elizabeth Cruise. Dr. Wes Drummond, a thirty-something hunk with short dark hair shaved on the sides and longer on top as was the style, meticulously observed every inch of Bonkers' exposed body. Taylor wanted nothing more than to cover the body to give Bonkers some dignity, but she knew that was futile and the doctor was only doing his job. It just seemed so intrusive.

"Has she been raped?" Chris asked, even though she knew the answer.

Dr. Drummond met Chris's gaze. "It's difficult to determine at this point. There's no tearing or bruising, but there appears to be lubricant in the vagina. She may have had consensual sex."

Chris shook her head. "She was asexual, doc." And, the lack of tearing and the lubricant were consistent with what was found on Raine.

"Preliminary cause of death looks like strangulation," he said. It wasn't a surprise given the bruises around her neck. "Rigor mortis is just beginning to set in, so I'd say no more than four hours since she passed."

It was noon, so she probably died around eight o'clock. Chris turned to Taylor who was writing notes on a piece of paper she got from a note pad in the kitchen. Why she insisted on doing this, Chris had no idea. Taylor had a memory better than an elephant's. "Check with the superintendent to see if you can get video surveillance footage of the lobby."

Taylor nodded and turned to walk away.

Drummond nodded to his assistant, a young man who didn't look old enough to have graduated from medical school. "Okay, let's turn the body."

Taylor walked back towards the doorway when she heard that. The surveillance tapes could wait. She needed to know if the Rune symbols were carved into Bonkers' chest.

The assistant put down the camera he used to take photographs of the scene and helped Drummond turn Bonkers' tiny form. Her chest area was covered in blood. You could see the cuts over her left breast, but you couldn't make them out with the amount of blood congealed and dried around the wounds.

"Fuck me," Chris said.

* * *

They left Bonkers' apartment armed with a CD of the building's video surveillance for the past two days right up until after Chris, Kate, and Taylor entered the building to do the welfare check.

"Let's go to your place," Chris said to Taylor. "We can check the video footage there."

"How are we going to find Silva?" Taylor asked.

"We don't need to find her," Chris said as she got in the car. "She's going to find us. She didn't ransack Bonkers' apartment, so I think Bonkers' told Silva what she was looking for wasn't there and she knows we took the duffel bag."

"I don't understand why she went after Bonkers, knowing we had the duffel bag," Taylor said. "It doesn't make any sense."

Chris glanced at Taylor in the rearview mirror. "What's your gut telling you?"

"I don't know. It's like she thinks the diamonds weren't in the bag."

"Like she has someone in the department who told her the diamonds weren't listed among the evidence we documented from the bag." Chris's eyes met Taylor's again. "Are you thinking St. James?"

"The thought occurred to me."

"Shit." Kate glared at Chris from the passenger seat. "We need surveillance on both of you wherever you go."

Chris reached over and took Kate's hand. "It will be fine. I've been doing this for a long time, babe. I'm not going to let Siobhan Silva get the better of us."

"Still, I'd feel better if you had protection. Back up at the very least."

"You're both welcome to stay at my place," Taylor said from the back seat. "I've got a state of the art security system."

Both Kate and Chris turned to look at Taylor. She shrugged and smiled. "You'd have twenty-four hour access to my gym, too." Once Gray and Callaghan left, she'd be alone in that big house and she wasn't looking forward to it.

Chris grinned at the thought of having full access to Taylor's home gym, but said, "I've got a security system, too."

"Yeah, but it sounds like Siobhan Silva is very well acquainted with security systems," Kate offered. "I doubt they would slow her down much."

"Where do you want to stay?" Chris asked Kate. "Where would you feel safest?"

"If you were at Taylor's, there'd be at least two of you there if she did manage to break in. Three if I'm there; four with Callaghan."

"Gray and Callaghan are heading back up to Bolton in the morning," Taylor said, grateful Gray wouldn't be in jeopardy.

"We'll think about it," Chris said. She couldn't make a decision about it with all the crap running around her brain. First things first, she thought.

As soon as they arrived at Taylor's, they began watching the video footage. Thank God it was on a motion sensor, so it only recorded when people were coming and going. The building had several cameras, covering the front entrance, the back entrance, the elevators, and the parking garage.

There was no sign of Silva until five o'clock that morning. She entered the building wearing dark coveralls and a baseball cap pulled low over her forehead, carrying the tool box Bonkers' described seeing at Raine's place. Silva used her body to block the camera's view from seeing what she used to unlock the door into the lobby. She could have used a key or a set of lock picks. If it was picks, she was damn good with them. She was through the door in seconds. The elevator door opened as soon as she pressed the button and she disappeared inside.

She exited the building via a stairwell and the back entrance at 8:35am.

"Three and a half hours," Taylor said.

With a clenched jaw and narrowed eyes, Chris looked up at Taylor. "Yeah. Poor Bonkers. Christ." Her hand stabbed into her hair and she dropped her head. She'd called Raine back while they sat in Bonkers' living room waiting for the forensics team to arrive. It was one of the hardest things she'd ever done in her life.

"Did she have family?" Taylor asked.

Chris shook her head, hand still planted in her hair. "She grew up in the foster system."

If her experience in that system was anything like mine, no wonder she was asexual, Taylor thought. It made her sick that Bonkers' life ended in the manner it did. No one deserved that, but it seemed ironically twisted that it happened to someone who swore off sex and probably for very good reason. "You have no idea how much I want Siobhan Silva to pay for this."

"Oh, I think I do."

Next on Chris's agenda was a search of the net for all robberies attributed to the Rune Crew. There was no doubt these two were professionals. They targeted expensive art work and jewels, hitting mostly private home collections. They hit a couple of art galleries, but the diamond heist was the only record of a jewelry store.

"I wonder if the other half of the diamonds were ever recovered," Taylor said.

"We need to talk to St. James, but before we do that, I need to update the Inspector." Chris called Cal Worthington and brought him up to speed. He ordered her not to approach St. James until Monday. She would obey him, but damn she wanted to flay him open.

"So, now what?" Taylor asked.

"I know I told you to take the weekend off, but I'm going to the medical examiner's office in the morning."

Taylor nodded. "I'll come, too." She didn't want a day or a weekend off. She wanted to find Siobhan Silva.

Chapter 16

The sky was dark and ominous when Taylor peeked out the living room window wearing jeans and her leather biker jacket. She looked at the warehouse across the street with new eyes, knowing the money to buy the building and convert it into a refuge for street kids was now within her grasp. She smiled to herself then turned as Grey made her way down the stairs.

"Good morning."

"Morning." Gray smiled and walked over to Taylor. "Are you going out?"

"Yeah, Chris is on her way to pick me up."

"We'll see you in a few days then." She wrapped her arms around Taylor, embracing her in a warm hug. "We'll be back down in time to go the Worthington's on Christmas Eve."

Taylor hugged her back and didn't want to let her go. It was only a few days and she supposed she needed to get used to living on her own again, but she felt lonely already. Since coming off the streets, she'd lived with Gray, Cail, or Chris. She had her own room at the Police Academy, but that was hardly living alone. There was always someone around, usually Cail. "I'll miss you."

Gray leaned back and bussed a kiss to Taylor's cheek. "And I you, little sister."

That brought a wide grin to Taylor's face. She splayed her hand over Gray's swollen belly and rubbed. "Take care of my niece."

"Always."

A horn blared out on the street and Taylor rolled her eyes. "My chariot awaits."

Taylor stepped outside and shuddered. The temperature dropped overnight to a bitter cold that made your nostrils stick together when you took a deep breath in. She jogged to Chris's car and doubled-checked the seat was all the way back before getting in. "Looks like it's going to snow again."

"Yeah." Chris leaned forward and looked up at the dark clouds. "Feels like it, too," she said as she pulled away from the curb.

"Have you heard anything new?" Taylor asked.

"Nothing much. She didn't leave any fingerprints behind and she cleaned up in the bathroom before she left. There were trace amounts of blood in the bathroom sink and in the drain." Chris shrugged, thinking this is exactly what Silva would have done to Raine if Bonkers hadn't interrupted her. "You don't have to come to the morgue, if you don't want. I'm not expecting any surprises."

It was the third time Chris had said that to her this morning. "It doesn't bother me, this kind of stuff." Taylor was more concerned about Chris. "I could go and get the information, Chris," Taylor offered. "You don't need to see your friend like that."

"I've already seen what Silva did to her."

"It's just her body, you know. She's not there. She's gone somewhere much more beautiful and peaceful."

Chris glanced at Taylor and smiled. "You believe that?"

Taylor had to believe Leila and Leiland were in a beautiful, peaceful place. "Don't you?"

"I don't know what happens to us when we die, but I don't believe we hang around our useless bodies. I'd like to think my mother has gone somewhere without pain and without a controlling asshole monitoring her every move."

"I'm sure she's much happier where she's gone."

Chris hoped so. Even though her relationship with her mother had been non-existent for the past sixteen years and a nightmare before that, she wished her mother well in the afterlife, whatever that may be. To change the subject, she asked, "Did you see Cail last night?"

"Nope." She still wasn't sure what to do about Cail. She wanted him back in her life, but she wasn't entirely convinced she was capable of a normal, healthy relationship.

"Well, you seem happier since he's come around a bit."

"I guess." Was it Cail coming back into her life that lifted her mood or was it the possibility of converting that warehouse? Taylor had no idea.

"Did you see the news?"

Taylor shook her head.

"They've been showing the footage of you and Cail going into the Gala with the caption, 'Love Rekindled?' And there's non-stop footage of the two of you leaving and comments about Cail's sobriety."

"He hasn't had a drink for several days."

"Yeah, that's good. See, you two reuniting has been good for both of you."

Taylor laughed. "I think watching himself on the videos and seeing what a total ass he made of himself was enough to make him stop drinking."

"Whatever works," Chris said, laughing too.

The Office of the Chief Coroner was a fairly new, state of the art facility in the Forensic Services and Coroner's Complex in north Toronto. Chris led Taylor to the autopsy suites and found the Chief Coroner, Dr. William Chan, himself. He waved them in and pulled the mask covering his nose and mouth down. A middle aged man lay on the stainless steel table in front of him, but he'd yet to make any incisions.

"Good morning, DS. Elizabeth Cruise is yours, yes?"

"Yep."

Chan was a good half a foot shorter than Taylor, making her feel like an ogre hovering over him. He tilted his chin up and met Taylor's gaze with eyes as dark as midnight studying her through trendy black framed glasses, a small smile on his face.

"I don't know you."

He was still wearing surgical gloves and Taylor didn't know what he'd touched with them, so she didn't offer her hand. "Constable Sinclair."

He continued to stare. "I'm Dr. Chan. Why do you look familiar?"

Taylor shrugged. She wasn't going to explain to him why her face was constantly all over the news, even weeks after Sarah Johnson was sentenced to prison.

"Huh," he said and turned to Chris. "I did Ms. Cruise's post this morning. Would you like to see the body?"

"If you wouldn't mind," Chris said. "I'd like to get pictures of the symbols carved into her chest."

"Ah, you know about the symbols? You've seen them before?"

He moved to a computer station and began typing on the keyboard, still wearing the gloves, and Taylor cringed. They were probably clean, but how could she know for sure?

"Yeah, in another case, but the victim survived," Chris said, moving to the screen and peering over his shoulder. He brought up pictures depicting the cuts on Bonkers' chest and scrolled through them.

"I can email these to you, unless you wish to take your own."

"No, these are fine. Can you tell what sort of blade was used?"

"V grind, possibly a survival knife. Very sharp. The offender probably sharpened it himself as I discovered trace amounts of metal shavings inside the wounds. The symbols were carved at an angle indicating a right-handed offender."

"What's a V grind?" Taylor asked.

Chan picked up a clipboard, turned the top sheet of paper over and drew a cross section of the knife blade with the thickness at the spine consistent until it got closer to the blade then it narrowed evenly on both sides down to the point of the blade. "This style edge dulls easily, so it's necessary to sharpen often," he explained.

"Anything else I should know, doc?" Chris asked.

"I'm sure you know about the vaginal penetration, otherwise why would you be on this case? What's interesting is there is no bruising, no tearing, so not consistent with rape. There were ligature marks on the wrists and blue fibres embedded in the raw skin from the nylon rope that bound them."

"So, she fought the bindings?"

"Some," Chan said. "Not enough to break the skin."

"Any other wounds?"

"Bruising on the neck consistent with strangulation, which is the cause of death."

"Did they strangle her by hand or did they use something else?"

Chan smiled up at Chris with a twinkle in his dark eyes. "Why do you say they and not he?"

Chris only grinned back and waited for him to answer her question.

"Hands. Small hands, consistent with a woman, small for a man."

"Were you able to get prints?" Chris asked, but she already knew the answer.

Chan shook his head. "No prints. Your offender gloved up. I sent swabs to the lab, so we'll see if *they* left any DNA behind."

"Can you tell if she was a virgin?" Taylor wasn't sure why she was asking. Curiosity more than anything, she supposed.

Chan's mouth dropped open. "She may have been as small as a child, but she was thirty-five years old."

"So?"

Chan opened the door to a walk-in freezer and disappeared inside.

He returned moments later pushing a stainless steel gurney with a black body bag on top. He unzipped the bag and spread the edges wide to expose Bonkers' small body. With the blood washed away, the Rune symbols were clear and precise over her left breast.

"She gave birth at least once, but there are signs of old trauma such as vaginal scar tissue. There's something else." He swung a huge magnifying glass on a long arm around and placed it over Bonkers' right thigh. "Take a look."

Taylor leaned over and looked through the glass. Dozens of fine white horizontal lines scored her thigh. "She was a cutter."

When she stepped back, Chris took her place and studied the lines.

"She was a cutter," Dr. Chan confirmed. "But, not recently. The scars are old. Most probably from her teens. I've put in a request for her medical records, but I don't expect them until mid-week."

"You'll keep me posted?" Chris asked.

Chan nodded. "And I'll send those pictures to your email."

* * *

"Well, that gave us a whole lot of nothing," Taylor said as they got back in Chris's car.

"It may have been what we expected, but it's not a whole lot of nothing. Every bit of evidence is needed to build the case for court. The fact that she's right-handed, even though most people are, still counts as points in the column leading to a conviction and the knife blade was the same type used on Raine. It's each little detail added to the whole that make or break a case."

"Tedious, is what it is."

"But necessary."

"I wonder what happened to her kid?"

The parallels to Bonkers' early life and Taylor's didn't escape Chris's attention. Taylor became pregnant with the child of her abuser, but he was stillborn. Despite how the child was conceived, losing him hurt Taylor tremendously. Since Bonkers never mentioned having a child, Chris assumed she gave it up for adoption or something. She didn't know whether to investigate Bonkers' childhood years or leave her to her secrets. "Why don't you dig into Bonkers' past? See if there's anything there we should be pursuing."

Taylor blew out a breath. Bonkers reminded her too much of her own childhood. If her abuser was still out there, she wanted justice for Bonkers. "Yeah, I'll check into it today."

"No, take the rest of the weekend off. Tomorrow's soon enough."

Chris pulled to the curb in front of Taylor's house and Cail stood at her front door with his hands shoved in the pockets of his coat and the collar turned up around his ears.

"Now that's love," Chris said with a smirk. "Standing out there in this weather, he has it bad."

"What is it they call that? Penance?"

Chris guffawed. "Oh, now I see why you're taking it slow. You want him to pay."

"No, I'm just leery of going through that pain again."

"I thought you liked pain," Chris teased, a wide grin on her face.

Taylor backhanded her upper arm, but couldn't help laughing. Then her face sobered. "I get why Bonkers cut herself. Physical pain masks emotional pain; takes it away for a moment."

The grin dropped off Chris's face. "Sorry, I didn't mean to bring up bad memories."

Others knowing the details of just how far she went to cope with her own pain was humiliating. Her face was on fire and she couldn't meet Chris's gaze.

Chris took her hand and squeezed. "I get it, Taylor. I never took that route, but I get it."

Taylor nodded and gave Chris a weak, pathetic smile. "I know." She squeezed Chris's hand back then released it and got out of the car.

"Hey." Cail smiled at her through shivering lips with a blue tinge to them. "Working today?"

"Not anymore? What are you up to?"

"I wondered if you wanted to go for coffee?"

She waved towards the front door. "Come on in, my little popsicle."

Cail snorted in a heroic effort not to laugh, but failed miserably. "Did you just give me a pet name?"

It took Taylor a second before she understood why he was laughing so hard. "Oh, my gawwwd. I didn't mean it like that."

Cail grabbed her and hugged her tight, his shoulders heaving. He hadn't laughed like this in ages and it felt great, especially with Taylor grinning in his arms, her face red and not from the cold. He could tease her about this one for years to come.

Cail settled onto the couch in the living room, his hands wrapped around his coffee mug, soaking up its warmth. "Have you seen the news?"

"Nope, but Chris gave me the highlights. Don't they have anything better to report on than our relationship?"

Cail laughed. "There's plenty to keep them busy, but they still can't resist commenting on us and the fact that I appeared sober."

Taylor reached for Cail's hand and entwined her fingers with his. "They'll forget about it if we ignore them."

"Yeah, right." He laughed again. "What are you up to today, Angel?"

"Hang on and I'll show you." She jogged up to her room and brought down the box from Crawford Publishing, placing it on the coffee table and pulling the files out.

"Working weekend?" he asked.

"Sort of. These are requests for appearances and interviews. I've got until tomorrow to go through them and give Emma a list of the ones I'll do."

Cail leafed through some of the folders. "Jesus, Tay. Some of these have a hefty fee associated with them."

"That's why I'm considering doing them."

His head whipped up and he stared at her with wide eyes. "Seriously? I didn't peg you for money hungry, Angel."

"I'm not. Not for myself, anyway. If I'm going to open a resource centre for street kids, I need money."

"Ah, now it's making sense."

Taylor pulled the file from Cheryl Starr and gave it to Cail. He took one look at the figure on the offer and nearly spit out his coffee. "Holy shit. You're not considering doing a documentary with Starr?" Even for the amount of money she was offering, it seemed too difficult a prospect for Taylor to consider. It would bring all of her past trauma to the surface.

"I already live with it, Cail," she said, reading his thoughts. "What's a bit of pain if it will pay for the resource centre?"

"Babe…" he started and was interrupted by the chiming ring of the doorbell. "Expecting someone?"

Shaking her head, Taylor got up and went down to the front door. She swung it open to find Will St. James leaning on the door jamb with a grin on his face. He wore a black wool coat with a thick royal blue scarf wrapped around his neck.

"What do you want?"

He pursed his lips into a mock pout. "Is that any way to greet a friend? It's freezing out here. How about inviting me in for a coffee or hot chocolate?" He shouldered his way past her and started up the stairs. "Nice place."

"Hey." Taylor closed the door and darted up the stairs after him, but he'd already rounded the corner into the open living space.

"Oh, sorry. I didn't realize you had company. Caillen Worthington, isn't it?" St. James walked over to the sofa and extended his hand to Cail. "Will St. James. I'm an old friend of Taylor's."

Cail took the offered hand and gripped a little harder than necessary. "It's Cail. I didn't realize Tay had any old friends."

"Oh, yeah. We went to high school together."

Taylor rolled her eyes and went to get him a cup of coffee. When she handed it to him, he was cozied up on the couch across from Cail, his coat and scarf hanging over the seat back.

"Working from home?" St. James asked, nodding to the files on her coffee table.

Taylor sat next to Cail. "Yep." He must have heard about Bonkers' death by now, but there was no way Taylor was going to feed him any details.

"Delacourte case?"

"No, its paperwork from my publisher if you must know." She smirked inwardly, satisfied she'd thrown him off. "Is that why you're here? Thought you'd stop by and try to weasel some case details from me?"

St. James shrugged and took a slow sip of coffee. "Actually, I stopped by to ask you out on that date you promised me."

The nerve, Taylor thought. "I didn't promise you a date."

The right corner of his mouth curved up and he stared at Cail for a moment then winked at Taylor. "Okay, sure. I should probably go."

"Yeah, you really should." Taylor waited for him to put his coat back on and escorted him to the door.

He turned to her before walking out. "Oh, one question. Where's Raine Delacourte?"

"I have no idea."

"Interesting," he said. "You see, last I heard, she was staying with Elizabeth Cruise and I'm certain Silva would have targeted her, not Cruise. So, where is she?"

Her gut told her this line of questioning wasn't right at all. Even if she knew exactly where Raine was, there was no way she would tell Will St. James. "I told you, I don't know." She pushed the door closed in his face.

Cail was waiting at the top of the stairs when she turned to go back up. "I hate that I can't see who's at the door before I answer it," she said.

"What the hell was that about?"

"He's sniffing for information on the case we're working, that's all."

"That man wants more from you than details of your case, Tay." He'd seen the way St. James's eyes followed her when she was in the kitchen making his coffee and he'd been pretty damn bold to ask her out while he was sitting right there.

Taylor huffed and climbed the stairs until she was nose to nose with Cail. "Do you think I'd even consider going out with him? With anyone?" She cupped his face in her hands, her thumbs brushing over his dimples. "There's only you for me, Cail. There will only ever be you."

Cail leaned forward, resting his forehead against hers. "Ah, God, Angel. You do my heart in sometimes." His lips brushed softly over hers. "What do you say we find an electronics store and get you a camera for your front door? I don't like that guy, Tay. There's something off about him."

"Which is why we're going out to get a camera, but I don't want something obvious."

"How about a light fixture with a concealed camera? You download an app to your phone and receive notifications when there's motion at the door."

She liked the idea of an immediate alert sent to her phone and being able to view the video anywhere, any time. They went outside and checked out the light fixtures. There were two, one at each side of the door. "There's no way I'm going to find a light fixture to match what's here, so I'm going to have to get two."

* * *

On the way to the electronics store, Taylor called Chris to update her on St. James's visit. She thought maybe she should have waited until they were in the office tomorrow as Chris wasn't pleased with the news. On the other hand, she would have been more upset if Taylor waited.

Cail purchased the light fixtures as his Christmas present to Taylor and installed them for her while she downloaded the app. When they tested it out, an alert sounded on her phone and she brought up the video of Cail standing outside the door grinning up at the camera. "It's bloody cold out here," he said. "Let me in."

Taylor laughed as she opened the door. "It works great. The video is very clear, too."

"Awesome," he said, grabbing her around the waist and pulling her in. "That's another present off my Christmas list. How are you doing with Christmas shopping?" He knew how she reacted in a grocery store, overwhelmed by the choices and anxious over the lack of escape routes.

"I'm done, I think."

Cail's eyebrows shot up. "You've done all of your Christmas shopping? Did Kate help you out with it?"

Taylor shook her head. "I made most of my presents."

"Drew them?"

"I'm not telling."

"I wish I was talented enough to make my own gifts."

"You are," Taylor said. "You could give people discs of your music."

"I haven't really played in a long time. I'm rusty, especially with this cast. If I was going to record my music, I'd need an instrument and the software and hardware to record it."

"You sounded amazing at Kate's birthday celebration."

"Why, thank you. My first fan." He grinned at her and gave her a quick kiss. "Let's go through your files."

They settled in the living room and Cail helped her go through each offer. She listed the pros and cons of each interview and appearance then created a yes pile and a no pile. When they were done, Cail handed her the pad he'd been writing on during the process. He'd listed the fee associated with each engagement and totalled them for her. "That's a shitload of money," he said. "Will that cover the costs of your warehouse?"

She shrugged. "I have no idea. I spoke to the real estate agent that I used to buy this place and he recommended a commercial real estate agent. I contacted him and he's checking whether the owner is willing to sell and at what price."

"When you buy it, and I have no doubt you will, I want to help. Will you hire your cousin, Nate, for the renovations?"

"It will depend on his quote. I'm going to get a few before I decide."

Cail grinned. "My girl's smart."

Taylor laughed and bumped his shoulder with hers. "If I'm going to do this, I'm going to do it right. I need to do some research."

"I'll ask around and get some recommendations for construction firms."

Taylor leaned in and kissed Cail's cheek. "Thank you. That will help."

"I told my parents I'd come for Sunday dinner. Will you come with me?"

"I've got some things to do here," she said. She just wasn't ready for a family event with the Worthington's. "Maybe next time."

She saw him to the door and thanked him for the Christmas present.

Cail's arms circled her waist and pulled her in. "I had fun today. It's nice to be able to hang out together."

"Yeah, it was nice."

"I've got a meeting with my sergeant tomorrow morning. I'm hoping to be able to go back to work, even though I'll be restricted to desk duties."

"A desk is better than sitting at home."

"Yeah. I'm getting pretty tired of that." Even packing up his apartment was getting boring. He brushed his lips over Taylor's then sank in to deepen the kiss. He kept it brief, otherwise he wouldn't be able to leave, then pressed a kiss to her forehead. "Love you."

"Love you, too."

Cail walked out into the bitter cold as fat snowflakes drifted down from above, a huge grin gracing his face.

Chapter 17

Taylor arrived at work early on Monday morning to update the board, adding Elizabeth Cruise's murder and saving Chris from dealing with it. She just finished when Chris wandered into the conference room carrying two Tim Horton's coffees. She handed one to Taylor and sipped hers as she studied the board.

"Do you think St. James is in cahoots with Siobhan Silva?"

Taylor was surprised by the question, although she probably shouldn't have been. "There's nothing in his files to indicate he's dirty, but those diamonds are worth a heck of a lot of money. It would be tempting, especially if he has medical bills from his mother's illness."

"Hmm." Chris took another sip of coffee. "I'm going to ask Brice to check into his mother's medical bills and his personal finances on the quiet." She turned to Taylor. "That's just between us."

Taylor nodded her assent.

"I've got a few things to take care of in my office. When Stone gets in, tell her I'd like to see her." With that, Chris walked out of the conference room.

Taylor followed her out, scanning for Detective Stone. Ambrose was at his desk, but Stone was absent. She went to her own desk and placed a call to Cheryl Starr from the National News Network. Cheryl answered on the first ring.

"Taylor?"

"Yes. I just wanted to let you know that I'll do your documentary."

"You will?" There was a quick laugh. "That's great. When can we meet to discuss the details and go over the contract?"

Taylor made arrangements to meet at Starr's office that evening. She'd emailed the list of engagements from her yes pile to Emma Brinkman the day before and called now to follow up. She got Emma's voice mail and left a message.

Stone still hadn't made an appearance, so she walked over to Ambrose's desk. "Where's Detective Stone?"

"Um, not in yet," Ambrose said, his eyes not leaving his computer screen.

"Well, when she gets in, can you tell her DS Cain wants to see her?"

His eyes widened as they shot up to meet Taylor's gaze. "Oh, alright."

Taylor shot him a quick glance over her shoulder as she made her way back to her desk. He picked up his cell phone and turned his back as soon as she began to walk away.

At her desk, she entered the name Elizabeth Cruise into the police database and got absolutely no hits. Not only did she not have a criminal record, Bonkers didn't even have an outstanding parking ticket. Neither was she listed as a witness or victim in a case. Whatever happened in Elizabeth Cruise's youth, it hadn't been reported to the police. Taylor picked up the phone again, this time placing a call to Social Services, requesting Cruise's records.

Chris approached Taylor's desk, scanning the office. "Where's Stone?"

"I don't know. Ambrose just said she wasn't in yet, but I think he called her."

"It can wait. We've been hailed to the Inspector's office." She nodded her head towards the elevators. "Let's go."

* * *

DuBois met them at the elevator and escorted them to a conference room, where they found Inspector Worthington sitting with Will St. James.

They took the seats opposite from St. James and the middle aged man with a receding hairline who sat beside him. Worthington sat at the head of the table and DuBois took the seat next to Taylor. Taylor looked over at Chris, not surprised to see her red-faced and seething, glaring across the table at St. James.

"Sergeant St. James is formally disputing being banned from your briefing on Friday, DS Cain," Worthington said.

"I told him the requirements to return," Chris responded. "Until he's willing to share information instead of withholding it, he's not welcome in my unit." Despite the ire so evident in her expression, Chris's words were delivered in a calm, authoritative manner.

"With all due respect," St. James began, "there is certain data I'm not at liberty to share."

"Then you have your answer," Chris said, turning to Worthington. "But, since we're all here, I have a few complaints of my own. Sergeant St. James has hampered our investigation by withholding details relevant to our case, ignoring my orders and turning evidence over to the RCMP which was our jurisdiction, and harassed my partner at her home for details of our case."

The balding man looked over at St. James and St. James shrugged. He turned to Worthington. "Would you give us a few minutes, please?"

"I'm sorry," Chris said. "Who are you?"

"My apologies." He stood and reached his hand over the table. "I should have introduced myself. Staff Sergeant David MacInnis. RCMP."

Chris shook his hand then waited as he offered it to Taylor.

Taylor stared at his hand for a moment before reluctantly shaking it. If it hadn't been rude not to, she wouldn't have touched him. As it was, she couldn't wait to go and wash her hands.

"You can use my office," Worthington said and escorted MacInnis and St. James out.

"What do you think he's up to?" DuBois asked.

"No good," Chris said. "If he was serious about this complaint, he would have brought someone higher ranking than a staff sergeant. He wants access to our case details, but he's not willing to make too big a splash about it."

Worthington came back in then. "What's this about St. James harassing Sinclair at home?" he asked, returning to his seat at the head of the table.

Taylor gave him a run down of St. James's impromptu visit the day before.

"So, why is St. James so interested in Raine Delacourte's whereabouts?" Worthington asked, shooting Chris a knowing look.

"He thinks she still has the diamonds," Chris answered. She stood, shoved her hands in her pockets and began pacing the room. "The thing is, Siobhan Silva saw us take the duffel bag out of Cruise's apartment, so either someone tipped her off that the diamonds weren't on the list of items recovered from the duffel bag or she found a way to hack into our files."

"You think St. James tipped her off?" DuBois asked.

"Him or someone else with access to our files."

MacInnis walked back into the room, ending their conversation. He took his seat at the table. "Sergeant St. James is working on clearance to share information."

"And if he doesn't get clearance?" Chris asked.

"Then we have a problem, DS Cain."

Someone's phone chirped and MacInnis pulled his cell phone out of the inside pocket of his suit jacket, swiped the screen, and began tapping it. "St. James has clearance," he said. "He'd like to meet you in your office in an hour, DS Cain."

"Make it my office," Worthington said. "One hour."

"Yes, sir." MacInnis tapped away on his screen with his thumbs and moments later it chirped again. "Confirmed." He stood, returning his phone to his inside pocket. "Constable Sinclair, I'll apologize for Sergeant St. James bothering you at your residence."

"Will you apologize for him for the death of Elizabeth Cruise?" Chris asked.

"I'm sorry that Ms. Cruise lost her life, DS Cain, but it's hardly Sergeant St. James's fault. His hands were tied."

Chris glared at MacInnis as he walked out of the conference room. Bullshit, she thought. "He wouldn't have gotten clearance that fast if it was an issue."

"I agree," Worthington said. "That was awful quick."

* * *

Chris scanned the unit as she headed for her office and yelled out, "Stone." She took her seat and watched as Stone appeared in her doorway, pale faced and wide eyed. She wouldn't say Stone looked disheveled, but the buttons on her blouse weren't lined up. "Close the door and take a seat, Detective."

Stone eased the door closed and sat in front of Chris's desk with her hands clasped in her lap.

Chris put a finger on the file folder on the corner of her desk and drew it in front of her. She didn't open it. She didn't need to. It was more for Stone's benefit, who'd know it was her personnel file. "You've been with my unit for two years, Detective. I'd describe you as a bulldog. You sink your teeth into a case and you don't let go until you shake everything out."

"Thank you, Sarge."

"You know what I'm going to say, don't you?"

"Yes, Sarge." Stone dropped her head. "I've been dropping the ball the last couple of weeks."

"Why?"

"I'm sorry. It won't happen again."

"I didn't ask for an apology, Danny. I'm asking what's going on?"

Stone's head popped up and she eyed Chris. "I … it's just some personal stuff."

It didn't surprise Chris that Stone was reluctant to talk. It was the way of things with police officers, as if everyone took an oath not to make excuses for having lives. "I can't help you if you don't talk to me. Something obviously isn't right."

Stone's eyes pooled. "Things are just a bit hectic at home. Paul left me, so it's just me and the kids."

"Couldn't handle having a cop for a spouse?"

Stone laughed, although neither of them found it funny. "There's a reason they say cops aren't a good bet for marriage."

"It's harder on our loved ones than it is on us." Chris flipped open the file folder. "You've got vacation time you haven't used." If she didn't use it by the end of the month, she'd just lose it. "Why don't you take the time, spend Christmas with your kids and come back in the New Year ready for a fresh start?"

"I didn't want to put in a last minute request so close to the holidays."

"You need the time, Danny. Take it."

"You're sure? I won't leave you stuck over the holidays?"

"We'll manage," Chris said with a grin. She picked up the first sheet of paper in Stone's file and handed it over to her.

Stone scanned the vacation request, signed with Chris's authorization, and looked up in surprise. "You knew all along I was having problems at home, didn't you?"

"I figured it was something like that." Chris got up and opened the door. "Now go home." As Stone was walking out, she added, "Oh, and you might want to fix the buttons on your blouse."

"Oh, shit." Stone looked down at her shirt. "I took Kaitlyn to the doctor's like this."

Chris laughed and leaned against the door jamb, watching Stone go to her desk and start collecting her things. Detective Blake wandered over and leaned against the wall next to her. "Everything okay with her?"

"It's a tough balance," Chris said. "Between work and home life."

Maryann Blake knew that only too well. Her husband left her because he thought she put her job before him. He was probably right, but it still hurt. "Yeah, cops and relationships are like oil and water."

"Most of them." Chris was betting on her relationship with Kate being one of the few that lasted.

"And, speaking of relationships, here comes yours."

Blake pushed off the wall and walked away, leaving Chris to watch Kate, resplendent in her crisp uniform, walking across the unit towards her. Kate's smile lit up the room when their eyes met.

"Got a minute, DS?"

"For you, always," Chris answered. She waved Kate into her office and closed the door.

"Sorry to barge in on the middle of your day, but I have some news and I couldn't wait to share it with you."

It had to be good news, as the grin remained on Kate's face and her blue eyes sparkled.

Kate reached into her pocket, pulled out a black leather wallet, and opened it to display her shiny new gold shield. "I've been assigned to Homicide beginning in the new year." She flew into Chris's open arms, laughing and crying at the same time.

"Congratulations, Detective. This calls for a celebration."

"And there'll be plenty of time to celebrate. I'm using up my vacation time, so I'll be off until after the holidays. This is going to be the best Christmas ever."

Chris's muscles tensed and she groaned. Kate was so into Christmas, but it was an anomaly to Chris. Now that she had Taylor, Gray, Kate, and the Worthington's, she didn't have a clue what Christmas would be like.

"Why does Christmas freak you out so much?" Kate asked.

"It's not Christmas, so much. It's buying presents for all those people and I don't have a clue what to get them."

Kate leaned back with eyes wide. "You still haven't been Christmas shopping, have you?" When Chris shrugged, she said, "Okay, that's it. I'm meeting you here after work and taking you shopping." She opened the door and threw Chris a grin over her shoulder. "Then we'll celebrate."

Kate stopped at Taylor's desk to say hello on her way out. Just like Cail's, Taylor's eyes looked a little brighter. "We saw Cail at my parents' last night for Sunday dinner. He seems much happier."

Heat flushed Taylor's face as she smiled up at Kate. "Yeah, we're trying."

"Well, *trying* becomes you." She grinned and walked away.

Kate's announcement gave Chris an idea of what to get her for a Christmas present, but she didn't have much time to pull it together. "Blake," she yelled then turned to open the web browser on her computer.

Chapter 18

On the way back up to Inspector Worthington's office, Chris told Taylor about Kate's promotion to detective and taking the rest of the year off. "I've got some vacation time left as well. Would you be okay working with Blake until I get back?"

"Sure." If anyone deserved a vacation, Taylor figured it was Chris. If it meant she had to work with Detective Blake, she'd do it for Chris.

"Cool. I'll be here until Christmas day, then you're with Blake. She's up to date on the Delacourte case."

Five chairs surrounded the round table in the corner of Inspector Worthington's office. When Taylor and Chris joined Worthington and DuBois, four of them were filled and the fifth one sat empty for over ten minutes.

"Maybe he's not coming," Chris said after a long silence.

"You wish," St. James said as he strolled into the room with a laptop bag slung over his shoulder.

"I do," Chris murmured with a smirk.

St. James took the remaining seat, setting the laptop bag next to his chair. He opened it, pulled out a thick file folder, and placed it on the table in front of him. "Ten years ago, the RCMP investigated a break in and theft at a prominent residence in Banff. You've heard of the Group of Seven."

"Iconic Canadian landscape painters from the 1920s," Taylor said.

Everyone stared at Taylor for a moment before St. James continued. "Yeah, that would be them. The Carmichaels owned a landscape by J.E.H. MacDonald, one of the Group of Seven artists, worth a few million. It was the only item stolen, which tells us the perpetrators targeted that specific painting. The thieves left behind a signature." He opened the file folder and passed a photograph around. The same four

Rune symbols that had been carved into Delacourte's and Cruise's chests were spray painted across a wall where it was obvious the painting had been hanging.

"It was a professional job. In and out with no one the wiser. The Carmichaels slept through it."

"If they were professionals, I take it there were more thefts," Chris said, playing dumb.

"There were. They were dubbed the Rune Crew. They hit a number of private residences and the odd gallery, taking either priceless art or jewels. They knew what they were going in for and took only one or two pieces. Then, about six years ago, Silva was arrested after assaulting Lily De La Cruz. We went to her apartment to arrest her and recognized a painting hanging on the wall from one of the Rune Crew heists. We obtained a search warrant for her apartment and two more of the stolen items were recovered.

"Silva spilled her guts on De La Cruz in exchange for a lesser charge and reduced sentence, but insisted she wasn't involved in the thefts. We went to arrest De La Cruz, but she was in the wind. We never found her, until Raine Delacourte put a picture of her in the newspaper with her memorial."

"Six years and you never got any leads on her whereabouts?" Chris asked.

"Whoever set up her new identity was good. So good, we'd like a look at the passport you logged into evidence."

Chris couldn't see any reason not to give him access to the passports, so she nodded her assent. "But, De La Cruz was dead," Chris said. "Why insert yourself into my investigation?"

"Five years ago, the Rune Crew stole forty-eight blue diamonds from a jewelry store in Banff."

"Okay. Still doesn't explain why your nose is stuck in my case."

"Siobhan Silva was incarcerated five years ago. We know one of the perpetrators was Lily De La Cruz. The second was shorter than Lily with an athletic build."

Chris laughed. "You think Raine Delacourte robbed a jewelry store?" She couldn't picture Raine stealing from anyone.

"She's top of our list at the moment."

"As far as I know, Raine didn't meet Callie until about a year before their wedding, which was three years ago. She couldn't have helped Callie rob that store."

"I need to interview Raine Delacourte. Even if she wasn't involved, she must have some information about it. At the very least, she knows the location of the diamonds. De La Cruz would have left them to her when she passed, if she hadn't already sold them."

"It's not Raine you need to talk to, it's Silva. And we would have had her in custody if you hadn't withheld vital information." Chris glared at St. James. "And Elizabeth Cruise would be alive." Everything he told them so far was public information, leading Chris to believe the whole clearance to share details bullshit was just that - bullshit.

"If Raine Delacourte was not involved in the theft, then Silva may lead us to the second perp."

Chris's face turned fire engine red and the veins in her neck throbbed. "The RCMP may think nothing of leaving dangerous offenders out on the street to do their work for them," Chris began as she rose from her seat, "but, the Toronto Police do their own investigating." She turned to Worthington. "Sir, we'll be in the field."

Taylor jumped up to chase after Chris as she strode from the room and caught up to her pacing in front of the elevator.

"I can't be in the same room as that asshole without wanting to ring his scrawny neck. I can't believe we've wasted the whole fucking morning with his bullshit."

"I don't understand why he had to get clearance to share information that is available on the internet," Taylor said.

"Exactly. It's complete bullshit. You know what I think, Sinclair? I think Will St. James wants those fucking diamonds." A grin spread across Chris's face. "How funny is it that he was just sitting about a foot away from them?"

* * *

Sergeant Colin Hayes, his ginger hair cropped short, tapped his fingers on Cail's personnel file and glowered at him across his desk. "You were given a conditional return to duties last month and, let's face it, your behaviour over the past couple of weeks is unbecoming of an officer."

He should have expected this, but, like an idiot, he'd come into the station expecting to be placed on desk duties until his broken arm healed. "Anyone who'd been through what I just experienced, would have reacted the same. The difference is the media were all over it."

"You're in the public eye with your association to Taylor Sinclair, Cail. You should know better than to give the media the opportunity to film you in that state. It looks bad on all of us."

"You're right, of course. I don't have an excuse, Sarge."

Hayes continued to tap his fingers on the file and consider Cail as beads of sweat formed over Cail's lip.

"You're receiving your second written warning and you haven't even got six months in yet. One more, Worthington, and you're out."

"Yes, sir. I understand."

Flipping the folder open, Hayes drew out a sheet of paper and passed it over the desk to Cail. Cail signed the warning and got to his feet.

"Report for night shift at twenty-three hundred hours. You'll work the front desk."

"Yes, sir."

Cail stepped out of the office and ran into Tara MacNeil, his partner. Or, she had been before he went off on sick leave. "Tara?"

"Hey, how's the arm? You coming back to work?"

"Desk duties. Night shift."

"Poor bastard," she said and laughed.

He didn't realized how much he missed riding with her until that moment. Laughing with her helped take some of the sting out of his visit with Sergeant Hayes.

* * *

"How is it you're not blind yet?" Chris asked.

Brice McLean's nose was only about an inch away from the laptop screen as his fingers flew over the keyboard.

"Ah, Cain. I wondered when you'd make an appearance." McLean leaned back in his chair and picked up the coffee cup from his desk. He took a sip then grimaced. "Ugh, it's gone cold."

"What have you got for me, McLean?"

He shuffled some papers around on his desk and then handed several sheets to Chris. "The mother has health coverage, so no major medical bills, and she has quite a bit in savings and RRSPs. St. James doesn't seem to be as money conscious as his mother though. He's basically living paycheque to paycheque."

"Aren't we all," Chris murmured as she scanned the documents.

"You'll see from his bank statements that he's got a hefty car payment and his rent is high. He spends a lot on clothes and entertainment, but nothing outrageous for his income."

No, Chris thought, not outrageous, but he was spending pretty much every penny he made. Even she managed to save a little bit each month and she was earning equity in her house instead of blowing it on rent. "Alright," she said and stuck the documents in McLean's shredder. "What about Silva's laptop? Anything?"

"Ah, now there's an interesting lady."

Chris snorted. "I wouldn't call her a lady."

"I haven't had much time to look at her files, but she had a lot of photographs on there. It looks like she's been doing some surveillance of you and Sinclair as well as several others who I haven't identified as yet."

"I may be able to help you with some of them," Chris said. "Any evidence she's a hacker?"

"I wouldn't say she has the technical know how for that based on what I've seen so far. Her browser history doesn't support that either. Again, she's been researching you and Sinclair and several others. I'll send you a list as soon as I get a few minutes here."

"If you haven't got the time, is there someone else you can put on it? It's kind of time sensitive. I need to know if there's anything on that laptop that will help us locate Siobhan Silva."

McLean smiled up at Chris and Taylor. "I just took on a new intern. She's working on her Computer Security and Digital Forensics degree at Ryerson. Want to give her a go?"

"Sure, why the hell not?"

McLean picked up his phone and dialed an extension number. "My office," he said and hung up.

Taylor looked over her shoulder at the woman rushing across the lab towards them. She was wearing a dark grey business suit, her blonde hair pulled back in a tight knot. She was a good ten inches shorter than Taylor, putting her at around five foot two, and couldn't have reached her twentieth birthday yet. Her eyes became wide behind tortoise shell glasses when she saw Taylor.

"Oh, I know you. You're Taylor Sinclair."

"Thanks for solving that mystery," Taylor said sarcastically. She was so tired of people saying stupid things to her.

"Sorry. I guess I'm fangirling."

Taylor stepped aside so she could enter McLean's office. He handed her Silva's laptop.

"Gayle Lansing, this is DS Cain and Constable Sinclair. They need an assessment of this laptop asap."

"Anything that can help us locate the owner is priority," Chris said. "But, any information you could give us would be helpful."

"Do you know who the owner is?"

"Siobhan Silva, aka Lian Logan. She's wanted for murder and

several counts of sexual assault."

Lansing tucked the laptop under her arm. "Give me an hour, two tops, and if there's anything on here, I'll find it."

"Where to next?" Taylor asked as she followed Chris out of the computer lab.

"We'll start with the place Raine met Callie."

"Where was that?"

"Les Beau's. Callie was working there part-time. Maybe they can tell us who she was hanging out with before she hooked up with Raine."

* * *

Cameron worked the bar and Gloria waited tables when they walked into Les Beau's. Chris approached Cameron and asked where Sammy was.

"She's in the back. You need her?" She nodded at Taylor, smiled. "Hey, Frigg."

Taylor frowned at her. "It's Taylor."

Cameron grinned and winked at her. "You look awfully damn good in that uniform, *Taylor*."

Chris grinned at Taylor's flushed face then turned back to Cameron. "How long have you worked here?"

"I don't know. Two, two and a half years. Something like that."

"I'll need to speak to Sammy."

"Sure." Cameron picked up a phone at the end of the bar with her back to Taylor and Chris.

Chris raised her eyebrows at Taylor. "Frigg?"

"Don't ask."

"She'll be right out," Cameron called from the end of the bar then leaned over to take the order of a woman sitting by herself.

The door next to the bar flew open and Sam rushed out, her face pale and her eyes wide. "Is it true? Bonkers? Did someone kill her?"

Chris walked over to Sam and held her wrists, looking straight into her eyes. "Who told you that?"

"Raine just called. She said Bonkers has been murdered. Is it true? God, Chris. Just tell me."

"Yes. We believe the woman you knew as Lian Logan murdered her on Saturday."

"Oh, God."

As Chris led Sam to a booth and sat her down before she fell down, Taylor went to the bar and got a glass of water from Cameron. She placed it on the table in front of Sam then sat opposite her.

"Does she have a last paycheque that she might come in for?" Chris asked. It was a long shot, but you never knew.

Sam shook her head. "We have direct deposit. There's no reason for her to come back here." She picked up the glass and took a few tentative sips.

"I'll need her banking information."

"Let's go back to my office and I'll get it for you."

Chris waited until Sam was seated at her desk before she asked her next question. "When did Callie Delacourte start working here?"

"Callie? Why?"

"Because she's connected to Siobhan Silva, aka Lian Logan. They knew each other when Callie lived out west."

"Is she the reason Callie moved here? She said she came to Toronto to escape an abusive relationship."

"Yeah," Chris answered.

"I don't understand any of this. Why did she go after Raine and Bonkers? Because they knew Callie?"

"No. It's more complicated than that. When did Callie start working here?"

"Shortly after she moved here. I think she took the job more to socialize than for the money. She didn't seem to be hurting for cash and the amount she earned here part-time probably didn't even cover the insurance on that car she drove."

"What kind of car did she drive?" Taylor asked out of curiosity.

"She had a sexy black Aston Martin," Chris said.

"Raine still has it," Sam said. "She keeps it in a garage. She won't drive it, but I think it's still too painful for her to sell it."

She'd have to look into that, Chris thought. The car was most likely the proceeds of crime. "Do you remember Callie hanging around anyone with Raine's build and height before they met? Say, from the time she started working here until about five years ago?" Chris asked.

"I don't remember her dating anyone back then. She was pretty messed up from the relationship she fled."

As if she just remembered, she got up and retrieved Lian Logan's file from a dented metal file cabinet and photocopied the blank cheque she had supplied for her direct deposits and handed it over to Chris.

"Thanks," Chris said. "You wouldn't happen to still have Callie's personnel file, would you?"

"I should have, but it will be down in the basement somewhere. It might take me a while to find it."

"Give me a shout when you do and we'll swing by to pick it up. Do you have a next of kin on file for Logan?"

Sam grabbed the file folder out of the cabinet again. "No. She wrote NA where it says next of kin."

"Figures." Chris stepped out into the hall and turned back when Sam spoke again.

"I hope you find Lian, Chris." Tears brimmed Sam's eyes. "She needs to pay for what she's done to Raine and Bonkers."

"We'll find her."

* * *

"I'll run Lily De La Cruz for known associates," Taylor said as they stepped out onto the sidewalk.

"Try Siobhan Silva as well. We'll apply for a warrant for Silva's bank records, too."

"Are we going back to the office then? Can we check the vape store across from her apartment before we go back? I'd like to check Cruise's apartment again, as well, to see if I can find anything relating to her past."

"Get anything there yet?"

Taylor shook her head. "I'm waiting on her Social Services records."

Chris shoved her hands in her coat pockets as they began the trek to the car. "Eléane's funeral is tomorrow."

"Do you still want me to come?"

"Kate's coming, but I figure the more the merrier. If I'm surrounded by friends, the bastard can't cause a scene."

The bruise on Chris's cheek, courtesy of Sebastien St. Amour, resembled dark clouds rumbling across the sky. If it came down to it, Taylor had no problem putting herself between St. Amour and Chris. "Then I'll be there."

They missed Siobhan Silva at the vape store by less than an hour. According to the clerk, Silva stocked up with enough juice to last her a few days. If she was going to return there, it would be on Boxing Day or the day after. She'd have to run it past Detective Blake, but Taylor planned on staking the place out if they didn't have her by then.

They crossed the street to Silva's apartment. The police seal was still in tact, so she hadn't gone back in. Taylor stood in the middle of the living room then turned in a slow circle. "I don't think she has a lot of money, so where would she go?" She closed her eyes, trying to picture Silva out there somewhere. "Would she stay in a car or is it too cold for her? Cheap hotel? Hostel?"

"Let's put that on the list," Chris said. "Call around to hotels and hostels and give her description."

Chapter 19

The silence inside Elizabeth Cruise's apartment sent shivers up Taylor's spine. She felt like some kind of voyeur looking through Cruise's personal belongings, but it had to be done. Inside a dresser drawer, behind a pile of neatly folded t-shirts, Taylor found a bundle of letters wrapped in a pink ribbon addressed to Melodie. There was no address and no last name.

She teased the ribbon off and opened the first envelope.

My Dear Sweet Melodie,

Today is your first birthday and I've thought of you every day over this past year. Are you walking yet? Have you said your first words? Oh, how I wish I could be there to celebrate all of your firsts.

Taylor's chest tightened as she folded the letter, unable to read more. She'd never written letters to her son, but she wondered every day about the boy he would have grown into; wondered who he would have become.

She took the last letter from the pile, opened it.

My Dear Sweet Melodie,

Happy 22nd Birthday my little love.

Taylor dropped down, her butt resting on her lower calves, with the letter fisted in her hand just as Chris popped her head in the bedroom door. "Find anything?"

Taylor looked up at Chris. "She was thirteen when she had her daughter."

"Oh shit, Taylor." Chris came into the room and crouched next to Taylor. "I can have Blake investigate Bonkers' past."

Shaking her head, Taylor handed the letters to Chris. "I want to do it. I need to do it."

Chris opened a few of the letters at random and skimmed through them. "We need to find out where Bonkers was staying at age twelve or thirteen."

"It will be in her case files. I should have them later today."

"I haven't read through all of the letters, but I didn't see any mention of the father."

Taylor winced. She was going to have to read the letters, all of them, all the way through. "Do you think I could take copies of the letters and read them at home tonight?" She couldn't do it sitting in the middle of the unit with all eyes on her.

"You don't have to read them, Taylor. I can get-"

"No," Taylor cut her off. She didn't need anyone picking up her slack because she was deemed too fragile, especially Detective Blake. "I'll read them."

Chris nodded, her respect for Taylor ever increasing. "Okay. Take the copies home."

* * *

Detective Blake shot out of her chair when she saw Chris and Taylor walking in from the elevator.

"Uh, Sarge. There's a lady waiting in your office. Classy. Long dark hair, brown eyes, mid-fifties, striking."

Chris blew out a breath and steeled herself to deal with Dr. Sylvie Raynard. "Thanks, Detective or should I say Detective Sergeant?"

Blake shrugged, struggled to keep the grin from spreading across her face and failed. "Yeah, I passed that puppy with flying colours."

Taylor stepped forward and offered Blake her hand. "Congratulations, DS."

Blake shook her hand, still grinning. "Thanks, Sinclair."

Chris wrapped her arm around Blake's neck and pulled her in with a quick laugh. "Yes. Way to go. Now I can dump all of the admin duties on you."

Blake's grin turned into a frown. "Hey, that's not fair."

"You gotta learn it if you want to command the unit. Why don't we meet up for drinks tonight to celebrate at Delaney's. Kate's celebrating, too. She just got her detective's shield."

"I'm in," Blake said, pulling out of Chris's headlock. "Do you hear that everyone?" she called out. "Drinks at Delaney's tonight."

A half-hearted cheer erupted from the detectives manning computers or talking on phones then quickly died out.

Chris rubbed her hand over Blake's head, messing her hair. "Congrats. I'm proud of you, Maryann." She was smiling when she strode into her office and saw Sylvie sitting in one of the chairs facing her desk with her coat lying across her lap and a thick manilla envelope sitting on top of it. "Sylvie," she said with a nod and took her seat behind her desk. "What can I do for you?"

Sylvie smiled, but her eyes were tired and droopy. "I was instructed to give you this upon Eléane's death." She hefted the envelope as if it weighed a ton and passed it to Chris.

"What is it?" Chris asked. She took the envelope then laid it on the desk in front of her.

"It's sealed, but I believe there is a copy of her will and some letters addressed to you."

"Why would she give me a copy of her will?"

"To ensure that you receive the things she wants you to have. She worried that Sebastien may contest the will because she's left everything to you. Her lawyer is aware of her fears and assured her there would be no issues, but she still worried."

"It doesn't matter. It doesn't change anything."

With a loud sigh, Sylvie got to her feet, draping her coat over her arm. "I wish it could. I wish there was some way of changing the past, Chris. Unfortunately, that's not possible." She stepped forward and laid a hand on Chris's shoulder. "You'll also find evidence of his abuse in that envelope - pictures of your injuries over the years, my reports from examining you, and notarized statements from your mother and I. Whatever you decide, I hope it includes finding a way to heal the damage we've all done to you." Her lips curved up, but there were tears in her eyes. She gave Chris's shoulder a gentle squeeze then flew out the door, graceful on her shiny black heels with her silk blouse billowing behind her.

"Fuck," Chris shouted and slammed her office door closed.

Taylor jolted at the expletive and the resounding bang. She glanced around the office area to see everyone else looking wide-eyed at each other.

"Give her a few minutes to cool off then take her a coffee," Blake said over her computer screen.

Taylor had been thinking the same thing, so she nodded and went back to her search. She couldn't find anyone associated with Lily De La Cruz or Siobhan Silva who matched the description of the shorter woman in the diamond heist. She went on Facebook and brought up Callie Delacourte's page which hadn't been deleted after her death. Taylor searched through her friends list looking for someone who matched the description they had of Sass. Her interest piqued when she found a woman named Angela St. James, an athletic blonde, but she could only see her profile picture as the account was private. She couldn't tell if she was short or tall.

Could it be a coincidence that she shared Will's last name? She brought up Will St. James's Facebook page and was disappointed to see that it was private as well. She couldn't view his friends list, pictures, or his relationship status.

She entered Angela St. James into the system for a criminal records check. She was squeaky clean, not even a speeding ticket on record. She had an Alberta drivers' licence and an address in Banff, Alberta. Her height was listed as five foot three.

"Constable Sinclair?"

Taylor glanced up from her computer screen to the officer with light brown hair and wire framed glasses holding out a thick manilla envelope. "Yes," she said and accepted the package. "Thank you."

He shrugged, turned, and shuffled away while Taylor opened the envelope, spilling the contents of Elizabeth Cruise's Social Services file onto her desk.

Chapter 20

Chris's door was open when Taylor approached with two cups of coffee and a file folder tucked under her arm. "Got a few minutes?" she asked before entering.

Chris waved her in, her eyes still glued to her computer screen. Taylor placed a coffee on the desk in front of Chris and took a seat across from her, patiently waiting for Chris to finish what she was doing. Her hair was standing on end, spiking up in all different directions.

"I don't think Silva made our home addresses," Chris said with her eyes still on her screen. "Her surveillance photos of us are mostly from Bonkers' place."

"Was there anything else of value on her laptop?"

"Nah, not really. She's got an iPhone. Lansing accessed her 'Find My iPhone' account, but the phone's turned off. If she turns on that phone, we'll have her."

"I found an woman who fits the description of Sass on Callie's friends list on Facebook."

Chris's eyes jumped from her screen to meet Taylor's. "Got a name?" She noticed the mug on her desk and picked it up to take a long gulp then leaned back in her chair with a sigh.

"Um, yeah. Angela St. James."

Chris's eyebrows popped up and her mouth dropped open.

"Can't be a coincidence, can it?" Taylor asked.

"No fucking way."

"No criminal record. Resides in Banff, Alberta."

"Which is where Will St. James was posted."

"And where the Rune Crew committed their run of thefts."

"He's in this. I don't know how deep, but that bastard is in this."

234

Chris needed to clear her head and think. Her mind was muddled by the envelope sitting in her desk drawer and all of the shit from her past spewing to the surface.

"Can we bring him in to interview?"

"I'll talk to the Inspector."

"Elizabeth Cruise's Social Services records came in. She was in a foster home for eighteen months, from age eleven through thirteen. She was placed in a group home when her foster father was arrested. She had a baby girl about six months after that and gave her up for adoption."

The pain and strain was evident in Taylor's face and Chris thought maybe she made a mistake in allowing her to follow through with Bonkers' past. "I can give this to Blake."

Taylor shook her head. With her belly churning, she turned pleading eyes to Chris. "The foster father was Gary Tremblant."

"Jesus fucking Christ." Chris shot to her feet. She knew the Tremblant case. She'd studied it after she learned Taylor had been placed in his care and raped. She would have recognized Bonkers' name. There was a child named Elizabeth in their care when Gary Tremblant was arrested for sexual assault of a minor, well before Taylor was placed in his care by a vengeful social worker, but it wasn't Elizabeth Cruise. "Elizabeth Cummings. Fucking hell." Her fingers stabbed through her hair as she paced. "She changed her name."

"Shortly after his arrest," Taylor said. "I checked. Gary Tremblant is still a resident of Palmerton Penitentiary. His trial isn't scheduled for another couple of months yet."

Chris dropped down in her chair and studied Taylor over her desk. "You can put this away. He's already been tried for assaulting Bonkers."

"It pisses me off that he got off so easy on those charges."

"He won't get off lightly this time."

"No. He won't." Taylor gathered up the file folder and her coffee then made her way to the door before turning back. "Listen, could you maybe stop offering to get Detective Blake to cover for me? I can handle this, Chris."

"I know. I just don't want to re-traumatize you."

"I'm where I belong, investigating sex crimes. It's what I know."

And how sad was that? "I feel kinda responsible for your emotional state because I brought you into this. I convinced you to become a cop and to come into sex crimes with me."

"In doing that you gave me a purpose for the first time in my life. All of the horrors I've lived through wasn't for naught because you've given the opportunity to use those experiences to stop monsters like Gary Tremblant, Sarah Johnson, and Siobhan Silva. And my emotional state is just fine." A smile tugged the corners of her mouth. "It will be even better when we turn the key to lock Silva in her cage."

Chris shook her head and couldn't suppress the grin spreading across her face. She was in awe of Taylor Sinclair and her strength. "Yeah, that will make my day, too."

"She's after the diamonds, but I don't get why she raped Raine Delacourte and Elizabeth Cruise. It's overkill. Totally unnecessary." The smile was gone and Taylor's eyes narrowed and hardened. "She raped Lily De La Cruz. It wouldn't surprise me if she's raped others."

"You ran it through ViCLAS. If there were any other like crimes, they weren't entered into the system. You also have to consider that Silva spent most of the time between her attacks on De La Cruz and Raine in prison."

Which is exactly where she needs to be again, Taylor thought. "I'll start calling cheap hotels and hostels." She opened the door to find Kate standing on the other side. "Oh, hey. Congratulations, *Detective*."

Kate grinned. "Thank you. I can't tell you how good it is to make detective before either of my brothers."

"Ha, I bet that will burn their butts."

"I'm going to make sure it does. At every opportunity," Kate added with a mischievous laugh.

Chris grabbed her coat and the envelope from her desk drawer then joined them at her office door. "We're going Christmas shopping. Are you going to meet us at Delaney's later?" she asked Taylor.

"I've got some things to do, but I'll try to get there."

* * *

Taylor stood in the middle of her living/dining area listening to the silence. She'd get used to living on her own again. Eventually. Maybe. With a sigh, she continued into her office and booted up the iMac. Since Chris left for the day, she didn't see any reason why she couldn't make her phone calls from home.

She opened her messenger bag to take out her list of hotels and hostels and stared in at the copies of the letters Elizabeth Cruise had written to her daughter. If she was that young woman, she'd want her mother's letters. She'd want to know her biological mother loved her, thought about her. Did she know she was adopted? Was she a tiny, fairy-like woman, just as Bonkers had been? She'd never get the chance to know her biological mom, thanks to Siobhan Silva. And that was a terrible shame from what Taylor knew of Elizabeth Cruise.

She leaned back in the chair and closed her eyes. *Where are you, Silva? What are you planning next? It would be harder for you to go for Chris because she doesn't live alone. Will you try for me?* She hoped so. She hoped Silva would make that mistake because there was no way in hell she'd allow Silva to make her a victim again. She was more than done with that.

After a good half hour of focusing in on Silva. All she could get was a vision of Silva walking the streets in a black jacket and watch cap, her hands tucked in the coat pockets and her head down. If she had the time, she'd stake out Silva's neighbourhood, because that's where she'd been wandering in Taylor's vision. Silva stuck to the areas she knew.

She made half a dozen calls to cheap hotels before her cell phone signalled motion at her front door. She opened the camera app to video of Cail grinning up at her. With a grin of her own, she went to the door and opened it. "The camera works great."

Cail stepped in and wrapped his arms around Taylor's waist. "I didn't even have to ring the bell." Leaning in, he brushed his lips over hers. "Missed you."

"You just saw me yesterday."

"Twenty-four hours. I was in desperate withdrawal."

Laughing she gave his shoulder a shove and closed the door. "Everyone's going to Delaney's later to celebrate Kate's promotion. Detective Sergeant Blake's celebrating as well. Do you want to go?"

"Ah, I heard my little sister got her gold shield. I didn't know about Blake. Good for her. I'll come for a bit, but I'm working the night shift."

"Oh." Why that depressed her, she didn't know.

"I got my wrist slapped for conduct unbecoming. One more screw up and I'll be looking for a new job."

"Oh, Cail. I'm sorry."

"Not your fault. I was an idiot. I guess I deserve the slap."

She couldn't argue with him there. "You just have to make sure you don't screw up again."

He tapped the tip of her nose with his finger. "Smarty pants. Anyway, I came by to see if you wanted to go for dinner."

"I was just going to get ready to go out. I'm meeting Cheryl Starr about that documentary."

"Why don't I tag along? Then we could grab dinner at Delaney's."

* * *

Chris dumped her shopping bags and the envelope Sylvie gave her on the kitchen island. "I suppose I have to wrap all of these."

"That's the idea," Kate said as she bumped Chris's shoulder. She picked up the envelope. "What's this?"

"Stuff from my mother apparently. A bunch of letters and a copy of her will. She asked Sylvie to make sure I got it."

Kate peered inside the envelope. "There are pictures in here."

"Yeah, you probably don't want to look at those. It's evidence in case I decide to charge Sebastien. Eléane and Sylvie's gift to me. I don't know what the hell to do."

Kate brushed her hands over Chris's cheeks then cupped her face, gazing into her deep brown eyes. "You don't have to do anything until you're ready. Just leave it. Think about it. If you decide you want to go through with it, I'm here for you."

"Thank you." She didn't want to think about it right now. Couldn't think about it without frying her circuits. "Let's get ready. I could use a few drinks after the past week."

"We'll take a cab." Kate brushed a light kiss over Chris's lips. "Then we can both have a few."

Chris wrapped her arms around Kate's waist and pulled her in close. "Or, we could be a bit late and have our own little celebration, *Detective*."

* * *

Taylor and Cail walked into Delaney's hand in hand to find it jam packed. For a Monday night, the place was hopping. Maryann Blake stood at the bar, already well into her celebration by the looks of her. Her arm was slung around the neck of a curly haired blond with the physique of Adonis.

Taylor recognized the faces of half the Sex Crimes Unit, including Danny Stone who leaned into Chris, her hands conducting a symphony as she spoke, with a serious expression on her face. Chris shook her head then gave Stone a hug, slapping her back with her hand. When she straightened, Stone wiped her fingers under her eyes and smiled.

Cail went straight to Kate, hugged her right off the floor, turning her in a circle. "Congratulations, Detective. I knew you'd ace that exam." He set her down, grinning, and reached for Taylor's hand. "Let's see it."

Kate rolled her eyes, but pulled out the leather wallet that held her ID and badge. She opened it then shut it quickly. "There. That's all you get."

"Hey." He grabbed the wallet from her hand and opened it. "Well, look at that, all shiny and new. Well done, babydoll." He leaned over and bussed her cheek while she grabbed the wallet back and stuffed it in her pocket.

"Congratulations, again," Taylor said.

Kate twirled in a circle then bowed. "Why, thank you." She lifted her beer from the bar. "Can I get you a drink?"

"Uh-uh," Cail said. "I'm buying this round."

Cail went to the bar to order drinks and let Maggie know they were there for dinner. She managed to find them a booth. Chris and Kate joined them as the waitress set a bottle of champagne and three flutes on the table.

Kate looked over at Cail with a raised eyebrow. "Not drinking?"

"Working nights tonight."

"Ah, lucky you."

"I'm not mixing drinks. I've got a funeral to go to tomorrow. You and Taylor will have to polish off that bottle of bubbly," Chris said to Kate

"Why?" Taylor asked. "We're going to the same funeral, aren't we?"

"You ever had a hangover, Taylor?" Chris asked, although she knew the answer.

"No, and I don't plan on having one tomorrow." Too much to do with Christmas coming and Siobhan Silva still loose on the streets of Toronto.

Chris grinned, deciding her mission of the night was getting Taylor drunk. "Just have a glass or two then. I'm sure Kate won't mind finishing the rest."

Since she'd already poured and drank half a glass, Kate just smiled. "Everyone ready for Christmas?"

Chris narrowed her eyes at Cail. "Why do people ask that? It just creates more pressure." She still had a couple of things to pick up, but couldn't do it with Kate around and time was running short.

"I'm ready," he said.

"Really?" Kate poured herself another glass. "What did you get for Taylor?"

Cail's back straightened, ready to surprise Kate with his practical and clever gift. "Security cams for her front door. Installed them already, too."

Kate rolled her eyes. "Oh, my God. You're terrible at this relationship thing."

"What? It's what she wanted."

Turning to Chris, Kate said, "If you bought me a security camera for Christmas, you can take it back and save yourself a few bucks."

"I didn't get you a security camera," Chris said with a cocky grin.

"Maybe you could talk to my brother about what constitutes an appropriate gift for your girlfriend."

"I like the cameras," Taylor said.

"See?" Cail brushed his lips over Taylor's temple. "I know my girl."

* * *

Both Chris and Kate stumbled into the house giggling like school girls. They just fell into bed when the doorbell rang.

"I'll get it," Chris slurred. "Who the hell's ringing the bell at oh dot thirty?" She pulled on track pants and a t-shirt and stumbled back down the hall. It took two tries to enter the code into her alarm system before she started to pull the door open.

"Chris, what if it's Silva?" Kate asked from behind her. She was wrapped in a cream bathrobe, her eyes heavy from too many drinks.

Chris nodded to the side of the door and Kate moved into position as she tightened the belt on her robe. Chris eased the door open, peeked out, and pulled it open. Raine Delacourte stood on her porch with a bright red, hard-cased suitcase at her side. "Raine?"

"I didn't know where else to go," she said. "I couldn't go to my place or to Bonkers' apartment. I didn't know where to go."

"You came to the right place." Chris pulled her inside, retrieved her suitcase, shut the door, and reset the alarm.

Kate stepped out as the door closed and Raine's hand shot to her chest. "Oh, hello." She turned back to Chris. "I'm sorry, I didn't realize you had someone here."

"It's fine," Chris said. "Raine, this is my girlfriend, Kate."

Kate smiled. "Can I get you anything? Tea or coffee?"

"Tea would be nice. Thank you."

Chris led Raine into the living room and took her coat. She sat on the sofa and stared at the twinkling Christmas tree in the corner of the living room. "I came back to organize Bonkers' memorial. I caught a cab at the airport and realized I didn't know where to tell him to take me. I'm so sorry to intrude."

"You're not intruding. It's good you're here." Better here than anywhere else in the city, Chris thought. "You can stay in our guest room tonight."

"*Our* guest room?" Raine glanced over her shoulder at Kate in the kitchen. "She's beautiful, Chris. I didn't know you were living with someone." Her hand patted Chris's thigh as she sat down next to her. "It's about damn time."

Chris's eyes travelled to Kate. "Yeah, it is." About damn time she made Kate an offer she couldn't refuse.

Raine wondered if Chris was aware of the dopey look of love that came into her eyes and smiled to herself. "You're in love."

"Head over heels." She grinned at Raine. "Never thought you'd see the day, did you?"

"Honestly, no. I didn't." Raine couldn't remember the last time she smiled or felt that surge of joy. "But, I'm thrilled I was wrong."

Chapter 21

Taylor jolted awake on the sharp edge of a nightmare at just past three in the morning. She made coffee, planning on taking a cup up to her bedroom to sit in her window seat. She went into the office instead, figuring hotels were open twenty-four seven. There was no reason she couldn't call them at this time of the morning. She picked up where she left off on her list.

She was down to her last call when a text message from Cail came through.

You up?

Smiling at her phone, she responded, *'Yeah, you?'* She had to laugh. He couldn't have gotten much sleep yesterday.

I'm dying. I'd give my left eye to be snuggled up in bed with you right now.

She was about to respond when another text came through.

Oh, shit, sorry. I should have picked another body part.

Taylor brushed her fingers over her scarred left eyelid.

Keep your body parts. I'm kind of partial to them all.

He texted a smiley face then several kissing faces.

She made the last call on her list, striking out on every one. She had to be staying somewhere. It was too cold out to be sleeping in a car. At least, it was too cold for people not used to living on the streets. She'd have given anything for a car to sleep in at times in her life, even in the dead of winter.

She got up and stretched. She still had time to go out for a good run before work. If Siobhan Silva was out there, watching her, all the better. She could rely on her intuition for that. If someone was watching her, she'd know.

* * *

"It's all about the diamonds. Callie must have mentioned them to you at some point." Chris picked up her coffee and sipped while Raine sat stiff shouldered, staring down at her hands.

Her head was clear this morning, which was a surprise after the amount of beer she consumed last night. "Did she ever mention someone named Angela?"

Raine's head flicked up and she met Chris's gaze for a moment before lowering her head again.

Yeah, you know her, Chris thought. Or, you know of her. "She may have referred to her as Sass."

When Raine didn't respond, Chris wanted to throw her coffee cup across the room. "Goddamnit, Raine. She's still out there. Until we have her behind bars, your life is in danger. Do you get that?"

Raine's head came up, slowly this time. "I don't have the diamonds."

Chris stabbed her hand through her hair. She wanted to say neither did Bonkers, but couldn't bring herself to do it. "I think she knows that. But, she wants to find out who does have them and you're her ticket to that." She set her coffee on the table and leaned closer to Raine. "What are you afraid of? Why won't you talk?"

"I …" Raine began then clamped down again. "Am I going to jail?"

"Why would you think that? You weren't involved in the theft of the diamonds."

"As an accessory?"

Chris shook her head. "Who the fuck told you that?"

"The police officer who came to my room at the hospital. The RCMP officer."

"St. James?" That fucker.

"Yes, I think that was his name. He said if I talked to you, I'd be arrested for obstruction of justice or something."

"Why didn't he want you to talk to me?"

"He said it was the RCMP's case and the Toronto Police had no business or jurisdiction to get involved in it."

"That's bullshit. You're not going to jail, especially if you tell the truth about what you know. What did you tell him, Raine?"

Raine sighed and, staring down at her lap, started to talk.

* * *

Chris walked into the Sex Crimes Unit wearing a black pant suit with a silk shirt in charcoal beneath it. A long, black wool coat was slung over her arm. She wasn't surprised to see St. James sitting at a desk on the far side of the unit with a direct view of her office door.

"Okay, listen up," she called out. "I've got a couple of announcements." She waited until the room quieted. "Detective Danny Stone has taken a cushy position with Media Relations." It would allow Danny to be home with her kids in the evenings and on weekends. Chris couldn't blame her for grabbing the opportunity. "Danny will be missed as a member of this team and I wish her well in her new position.

"Secondly, I will be taking a week's vacation beginning Christmas Day. I'll be in most of today and for a few hours tomorrow morning, then Detective Sergeant Blake will be in charge.

"Blake, my office. Sinclair, I need coffee."

Blake followed Chris into her office and waited while she hung up her coat. "Have you got court today?" It was rare to see Chris dressed up.

"No, a funeral."

"Oh. Anyone I know?"

Chris shook her head, unwilling to explain the whole situation with her estranged family. "I need to bring you and Sinclair up to speed with the Delacourte/Cruise investigation. This probably isn't the best time for me to take off on a vacation, but I trust you. If anyone can wrap this shit up, it's you."

"I appreciate your confidence in me, Sarge."

Taylor stepped in balancing three mugs of coffee. She brought one for Blake too, hoping to get on her good side. She set the coffees on Chris's desk, picked up her own, and started to leave.

"Close the door and take a seat, Sinclair. I need to give you and DS Blake an update."

Taylor did as she was asked and took a seat next to Blake in front of Chris's desk. Chris remained standing, pacing back and forth.

"Raine Delacourte showed up on my doorstep last night. I sat down with her this morning and interviewed her. It turns out she was aware of Callie's previous career as a thief. All she knows is what Callie told her, so it's essentially hearsay. She stated Callie and Siobhan met in college. They began their string of thefts after Callie, or Lily at the time, laid out a plan to steal a painting from a house she'd visited during a wedding. Raine didn't know how the Runes came into play, though Silva was apparently into Runes.

After Callie moved here, she decided to do one last job - the diamonds. She thought committing another heist while Silva was in prison would remove the suspicion from them. Raine doesn't know who she did the job with. Apparently, they split the diamonds. Callie held on to hers, waiting for the heat to die down."

"Does she know how Will St. James ties into all of this?" Taylor asked.

"She never met him before he visited her in the hospital and threatened her with accessory and obstruction of justice if she talked to the Toronto Police."

"It's not looking good for him," Blake said.

"No, but I still don't have anything solid on him. I've requested the case file from Inspector Harmon Jessop, St. James's superior in Banff, and should have it within the hour." Chris glanced at her watch. "As I'll be out of the office for a couple of hours this morning, you can read through it, Blake."

"In other news," Taylor began, "I called every hotel and hostel I could find and drew a big blank. I went through Silva's neighbourhood on my run this morning. I know she's hanging in that area, but I didn't see her or get a vibe of where she might be staying."

"Any Air BNB's in that area?" Chris asked. "Rooms for rent on a short-term basis?"

Taylor frowned. "I never thought of those."

"Check into it." Chris took a last swig of Taylor's excellent coffee. "While you're doing that, I'll update the inspector."

"Mind if I go with?" Blake said as she rose to her feet. "It wouldn't hurt for me to get some experience reporting to the brass."

Chris opened the door to find Gayle Lansing standing there with her hand up as if she was about to knock.

"Oh, pardon me, Detective Sergeant. I wanted to give you an update on what I found on Silva's laptop."

Chris took a step back and motioned Lansing in before closing the door again. "What have you got?"

"There were several files deleted on Thursday at approximately 1900 hours."

"Uh-huh," Chris said. That would have been when St. James was in possession of the laptop. "Were you able to retrieve those files?"

"Well, one of them was a thread of text messages. The messages are unretrievable, but I've got the number they were to or from."

"Text messages? On her laptop?"

"Yes. She synced her iPhone to the MacBook, so any text messages to her phone also come into the message app on the MacBook."

"Okay."

"The thing is, the number is registered to an RCMP officer."

"Let me guess," Chris said with a sneer. "Will St. James."

"Yes. That's right. I was able to retrieve the other deleted file. It was a screen shot of a memorial on the Toronto Star website."

"Callie Delacourte."

"Right again."

"Thank you, Ms. Lansing. That's very helpful."

"You're welcome. Um, there's one more thing." She set the laptop on Chris's desk. "May I show you?"

Chris nodded while Lansing opened the laptop and tapped on the keyboard, opening a website. An image displayed on the screen. A live shot of Chris's office.

Chris looked from the laptop up to the bookcase on the wall behind her desk. She walked over to it and held her finger up as she scanned the shelves for a camera.

"A little to your left," Lansing said.

Chris moved her finger to the left.

"Right there."

She stopped and pulled out a hardcover book on interrogation techniques. Inside the book was a small camera with the lens facing the spine of the book. "Son of a bitch. Is that recorded or only in real time?"

"It's backed up to the website."

"When was it installed? Can you tell?"

"Yes, ma'am. Last Wednesday at approximately 0300 hours."

"The same day St. James arrived." Fucker. She opened her office door and looked across the room to the desk St. James was using. He wasn't there. She handed the book to Lansing. "See if you can track that camera. Let's see if it's an RCMP device."

"Ah, will do, but I can tell you right now it's a cheap, electronics store type camera."

"Does it have audio?"

"No, just video."

"Well, that's a relief."

When Lansing left, Taylor asked, "Was that a real book?"

Chris shook her head. "No."

"That's too bad. I would have like to have read it."

Chris and Blake broke out laughing.

* * *

It didn't take long to update Inspector Worthington and Inspector

DuBois. Worthington told Chris to send him a copy of the RCMPs case file and he'd call Inspector Jessop himself.

When Chris got back to her office, Lane appeared in her doorway in a sleek black dress. She took one look at Chris's outfit and said, "You're going to the funeral."

"Yeah."

Lane took a seat, crossing her legs at the ankle. "I don't know whether to go or not. I'm so damn angry with her."

She should have thought to ask Lane. If she hadn't been so screwed up by all of it, she would have. "I've got Taylor and Kate coming with me for support. It would be nice to have you there, too."

Lane's lips curved up slightly. "Well, you've just given me a good reason to go."

Chris lifted a shoulder then let it drop. "Up to you."

Lane stood, went around the desk and laid a hand on Chris's shoulder. "Why are you going?"

"I don't know, exactly. She was my mother and, in the end, she tried to make amends for her behaviour. I don't know if I can ever forgive her or squash the resentments I have towards her, but I feel like I should go." She couldn't face the guilt if she didn't.

"Then I'll go for you. Call me when you're leaving and I'll meet you in the garage."

When Lane left, Chris opened her email to find the Rune Crew file in her inbox. She forwarded it to Worthington, Blake, and Sinclair then opened the attachment to scan the file. As far as she could tell, he'd done a thorough investigation. The only issue was St. James hadn't been able to identify the second subject or locate Lily De La Cruz. And that was just bullshit, she thought.

"Sarge?"

Chris glanced up at Taylor. "Yeah?"

"It doesn't look like that area runs to Air BNB's, but there were a few rooms for rent by the week that I'd like to check out. Maybe we could hit her neighbourhood with a photo after the funeral."

"Yeah, let's do that."

"I brought a change of clothes-"

"No, stay in uniform and we'll hit the streets right after the service." Chris closed out her email. "The name of the insurance company that insured the diamonds is Alberta Alliance. Find out what you can."

"Right." Taylor went back to her desk and Googled Alberta Alliance then picked up her phone and called their offices in Banff. It took several minutes to get through to someone who had any information on the diamond heist, but when she did, she hit pay dirt.

She went back to Chris's office. "Sarge?"

"Yeah."

"Alberta Alliance hires private investigators to recover stolen goods. They get a nice finders' fee."

"Yeah, I think that's standard."

"Yeah, but fifty percent of the diamonds were recovered and a million dollar fee was paid to the private investigator who brought them in."

Chris just stared at Taylor, waiting for the punch line.

"The P.I. in this case was Angela St. James."

"Fucking A."

Chapter 22

The sidewalk was lined with reporters as the four women walked, shoulder to shoulder, through the mob and started up the steps to St. Patrick's Catholic Church. Three sets of double doors spanned the top of the stairs under curved grey stone archways, the centre set gaping open. They were almost to the top when two burly men in identical black suits stepped out and blocked their entrance. Both men were tall with broad, bulky shoulders and short dark hair. Armand and Alexandre St. Amour glared at their sister.

Armand took one step forward. "You're not welcome here."

"Then you shouldn't have made it into a public spectacle," Chris said, glaring right back.

Taylor and Kate stepped in front of Chris, one from her right and one from her left. "You can't prevent anyone from entering a church," Kate informed Armand. "Step aside."

Alexandre snorted out a laugh and flexed his muscles in his dark suit as he stepped up next to Armand. Chris pushed between Kate and Taylor. "I don't think your father would appreciate a scene with the media two feet away." She glanced over her shoulder at the crowd on the sidewalk below. "Either you step aside, or I make sure they know exactly why you don't want me here and how I got this bruise on my face. What would that do in his bid for the Ontario Premiership?"

The brothers looked at each other, grim faced. Alexandre turned to Chris, sneering. "Wait here." He turned and disappeared through the double doors.

"Aww, he needs to check with daddy," Chris said and received a death glare from Armand as Taylor and Kate laughed.

By the time he came back, there was a line up on the steps behind them. Alexandre looked at Armand, nodding his head toward the inside of the church. The brothers walked back inside.

"Assholes," Kate said.

"You won that round," Lane said. "But, you need to be careful, Chris. They won't take that lightly."

She didn't imagine they would, but she wasn't the defenceless kid she used to be either. She almost wished one of them would try something then remembered where she was. She hadn't been to church since her parents disowned her, but it didn't diminish the fear of God that had been instilled in her as a child. Her eyes drifted up to the alter at the front of the church. "Sorry," she whispered and barely managed to refrain from crossing herself.

They found a seat midway down the aisle.

"You should walk right up to the front and take a seat with the family," Lane whispered.

"I wouldn't sit with them if you paid me."

* * *

The service seemed to go on forever. Chris couldn't wait to get back outside and take a long inhale of crisp, cold air. As she stepped through the doors into the foyer, Armand came out from behind the door, grabbed Chris's arm, wrenching her shoulder, and forced her through a door across the hall. Taylor and Kate were right on their heels, but the door slammed in their faces. The click of a deadbolt sliding into place echoed through the anteroom.

Armand twisted her arm behind her back as he shoved her to the floor at her father's feet in the dark, wood panelled office. She swore she heard something pop in her shoulder, but she'd be damned if she let Sebastien see her pain. Armand went to stand next to his brother at the door and Chris laid her hand on the grip of her weapon, stifling a wince as a sharp pain shot from her shoulder to her fingertips. Sebastien St. Amour stood, leaning against an ancient, intricately carved desk with his arms crossed over his chest. She lifted her narrowed eyes to his.

"Assault, abduction, and forcible confinement of a police officer."

Sebastien sneered down at her. "Do you really think you could make any of that stick?"

A loud bang on the door reverberated through the room, and Chris's bones.

"Do you really think I can't?"

Another boom shook the room as Taylor and Kate burst through the door. Both had their weapons out and trained them on Alexandre and

Armand.

Chris drew hers out of its holster and aimed it at Sebastien's face using her left hand to support her right forearm. The urge to pull the trigger had her finger twitching. Or maybe it was just the pain. She got to her feet and began backing up towards the door, keeping her eyes on Sebastien. She had no doubt all three of them were armed.

"A word of caution," Sebastien said in a calm, quiet voice. "Keep you mouth shut and stay away from my family."

"Or what?" Chris asked.

Sebastien's response was a lewd smile.

As they stepped outside, Chris hoped that was the last time she would step foot in a Catholic Church. She drew in the cool, crisp air she'd been desperate for.

Kate squeezed her hand. "You okay?"

She nodded and they started down the steps with Lane and Taylor behind them and rows of reporters in front of them. God, she was tempted to walk up to them and start blabbing. It would serve Sebastien right. "Fucker."

"That's twice now we should have arrested him, Chris. I don't like letting him get away with this shit."

Chris twisted her lips up in a tight smile. "Neither do I." They turned left on the sidewalk, heading away from the reporters.

"Taylor. DS Cain. Can you tell us your connection to Eléane St. Amour?" A reporter shouted.

Would love to, Chris thought. "Just paying our respects." She reached in her pocket for her keys and another sharp pain sliced through her shoulder. Damn it. "Fucker," she muttered again. She reached back with her left hand and passed the keys to Taylor. "You drive."

Taylor's mouth dropped open, but she didn't say anything. Chris was looking a bit pale. Besides, the front seat was more accommodating to her long legs. She turned to Lane. "Something's not right."

"I noticed," Lane said. Chris thought she was doing a fine job disguising her pain, but her face was pale with a green tinge to it and she was favouring her right arm. "I don't care what she tells you, you're driving us straight to the hospital."

Oh, crap.

* * *

When Chris didn't resist going to emergency, Taylor thought it must be bad, but thankfully that wasn't the case. Her shoulder had been wrenched badly, but would just need time to heal. In the meantime, she wore a sling to immobilize it.

There was a reason for Chris's lack of resistance. She wanted her shoulder examined to document the injury. She had Kate photograph the bruises on her arm and requested a copy of the CT Scan from the doctor.

Then she placed a call to Inspector Worthington, asking him to request an audience for her with the Chief of Police for a personal matter.

"What are you up to?" Kate asked.

"We haven't arrested him yet, but that doesn't mean we're not going to. I just need to ensure it's airtight and he can't weasel out of it."

"So, what? You're going to ask the Chief to make sure his contacts don't squash his charges."

"Yeah, that and I'm going to arrange for him to be arrested in the presence of the media." She'd use Taylor's contact with Cheryl Starr from the National News.

"Shit, Chris. This is just going to piss him off even more." She rested her hip on the edge of the gurney and clung to Chris's good hand. "And that scares the shit out of me."

Chris raised Kate's hand to her lips, pressed a kiss to her knuckles. "Have I told you yet today how much I love you?"

"Hmph," Kate said. "Love you, too."

"I'm not a scared kid anymore, Kate. I'll be damned if I let him intimidate or threaten me. I think it's time *he* learned to fear me."

The edge of Kate's mouth curled up. "Now, that I like."

To Chris's astonishment, Inspector Worthington called her back within minutes to inform her the Chief would see her as soon as she got back to Headquarters.

Taylor and Chris dropped Kate and Lane off and rode the elevator up to the Sex Crimes Unit. Chris dropped her coat off in her office and approached Taylor's desk. "I need you to write up witness statements. One for today and one for when he backhanded me at the hospital."

"You're going to arrest him?"

"I'm working on it. I'm going up to see the Chief. When I get back, we'll hit the streets, see if we can find Silva's hole."

Taylor watched Chris walk away. She was one tough cookie, but she couldn't help the fear crawling up her spine and tingling the back of her neck. Sebastien St. Amour wasn't someone to mess with.

Chapter 23

Chris gave Chief Maddison Clark the condensed version of her family history then detailed the events at the hospital when Sebastien clocked her and the incident at the church. She explained Sebastien had connections he would use to get the charges dropped.

"What connections? Who?" Clark frowned at her. "I can assure you he has no ties to this office."

"I'm sorry if I inferred he did. I came to you because I'm certain he doesn't. I know he's got strategic connections, but I don't know who. I'm hoping laying these charges will flush them out and I can deal with them individually."

"How?"

"Simple. I'll pay them a visit and explain that I'll reveal the identity of those protecting him to the media if his charges are dropped."

Clark tapped her pen on the date book laying open in front of her. It wasn't a bad plan, but definitely not worth the risks, and there would be risks for Chris, for a few measly assault charges. "If we do this, Cain, we charge him with everything, including the abuse when you were a child."

Chris slumped back in her chair. She knew Clark was right, but damned if she wanted the whole media circus Taylor went through and that's exactly what she could expect. The alternative was to do nothing and let him become the next Premier of Ontario. And that just didn't sit right in her belly. "Can I have a few hours to think it over?"

"You may," Clark said as she stood. She knew the evidence was there after reading the medical reports herself. Add to that Dr. McIntyre's testimony and they had a solid case. "But, you've already made your decision, Detective Sergeant."

She supposed she had. "Yeah, but I need to work out the details.

This is going to be one hell of a media shit show and I'm going away on vacation the day after tomorrow."

"Maybe you should consider waiting until after your vacation to follow through."

Chris kind of liked the idea of being out of the country while the shit hit the fan, but that would be the coward's way out.

On the way back down to her office, she called Lane's receptionist and made an appointment for the end of the day. She slipped into her office, grabbed her coat, and turned to find Taylor in the doorway.

"Statements?"

"Emailed to you. I wanted to ask you about the letters Bonkers' wrote to her daughter."

"Oh, yeah. I don't suppose we need those now."

"No. May I contact her daughter and offer them to her?"

"Taylor, we're not even sure if she's aware she's adopted. It could be traumatic for her."

"I know. I thought I'd go see the parents, ask their permission." At Chris's hesitation, she added, "If I was her daughter, I'd want the letters. Her birth mother loved her very much. She should know that."

Hell, she had to be proud of Taylor for the great compassion she had despite a shitty life. "Yeah, go ahead."

* * *

As Taylor drove them to Silva's neighbourhood, Chris updated her on Sebastien and her plan to prevent him from weaselling out of the charges. Taylor remained silent, even after she finished.

"You don't like it." Chris finally said, her nerves ratcheting up with every moment of silence.

"I don't like the position it puts you in. He's dangerous, Chris. We both know that."

"Yeah, but if this plays out like I hope it will, he won't be able to touch me from a cell."

"Armand and Alexandre will still be walking the streets. He'll have them do his dirty work."

"They try anything and they'll be joining him in a cell." Fuckers. "I'm not going to let him hurt me again. Fuck that. I'm damned sure not going to run scared. I'm not that weak kid anymore. Sebastien St. Amour will learn that pretty damn quick if he tries to fuck with me."

Taylor nodded as she pulled into a parking spot at the curb. It was the determination in her voice, laced with a bit of anger, that convinced her Chris was more than ready for this. "Okay. Whatever you need,

I'm here."

"Just like that?"

"Of course." Chris had been there for her when it became public knowledge that Sarah Johnston molested her for years, so it was the least she could do. Besides, they were friends.

"Alright. I need to set up a meeting with Cheryl Starr."

"Oh, boy. You're really going to do this."

"I'm going to make damn sure the charges stick is what I'm going to do."

They spent the next two hours talking to people on the street, in the shops, and at the rent by the week places Taylor found online. Silva had been in a few of the shops and a few people recognized her, but no one had seen her within the past day and she wasn't staying at any of the rental places.

"We should hit the gay bars," Taylor suggested. "She could have picked someone up and is staying with her."

Chris smiled as she absently rubbed her shoulder. "Let's go back to Les Beau's. Chances are, if she picked up, it would have been there."

Sam was working the bar, so Chris headed straight for her.

"Hey, I have Callie's file for you. I called and left you a message."

"Yeah, sorry. We've been busy."

Sam nodded to the sling, visible through Chris's open coat, and at the bruise on her cheek. "Looks like it. What happened now?"

"Ran into some shady characters. Listen, was Siobhan Silva dating anyone, interested in anyone?"

"Siobhan? Oh, Lian, right." Sam swiped a rag over the clean bar. "Not that I know of." She called across the bar for Gloria and waved her over. "Did Lian have the hots for anyone?"

"Hard to tell with that quiet little mouse. Her eyes were always scoping, if you know what I mean. But, I never saw her make a play for anyone."

"Did those eyes scope anyone in particular?" Taylor asked.

Gloria grinned and ran her eyes up and down Taylor's long body. "Besides you, you mean?" She giggled as Taylor's colour rose. "Oh, she couldn't take her eyes off you the night you were in." The smile dropped away as she remembered Lian looking like that once before. "Actually, she was very attentive to a dark haired woman who came in a few times. I don't know her name and I haven't seen her in a week or two."

"Description?" Chris asked.

"Long, dark hair, brown eyes. Maybe five-six, five-seven. Slim build." She smiled again with a little seduction behind it. "Small breasts, lush lips."

"She come in with anyone?"

"No, I don't think so. Sat at the bar, alone, drinking Bud Lite from the bottle."

"Okay. Thanks." Chris and Taylor stepped out onto the sidewalk with the sun peeking out from behind the clouds. "So, what did we learn, Sinclair?"

"That Siobhan Silva has a type - slim brunettes with small breasts." Callie Delacourte, the woman Gloria described, and Taylor all shared those traits.

Chris laughed, shoving one hand in her pocket and using it to keep her coat from blowing open as they made the trek back to her car. "Besides that?"

Taylor shrugged. "Silva may be shacking up with the woman Gloria saw?"

"Possible."

"Impossible to track her down with a vague description."

"Yeah, but we won't need to track her down. Silva will make a play for one of us. She has to figure we have the diamonds and that's what she's after."

"Then why rape Raine and Bonkers? Why kill Bonkers?" It made no sense. She could have gotten the information she wanted without resorting to such violence.

"I figure she acquired a taste for it when she raped Callie. Or Lily. She thinks she can get the location of the diamonds by hurting them, so why not have a little fun while she's at it?" She hit the remote to unlock her vehicle, tossed the keys to Taylor, and climbed in the passenger side, gazing straight ahead. "Check with Missing Persons to see if they have anything that matches with the description of the woman that Gloria just gave us."

"You think Silva may have assaulted or killed her?"

"Silva's not going to stop. If we don't find her, she'll kill again."

"Then we need to find her, before she hurts anyone else."

"We will. She'll come to us." She just hoped it was her Silva came for and not Taylor.

* * *

After checking with Missing Persons and getting nothing, Taylor sat at her desk and dug deeper into Angela St. James's life. Her net worth was somewhere upwards of fifty million dollars. That's a heck of a lot of recoveries, she figured.

Why didn't Will St. James's finances show some of that wealth? Wouldn't he have gotten some kind of settlement in the divorce?

She had her own private investigations firm, Keller Investigations. Small, but very successful with the majority of her business focused on recovering stolen goods for insurance companies Canada wide. She used her maiden name for the business, so why wouldn't she take that name back after the divorce or change the business name to St. James Investigations? Didn't matter, Taylor thought.

The business address was a post office box. Did that mean she worked from home or a virtual office? Taylor wondered. Keller Investigations' website listed services, an about page, and testimonials from clients, which Taylor spent several minutes perusing before deciding it seemed legit.

She'd pass it all by Chris because she couldn't figure out where Angela St. James played into this whole thing. Did she steal the diamonds with Lily De La Cruz or did she just recover half of them? How was Will St. James involved?

She picked up her phone when it rang, still pondering the St. James connection. "PC Sinclair."

"Taylor, it's Emma. I couldn't get you on your cell."

"Ah." Taylor pulled her phone out of her pocket and discovered the battery was dead. "Sorry. I need to charge it."

"I need to talk to you about this charity. I've got people calling up wanting to donate. You'll need to set up a non-profit business account and we need a name."

"People are calling up to donate?"

"After your speech the other day, the phone's been ringing off the hook. We can discuss fundraisers, too, but we need the name of the centre."

Taylor pulled her glasses from her face and rubbed her eyes. "Beneath My Wings."

"Beneath My Wings," Emma repeated. "I love it. It speaks of protection and a safe place."

"It's a song Leila used to sing to me."

"Right. Wind Beneath My Wings."

"Yeah, that's it."

"That's great. Set up the account and apply for a business number. I'll let people know to make their cheques out to Beneath My Wings."

Taylor rubbed her eyes again. Accounts, business numbers ... how was she supposed to know how to do all that? "Okay, fine." Cail would know or at least he would point her in the right direction.

"You could organize an event in the spring to raise money and awareness. What do you think?"

Holy, crap. She rubbed at her chest which grew tighter the more Emma talked. "Em, how am I supposed to figure all of this stuff out, work full time, and get a resource centre up and running?"

"Easy. Hire a PA."

* * *

"How's the shoulder?" Lane asked as Chris walked into her office.

"Sore, but I'll live." She sat in one of the comfy, white leather chairs and leaned back. "I talked to the Chief about arresting Sebastien. I thought if we hit him with assault charges, we may flush out the contacts protecting him."

"And?" Lane already talked to Chief Clark, but she wanted to hear it from Chris.

"She thinks if we're going to take the risk, we should go all the way and include the charges of child abuse."

"If *you* are going to take the risk, not we. He's a dangerous man and if the charges somehow don't stick or he uses his sons for retribution, you're putting yourself in grave danger, Chris."

"So, you think I shouldn't pursue the charges?"

Lane walked to her window and stared out. It was such a blurred line when you were dealing with someone you cared for deeply. "No, I think pursuing the charges is necessary. I'm just scared to death for your safety."

Chris got up and walked to the window, stood next to Lane and stared out at the growing darkness. "I'm not that kid anymore. I know how to protect myself."

"I know that." Lane slipped her hand into Chris's. "And still." She shook off the feeling of apprehension with a sigh. "You sure you're ready for this? You've been so resistant to talk about it all the years I've known you."

"I don't know that I'm ready, but it's time." Not just for herself. For every citizen of the province who would be under his rule if he made Premier. "We have enough to charge him with physical and sexual abuse of a minor."

"We do." With Chris's medical records from the night she was disowned by her family, her testimony, plus Lane's own testimony, there was enough to get a conviction.

"We have more."

"More?"

"My mother and her friend, Dr. Sylvie Raynard-"

Lane's mouth dropped open. "I know Sylvie."

"I figured," Chris said. "They put together a package for me with pictures of my injuries and Sylvie's reports every time she treated me. My mother kept records of every time he hit me as well. I have notarized statements from both of them."

Lane continued to stare out the window and said nothing for some time. "She did care."

"She was basically his prisoner for the past thirty years. She tried to get away with me a few times, but he always found her. When he brought us back, it wasn't her he hurt."

Lane closed her eyes. "I could have helped her, if she'd only said."

"Yeah, me too."

"So, you'll put him away. As long as whoever he has protecting him doesn't get in the way."

"I think I may have some leverage there, but I need to know who they are first."

"The Chief said you're taking a holiday. Will you wait until you come back?"

"Yeah."

"Good." Some of the tension drained from Lane's shoulders. At least Chris wasn't rushing into this hastily. It gave them time to form a plan to ensure Chris's safety. "It's good you're going on a vacation. I've never known you to take one before."

Chris laughed. "I've never wanted to go on one before. It's Kate's Christmas present, so she doesn't know yet."

Lane's brows shot up and she grinned. "Where are you going?"

"The beach. Mayan Riviera or some shit, near Cancun."

"Oh, it's lovely there. I hope you both have a great time." She wrapped Chris in a warm hug. "Merry Christmas."

"Yeah, Merry Christmas." Chris patted Lane's back awkwardly. "You going to the Worthington's?"

"No, my kids are home for the holidays, so we're going to have a quiet celebration at home."

"Ah, so no hot dates for you?"

Lane laughed and gave Chris's good shoulder a light slap. "I may be getting older, but I'm not dead."

"All the power to you." Chris shot her eyebrows up and down, grinning. "Wish your kids a Merry Christmas from me."

"Will do. Enjoy your holiday. While you're away, I'll look over your medical reports and statement from the night they threw you out and talk to the Chief about his contacts."

Chris gave her another one armed hug. "If we do this, I'm going to need you."

"I'll be here. Right here."

Chapter 24

Taylor followed a flagstone path to the granite steps leading to the front door of a large house decorated with hundreds of clear Christmas lights giving off a soft, warm glow. A Christmas tree, also decorated with clear lights, was visible through sheer curtains. A pine wreath with pine cones, holly berries, and red ribbon hung on a dark red door. Taylor gave it three good knocks.

The woman who answered wore charcoal slacks with a cream blouse and a red apron. Pearl drops hung from her ears and her highlighted blonde hair was pulled back in a messy knot.

"Mrs. Henderson?"

"Yes?"

"My name is Taylor Sinclair. I need to speak to you about your daughter."

"Mel? Is she okay? I know who you are. You're a police officer. Has someone hurt our Mellie?"

"No, she's fine."

"She's not here."

"It's you and your husband I need to speak with."

"You're sure she's alright. She's working tonight. I can call her."

"She's fine, really. I'd like to talk to you about her adoption."

"What? Why? It was a legal adoption."

"This is kind of awkward. Let me explain. Melodie's birth mother passed away recently and I've come into possession of some letters she wrote to Melodie."

She opened the door wider and motioned Taylor in. "Maybe you should come in. I'll make coffee."

She led Taylor into the living room where the tree glowed brightly, setting off the red, gold, and crystal decorations. There were more presents beneath it than Taylor had seen in her lifetime. She supposed it was pretty and the warm light was calming.

Mrs. Henderson came back in with a tray of coffee and her husband, a man in his late forties with light brown hair and a slight bulge in his belly. "This is my husband, Jack. Jack, Taylor Sinclair."

Taylor stood to shake his hand while Mrs. Henderson poured coffee.

"I don't understand why you're here. Carolina said you wanted to talk about Mellie's birth mother."

"Yes. Elizabeth Cruise was killed a few days ago."

"Can you tell us what happened? Was there an accident?" Carolina asked. She poured three cups of coffee and handed one to Taylor then set the cream and sugar next to her cup.

"No." Taylor hadn't done a notification before and this was very much like that, even though these people probably never met Elizabeth Cruise. "She was murdered."

"I'm sorry to hear that, but Mellie has never met her."

Taylor added cream and sugar to the coffee then sat back in her chair. "I know. I came into possession of some letters Elizabeth wrote to Melodie and I thought Melodie should have them, but I wanted to check with you first."

"Why do you think she should have them?" Carolina asked as she took a plate of cookies from the tray and set them in front of Taylor.

"Elizabeth wrote one letter each year, on Melodie's birthday. It's plain in the letters that she loved Melodie very much. She was very fortunate in her adoptive parents, but it might be nice for her to know that her birth mother loved her, too. To know that she wasn't given up because she wasn't wanted, but because Elizabeth wanted her to have a better life than she was able to provide."

Carolina and Jack looked at each other, nodded and smiled.

"She knows she was adopted," Carolina said. "We've been very honest with her there. We told her if she ever decided she wanted to meet her birth mother, we would support her. She hasn't asked. We figured at some point she would, but she wasn't ready yet."

"And now she'll never get that opportunity," Jack said, his brown eyes sad. "You want our permission to give her the letters?"

"Yes. Or I could give them to you."

"Would you mind?" Carolina asked. "She'll need to be told her birth mother is gone and that will be upsetting to her. We'd like to break the news to her ourselves."

Taylor reached into the inside pocket of her long leather coat and pulled out the stack of letters wrapped in a pretty pink ribbon. She passed them to Carolina and stood, having barely sipped the coffee. The Henderson's had some reading to do and she left them to it.

At the door, she turned back to the couple standing side by side, arms wrapped around each other. She envied them, the love so obvious between them over twenty years into their marriage. "I just want to say Mellie is very blessed to have you both for parents."

"Oh, we're not perfect," Carolina said. "But, we love her with all our hearts."

Taylor took a deep breath as she walked back down the flagstone path. It was pointless to wonder what her life would have been like if she'd had parents like the Hendersons or the Worthingtons. Or to wonder at the life her son would have had with the Ripkins had he survived.

Instead of going home to an empty house, she made a quick stop at a toy store, drove to the cemetery where her son was buried, and wandered through the grounds until she came to a gleaming white marble headstone. It was marked simply with his name, Leiland Ripkin, with one date below it - the day of his birth and his death.

The last time she'd been here was for his funeral. She hadn't been able to bear the thought of coming back. She dropped to her knees and ran her fingers over his first name. Somewhere out there was a similar marker with the name Leila Sinclair on it. She'd spent too many hours wandering through cemeteries like this one looking for a marker bearing her sister's name and still she didn't know where Leila was. "I'll find you," she whispered.

She took the toy train from her pocket and brushed the snow from the top of the headstone to rest it on top. "I'm sorry I haven't come before now. I don't have an excuse, I just didn't know what to say to you." But, now she did. "I love you, Leiland. I'll always love you."

She adjusted the train, so it sat just so on its perch. "And one of these days, I'll bring your Aunt Leila here to watch over you. Maybe you've already met her, up there in heaven." She smiled at the thought. "If that's so, I know you're well taken care of and well loved." She closed her eyes and tilted her face up to the bright moon. "Love you both."

* * *

Taylor stepped out of her nice, warm car into the arctic air and blowing snow in the Worthington's driveway at seven o'clock in the morning. She dropped off her presents before heading to work, so they wouldn't be sitting in her car for the next few hours.

She went straight up to Lane's office when she arrived at Headquarters and tapped on her door.

Lane looked up from her computer and smiled. "Hello, Taylor. What can I do for you?"

"Uh." Taylor took a step forward, carrying a canvas wrapped in shiny red paper with a cream bow fashioned out of ribbon. "I just wanted to drop off your Christmas present."

Lane got to her feet. "Taylor, you didn't have to do that."

"It's the least I could do after everything you've done for me this year." She laid the canvas on Lane's desk.

"Can I open it now?"

"Yeah, sure." Taylor shrugged.

Lane wasn't as careful at opening presents as Gray. She tore into the paper and ripped it wide open making Taylor laugh. When she revealed the painting beneath the paper she gasped. They'd all gone for a walk on a Provincial trail when they were up at Gray's house in Balton a couple of months ago. Lane had been in awe of a young buck they'd seen come into a clearing to graze for a few moments before wandering off. She'd painted the buck with its beautiful tan pelt and fuzzy, budding antlers as he gazed up at them from where he stood majestically in the clearing. It was signed at the bottom right corner in the way Taylor signed all of her paintings - T. Grace Sinclair.

"Oh, Taylor, it's beautiful. And such a lovely memory."

"I thought you'd like it."

"Can I put it up in here? In my office, where I can see it everyday and my patients can admire it?"

"It's yours. You can put it wherever you want."

Lane embraced Taylor and whispered, "Thank you, so much."

* * *

Blake was already at her desk, so Taylor made her a coffee and took it to her before settling in behind her computer.

Blake held her mug in both hands and propped her booted feet up on the desk. "You planning on working tomorrow?"

"I guess. I'd really like to find Siobhan Silva."

"Any ideas on where she is?"

Taylor updated her on the idea she may be staying with a girl friend.

"We could stake out the neighbourhood. We know she keeps coming back to that vape store."

"It'll be closed tomorrow. It's Christmas." Today, she thought.

Today's when everyone would be out doing last minute shopping before everything closed down for the holiday. Today was their best shot at spotting her on the street.

"Where's my coffee?" Chris asked as she walked up to Taylor's desk.

"I'll make you one on one condition?"

Chris raised an inquiring eyebrow. "Condition?"

"I want to spend the morning on the street. In Silva's neighbourhood."

"No can do. I need to spend the morning with Blake going over everything she'll need to take care of while I'm away."

Taylor only stared at her. If she was with Blake all morning, Taylor was open.

For fuck sakes. Chris rolled her eyes. "Change into plain clothes. If you spot her, you call for backup. Eyes only until they arrive."

"Ten-four, Sarge."

"And call me. I mean it, Taylor."

* * *

Taylor wore a black watch cap in an attempt to conceal her identity and added a pair of mirrored aviator sunglasses. She checked the coffee shops and diners first as that's where she would have headed this early in the morning. She didn't see any sign of Silva, but the coffee she bought for herself kept her hands semi-warm.

When the stores began to open, she hit the vape store. They hadn't seen Silva and didn't expect her in until after Christmas.

She checked a few more places, showing Silva's picture. She'd frequented the small market on the corner, but they hadn't seen her in a few days. She received similar responses from the variety store and a pharmacy. Either she was holing up somewhere or she'd changed locations.

Taylor went back to the vape store and took up a position where she could monitor the street. Her eyes scanned continuously, taking in the last minute shoppers walking in pairs or small groups, people walking with their heads down against the cold, their steps brisk. A nearby novelty shop was playing Christmas music, piping it out to the street. In Christmas's past, this had been one of her favourite pastimes - watching people rushing around, some smiling, some scowling. Many wore Christmas colours, Santa hats or reindeer antlers. Some were drunk, some stoned out of their minds.

Her cell phone rang, startling her. Chris checking up on her, she thought, and answered, "Sinclair."

"What are you doing?" Chris asked in an annoyed tone.

"Standing in the vape store watching the street."

"No, I mean why aren't you at the Worthington's? You were supposed to be here at eleven."

Where had that time gone? she wondered. "I thought I'd keep watch for a while longer."

"Are you avoiding coming here?"

Taylor rolled her eyes, but Chris wasn't wrong. "What do I know about family Christmas's?"

"About as much as I do probably. Get your ass over here."

The whole gift thing made her uncomfortable, both the giving and the receiving. Then, everyone wanted to hug you and how do you get out of that without seeming rude? "Maybe I could just keep an eye out here for a bit longer."

An audible sigh came over the phone. "Taylor, give it up for the day. We'll get her. She'll come to us."

Easy for Chris to say as she'd be in the sunny south starting tomorrow. What if she showed up at Chris's and no one was there? Then what would they do?

Chris sighed again at Taylor's silence. "Get your ass over here, Sinclair. That's an order."

The call ended and Taylor frowned at her phone. That wasn't fair. Now she had to go. She went to the counter and gave the man behind it her card. "If she comes in, text me. Don't let her know I was here looking for her, just notify me when she comes in."

"Right. Will do."

She was at the door when he called out again. "Merry Christmas."

Taylor turned back, smiled. "You, too."

Chapter 25

Silent Night played behind the voices chattering away in the family room as Taylor walked into the Worthington's. The house smelled of apples and spice. And turkey. Rose took her coat and led her through to the family room where everyone was sipping from steaming mugs and nibbling on Christmas baked goods, veggies and dip, cheese and crackers, some kind of Mexican salsa mix with tortilla chips. A lot of food, Taylor thought, considering they'd be eating a big turkey dinner in a few hours.

The mountain of presents surrounding the tree had grown exponentially since she'd stopped by that morning, like a big wave of presents pushed into the middle of the room.

"Sorry I'm late."

"You're here. That's all that matters," Rose said.

Cail came in from the kitchen, gave Taylor a quick peck on the lips and handed her a steaming mug. Whatever was inside it seemed to be the source of the apples and spice scent. "What is it?"

"Hot apple cider." He tapped her nose with the tip of his finger. "You'll like it."

"What's in it?"

"Apple cider," he said with a grin. "And a stick of cinnamon."

"Oh." That explained the piece of wood floating around in it. "It's non-alcoholic?"

Cail laughed. "Did you want alcohol in it?"

"No." She felt like an idiot even though no one was paying her much attention. She took a seat next to Cail on the couch and tuned into the conversations around her.

Chris was filling Callaghan in on the Silva case as Gray listened intently, probably figuring the angles to turn it into a novel. Kate,

Dave, and Cal were in a heated discussion about some sports team Taylor had never heard of. She wasn't even sure what sport they were talking about.

Cail took Taylor's hand and whispered, "You okay?"

She nodded. "Yeah, fine."

"You look a bit like a deer in the headlights."

"Just listening." She blinked a couple of times, hoping she didn't look quite so stunned, then nodded to the tree. "That's a lot of presents."

"Well, there's nine of us, all buying presents for each other."

"Speaking of which ..." Kate grinned at her mother. "Can we open presents now?"

"I swear you're still like a kid when it comes to Christmas," Rose said with a warm smile. "Cal, dear? Why don't you play Santa? We'll start with the stockings."

Stockings wasn't quite the right term for the huge red sacks Cal began to distribute to his children then to Chris and Taylor. Taylor just stared up at him, figuring she probably looked like that deer in the headlights again. "You didn't have to do this."

"Of course we did," Rose said. "We always do stockings for our kids."

Cal brought one more out from behind the tree except this one was a cream colour with abc blocks and assorted kids toys decorating the outside. He gave it to Gray. "For the baby."

"Oh, my. That's very sweet, but you really didn't have to go to all this trouble." She grinned at Cal then Rose. "But, I'm thrilled you did." She began to meticulously untie the fancy ribbon.

Taylor waited until everyone else began to open theirs before she started in on hers. At least she didn't have to do it alone with everyone's attention on her. She pulled open the sack and peeked at the dozens of wrapped presents inside. She only brought one present for everyone and felt miserably guilty.

Cail didn't like the look on Taylor's face, as if she was being tortured. "It's just odds and ends. Stuff we need or fun, silly things."

She nodded and unwrapped the first present she pulled out. Her face turned the colour of Santa's suit as she realized it was three pairs of the lacy boy shorts she preferred from Victoria's Secret. She was still embarrassed when Kate held up some fancy thongs - deep red with black lace and bows.

"Whoohoooo," Kate said, laughing as she twirled them around on her finger.

"Nice." Chris grinned and everyone broke out laughing.

The next present Taylor unwrapped contained a black long sleeved t-shirt and pants in that soft, wicking material.

She was trying to figure out where she would wear them when Rose said, "They're for under your uniform to keep you warm. They're women's small, extra tall, so they should fit."

Never in her life had anyone thought to buy her clothes to wear under her clothes to keep her warm or go to the lengths of finding extra tall which couldn't have been easy. She looked up at Rose, her eyes burning as she clutched the garments to her chest in tight fists.

Everyone else busily tore into their own presents or watched the others unwrapping, but Rose held her gaze, smiling, but with sad eyes. Taylor didn't know what to say, didn't have the words. Thank you didn't seem to be enough.

Cail glanced over at Taylor then put his gifts aside. "Tay?" Maybe this had been a bad idea as she looked completely overwhelmed. She'd only opened two of her gifts and the huge sack sat at her feet filled to capacity. He ran his hand up and down her back. "Angel? Too much?"

Less than a year ago, a bag less than a quarter of the size of the sack in front of her would have held all of her belongings. Did people do this every year? It seemed so excessive. She would have been more than happy if all she received was the top and pants to keep her warm.

The room burst out with laughter again and Taylor looked over at Gray who held up a baby onsie with a horizontal bar that was three quarters blue and one quarter black. Above the bar, it read, 'Diaper loading' and beneath it, 'Please wait...'

Taylor smiled, still clutching the clothes to her chest.

Gray held up another onsie. This one said, 'I'm not just milk drunk, I'm tit faced.' Everyone cracked up and Taylor couldn't help but join in.

"Where on earth did you find these?" Gray asked. "They're hilarious."

"Oh, here and there," Rose said. "I was worried you'd be offended."

"Not at all. I love them." She held up another one with arrows pointing to each of the arm and leg openings, labeled either arm or leg. In the middle it said, 'You can do this Dad'. "I think this one is my favourite." She nudged Callaghan with her shoulder.

"Hey." Callaghan pouted. "I'm sure I can figure it out without instructions."

"My favourite is the tit faced one," Chris said with a cheeky grin and Kate slapped her upper arm. "Do you think I could get a t-shirt with that on it?"

When everyone went back to their sacks, Taylor's was no longer at her feet. She looked around and Cail patted her thigh.

"You can open it later."

She slid her hand into his and relaxed into the back of the couch. "Thank you." Cail's understanding was a gift all its own.

Rose got up, heading into the kitchen, and Taylor followed her.

"I need to apologize," she began.

"No." Rose stopped in the middle of the kitchen and turned back to Taylor. "It's a lot, I understand."

"I don't want to seem ungrateful. It's just … I guess I'm not used to receiving so much. No one's ever given me anything like that before. Well, except Gray when she bought me a bunch of clothes, but no one's ever bought me stuff to keep me warm. I love them. Thank you doesn't seem to be enough."

Rose reached up and laid a hand on Taylor's cheek, astonished no one had ever given this poor girl what she considered necessities. "You're more than welcome. It does my heart good to know how much you appreciate them." She dropped her hand and opened the oven to check on the turkey. "I heard about your plans for a resource centre for street kids and I'm so proud of you. If you need any help, you just let me know. I've worked with a lot of charities. I'd be happy to organize some fundraisers."

And that was another gift. Her hand covered Rose's. "Thank you. It means a lot to me that you'd offer and I can certainly use the help."

* * *

She managed a bit better with the individual gifts, especially when it was time to give out her own. Rose and Cal opened theirs together and Rose gasped when she pulled the paper back and saw the painting - the Toronto skyline at night with the faces of her three children in the dark sky above wearing their police caps and uniforms. Cal's eyes shone with pride as Rose's filled then overflowed.

Rose motioned to the painting over the flickering fireplace. "Would you?" she asked Cal.

He removed the painting above the mantle and replaced it with Taylor's as everyone stood to get a better view.

Cail wrapped his arm around Taylor's shoulders. "That's amazing, Angel."

"That," Cal stabbed his finger towards the painting, "is priceless." He turned to Taylor, not caring about her hephaphobia, and hugged her tight. "Thank you."

Her body was rigid until he released her and Rose took his place. "Now it's my turn to tell you that thank you isn't enough. It's the best present ever."

"You're welcome." She'd be glad when all this gift stuff was over.

Chris and Kate opened their painting next and laughed as they looked for all the leaves poking out from various places on their bodies as they walked, hand in hand, down the path on a Provincial trail in Balton. They'd all had a leaf fight at the top of the trail, shoving leaves up each other's shirts and down their pants. It was the most fun Taylor had ever had.

Then Gray and Callaghan opened the painting Taylor did for the baby's room with a fairy in a bright purple dress sitting on a big, red toadstool. A golden light glowed behind her, fading into a bright green forest behind her and a sparkling, brilliant blue stream at the base of the toadstool. Her gossamer wings were nearly transparent except for the tiny golden lines intricately painted within them.

"I figured babies like bright colours," Taylor said as Gray and Callaghan gaped at the painting. "She'll watch over Gracie while she's sleeping."

Gray's head came up slowly, her bright blue eyes glinting with tears. "It's beautiful."

Taylor figured the one thing Dave would like a painting of most was himself, so she painted him in uniform with a cocky grin on his face. "Cool," he said and laid it at the side of his chair without another word or an acknowledgement of Taylor.

It didn't bother her or surprise her. She got Cail's gift out next and brought it over to him.

"What? I don't get a painting?"

"Sorry."

She sat down next to him and watched as he ripped the paper off the large box then reached into his pocket for a utility to cut through the tape.

When he opened it, he just sat there staring at the Gibson acoustic guitar with mother-of-pearl doves inlaid along the fret board and pic guard. It was exactly like the one he sold to get through his last semester at law school and he knew how much it was worth. "Jesus, Tay. You didn't have to do this."

"After I heard you play at Delaney's, I wanted to."

"What is it?" Rose asked. "Let us see, Cail."

He pulled the guitar out of the box and held it up.

Rose gasped again. "Oh, Taylor." Her hand covered her mouth as her bright blue eyes pooled.

"Holy shit," Kate said. "It just like the one you had."

"Play something for us, son," Cal said with a warm smile.

Cail spent a minute tuning it while Rose turned off the Christmas music playing in the background. Grinning, he started to play a tune then sang *All I Want for Christmas is You* to Taylor.

Cal's gift to Rose came in an envelope. She opened it and pulled out a Christmas card. Inside the card was a picture of building on a beach.

"It's lovely, but I don't understand," Rose said.

"It's our condo in St. Pete's for the next three months."

Rose's mouth dropped open. "You put in for retirement?"

He shook his head. "I'm taking a leave of absence, a trial retirement."

She nodded then went to him and sat on his lap, wrapping her arms around Cal's neck. "Thank you. It's perfect."

She remained on his lap while Chris gave Kate an envelope. Inside she found the eTickets Chris had printed off. "Mexico? You bought us tickets to Mexico?"

"It's an all-inclusive in Playa del Carmen, near Cancun."

"But, I'm starting in homicide in the new year."

"Yeah, but you're off for the next ten days and I had some time coming."

Kate studied the tickets again. "Oh, my God. We're leaving tomorrow morning." She threw herself at Chris forgetting about her tender shoulder. "I haven't been on a vacation like this in years. Thank you, thank you, thank you." With each thank you, she kissed a different spot on Chris's beaming face. "Oh, my God. We hardly have time to pack."

Chris laughed. "How much time can it take to throw some stuff in a suitcase?"

The Worthington's howled with laughter.

"We're talking about Kate here, Chris," Cail said. "You may miss your flight."

When all the gifts were opened, Cail took Taylor's hand and led her up to his room to give her one more gift. "I figured you'd want to open this one in private."

She carefully removed the bow and the wrapping paper then lifted the lid on the small box. Inside was a cheque made out to Taylor in the amount of twenty-five hundred dollars.

"I know it's not much, but it's a donation for your refuge."

Her breath caught and her eyes stung. "Cail, you can't." He still had a massive student loan debt from law school. He couldn't afford to give away so much money.

He took her hands in his. "I wanted to give you something that meant something to you."

"It does. It means everything that you would think to do this, but I'd rather you put it towards your loans."

Shaking his head he said, "No. I had some extra cash because I haven't had to pay rent and I'll be able to save more staying at my parents for a few months while they're away. I want to contribute, Tay. It means a lot to me even if it's just a small amount."

She still would have preferred if he put it against his loans, but she recognized his need to contribute. "Thank you. It's the best present ever, but…"

"No, Angel. No buts."

She looked up at him with a twinkle in her eyes. *"But … you need to make it out to Beneath My Wings,* so I can write you a tax receipt."

"Beneath My Wings," he repeated with a grin. "It's perfect."

She wrapped her arms around his neck and hugged him tight. "Thank you, so much." It was like the old Cail was back. The one who was patient and empathetic and compassionate. She just hoped he stayed. "I've got something else for you, too." She stepped away from him and reached into her pocket. "It's not really a gift though. It's already yours." She handed him his watch.

"Ah, God." He looked at the watch for a moment. "I don't deserve this." Then he gave her a cheeky grin. "But, I'm not giving it back. And I'll make damn sure I don't lose it this time."

Chapter 26

After dinner, the women went into the kitchen to tackle the dishes while the men sat in the family room holding their full bellies.

"Dave didn't buy one gift," Kate complained. "I swear to God, next year I'm not getting him anything. Selfish bastard."

"Don't be too hard on him," Rose said as she loaded plates into the dishwasher.

Kate leaned back against the counter and crossed her arms over her chest. "Don't you get tired of babying him? Maybe a little tough love would be good for him."

Rose straightened and laid her hand on her lower back trying to ease the ache. She'd had this argument too many times to go through it again. "Maybe it would." Lord knew nothing else had, but there was a reason they put up with so much from their younger son and Kate knew it. "Now's not the time though."

Kate rolled her eyes behind her mother's back. "It never is," she muttered and picked up a tea towel to dry the pots and pans Taylor was washing.

"I'm sorry if this upsets you, Rose," Gray said. "But, I have to agree with Kate. I mean, most of us bought our gifts and it's not like we spent a huge amount of money, but Taylor made hers and it had to have taken her hours and hours. If he was my son, I'd have taken him by the ear, stood him up, and made him say thank you."

"You don't understand. None of you understand."

"Mum," Kate said, her eyes oozing sympathy. "Look at who your talking to. All three of them."

Rose looked at Gray, knowing her story. She looked at Chris, knowing her story. Then at Taylor, knowing hers, and dropped her head in shame. "I owe all of you an apology. I'm sorry."

"He was sexually assaulted," Chris stated.

Rose's head flew up and she glared at Chris. "Don't let him hear you say that. Don't ever let him hear you say that."

"I'm sorry, but it doesn't excuse that kind of behaviour. Maybe he uses it as an excuse to behave like an asshole, but it doesn't make it okay."

Taylor's phone signalled an alert. "Oh, geez. I'm sorry. That's the motion sensor on my door cams." She took the tea towel from Kate, dried her hands, and pulled her phone out of her pocket. She opened the camera app and stood watching the footage from her front door. "Chris?"

"Yeah." She got up from her perch at the island and went over to look at Taylor's phone.

The video showed a person wearing a dark ball cap pulled low on their forehead wearing a dark puffy coat and carrying a blue-green tool box.

"Silva," Chris said.

They watched as she used lock picks to open the door then disappeared inside. Chris was on her phone before the door closed. Kate rushed out to the family room for her father and brothers.

"I've got two unmarkeds heading over to watch the front and back of the house in case she comes out before we get there," Chris said as soon as she ended her call. Here's what we're going to do." She pointed at Taylor. "You're going to drive in the back like normal only you'll have Cail and Kate in the car with you. Go in through the garage, but be careful. She'll be lying in wait where she can surprise you and knock you out."

"The hell she will," Cail said.

"I'll be on the front door," Chris continued.

"I'm with you," Callaghan said.

"As am I," Cal said. He cuffed Dave up the back of his head when he stood there saying nothing.

"Ah, yeah, me too." He rubbed the back of his head, pouting.

"You don't want to call in the Emergency Task Force?" Cal asked.

"There's enough of us to handle one small woman. As far as we know, she'll be carrying a knife, but she doesn't have a gun." When she got a nod from him, she went back to planning the op. "Clear the basement then unlock the door for us on your way up the stairs."

"You don't think she'll be in the basement," Taylor stated.

"I think she'll be in your room, setting up. Will she hear the garage door from your room?"

Taylor shook her head.

"And your room faces the front, so she won't see you." She nodded, paced back and forth. "Yeah, she'll be in your room. She won't be expecting you home from work for another hour or so. Be as quiet as you can. Shoes off. Callaghan, Dave, and the Inspector will clear the main floor while we head upstairs. We clear every room before we hit Taylor's.

"Any questions?" She was met with silence. "Okay, let's clear out."

Gray and Rose stood at the front door as they all drove off.

"I hate being the one left behind," Rose said.

Gray smiled. "We could take your car, park in the laneway across the street from the house."

Rose gaped at Gray. "Callaghan would kill me. You're about two months away from delivering a baby for goodness sakes."

"It's not like we'll be in the danger zone."

Rose put her hands on her hips, staring out the door. She really did hate being left out of the action all the time. "Okay, but we park well away from the house."

Gray's smile spread into a grin. "I'll get my coat."

* * *

Taylor had her earphones in with Chris on the other end of her phone. As she approached her back gate, Cail and Kate bent over in the back seat. "Driving through the gate."

"Ten-four. We're walking up the street, almost at your place now."

Taylor pulled into the garage and they all got out of the car, pulling their weapons out as they approached the door leading to basement level of the house.

"Entering the basement," Taylor whispered.

"Ten-four. Keep the line open."

Kate eased the door open and Cail and Taylor went in, one to the right, one to the left, weapons raised as they scanned using only pen lights. It was mostly open space except for a small powder room and the utility room. Kate checked the utility room and Taylor the powder room and they all met back at the bottom of the stairs.

"All clear," Taylor whispered. "Heading to you."

She let Chris, Cal, Callaghan, and Dave in and they all toed off their boots. They tip-toed up the stairs with Cal, Callaghan, and Dave breaking off as Chris, Kate, Cail, and Taylor headed straight up to the second floor.

The whole time they were clearing the second floor, Taylor was thinking this was too easy. Would Silva really just walk in, expecting to overpower her? By the time they cleared all the rooms except Taylor's, Cal, Callaghan, and Dave joined them. The door was closed and she'd left it open.

Kate stood against the wall and put her hand on the door knob as Chris counted down with her fingers - three, two, one. Kate threw the door open and Chris, Taylor, and Cail burst through the door, weapons up. The rest piled in behind them.

A soft light beamed from one of the bedside lamps. Silva stood on the other side of the bed in the process of tying a blue nylon rope to the post on the headboard.

"Hands above your head," Chris shouted.

Silva dropped the rope and slowly raised her hands. "Jesus. How many of you are there?"

Taylor circled the room, her weapon trained on Silva until she was behind her. She secured her hands in cuffs then performed a body search. "Siobhan Silva, you're under arrest for two counts of forcible confinement, assault with a weapon, sexual assault with a weapon, and one count of murder. You have the right to remain silent." She read her the rest of the Miranda Warning and led her out of her room. She didn't want Silva or her sick box of tricks in there.

"I want a lawyer. How the hell did you know I was here?" Silva asked as Taylor led her down the stairs.

"We're pretty smart cops," Chris said from behind her. "Take her outside," she told Taylor. "Tell the officers in the unmarked unit to take her in to Sex Crimes and have her put in an interview room. I'll call in forensics to process the scene."

Taylor winced as she glanced over her shoulder at Chris. The arrest had been easy, but now she had to deal with strangers pawing around in her room. She had a feeling it was going to be a very long night.

As she was passing Silva off to the two officers from the unmarked unit, Gray and Rose walked across the street.

"What are you doing here?"

"We were feeling left out," Gray said with a sheepish grin. "Everyone okay?"

"Yeah." Taylor looked up to her bedroom window. Her sanctuary wasn't faring too well though.

* * *

Taylor went back up to her room and found Chris leaning over the

Mastercraft tool box.

"We've got her knife. V grind blade," Chris said. "Strap on, lube. She's toast."

Taylor pointed to a white jug sitting next to the toolbox. "And the disinfectant."

"Yeah. That's going to have Raine's prints on it."

Chris pulled her cell phone from her belt when it began ringing. "Cain."

"Hey, it's Constable Allen."

"Hey, what's up?"

"I just got a call for a welfare check. Michaela Brighton was supposed to fly out to Halifax yesterday to spend Christmas with her family. She never made the flight and her family hasn't been able to contact her."

"Yeah?" Chris had a sinking feeling in her gut.

"She's one of yours DS. Same MO as Delacourte and Cruise. Only this one has been dead for at least a few days."

"Describe her for me," Chris said.

"Long dark brown hair, brown eyes. Slim build and about five foot six, a hundred and twenty pounds."

"Damn it. I'm on my way." She hung up and turned to Taylor. "I think we just found the woman Silva was paying attention to at Les Beau's."

* * *

Allen was at the door when Chris and Taylor arrived at the brown brick townhouse just a block from Les Beau's. They signed in and donned paper booties.

"You'll want to take a look in the kitchen, DS," Allen said, looking at Taylor with a pained expression.

"Yeah? Thanks." Chris motioned for Taylor to enter first in case she was hit with a vision. She wasn't wrong. Taylor took two long strides inside the door and froze. Chris laid a hand on her back and waited. When the tension of her muscles began to ease, Chris said, "Tell me."

"It's her," Taylor said. She got the same feel as she did at Raine Delacourte's. "Took more time with this one." She shook her head. "No, I think it started off as a hook up before we found Silva's apartment. She came back and the vic let her in."

"Okay," Chris said. "Let's take a look in the kitchen first."

They walked up a short set of stairs to the main level and made their way to the back of the house. In the brightly lit kitchen with white appliances and cupboards and grey counters, they found what Constable Allen had been referring to. On the kitchen table, today's edition of the Globe and Mail newspaper sat, surrounded by photographs of Taylor's house. In one of the pictures, Taylor was leaving the house in her running gear. In another, she was answering the door to Cail.

"Well," Taylor said. "It's not like we have to worry about her getting to us now."

"No. And now we know where she's been staying."

"I don't know how she could stand the smell," Taylor said. Even from down here, she could smell death and decomposing flesh.

They headed upstairs and found Michaela Brighton in the master bedroom, arms and legs still tied to the four corners of the bed with blue, nylon rope. Her brown eyes were glazed over, petechiae evident in the whites.

The Rune symbols had been carved into her chest.

Taylor peeked into the en suite. "She didn't bother to clean this one up." Dried blood smeared the white counter and sinks. Several towels littered the floor, but they were black. Forensics would find any blood evidence on them.

"Thought she had time," Chris said. "Let's head into the office and let forensics do their thing."

* * *

Chris brought the CCTV image from Interview One up on the computer in her office and turned the screen so Taylor could also see Silva pacing the small room, her arms flailing around as she spoke to herself.

"She's trying to concoct a reasonable explanation for being in your house," Chris said.

"She won't come up with one."

"No. We've got her cold on Raine's assault. DNA from the hair in the cap she left behind will match. We'll get a match on Bonkers, too. There was saliva mixed in with the blood on her chest."

Taylor screwed up her nose. "She licked the wounds?"

"Looks like."

"That's just … gross." All that food they'd eaten for dinner turned in her belly with the thought of Silva licking Bonkers' blood. To take her mind off it, she turned her attention back to the CCTV image. A forensic tech entered the room and took Silva's boots from her and got a DNA sample. They'd check her boot prints against the print lifted from outside Raine's window.

They also had enough evidence from the Michaela Brighton scene to get a conviction. Siobhan Silva's fingerprints were all over the house.

One of the uniformed officers who brought Silva into Headquarters tapped the doorframe with his knuckles. "Excuse me, DS Cain."

"Officer." Chris nodded in greeting and studied the sandy haired young man, tall, slim, and grim faced as he shuffled back and forth from foot to foot. "What can I do for you?"

"Um, I thought you should know, we gave the suspect the opportunity to call a lawyer."

"Okay. Thanks."

He scratched his head. "The thing is, the number she called didn't come back to a lawyer. The number is registered to a cop."

Chris narrowed her eyes, knowing exactly where this was going. "Spit it out, officer. Who did she call?"

"Some RCMP guy. Sergeant Will St. James."

A slow smile crept across Chris's face. "Perfect. Do me a favour. St. James is not authorized to see Silva. When he arrives, tell him he can't take any weapons or electronic devices into interview then show him into Interview Three."

"Ten four, DS."

"And make sure you lock the door behind him," Chris added with a smirk.

He nodded, spun on his heal, and headed back toward the interview rooms.

"You're going to interrogate him?" Taylor asked.

Chris's smile widened. "No. *We're* going to interrogate him." She put the CCTV camera on split screen between Interview One and Interview Three.

Chapter 27

"How do we interrogate him?" Not only was Taylor inexperienced in interrogating suspects, she had no idea how to interrogate a cop. He'd know the interrogation techniques inside out.

"Don't worry. I'll take the lead. I'm going to try to get him to talk himself into a corner."

"It's harder, isn't it, when we don't know the extent of his involvement?"

"He'll want to know what we know and that will work in our favour. I'll use it as leverage."

Gayle Lansing wouldn't be in the office this late on Christmas Eve, so Chris sent her an email, hoping she'd respond, asking if she tracked the camera. Not only did she respond, she did so within seconds, stating the camera was purchased at an electronics store on Queen St. on December fourteenth. She got another email from Lansing moments later stating, "I've been going through the footage from the camera. The attached clip is from the time the camera was installed."

Chris clicked on the video. The dark image blurred before the camera steadied on a face. The lights were off in the office, but the person was staring directly at the camera, as if she was sliding the book into place on the shelf. Then she turned and walked out.

"How the hell did Siobhan Silva get into a secured area of Headquarters at three o'clock in the morning?" Chris asked.

"Well, she's a professional thief, isn't she? If she can break into Art Galleries and stuff, she can break in here."

Chris shook her head. "Un-fucking-believable." She sent a quick email back to Lansing thanking her. Then she emailed Brice McLean, letting him know Lansing had done an exemplary job. When she tuned back into the CCTV footage of the two interview rooms, Silva paced back and forth in her stocking feet. The door to Interview Three opened and St. James walked in, looked around the empty room in confusion, then swung back around to the door as it closed in his face. He grabbed the door handle, yanking on it, and started pounding on the door.

Chris grinned. "Got him right where we want him now."

"Oh, boy," Taylor said.

* * *

Taylor didn't want to tread into the interview room with St. James. He was still raging mad at being locked in there. Chris, on the other hand, couldn't wait. She unlocked the door and strolled in ahead of Taylor.

"What the hell do you think you're doing?" St. James yelled.

Chris grinned. "You're being detained on suspicion of aiding and abetting Siobhan Silva."

"Are you fucking kidding me?"

"Sit down, St. James." Chris's grin was gone, replaced by an ice cold glare.

To Taylor's surprise, St. James dropped himself into a chair. She took a seat next to Chris, across the table from him.

Chris recited the Miranda Warning. "Do you understand your rights, Sergeant?"

He laughed. "Is this a joke?"

"Yes or no?"

"Of course I understand my rights. And no, I don't want a lawyer. I don't need one because you're about to make a fool of yourself, DS."

"Okay, make a fool out of me, St. James. Explain to me why you deleted files from Silva's computer while it was in your possession."

He stared blank-faced at Chris.

"That's tampering with evidence," Chris said. Apparently, he was taking his right to remain silent to heart. "You didn't tell us twenty-four of the diamonds were recovered. What was the name of that agency, Sinclair?"

"Keller Investigations," Taylor answered.

"Yeah, that's the one. Angela St. James was the P.I., right?"

"That's right."

"How is it your wife recovered half of the diamonds in a case you were investigating and received a big, fat finders fee?" Chris asked.

St. James laughed again. "You think my ex-wife had anything to do with this?"

"She fits the description of the second perpetrator."

"She has an air tight alibi, DS. At the time of the diamond heist, she was in bed with me. It was our first night together, so we didn't get much sleep." He grinned and winked at Chris.

"How reliable is that alibi if you're covering for her?"

He lost the grin. "You can't honestly believe either of us are involved in this? It was Ang who discovered the safety deposit box where De La Cruz left half of the diamonds for Silva. She makes a damn good living recovering stolen goods. She doesn't need to steal."

"Why did you delete the files?"

His mouth firmed to a fine white line.

"Why did you make a big deal about getting clearance to share data with us then feed us a bunch of bullshit that's public knowledge?"

St. James glared at Chris, but didn't answer.

Chris stood, bracing her left hand on the table as she leaned forward, her right arm snugged close to her body in the sling. "Are you working with Siobhan Silva to locate the remaining diamonds?"

"No. Silva was supposed to be working with us to locate them, but she went off the grid. We didn't expect her to sexually assault Raine Delacourte. We sure as hell didn't think she'd go after Cruise."

Chris sank back down into her chair. "You fucking idiot."

"She was supposed to get Raine to admit to the jewelry store robbery with De La Cruz. That's it."

"Raine didn't even meet Lily De La Cruz until about a year after the heist."

"Raine Marquez flew to Calgary on the same flight as Callie Delacourte a few months before the heist and flew back to Toronto on the same flight two days after it. They sat together in first class on both flights. They knew each other, DS. Well enough to pull off one of the most notorious heists on record in Canada. The diamonds they stole were worth upwards of fifty million dollars."

Chris looked at Taylor then got to her feet. "Excuse us for a moment." She went out into the hall with Taylor and locked the door behind her. "Get a couple of uniforms over to Samantha Ward's apartment to pick up Raine and have her brought in to Interview Two."

"Sam from Les Beau's?"

"Yeah. We're going to get to the bottom of this shit show once and for all."

"Do you think Raine helped Lily De La Cruz steal those diamonds?"

Chris swiped her hand through her hair. "She's been hiding something from the beginning, so yeah, I think she's involved."

"When we walked into her bedroom and I got a sense of what happened in that room," Taylor began. "I knew the offender called Raine by a name other than her own, but I don't know if it was Sass. It may have been a ruse to throw us off."

Chris nodded. "That makes sense, since we haven't been able to find anyone named Sass who's connected to this." She waved her hand towards the end of the hall. "Get the uniforms to pick up Raine. Sam's address will be on file."

Taylor walked away and Chris headed for the break room to make coffee.

* * *

They went back in to Interview Three with St. James while they waited for Raine to be brought in. Chris set a cup of coffee on the table for him and took a sip of her own. It wasn't as good as Taylor made, but it was still way better than the sludge the department supplied.

"What did Raine tell you when you interviewed her at the hospital?" Chris asked.

"She'd just come out of surgery, so she was pretty groggy. She wasn't making much sense. When I went back the next day, she was gone. Then I went to Cruise's apartment and she wasn't there either."

"Did you tell her not to talk to the Toronto Police?"

"No. Did she say that?"

"Why did you delete the files?"

He didn't answer.

"Who's Sass?"

"Hell if I know. It's not a name I ever heard before Raine Delacourte stated Silva called her that."

"Why did you feed us the bullshit about getting clearance?"

He took a sip of coffee then stared down into his cup.

"Answer the damn question."

St. James looked up at Chris and smiled. "How about you let me make a phone call and maybe I'll be able to answer?"

"A phone call to whom?"

"My commanding officer."

"Maybe you could send him a text then you could delete it afterwards."

He slumped back in his chair. "Do you think the TPS will hire me when the RCMP kicks my ass to the curb for what I'm about to tell you?"

Chris shrugged. "Maybe."

"Hell, I'm up a creek for what I've already told you. I gave you the run around because when I asked for clearance, it was denied. I didn't want to be kicked out of your unit, so I bullshitted."

"They didn't want you telling us you were working with Silva."

The edges of his mouth curled up. "Bingo. I deleted the files on Silva's computer on orders from my Commanding Officer."

There was a tap at the door and Chris nodded at Taylor. They both got up and went to the door.

"Cain?" When Chris turned around, St. James asked, "Am I free to go?"

"Not yet." If she could corroborate what he'd told them, then she'd set him loose, but not before.

He nodded, turned his coffee cup round and round on the table then looked up at her with puppy dog eyes. "Well, just so you know, this is the last Christmas I'll get to spend with my mother."

"Lucky you," she said. "I went to my mother's funeral yesterday."

* * *

Raine stared wide-eyed at Chris as she read her the Miranda warning. "Do you understand your rights?"

"No, I don't understand any of this. Why am I here? What's going on?"

"We just have a few more questions. This is standard procedure in interview. Do you understand your rights?"

"Yes, I understand."

"You know, I've been distracted during this entire investigation with some personal crap. I haven't been on my game. But, right from the start we knew you were hiding something."

"I'm not hiding anything. I told you everything I know the other day."

Chris held up her hand, palm out. "No more lies, Raine. I really can't take anymore bullshitting. We've been gathering evidence since you were assaulted. The RCMP has been collecting evidence on the diamond heist for five years. What do you think they found?"

"I don't know what you're talking about."

"No? You don't remember flying out west with Callie five years ago? Sitting next to her in first class? Flying back with her about three months later, two days after the diamond heist? We know you did that job with her, Raine. It's going to feel a lot better once you come clean."

That weight you've been carrying around will fall away. You know it will.

"You made up the name Sass," Chris continued. "You just said that to throw us off. It was Lily, wasn't it? She said, 'Why Lily? She wasn't yours.' That's what Silva said, didn't she?"

Raine's shoulders hunched over as she stared down into her lap.

"I can see the stress and guilt weighing on you, Raine. Telling the truth will relieve all that pressure. You want this to be over and done with, don't you? Tell the truth and you can start to put it behind you.

"You're a good person. I've known you for a long time. I know you're kind and nurturing."

Raine lifted her head and looked Chris in the eye.

"Maybe Callie convinced you to help her, so she could put her past behind her. One last job, so she could be free. You'd want to help her cut her ties with an ugly past."

"I wanted to help her. That woman left her scarred, inside and out. Now I know how she felt."

Chris got up and slid her chair around the table to sit next to Raine. She took Raine's good hand in hers and spoke in a soft, comforting voice. "You'd never stolen anything before, had you? Just this once to help a friend?"

"I did it for Callie."

"That's right, you did it for Callie. Let it out, Raine. Set yourself free."

"If I'd just given that bitch the stupid diamonds, Bonkers would still be alive." Raine sighed, looked Chris in the eye, and confessed.

Chapter 28

Chris opened the door to Interview Three and glared down at St. James. "We've got a full confession from Raine Delacourte on the diamond heist."

"Told you," he said with a smirk. He stood and stretched. "I'll need my phone and my weapon. I'll be taking Delacourte into custody."

"You know," Chris said casually. "I knew you were off from the start. It was in the way Sinclair reacted every time you were around."

St. James clenched his fists, glaring at Chris. "You fucking bitch."

"Did you think Sinclair wouldn't tell me what you and your buddies did to her in high school?"

"I didn't do anything. I couldn't stop them."

Yeah, right, Chris thought. "Then the whole thing with not having clearance to give us details of the diamond heist. I contacted your commanding officer and he sent me the whole file."

"You spoke to Jessup? You had no fucking right." His face turned a deep magenta, the veins in his neck corded and pulsing.

Chris figured it was time to stop playing with him or she'd give him a heart attack. "Delacourte has been turned over to the local RCMP detachment. Inspector Worthington notified your CO that the Toronto Police are charging you with accessory in the rape of Raine Delacourt and the rapes and murders of Elizabeth Cruise and Michaela Brighton."

"I don't even know anyone named Michaela whatever."

"Her body was discovered this evening," Chris said. "Another one of Silva's victims that would be alive today if you hadn't held back on us."

"What the fuck have you done?" St. James screamed.

Chris smiled. "Did you think we wouldn't verify your story?"

St. James lunged at Chris. Taylor shot through the door and tackled him, taking him down hard to the floor, knocking the wind out of him. She had his arms behind his back and cuffed before he knew what hit him.

They walked him down to the front desk and turned him over to the RCMP officers who were waiting for him.

"We'll ignore the assault of an officer," Chris said. "I figure you're in enough trouble."

St. James started to walk away sandwiched between the two RCMP officers then stopped and turned back. "Will you at least answer one question for me?"

"Maybe," Chris said.

"Where are the diamonds?"

Chris grinned. "We've had them since Raine was discharged from the hospital."

"They were in the duffel bag?"

"They were in the safe in Worthington's office. At one point, you were sitting about one foot from them."

The look on St. James's face could only be described as defeat. It would be up to the RCMP to investigate whether or not he was after the diamonds. Chris was confident he was. Why else would he have teamed up with Silva?

On the way back up in the elevator, Taylor asked, "Do we even need to interview Silva?"

"No, but we may as well make it three for three. Nice tackle, by the way."

"Thanks," Taylor said. "I figured you'd been injured enough this week."

"Ah, well. I've got a week to recuperate on the beach anyway."

* * *

Siobhan Silva shot to her feet as Chris and Taylor entered Interview One. "It's about time. Do you have any idea how long I've been waiting in here?"

They took their seats at the table and Chris said, "Sit down, Silva."

"No. I called for a representative hours ago."

"Yeah, St. James won't be coming to your rescue. He's been taken into custody."

Silva sank down into her chair.

"You may as well come clean now," Chris began. "What do you think is going to happen when the DNA results from the hairs on the cap you left behind at Raine Delacourte's comes back? Or the match from your boots to the print we lifted outside of Delacourte's office window? Or how about the saliva from Elizabeth Cruise's chest? Then there's the blood on the knife we collected from the toolbox you brought to Constable Sinclair's. Plus, both crimes match the MO of a crime you were convicted of six years ago."

"I want a lawyer."

Chris looked over at Taylor. "Well, shit. She just ruined our fun." Turning back to Silva, she said, "Added to the charges Constable Sinclair previously listed are the forced confinement, aggravated sexual assault, and murder of Michaela Brighton."

Chris and Taylor left the room and Chris arranged for uniformed officers to take Silva to booking.

"Why don't you go home and pack and I'll write up the reports?" Taylor said.

Chris looked at her watch and winced. "Shit. I didn't realize it was so late."

"Go on. Have a great vacation."

Wrapping her good arm around Taylor, Chris said, "Merry Christmas."

"Yeah. Merry Christmas."

"When I get back, we'll be dealing with Sebastien."

Taylor nodded. "I'll be here. Anything you need. In the meantime, try not to think about it. Just have a good time."

"You sure you're okay doing the reports?"

"I got it. Go home."

"Yeah. Going." She grabbed her coat from her office and returned to Taylor's desk. "Thanks. For everything."

"Anytime."

"Take tomorrow, or today I guess, off. Don't come in until Boxing Day. I'll give Blake a call and update her. That's your first official active case in the bag. Well done, Sinclair. I'd give you a gold star, but ... you know ... I don't have one."

She strode away, laughing.

Taylor called after her, "You're getting punchy, DS. Try to get some sleep before you start drinking margueritas on the beach."

"Oh, margueritas on the beach? Here I come! Whoohoooo."

Taylor snorted as she watched Chris disappear around the corner.

Half an hour later, she was about a quarter of the way through her reports when she caught movement out of the corner of her eye and looked up to find Cail approaching her desk. "What are you doing here? It's the middle of the night."

He set a thermos of coffee on her desk and leaned over to brush a kiss against her lips. "Merry Christmas, Angel."

"Mmm. Merry Christmas. My first ever Christmas kiss."

"Let's make it a tradition."

"I still have quite a bit of work to finish up."

"I'll keep you company. Your gifts are in my car, so I thought I'd escort you home and carry them in for you."

"Aren't you working tomorrow?"

"Nightshift," he said with a grimace. "I think the sergeant is punishing me."

"Seems like."

It took a little over an hour to finish and file the reports. Taylor stood, stretching. "Now I need to go home and deal with my room."

Cail helped Taylor into her coat. He knew how having the forensics techs in her room would effect her. She wouldn't rest until she put the room to rights. He took her hand as they walked to the elevators. "I'll help you clean."

"You will?"

"Yeah."

"How did you know I was still here?"

"I asked Kate to text me when Chris was on her way home. She said you were staying to write the reports, so I came up."

"Huh."

They got in the elevator and Cail pushed the button for the garage.

"Maybe after we clean my room you can play me a song."

"It would be my pleasure."

"Then maybe we could have Christmas sex."

Cail grinned as he stared up at the descending floor numbers. "Best. Christmas. Ever." It was made even better at the raspy sound of Taylor's laugh.

* * *

Gray saved her present to give to Taylor in private. On Christmas morning, they sat in Taylor's living room and Gray handed her a box wrapped in gold paper with a huge lacy bow in silver.

Taylor unwrapped it carefully and lifted the lid from the square box. She moved the gold tissue paper around until she exposed the piece of paper perched in the tissue. "You and Cail," she said. "You know me so well." She lifted the cheque out and her eyes popped out at the amount. It was for $100,000, made out to Beneath My Wings. "Holy crap." She wrapped her arms around Gray and just hung on for a few moments. "Thank you so much."

"My pleasure. There's one more thing in there. The donation was a last minute addition."

Taylor straightened and pulled the tissue paper out of the box. Sitting on the bottom was an envelope. She removed the card from the envelope. The front had a picture of a baby on it. Taylor's brow furrowed and she opened the card. Her eyes pooled as she read what Gray had written inside.

Taylor,

Other than Patrick and I, no one would make a better guardian to our daughter than you. Would you do us the honour of being Gracie's Godmother?

Taylor's eyes burned as she threw her arms around Gray again. "Yes, yes, yes. I would love to." She had no idea what it meant to be a Godmother, but it sounded wonderful.

After Gray and Callaghan left to spend Christmas with his family, Taylor led Cail up to her bedroom and opened her closet door.

"What's all that?" he asked. The floor of her walk in closet was covered in shopping bags.

"Blankets, sleeping bags, winter coats, hats, and mitts." She looked up at him with a shy smile. "I also have a bunch of Tim Horton's gift cards. Would you spend the afternoon with me handing this stuff out to the homeless?"

Cail shook his head, in awe of the woman standing beside him. "It would be my honour."

ABOUT THE AUTHOR

Wendy Hewlett is a British born Canadian author who began writing in earnest in 2011 with *Saving Grace*, the first book in the Taylor Sinclair Series. She enjoys writing strong female protagonists in the mystery/crime fiction genre.

She has enjoyed many exciting jobs including working on cruise ships in the Caribbean, Security & Fire Supervisor at General Motors Canada, and Clinical Associate (Addictions Counselor) at a private Addiction Treatment Centre.

She has one son who she credits as being her finest achievement.

She dreams of spending a year exploring and writing in her birthplace, Scotland, as well as England and Ireland.

Look for *Saving Grace, Unfinished Business*, and *Runed* at your favourite online bookstores.

Book 4 in the Taylor Sinclair Series is due out later in 2019. Wendy also plans to publish several unrelated novels in 2019.

Visit the author's website at: wendyhewlett.com and sign up for her Monthly Newsletter to stay up to date on news, new releases, giveaways, and more.

Follow Wendy on:

Reviews are the bread and butter of an Indie Author's career. Please take a moment to write a quick review on Amazon, Goodreads, or your favourite online book retailer. It is greatly appreciated and allows Wendy to continue writing and publishing page-turning novels with wonderful, strong female protagonists.

Made in the USA
Lexington, KY
25 March 2019